To those who have loved me, and those who have wished me ill.

You have forged my pen of perseverance, will, and compassion, the strongest weapon against prejudice, hate, and malice.

With that pen, I will create passionate heroes, sadistic villains, and an escape for those in need.

Thanks to Shay, who has kept me above the water when I thought I was drowning.

You are the light in my darkness, the love of my life, and my best friend.

You are my firefly.

FRAY!
THE LEGION OF HEROES

Book 1

Quillan Ink

Quillan Ink Publishing, LLC

1

The Boy Behind the Mask

Chapter 1

Back to Hell

Content Warning: Contains bullying, self-doubt, and abuse.

Belmont High: a place for happiness to die, I thought with a scoff. It's what my friends and I would say about this place. Often. The school's motto had always been "Belmont High: a place for students to thrive."

Not for kids like me, though. Not for the minority here in the small city of Old Belmont. A goth kid with an interest in piercings and heavy music, living in a conservative, religious city on the edge of ruin. I was the punch line to a bad joke.

And it made me sick.

As Johnny's condescending tone bellowed near the entrance of the school, I knew I was about to make yet another poor choice. I couldn't quite hear what he was saying, but his voice had been a plague on my daily life.

Today was the first day of my sophomore year, which I had been fearing for the entirety of summer vacation—because of *him*. My hands trembled, and my heart sank as I got closer to the end of my peace. There were the same old security doors with the same old chipped paint, begging for me to suffer behind them.

Freshman year had been stressful for several reasons, but mostly because Belmont High was different. Our city had two elementary schools, Southwest Elementary and Northeast Elementary, which bled into two different middle schools. From there, though, the two merged into the intimidating two-story Belmont High where the bullies had already taken hold, waiting for my arrival.

Belmont High was beautiful. Gothic-style architecture and black-painted brick made this building feel like a different world. We had been given a tour in late eighth grade, so I knew that there were four different wings, one for each grade level. Old Belmont was proud of this school's history. It had once been a massive church, but in a drastic turn of events, it was now our one and only high school.

After checking my eyeliner in the reflection of the window and brushing my long black hair out of my eyes, I fixed the folded sleeve of my black, metal-band t-shirt. I pushed my round, full-framed glasses up and looked forward.

"Did you not hear me, nerd? I said I forgot my pencil. Give me one!" Johnny said. I glanced behind me, catching a glimpse of what was going on.

Johnny's spiked, naturally red hair pulled my attention to the left. Freckles flaked his skin, and as he caught my eye, he grinned, baring dirty yellow teeth. Alarm shot through my body as I looked away from him, fear coming on like a sudden cold.

He turned his attention back to the boy he was yelling at, and I closed my eyes for a moment; I didn't want to hear someone else getting pushed around. I didn't want to stand by as someone was getting hurt, and that's the reason I was always getting into trouble. My few close friends and I had been dealing with Johnny and his crew for years now, and all we'd ever needed was someone to stand up for us.

"Come on, man. You can't just take my stuff all the—"

Johnny's sharp voice interrupted the kid. "Give me the bag!" Johnny demanded. I heard a loud smack, followed by the sound of the kid's glasses clattering against the ground. I sighed, turned around, and clenched my fist. My fear had disappeared as fast as it had arrived, and now I was seeing red.

Johnny turned his attention to me. "What are you looking at, Tony?"

I looked at the guy getting bullied, who was now picking up his blue and gray backpack off the ground. His pale skin was now red, and his eyes swelled as he was about to cry. He looked up at me for a moment, and then back at the ground, frozen in place.

"Leave him alone!" I said. "Don't you ever get tired of pushing people around?"

Johnny laughed and stormed toward me. As he got into my face, I was reminded that he was the same height as me, about 5'10". "Don't you ever get tired of getting beat up?" he asked.

I tried to keep my fists clenched, but as I felt the heat from his face hitting mine, my fire went cold. Johnny scared the shit out of me, yet I continued to try and stand up for the people he was bullying. There was only one problem.

It never worked.

I faltered, took a step back, and loosened my hands. Johnny's piercing blue eyes stared into mine with such intense malice that I wanted to puke. My insides twisted as he stood, still smiling.

Suddenly, his fist hit my cheek, throwing me off balance and making me fall on my ass. I covered my face, clamming up as I found myself unable to fight back. I awaited another strike, but he rummaged through my bag instead, stealing the zip-up bag of pencils it held inside.

He ran off, and as I sat up, the kid was also gone without a trace. I sighed again, looking down at the sidewalk. I stared at it, wishing I could make a difference to those who needed it. But they didn't seem to care either.

After getting up from the ground, I tried to prepare for the year to come. Could I make it through? I forced myself to enter the building.

The lobby was also something I'd marveled at upon our introduction. As soon as you opened the doors, you could see the tall glass windows of the main office with a staircase on either side of it that led to the junior and senior wings. A large golden chandelier drooped from the ceiling.

I sighed yet again, knowing I was in a lot of trouble this time as the principal motioned for me to come into his office.

Principal Jackson was a tall man, about 6'3", and had a very neat appearance. His cleanly shaved face and short, slicked-back auburn hair had been his look since he started here two years ago.

"Starting early this year, are we?" he asked me, seemingly upset.

"Trust me, I don't want to be here either," I said. As I realized the words seemed rude, I put my hand on the back of my neck, trying to backtrack. "Yeah… Johnny was bullying someone and I tried to stop it."

Principal Jackson sighed. "I don't want to hear it, Tony. You know Johnny has a rough home life. I know he bothered you last year, but he told me you attacked him out there," he said.

"Attacked *him*?" I threw my hands up in aggravation. "He's been bullying me for years! Look at my face; he hit *me*!" I paused for a moment, trying to figure out what to say.

There had been many opportunities for him to understand that Johnny bullied us, but Johnny and his friends were smart enough to avoid trouble most of the time. With my peculiar appearance and the lack of cameras, it usually leaned in his favor. It was one of the downsides of living in a city like Old Belmont.

"This quarrel with Johnny needs to end. You've been in my office on multiple occasions, all regarding him and his friends. I understand that Johnny is a troubled child, but I can't have you starting fights with him anymore. With all due respect, you need to start minding your own business before you ruin your life academically."

I jumped to my own defense before he could spew another degrading word to slander my character. "My grades are perfect. I'm literally ahead of the rest of my class!" The situation was aggravating. I had never been below an *A* in any of my classes, and I had even taken extra courses over the summer to get out of school sooner.

"I'm not talking about your grades; those are great, and you have almost enough credits to be considered a junior. I like you, Tony, and I don't want to see you throw your future away because of a bully. Despite that, I'm giving you a warning today. If you start any more fights, our next visit will be talking about expulsion."

My eyes widened, unsure of what to say. "I understand. I'll stay out of trouble," I said, defeated.

"On another note, I understand that Johnny is a problem here. He's got quite the record from Southwest Middle School as well. We've been working with him, along with attempting to get in touch with his parents to push him in the right direction. If you ever need to talk, our counselor is always available. Go ahead and head to the cafeteria; there's still a couple of minutes before class," Principal Jackson said.

Before I could turn, he cleared his throat. "I believe in you, Tony. Here, keep it," he said, holding a purple mechanical pencil out to me. I looked at it and nodded in acceptance.

I grabbed the pencil and left his office, disregarding the idea of going to the counselor. I'm sure it helped some people, but this school had already proved I wouldn't be one of them.

I was immediately bombarded with the roaring of students eager to be back with their peers. I scouted through the toxic river of kids, searching for my friends, and then I saw the bright-orange hoodie and baggy ripped jeans of Talida, which were easy to spot in the crowd. Her hair had remained the same for as long as I can remember. It was light brown with a bobbed cut that gave a rounder look to her face, letting her bright-blue eyes shine with the hope that this year would be better than the last eight.

Standing next to her were my other two friends, Shawn and Aiden, both of whom had dark-brown hair. Shawn's broad shoulders and Aiden's chunky build emphasized Talida's slender figure. Shawn had short curly hair, and Aiden let his shaggy hair grow out to the bottom of his neck, barely touching his marching-band shirt. His acne had calmed ever so slightly, leading me to believe he had been trying to do something about it this year.

Shawn was an inch shorter than me while Aiden was just barely taller than Talida. I noticed Shawn had gotten an all-white, hooded vest over the summer, showing off his toned arms. He was in shape but not athletic. They turned to me, and all three of them gave a quick smile; they had been waiting.

"Tony!" Shawn and Talida shouted across the room, followed by Aiden's gaze.

"Hey, guys! How was your summer?" I asked as a grin crept across my face. Despite the difficult morning, they were always able to raise my spirits.

"It was good," Shawn said. "I finally unlocked all the characters in *Immortal Fighter*. Grudgematch being a playable character was a surprise, though."

I smiled. We had played that game together for a long time, but they had dropped a new DLC over the summer with ten unlockable fighters. I had come across an article that spoiled the secret playable hero, but I kept that information to myself.

Talida's mouth widened in shock. "I've been trying all week to unlock everyone! I got close, but I had no idea he was the secret warrior. I spent most of break helping my dad get his greenhouse up."

"Mine was great until I had to come back to this hellhole," Aiden said with negativity practically rolling off his tongue.

I nodded in agreement to Aiden. I didn't want to be in school longer than I had to, which is why I had taken a science course over the summer along with doubling my history and math classes last year.

"I didn't get a chance to play a lot this summer," I said. "The last time I played was when we were at Shawn's house. I'll be honest—I spent most of my time drawing and trying to forget having to come back." I smiled, knowing our friendship had continued to grow despite the bullies. The four of us sat down, tossing our backpacks to the side.

Not a lot had changed over the years. The students didn't like that I was goth, made fun of Shawn for being a geek, frowned upon Talida for being poor, and took cracks at Aiden's weight and autistic mannerisms. His aggressive acne had been their target last year. We still weren't popular, and we could never imagine it differently despite the want for change.

"I wonder where Johnny is," Talida said.

"Maybe he moved away and took his trolls with him," Aiden muttered in a hushed tone, mostly to himself as he added shading to the scales of a black dragon he was drawing.

I sighed. "I ran into him outside, bullying someone. It would be the best gift ever if they would just leave," I said.

"Or just disappear. I don't care how," Aiden muttered under his breath hatefully. "Die even."

Shawn chuckled at Aiden's remark and then realized what I had said. "Wait, he's starting shit already?"

"Yep, and this time I'm in a lot of trouble for stepping in. The principal gave me a warning and told me that if I started any more fights, he would talk to me about expulsion."

A shriek left Talida's mouth. "What? Are you kidding me? And what about *him*?"

I rolled my eyes. "Said he was gonna look into counseling."

Aiden choked on his drink, coughing for a moment as the others groaned in disgust. "Counseling? Yeah right," Aiden said. "You better not get kicked out."

"Dude for real!" Shawn added.

I yawned. I was having a hard time staying awake, even after all the drama. Between the fear of coming back to school and a bad nightmare from last night, I was very tired, and it was causing me to zone out.

"You okay?" Aiden asked, seeing my mind trailing off again.

I looked at him, my thoughts being pulled back from my memories. "I will be," I said. "I've been having problems sleeping."

"Due to coming back?" Aiden asked. I shook my head as the other two jumped in.

"Was it the cloaked dude again?" Shawn started, looking concerned. I had been struggling with nightmares for several years now, all involving the same thing. Somewhere, some way, a cloaked figure would be involved. It always sent shivers down my spine every time I saw it as if it were a threat to me.

This figure was the only thing that connected these nightmares, and he was always the same. Under a black cloak with glowing yellow eyes and two glowing nose slits. I've never been able to make out the rest of his face.

"Yeah. It was a scary one, but I'd rather not go into detail right now about it," I replied, starting to visibly shake as I remembered it. "I'm more focused on how I'm going to survive three more years without Johnny getting me expelled."

"You know, my dad says recurring dreams have an important meaning. Maybe you should see someone about it to see if there's something that can make them stop," Talida said.

"Maybe I should. I think they're getting worse."

"We're always here for you," Aiden said. "To get off these scary topics, did you all watch the new Grudgematch movie over break?"

Shawn slammed his hands on the table. "Yes!" he said. "I took Talida to watch it. He's the greatest superhero of all time! He's one of the few heroes that are shown as gritty and violent. I love it!" He nudged my arm. "You totally should have gone, man!"

I smiled. I had been wanting to watch it, but my parents had kept me pretty busy over the summer. The night my friends went and saw it, I wasn't able to get away. "I'm sad that I missed it."

As Aiden started his bombardment of questions about what they thought of it, we were interrupted by the bell.

It was time to head to class, so I grabbed my backpack and began to walk down the long, crowded hallway. Johnny walked up beside me and smiled as he shoved me into a white concrete wall covered with bulletin boards and posters.

"Move!" he yelled obnoxiously, right in my ear. I jerked away, my ear ringing as he sprinted down the hallway with his two thugs following suit. Not much had changed about Rob and Grey over the years either.

Grey reminded me a lot of an ogre; he was big, not too bright, and followed orders. Rob, while following the same master, was much taller and crafty. If any of the three could think of a way to not get in trouble or to think of ways to cause distress, it would be him.

I sighed as I entered the classroom on my right.

I examined the room, unhappy to realize who else was in my class. Johnny was sitting right behind the last open desk with a vindictive grin. He leaned back in his chair, putting his hands behind his head. Rob was in the back corner, mirroring how I had met him the first time. I frowned, walked toward the desk, and sat down.

Mr. Karson walked in and stood in front of the whiteboard.

My teacher started to write math review problems on the board, and I knew this was going to be a relatively easy day. "I want these problems finished by tomorrow," he told the class sternly.

I pulled out a couple of binders from my bag, one for math. The other was a personal project I had been working on, involving a few printed character designs and a short story. I had been trying to further my graphic design over the summer with a tablet I had talked my parents into buying me. I'd always wanted to be a digital artist, so I decided it would be a good idea to design a few characters with a new coloring technique.

The designs were botched, to say the least, but I was hoping if I mastered the new ideas, one day I might be able to be a graphic designer for a game company.

I wrote down the math problems in a notebook so that I could finish them tonight. I had completed a few of them, but Johnny's gaze from behind was beginning to burn a hole through the back of my skull. As I put away my binders, I excused myself to use the restroom.

As I sat in the bathroom, wondering how I was going to survive the rest of this year, paranoia set in. The realization that I probably shouldn't have left my belongings in the classroom followed. I calmed myself, knowing the teacher wouldn't allow anyone to get into my bag. I hurried back.

As I neared the door, I could hear the students inside cackling over something. Fear shot through me.

Surely, it wasn't about me.

I entered the room, and to my dismay, Johnny was standing in the front with my open binder.

My eyes widened, and as my mouth opened in horror, I looked at the teacher. He sat in his chair, roaring in laughter like the rest of the class. *How could he?* I thought. Of all the people, I shouldn't have to worry about him.

"Listen to this!" Johnny yelled out, preparing to read more of the story I had written. He showed the class a picture of a character dressed in black and white, which happened to be referenced from me. I wanted to run up and hit him. My whole body was now fuming in anger and betrayal.

"Stop!" I squeaked, clenching my fists. The class chuckled at my pain.

Johnny continued to read. "I used my new abilities to walk through the wall. Now that I can phase through solid objects unseen, I can become a real-life superhero like Jake!"

Johnny burst into laughter, unable to read more.

Amused, he yelled out, "Tony thinks he has superpowers!" The room erupted. As everyone laughed at me, I sat down at my desk, covering my head as I leaned on the table. Trying to hold back the wave of gloom about to hit me, I began to question what I'd done to deserve all this.

"Okay, Johnny. Sit down," Mr. Karson said.

"Don't cry, Tony!" Johnny hollered as the classroom began to calm down. "I like the story—I really do! Be careful with your powers, though. Wouldn't want to get caught in the girl's locker room!" He started to head back toward his desk, and I now couldn't prevent the sobbing.

"Ew—what a pervert!" Rob blared from the back. "You ladies better watch out!"

I lifted my head, my face now red and full of tears while I ugly-cried. "I'm not a creep," I whimpered. "That's not what the story's about..." As I looked around, several boys were looking at me with surprised disgust. Girls were now whispering back and forth, looking at me like I was some sort of sick deviant.

I continued hiding, speechless, waiting desperately for the bell to ring. I wanted nothing more than to disappear right now and escape this atrocious character Johnny had turned me into.

As everyone settled down, the bell finally rang, and I ditched. I went home, avoiding my friends, ignoring my cell phone, and making sure to take my time. I would deal with the aftermath tomorrow, when I was sure I would have a hundred unread messages on every device I owned.

As I walked, I wished that my life would change. If only I could actually have those powers, Johnny would never be able to bully me again. I could turn the entirety of Old Belmont around, or I could burn it to the ground.

After several hours of wallowing, I arrived home.

"How was school?" my dad asked, the words seeming strange and unfamiliar. Both my mom and my dad were in the living room. My father was a little bit taller than me with broad shoulders and short black hair, unlike my mother's blond curls. I thought for a moment, unsure if I should reveal the day's events. He never cared, usually summarizing my problems as "exaggerations."

"It was okay," I said simply as I headed toward my room.

The energy shifted, and Mom left the room without a word. I heard their bedroom door close. Hard. My adrenaline spiked, signifying that I was in a lot of trouble.

"Your principal called me," he said before I could speak, "and told me that you ditched school this morning after confronting Johnny again."

I opened my mouth to speak, but the words came out weak. "I had a bad day. I'm sorry."

My dad laughed and looked away. He started to shake his head as he pursed his lips. "Unbelievable. What the fuck were you thinking? Quit butting in where you don't belong! I've told you so many times that what that boy does is none of your business." The statement triggered me, and I was unsure how to respond.

"But it *was* my business…"

"Yeah? Tell me how."

"He made it my business. I can't just sit back and watch someone get bullied." I shifted on my feet, preparing to change the subject. "You know, I would have liked it if someone ever stood up for *me*," I said, beginning to fumble through my words as my anger rose.

"Let someone else deal with it next time instead of acting like you're some kind of fucking hero!"

I clenched my fist. "Who else is there?" I yelled. "Who's going to help them? Who's going to help me?"

My dad's words bellowed through the house, his face blood red as his frustration rose. "How about a *teacher?*" he snapped. "That's what they're there for, Tony. If you have a problem, you tell someone higher than you."

I snorted, the statement being ridiculous. "Well, the teacher sure as shit didn't care about me today while he was laughing at me with everyone else." I swallowed, trying to avoid thinking back on the situation.

"Look at where they're coming from. Maybe if you didn't go to school dressed like a delinquent, you wouldn't get treated like one. You act like you're some kind of victim. You're the one starting the problems!"

His toxic words infuriated me. They made me want to lash out, but I couldn't bring myself to say what I wanted to. "I'm just trying to be me. What am I supposed to do when the whole world is against me for no reason?"

"You're supposed to change! You're supposed to grow up, get a job, and act like a normal fucking person. Let go of this attention-grasping, artsy, *freak* phase and quit wasting your life on video games." His words stopped, and I felt myself ready to explode. He didn't like me; he liked the image of the son he wanted me to turn into.

"And grow up to be what exactly?" I said quietly, my words surprisingly stable. His eyes shrank to a slit, warning me to be careful. "Grow up to be like you? Someone who only cares about fucking image?" I snapped, surprised the words made it out at all.

My dad took two steps toward me, fuming.

Then the back of his hand hit my cheek.

My eyes widened, surprised. The entire room went silent. I looked up at him, confused and scared. He had never hit me before. I turned around and sprinted toward my bedroom.

"If you don't change, you're going to ruin your fucking life!" he screamed from the living room.

I whispered my next words, not daring to let him hear me. "What good is the life I'm heading for if I'm hiding in the shadow of who I'm supposed to be?" All of this because I was different. All because I was weird.

I passed my brother's room, seeing him and his two friends playing on their console. He gave me a sympathetic smile, and then turned back to his game. There was nothing he could say. He had heard it all.

Now, making it to my room, I threw my backpack against the wall. All I've ever wanted is to freely be myself. I've done nothing to be considered a delinquent in the past, yet this whole town wants me to think that I'm some kind of criminal. All I want is peace. All I want is for this shitty life I have, to change.

I climbed up the ladder to lay in my bed, looking around from the top of my mattress on stilts. I looked at the desk on the other side of my room and saw that my tablet was gone. *He must have taken it.*

I frowned, and started to cry, my cheek stinging and red. I touched it, still not able to believe it had happened. Out of all the emotional abuse my dad had put me through, he had never hit me. Not until tonight.

I looked at my walls covered in pictures I had either designed or found for inspiration. One poster stood out from the rest. My limited-edition poster of Grudgematch in a typical superhero post, hands on waist and standing proudly against the evil in his city.

I wanted to be like him.

I wanted to be able to make this world a better place.

I threw on a pair of headphones and drowned out my sorrows with the sweet sound of heavy metal. Music and my friends seemed to be my only allies in this life. As I drifted to sleep, I clung to the idea of a better tomorrow.

* * *

My eyes opened, my body numb as I wondered how long I had been asleep. As I looked at my alarm clock, it had only been half an hour. *What the hell?*

An eerie instrumental played in my ears, and I pulled my headphones off.

I questioned if it was actually 4:30 in the morning, but the sun was still out, showing me otherwise. I felt like I'd slept for hours. I got out of bed and headed for a drink of water. As I turned the knob, I realized the sink in my bathroom was broken. I sighed and decided to head for the kitchen. As I made my way down the hall, the house was eerily quiet. I debated going back to my room so I wouldn't have to pass my dad to get to the kitchen, but I decided to go on.

I looked into my brother's room, and the three of them were now staring at a blank screen, holding controllers. I chuckled. "What are you guys doing?" I asked, the situation being very odd for them.

They sat still for a moment, and then one of the friends slowly turned to look at me, revealing dead white eyes. I jumped back, appalled by the vision. "What the hell?" I exclaimed.

"He sees everything," the friend said back, not making much sense. Was this a joke? Where'd he get the contacts? I shook my head and chuckled. It was a good prank, but I was still uncomfortable as I headed toward the living room.

When I got to the living room, I realized it wasn't a prank. Was this… another nightmare? My dad sat in his chair, tapping the same letter again and again on his work laptop, staring at the screen with the same glazed-over eyes. As I looked up, I saw my mom in the kitchen, scrubbing a pan with a spatula in the same spot, over and over.

"Am I…dreaming?"

Upon the words exiting my mouth, they looked up at me, sending shivers down my spine. As I took a step back, my mom walked into the living room. My dad dropped his laptop off the side of his chair with a thud and slowly stood up.

"What is this?" I asked myself, questioning if this *was* another nightmare. As soon as the thought crossed my mind, my vision flickered.

"He's real," my dad said in a monotone voice. The quiet words wrapped themselves around my lungs and squeezed. As horror coursed through my veins, I struggled to keep breathing. I turned around to head back to my room, and then I realized my brother and his friends were now standing behind me, crowding me as if they were a small horde of zombies.

Their eyes flashed yellow, and their jaws unhinged and stretched. They began aggressively screaming the words, "Veka's coming!" I looked around frantically, not sure where to go or what to do. Nor did I know who Veka was. I began to hear other voices. It felt like they came from a world outside this nightmare.

"Wake up!" a girl hissed. "We can't protect you here!"

Just as I was about to book it, the world around me faded to black as if I were about to wake from a dream. A sense of relief flowed through me, knowing I was about to wake up, and then a hand laid itself on my shoulder. It gripped me, and my skin numbed as if winter itself were touching me.

I was spun around, now looking at the cloaked figure in this dark room. As I tried to focus on his face, the lower half was still shrouded in an unnatural darkness. His yellow eyes and nose still split through the dark, sending me into yet another panic.

All the voices I had heard tonight mixed in an overlay of words, expelling themselves from the cloaked figure. "You're not going anywhere!" he hissed, his hands forming a tight grip around my neck. The pressure on my skin didn't feel like a dream. My muscles tightened, as if my blood was going to be sucked right through my skin.

I started swinging my arms. Anything to loosen his grip. As my fists slammed against his seemingly stone body, I was unable to make any progress. I looked into his snake-like eyes, close enough to be able to see a red ring around his slit pupils. It felt as if I was staring into fear itself. As my body began to numb, I raised my hands and pressed my thumbs into those petrifying eyes.

He grunted, his grip loosening enough for me to escape. His head snapped to a slant as his eyes reopened. The darkness lifted, revealing a horrifying grin with two long fangs and sharpened, stained teeth.

I woke up, gasping for air as the remnants of pressure remained on my throat. Now sitting up, shaking with adrenaline, the figure's grin lingered in my mind. I'd never seen his mouth before, and I wondered what it meant that I was seeing it now.

The idea that these dreams meant something scared the hell out of me.

That name. Veka. Was that the cloaked figure's name? I pondered this question for just a moment. I knew it was.

I looked at my clock. *Three in the morning,* I thought. I sighed, covered in sweat for the second night in a row. As my legs dangled over the edge of my bed, hot air from the heater vent slammed against my shins. *Why is the damn heater on?* I thought. I hated the heat, and my parents had always insisted that it be turned on at night.

I started to calm down, and I peeked across my bedroom, scared I'd see him again. With luck, I was now alone in the dark. I guess I didn't need any more sleep tonight.

Chapter 2

Trapped in a Haze

I stood in front of the school door again, hesitating to enter. Not only did I want to avoid the bullies, but I would also need to explain to my friends why I disappeared. *I didn't even text them back,* I thought, cringing. They had tried to call several times, but I had ignored it. I had never gone home without talking to them before they got on their bus. *What do I even say?*

I grabbed the frayed end of my arm warmer, picking at it with my black pointed fingernails. I looked down at the ground, ashamed of myself. Along with being embarrassed, I was also dead tired from another spell of nightmares. Would I ever get good sleep again? Maybe I should just leave. I shook my head. No, I couldn't let my grades slip. Maybe I could graduate early and leave the bullies behind.

I sighed, thinking about my friends and the argument I'd had with my father. I didn't honestly care if I ever went back home after he hit me, but I didn't want to leave my friends alone with Johnny. Despite my parents' opinion about me, I still felt I needed to prove something to them. I couldn't even do that right.

I pushed my way into the building. Every year—no...every day was getting harder to endure, but I needed to push through. I wasn't alone in this. My friends had always been here for me. I started to think about when I met them. I had stood up for them too.

* * *

The first person I met was Shawn. It was in third grade when I had my first interaction with him in the classroom. He had been homeschooled for the first couple of years and ended up living just a few miles away from my house to the south.

I sat at my desk in English class. "When you finish your story, don't forget that I asked you to draw a cover for it as well," Ms. Sharp said, leaving the room for a moment. I was struggling to finish my short story, but I had already nearly completed my cover. My eyes roamed around the classroom for inspiration. I wanted to see where everyone else was on this project.

A kid sat next to me. He had medium, curly dark-brown hair and a slightly round face. He was already starting to draw his cover. It was clear that his story was already finished, judging by the quarter inch of lined paper underneath. As I looked at his picture, it looked like a superhero with four arms and antennas, based off him. *The Adventures of Beetle Boy,* I read in my mind. My mouth widened, and I looked at my own cover, which was a superhero in a red suit with an "AB" on his chest, based off me. *The Adventures of Amazing Boy.* I quickly saw that the pencil he was using had a name on it. Shawn Dewman.

I opened my mouth to say something, but a massive kid with blond hair towered beside him, snatching the pencil out of his hand. Confused as to why he did that, I was quickly answered by his mischievous grin. "Give it back, Rob!" Shawn said. With a huff, he held the pencil back out to him. As Shawn reached for it, Rob quickly pulled it out of reach, and he snapped it in half.

Rob tossed the broken pencil onto the teacher's desk, and Shawn became beet red. "My grandpa gave that to me." The words were angry but quiet. "I hate you." His fists were clenched under his desk. He was scared of Rob. I shook my head, reached into my bag, and grabbed my own set of special pencils covered with superhero comic panels. My favorite thing about them was the colored erasers, matching the different hero on each of the pencils.

"Here," I whispered, putting one on his desk. "I'm sorry he did that." He looked up at me, confused, but he unclenched his fists. I smiled, happy that I could raise his spirits. "I like your cover. I wrote a story about a superhero too. Look! Our titles are close to the same."

A smile found its way onto his face. "No way, thanks! If only I had powers like in my story, I could defend myself against him," Shawn said, nodding toward Rob who was now in the back of the classroom.

"Yeah, if we both had powers, we could fold him up like a pretzel and toss him out the window. He probably can't even read," I added. His face purpled as he restrained a guffaw, trying to stay quiet so that Rob wouldn't hear us. He was smiling now.

"What's your name? I'm Shawn Dewman."

"I'm Tony Jensen." As we began to talk, we found out we were a lot alike. We both liked the same cartoons and stories, and I found out he lived close to me. We became friends right then, and he was the first one who stuck around.

Once the teacher came back into the classroom and found the pencil, Shawn was given his first warning. As Shawn and I tried to explain what happened, the teacher shut it down, stating that it had Shawn's name on it, so he was to blame. The rest of the class period, Shawn was back to clenching his fists.

Shortly afterward, I ran into Talida, who had just moved to the US from Japan. She wasn't like the rest of us here in southwest Old Belmont. She had arrived with duct-taped shoes and an All-Mart plastic bag instead of a backpack. I later learned that she lived in northeast Old Belmont, but her family splurged for their daughter to go to the southwest school. They wanted the best for her, even though Northeast Elementary was much closer. Aiden was much the same. We found him sitting against the wall at recess, drawing. After meeting Johnny and his group soon after, we were united, and the rest was history.

* * *

Now inside and past the lobby, I looked across the cafeteria. Before I found my friends, Shawn came running up to me. His eyes glowed as he made his way over.

"You're here!" Shawn yelled, giving me a fist bump. I smiled, seeing Aiden's default frown turn into a smile as he and Talida whipped around to see me.

"What happened, dude? Are you alright?" Talida asked.

"You left us!" Aiden said, punching me in the arm. I chuckled.

"I'm okay, guys. I'm sorry I disappeared on you. I had a horrible day yesterday," I said, holding the back of my neck nervously. "I couldn't bring myself to look at my phone. I'm really sorry."

"Did something happen with your parents or here at school?" Shawn asked me. "We all get days like that; don't worry about it."

Aiden interrupted, "If it had to do with either of those, it must have been a rough one."

"Both, unfortunately. I left my character binder in the math classroom, and when I got back from a bathroom break, Johnny was reading from it. The whole class was laughing about it! I was in a bad headspace after that so I ditched my classes. The principal called my parents about the situation, and then my dad blamed it all on me. He called me a delinquent, and you guys know how much I hate that word."

I paused, knowing more had happened but not wanting to tell them. *And he hit me.* "I'm—roughed up about it," I explained, trying to hold back how bothered I was about the incident. "And Rob made me out to be a pervert."

"That is so *messed* up," Aiden said, visibly upset. He started to pace as his smile disappeared, becoming jittery. It was then that they all started to stare at me.

"So, what happened to your face?" Shawn asked me, his eyes widening. "Is that from Johnny?" I reached up to my cheek, clenching my jaw. I hadn't noticed a bruise, but then again, I hadn't checked the mirror.

"Yeah…" I trailed off, knowing that was a lie. While I was bothered by the memory, I still didn't feel right lying to my friends. We shared everything, including the bad. I sighed. "No. When I tried to verbally defend myself last night, my dad hit me." It was hard to say the words, but I knew I needed to.

They all gasped. "Are you serious?" Talida yelled, her fists tight at her sides.

"What the hell, man? Your parents have no right to call you that, and they have no right to put their hands on you!" Shawn exclaimed, shaking his head and clenching his fists. "I wish we could do something about them… at least Johnny and his friends." His thought trailed off as if he were lost in some fabricated fever dream. He was likely thinking of a way to turn the tables.

"Fuck them," Aiden swore. "No, seriously. Fuck them."

"I agree with you. It's hard to want to even go back home. He's never done that before, and I don't know what to do. Not to mention Johnny and his goons are starting hard this year. If they continue, they're likely going to get me expelled."

Talida threw her head back, letting loose an aggravated screech. "God, they just don't know when to stop, do they? Are we seriously going to have to deal with them until we graduate?"

"Yup. And that's if we get lucky and they move out of Old Belmont," Aiden muttered, rubbing his ear.

"It'll end eventually," I started. "We just have to stick together. Maybe we can all graduate early and get the Hell out of here. As for my parents, I'll prove them wrong." My friends smiled, hanging onto that thought as we sat down for breakfast.

"You look tired, man," Shawn said, his voice dropping in concern. He looked me in the eyes. "We're in this together. Always will be." He raised his fist again to me.

"You all sure know how to raise my spirits. I'll be okay. I had another nightmare last night too. Only this time I saw his grin. The cloaked figure was choking me and threatening me after another ordeal involving the yellow eyes. It was bizarre, and I wasn't about to go back to sleep after that," I said, tearing the blue film off my carton of Frosted Flakes and pouring in the milk. I bumped his fist again.

Aiden groaned, followed by the others. "Do you think your bad experiences and thoughts are being manifested into this cloaked figure you're always talking about? I know he's not real, but do you think that's what those thoughts have formed in your brain?"

"You're really into this idea of manifestation lately, aren't you?" Shawn asked, chuckling. Talida giggled. He had been going on about it all summer, talking about using energies to try to create a better future. I liked the mindset and agreed with him, but we had been giving him flak for how often he had mentioned it.

"Come on, guys! I really do believe we can change everything if we just put our energies together. All this negativity has to go somewhere, right? Maybe we are manifesting this monster Tony keeps seeing!" Aiden said, starting to bite his nails.

"I think he has a point. I do really believe in energy, and he may be onto something. This cloaked figure in my nightmares became more prominent when I experienced higher amounts of stress. Maybe I *am* creating this monster that's trying to snuff me out with the power of our emotions," I said, starting to be concerned. In my eyes, energy wasn't something to mess around with.

Aiden's smile returned to his face as Shawn apologized. As the bell rang, I stood up to dump my tray. "Thanks, guys. I appreciate you all," I said as they began to head to class.

"See ya!" Talida called out, smiling.

"Goodbye!" Aiden blurted out, heading down the hallway with Shawn.

I walked into my classroom and was met with giggling. *Already?* I thought. I pretended not to hear it, sitting down at my desk. I pulled out my homework, having almost forgotten about it. Mr. Karson retrieved our papers, and started another review lesson.

Rob let out a fake moan, and I rolled my eyes. "I'm gonna ghost!" he yelled out, being met with an explosion of cackles. I sighed, knowing I wouldn't be able to free myself from the torment.

"That's enough!" Mr. Karson snapped, his voice piercing the laughter and sending the room into a disturbing silence. It would have been nice if he'd stopped it yesterday. I harshly let out a deep breath through my nose.

After his lesson, I got up to go to the bathroom, with my belongings this time. I headed to the freshman hallway. Off of it was the bathroom that was usually empty, and my only place of solace.

I closed the stall door. After hanging my backpack on the coat hook, I sat down. Remembering yesterday I knew I had to keep all my possessions with me in hopes of not reliving that horrible situation.

The laughter kept repeating in my mind, making me want to cry all over again. *Not here; you're not safe here,* I thought, swallowing my pain.

I crawled out of my nightmarish thoughts to the situation at hand. At least I was away from him. Johnny's face was fresh in my mind. It seemed pathetic that I had to go to the bathroom to get fifteen minutes of peace. Suddenly, someone else walked in, and my body went on high alert. If it were one of the bullies, they couldn't find out I was here. The last time I was caught in the bathroom, it was by Johnny and Grey, who had pulled down my pants and tied my hands to the toilet with my head dipping in and out of the water. It had been one of the most humiliating experiences I had ever dealt with at Belmont High.

I shuddered at the twisted memory of the counselor coming into the bathroom to untie me.

As I listened to them standing near the urinals, I recognized their voices, sending me further into distress. I lifted my legs slowly, leaning them against the cold metal around me.

"I can't wait for today to be over. I'm just going to drop out and be a mechanic or some shit, so why do I have to sit through algebra," Grey said.

"Because, dumbass, the basics are important. I'm trying to actually be somebody in my life. How am I supposed to outsmart people and get ahead if I have the wits of a deaf mockingbird?"

A grunt escaped Grey as if he disagreed, but he made no reply to the re-mark. "Do you want to skip class and go to the gym? It's empty at this hour, and I've got some bud behind the stands."

"You're hiding drugs in the gym? Are you stupid? If you light that up, the whole school will smell it."

"No, of course not. Beer. I got beer."

"Whatever, dude. Let's go. Art class is next anyway. I'm down for a drink."

As I sat silently, holding my breath, I was finally able to let out a deep sigh when they eventually left the room. *That was close.*

As I tried to relax and stay out of my head, I scratched the back of my neck, my pointed black fingernails scraping against my skin. It was amazing I wasn't more messed up than I was.

As I attempted to stay positive, my parents' voices echoed in my head. Not only from last night's ordeal but all the previous ones as well. They've called me a delinquent and a fuck-up on many occasions. I sighed as I looked at my hands. I leaned my head against the cold metal of the stall, not having realized how tired I was from the night before.

Were they right? Was there only despair and failure in my future? If I ran away from this place, would anything change? No, probably not. A tear fell down my cheek. I hated myself. This world would be better without me tainting it. My skin started to feel heavy. Heavier than my thoughts. As the relaxation from being alone mixed with my adrenaline dropping, my brain began to feel foggy. Soon, my eyelids flickered, and I fell into the dream world once more.

* * *

A fabricated memory was placed in my mind. My family and I had supposedly watched a movie the night before, so it made sense that I was now waking up on the couch in the living room. As I glanced around, everyone had gone to bed, and now I was the only one in here. Darkness surrounded me, and I had the urge to look at the television that was in the middle of the wall across from me.

Right in front of the screen stood a figure in a black cloak. A visible, black aura rested like a fog around him. It wore a hood over its head, and I couldn't determine its features. The figure's build pointed toward being a male, but I was unsure. I only saw its terrifying slit eyes, which glowed a beaming yellow as if they would pierce my soul. The piercing eyes were accompanied by two glowing slits for a nose, like those of a skull. They squinted, filled with an evil I dared not endure. The petrifying grin that went with it, shrouded by shadow, was left to my darkest bouts of imagination.

Cold seemed to emanate from the figure. It was as if my surroundings were starting to frost over. It wasn't only the uneasy chill; something else more sinister and malicious lingered in the air around me. My breath was suddenly visible, and I was starting to shiver.

I stared at him, my insides twisting and dropping as I questioned if what I was seeing was real. I screamed, jumping off the couch as I leapt toward the light switch. As I glanced over my shoulder to see if he was still there, the figure was gone without a remnant of the evil that had *just* been in my living room. My mom came running. "What's wrong?" she asked.

In my panic I questioned if I should even tell her. Would she believe me?

"That cloaked figure was in front of the TV!" I wailed, still shaking in fear. I had told my parents I'd been having a hard time sleeping and about this recurring villain of the night. They hadn't taken it seriously, telling me that my stress was giving me nightmares. I believed them, but that didn't help eliminate the issue.

"We're going on about this figure again?" my mom asked with an annoyed undertone. She was sure that I'd been "seeing things." She probably believed that this situation was just another example. Still...I knew this couldn't have been a hallucination; it was much different.

I sighed. It felt so real. It *looked* so real. Why would I have lied about seeing it?

My mom let out a deep breath, calming down from the elevated mood she had been in. "Oh, honey," she said, pulling me in close for a hug. She held me tight—and long enough for it to become uncomfortable. As I questioned when she was going to let me go, she took another breath in.

She giggled.

"There's no one here to help you," she whispered in my ear. Her voice was empty.

As if it weren't hers.

My entire body clenched, and I pulled away as goosebumps crawled along my skin. In a burst of energy, I screamed, looking at her.

Her eyes flashed yellow as she smiled.

Her jaw unclenched. She lurched forward in a chomping motion.

* * *

I shuddered awake, frantically trying to figure out where I was. Tethering myself back to reality, I wondered how long I had passed out in the stall. I worried I would get in trouble, but as I remembered the recent events, I didn't think I cared.

As the next few minutes went by with me bathing my mind in horrible past experiences, I started to hear teachers yelling. I couldn't make out what they were saying, but it was loud and sounded like something was going on. Maybe I should spend a couple more minutes in here. Did Rob and Grey get caught? The gym was down at the end of the hall on the other side. Or maybe someone started a fight; they usually met up in this hallway for that.

The yelling continued, and people were rushing around. When I tried to check my phone for the time, I was met with a black screen. *Of course my phone's dead. Have I been in here too long? Is this the class change?*

A couple more minutes went by, and a voice came over the intercom. "Everyone needs to evacuate immediately. There's a fire in the freshman hallway, which is an immediate threat. This is not a drill." The voice seemed panicked, and as I realized the fire alarms weren't going off, I became confused. *Are they broken? Is this real?*

As I rushed to finish up, I smelled smoke. It wasn't the pleasant aroma like sitting around an open flame on a camping trip. It was the kind of odor that came from plastic and other dirty objects catching fire. Opening the stall door and looking around, the putrid fumes were coming in through the top of the entry door.

"Oh goth!" I exclaimed. I had started saying goth instead of god a long time ago as a joke, but now it had been burnt into my vocabulary, and I said it unironically.

As I tried to think of the quickest way out of the building, I realized I would need to get through to the end of the hallway to the big glass door. The smoke was already getting to me, and as I freaked out, trying to breathe, I ripped off one of my arm warmers and ran it under the faucet. Wrapping it around my face, I knew I didn't have much time; with the smoke coming into the bathroom like it was, the fire had surely spread quickly.

Without thinking much more about the dilemma at hand, I sprinted into the hallway, booking it for the door. Almost immediately, my eyes began to water as I was bombarded by a cloud of black smoke. As it struck me, it was almost as if it took form. I half-expected it to grow teeth and attack me, for it was the closest thing I had seen to a real fire elemental.

Fear coursed through me as I got about halfway to my destination. I couldn't open my eyes well now, and I was beginning to cough as my wet arm-warmer failed me. *I'm so close,* I thought. *I have to make it through.* As I trudged between the flaming walls, a scream filled my ears. *Oh no!* I looked around, frantically, my eyes widening with the realization that someone else was still there. I wasn't sure what to do and my heart rate spiked.

"Hey! I'm in the hallway!" I tried to yell. The screaming turned into cries for help, and my breathing quickened. *I have to do something!* I spun to the left, and then the right. Where was the yelling coming from? As they cried out again, I pinpointed its location. My dad's voice echoed in my head, telling me that it wasn't any of my business. I shook my head, defying that thought. I had to do something.

I sprinted toward the room on my right. The door was closed and on fire. I knew that if I took the time to reach them, I would be putting myself in grave danger. No one in this school had ever helped **me**; my three friends were the only ones who had ever stood by my side. Everyone else looked down on us, and I certainly didn't owe them anything. *I have to help them,* the voice in my head said. They might not do it for me, but that didn't mean I shouldn't do it for them. How could I ever live with myself if I didn't help those in need? How could I ever be like Grudgematch? I reached for the door with a cough and then pulled away.

"Help! Are you out there?" I heard as the person behind the door hacked up a lung.

My teeth clenched, and my eyes narrowed. I could make a difference. What kind of person would I be if I left them here? The voice sent shivers down my spine, and it was almost as if my body moved on its own when I slammed my side into the flaming entry. The door burst off its deteriorating hinges, making me wince. Getting a nasty burn on the side of my arm, I ran into the room, trying my best to look for the person in trouble through the malicious haze.

As my vision shook, threatening to spin my surroundings, I began to hallucinate. Faces began to appear in the smoke. Twisting and turning, these living flames billowed around the corner, releasing themselves from the room.

I ran over to some fallen debris, and attempted to lift a cabinet that the boy was stuck underneath. The kid was short with shaggy brown hair and a thin frame. I knew him as Milo Sanchez; he was on the wrestling team and had always picked on Aiden for his weight. Our last interaction was him tearing Aiden's drawings apart.

As much as I wanted to leave him, I couldn't bring myself to do it. He gave me a confused look as I struggled to lift the rubble. His nose wrinkled, and his eyes glazed over in fear, unsure of why I was helping him. He knew I had recognized him, and what he had done in the past seemed to shake him to the core as he thought that I might be there to enact karma.

I coughed and pushed, sending my body into a light-headed state. Just when I thought I wasn't going to be able to release him, Milo was able to yank himself free. He stood up, looked me in the eyes, and then scrambled away. I followed, but he left me behind as I struggled to stand up straight. *Am I going to die?* I thought, slogging through the flames. I fell to the ground, unable to breathe. I tried to crawl forward, but now the smoke was taking the form of people, and I could hear laughter.

"You're never going to amount to anything," I heard a voice say from within the dark billows of smoke. I crawled, now starting to lose consciousness. I was able to make it near to a corner and saw what looked like a tall shadow run around it. I managed to get to my feet, first leaning against the wall and then bouncing the opposite direction as I smelled the hair on my arms being scorched off with my roasting skin.

A loud blast filled the room, sending a liquid into my face. "What the…" I tried to say. As the liquid hit my eyes and mouth, it started to sting. I screamed in agony, not knowing what to do. I couldn't open my eyes. I couldn't see, I couldn't breathe, and now I was sure I was going to die. I fell to my knees, my entire body locking up in pain.

"Shawn! Aiden—anybody!" I was able to call out from the floor. Tears rolled down my face, and I began to sob. My cries sputtered as they were interrupted by violent coughing. "I'm scared…" I whimpered. "I'm not ready to go." My body began to lose function. I fell to the floor, and then I wasn't able to move at all. It was as if I was paralyzed. As my body forced me to take a deep breath in, I fell into darkness.

Chapter 3

Second Chance

Consciousness returned slowly. In a realm neither awake nor asleep, I hovered in darkness.

"Where am I?" I asked myself. It felt as though I had entered a dream. I had no feelings, and I was in a black space. No walls or any signs of one. It was pitch black. *Am I dead?* I thought as I walked forward, leaving violet, glowing footsteps behind me on the newly formed floor. My thoughts echoed back as if I had spoken them aloud.

A presence emanated before me; almost as if *something* or someone were here with me. I had a sudden urge to reach for it, and as I extended my arm, it felt like my hand was reaching into a wall of ice water. Suddenly, a figure stood in the distance. Alarm shot through me, but this wasn't the figure I was used to. It was a man in a black, crystalline suit of armor. A large sword was sheathed on his back, and none of his skin was visible. He looked like a crystalline ninja. Or a Batman type, which made me chuckle. I cocked my head in question and took a step back.

"You're—different than the rest," the man said in a commanding, stern tone. He took a step toward me, and I quickly noticed the bright gold medallion across his chest with the letters *BW* engraved. A massive black cape flapped behind him from an invisible wind. I didn't know what to say, so I remained silent. "You and I have a lot to talk about, Tony. I'm not sure how long you have here, or how you connected with me, but I need you to know that your life is about to change forever. You know not what you wield, but you will soon understand."

"What do you mean? Who are you?" I asked, now stepping toward him.

"You wanted a second chance. I see that in you. My name is Blackwell. You must listen closely. The connection is weakening. Do not underestimate yourself, Tony."

"Wait," I interrupted. "How do you know that?"

"I see it within your mind. I see your pain, your happiness, your hate, and your love. There is a divide. Two paths stand before you. That of a villain, and that of a hero. One future choice will forge which path you take." His voice trailed off as he started to fade from my vision. I could no longer hear him. I started to sprint toward him, but despite every step, I made no progress.

"Wait! What choice? What do I need to do?" I screamed into the darkness. I reached forward, as if to pull him back toward me, but he was gone.

My body was thrown forward like someone had slammed on the brakes of a car, sending me to a screeching halt in the black void in front of me.

My eyes opened again. I was now in a dark hallway with black bricks. I was cold and wet, like the moment after you jump into a cool swimming pool where the full-body bliss surrounds you beneath the water. My dream had changed. I felt like I was in the real world, yet I was unable to drag or control my body as I walked next to someone. I became quickly aware that the body I inhabited wasn't mine. It was as if I was looking through the perspective of someone I didn't control. Like watching a movie through the eyes of a side character.

As I walked through this brick hallway, bright, oddly yellow torches lit up as I passed them. I continued down the corridor, past what seemed to be dark prison cells on both sides. Moans of agony filled the air as I passed them. As I headed further in, a pungent smell of mildew mixed with rotting flesh caused me to want to gag, but my body didn't react; I was trapped in this vessel I couldn't control.

It was then that I noticed someone was walking next to me. A towering figure. I would have leapt back in terror if I were able. I saw its two beaming yellow eyes and the two, bright-yellow nose slits I had seen in dreams for the last couple of years. But the rest was still unclear. His name was Veka. I was sure of it now, whether or not it had clicked from my previous nightmare or from the mind of the person I currently inhabited in this strange state.

"Please, I haven't had food in weeks," a woman said, sobbing in pain. I peered into the cell on my right where she was. It was a horrifying sight. I had never seen anything like her except in movies; she was skeletal in shape, only a thin layer of skin stretched over her bones.

"If you survive a few more months, I will set you free," Veka said in a scratchy, echoing voice. She sank into her cell, defeated as she started to cry again.

What kind of horror was this? Was I in hell?

"Please let me go! I have two kids, for Christ's sake! *Let me go*!" a man yelled through tears from a cell on my left, reaching for his head and yanking out his hair.

"I want to die!" a heartbroken man screeched from a cell on my right, grabbing the bars of his cell and yanking on them. "Kill me!" He screamed, his rotting eye sockets projecting terror into my mind.

"Please, god of the damned, end my life," an older man pleaded with his frail voice, latching onto the metal with a rotting, festering fist.

As we reached the end of the corridor, we arrived at a charcoaled, heavy metal door. Veka reached his hand out from underneath a black cloak and rested it on a biometric scanner. He had a dark purple tone to his skin with sharp black fingernails. What is he? Is he a demon? I was horrified. Is this what hell is? What did I do to be sent here?

The scanner lit up yellow as four loud deadbolts unlocked. The door swung open, and it revealed another man, who looked to be in his forties with tan skin and wiry black, overgrown facial hair, dusted with strands of gray. His arms were chained behind his back, similar to a straight jacket but much harsher. He had a collar around his neck, chained to the wall. It was apparent that this man had tried to escape—many times—for the chains were stained in what could only be his blood.

I stood over on the other side of the room as a high-strung cackle left the cloaked figure's lips. "Ah, good morning," Veka said in a scratchy voice. He reached his hand out and grabbed the chained man's beard, lifting his head to look into his eyes. I could see the prisoner's eyes from where I was standing. They were a beautiful brown, but behind the beauty was determination. This man wasn't broken of hope just yet.

As I marveled at this fire still in his eyes, I couldn't help but wonder why he was in here.

"Is there anything I can do to make your stay more comfortable?" Veka asked, pausing a moment for him to respond. "Perhaps a television to watch your hopeless, 'special forces' fall apart? I can get you the best quality TV so that you can see every…detail…of each and every one of your members' deaths." He paused for a moment, letting go of him and pacing around the room.

Veka chuckled softly. "You know, it's funny; you're just going to be locked in this room while my Followers do the work, and then I will kill you myself, ending this whole charade you created with just one, quick, slash."

The prisoner yanked himself forward, straining his chains as far as they could go toward his captor. "You will not get away with this! I will escape, and when I do, you will pay for your atrocities. You're a monster, Veka!" he said with ferocity.

Their bickering continued, but the voices faded and became distorted. The color in my vision became oversaturated and disfigured. My ability to understand what was now being said, was gone.

Everything then brightened to a pure white, and my ears began to ring.

* * *

My vision returned to me, first coming in shapes and then colors. I realized I was laying in a small hospital bed. As I sat up, my head was assaulted by a colossal migraine, and my entire body ached like I had the flu. Groaning in pain, I lifted my hand to rest it on my flaming forehead, only to feel a rough, thin cloth wrapped around it. A burning—but tolerable—sensation shot through my back and throughout my muscles. As I wiggled in search of a comfortable position, I realized I wasn't going to find one.

I looked around, seeing the IV attached to my arm, and my eyes wandered to the skin on that arm. I was pale. Like, vampire pale. My hands also appeared to be too large, and I questioned if they were even my own. I wondered how long I had been out. I quickly noticed my once black fingernails were now bare and cut short. The voices of doctors echoed across the hallway outside my hospital room, arguing back and forth amongst themselves.

"What was that dream?" I said to myself. The voice that left my mouth made me jump. *That's not my voice...is it?* My voice was several octaves deeper than it had been before I woke up. I returned my hand to my forehead weakly. I had lost a lot of strength, and my memory was foggy. I slid my legs to the side of the bed and rubbed my temple in thought. A soft beeping sound, hardly noticeable, began going off, and I looked around, curious. Shortly after it began, a large doctor walked in wearing a long, white coat. He was bulky, but he wasn't overly obese. He was followed by several others.

"Was that a nightmare?" I asked myself quietly, trying to piece together what I had witnessed. I was surprised of my deepened voice. *It was so vivid,* I thought. Who was that guy in the cloak, Veka? Who is Blackwell? Having seen Veka multiple times now, in more vivid situations, I was beginning to worry that he was real. I shook my head. They were likely just lore created by my mind to make my nightmares more realistic. How could someone like that be real? But why did he keep showing up?

Before I had a chance to question what "Blackwell" had told me, the doctor started to speak. "I see you're awake, Tony. I'm Dr. Christopher Mellark. How are you feeling?" he asked, sitting down on a round, wheeled stool. At the sound of my name, my memories of what had happened rushed back, overloading my head, and I zoned out for probably a minute or two. When I finally came to, the doctor was looking at me, snapping his fingers to try and bring me out of my haze as he observed my reactions.

"Sorry, what did you ask?" I asked, embarrassed for not remembering the simple question.

"It's no problem, Tony. I asked how you were feeling," Dr. Mellark replied, smiling back at me. His voice was light and inviting.

"Very weak; lifting myself is a struggle," I replied, gauging myself as I tried to lift my arms. I was lightheaded while sitting up, and it felt as though somebody was trying to pull me back down.

"Weakness is normal. It's a miracle you're able to sit up," he said. Before I had time to be confused, he began to speak again. "I need to get you caught up with the recent events. Take as much time to process this information as you need. Tony, you fell victim to a school fire, and despite our best efforts, you have been in a coma-like state for the last two years. Being able to sit up is a great sign, and we are going to have to run several tests along with several months' worth of physical therapy to get you back in your best health," the doctor informed.

At this point my head was spinning, and I couldn't breathe. *Two years!?* I thought. Were my friends okay? Did they even remember me?! I was having trouble speaking because of the thought of losing my best and only friends. And what about my family? As the thoughts continued, I was now experiencing a full assault in the pit of my stomach. I didn't want to lose them. The back of my throat tightened, threatening to make me lose what little calm I had left.

Dr. Mellark smiled. "I understand that this is a shock. We are here to help you in any way we can," he said. "These doctors are going to have to ask you several questions, and then we can begin with the process to get you out of here," he said, very confident in his ability to put me back on my feet. He stood and left the room, leaving me for the others' questions.

* * *

After what felt like a few hours of questions revolving around what I experienced during the fire and my current physical condition, Dr. Mellark returned to notify me of what to expect in the months to come.

"We will conduct a physical test today, and if you pass, we will allow you to leave the hospital over the weekend to make your necessary living arrangements. You will need to arrive at the EPT wing of this hospital Monday at 8:00 in the morning, where we will begin your physical therapy," he started.

In surprise, I cocked my head. "Wait, I can go home? Why are they letting me leave before the therapy?" I asked.

"That will only happen if you're able to pass the test. Physical therapy will be a long process, and I doubt you want to stay at the hospital any longer than you have to. Take that time to catch up with your friends and gather whatever information you'll need for afterward. This is a very important step for you, and we want to make sure you have what you need," Dr. Mellark said. Still a little confused, I wasn't sure why my parents couldn't bring me my necessities.

"Will my parents not be able to bring me the stuff? I mean, I'd like to go home and get them myself, but I'm confused," I said, rubbing my temple again. I had been in the hospital a couple of times, and my parents would normally bring me whatever I needed. As the doctor became silent, and Dr. Mellark looked to the others with a questioning gaze, my heart turned to stone. "Are my parents—okay?" I asked hesitantly.

The room had fallen into an unnerving quiet as those in the room sent shocked glances between one another. As a few of them raised their hands in the air in question, Dr. Mellark let out a sigh.

"I apologize. I was told that the others would update you on your current situation." Dr. Mellark pulled his fist up to his lips and cleared his throat, causing me more anxiety. As I began to think my parents were dead, I started to pick at my cuticles. The truth turned out to be significantly worse than I expected.

"About nine months into your coma, your parents had to make a difficult choice. You were showing signs of severe physical deterioration. Many doctors believed you would not come out of the coma alive. Your parents made the decision to pull the plug. It was not an easy decision, and it wasn't what they wanted to do. However, a man named Terrance King learned of your situation, and he spoke with your family. They came to the decision to let Terrance adopt you, and he also took over your coma responsibilities."

My mouth dropped. I didn't know what to say. I looked around the room as if the answer lay within it. My instincts kicked in, and I blurted out, "I'm not leaving with someone that's not my family." The thought of living with a stranger after this already life-altering situation sent me into a downward spiral. The fact that my parents had abandoned me threw me into a fresh pit of despair. Tears started to roll down my cheeks.

My feelings were conflicted. Part of me asked why they would have let me die rather than pushing forward. I asked myself if they loved me at all, but logic made an appearance. I had been looking horrible in everyone's view, and I had been told how expensive it was for an overnight stay in a hospital. Being on a constant IV and there every day for nine months? No one in their right mind would have continued to attempt to pay that. I couldn't hold this against them. I knew it wouldn't have been an easy situation for them to be in. I knew that if they were loaded, they would have continued to hope for my recovery.

But if Terrance had offered to pay for everything and relieve them of the financial situation, why had they let him adopt me?

"We understand—"

"No. You don't. You're sitting here telling me that I've been asleep the last two years, and my parents abandoned me when it got hard. What am I—"

"Tony, this is a lot to handle at once, but everything is already in order for you to pick up where you left off. I'm not asking that you leave with a stranger. I am simply stating that the stranger saved your life. Terrance fought for you. He insisted that he would put all the remaining financial burden on himself rather than your family. No strings attached."

Dr. Mellark had his hands up, trying to calm me down. As he took a breath, I had to ask the question still lingering on my mind. "Then why did they let him adopt me? Why is my family not here still hoping that I'll wake up, if Terrance decided to pay for everything?"

Dr. Mellark's gaze turned hard. More bad news, I was sure of it. "From what I understand, it was easier for Terrance to handle the finances of your situation if you were a part of his family rather than your own. Why your family hasn't been in contact after that, I am unsure."

I gulped. That is what I didn't want to hear. I opened my mouth to speak, but nothing came out. My throat tightened, and I sat there in silence before Dr. Mellark continued.

"Despite that, Terrance insisted that you would be given another chance."

The words of Blackwell in my dream were mirrored in what I had just heard. I wanted a second chance. But I was still unable to speak the words aloud. I lifted my chin, seeing that this was exactly that. I was afraid, and more alone than ever, but it was also time to turn my life in the direction I wanted it to go. "Alright," I muttered. I cleared my own throat, breaking the phlegm away as if trying to break loose the restraints of my previous life. "What's the next step, then?"

"Upon passing the test to leave, you will have your weekend free to gather what you wish to return to the EPT wing Monday morning. We ask that you come alone, and you won't be allowed visitors while in rehabilitation.

More will be explained as to why once you arrive."

I nodded, trusting that he would explain it further. The idea was odd to me. I had never been told people weren't allowed to come see me. Especially for something like rehabilitation.

Dr. Mellark walked closer to me, sitting on the edge of the bed as his topic changed. "You're a remarkable young man, Tony. Most adults don't come out of their comas being able to sit up and talk. Most patients lose a lot of their memory, and some even require relearning basic functions. I don't know much about you as a person, but I'm sure you are destined for great things. Don't waste your second chance." He slapped his legs and stood again. I followed his movement as he made his way in front of me.

"Now, for the other details: The hospital has given you the go-ahead to allow you back into school once you are done with your physical therapy. When you go back, you will have locker number 238. This information will be given to you before leaving the hospital. We are pairing you with Mr. Karson, and he will serve as your guidance counselor. His job is to keep a closer eye on you than the rest of the students so that you can have the best opportunity to catch up with your class."

I sighed with a not-so-hidden grunt. "Great…" I whispered to myself.

"Is something the matter?" Dr. Mellark asked, seeming concerned.

Hardly realizing he had heard me, I shook my head. "I just don't like Mr. Karson. He's given me issues in the past."

"Hmm. I'm sorry to hear that. I will warn you that you won't be having any more problems with school. The teachers have been coached on understanding when students are being bullied, and a zero-tolerance policy has been put in place now."

I rolled my eyes. *Zero-tolerance… Yeah, whatever.*

"Now, I do understand that most of the time, these programs don't do much good, but you've got something else on your side. That will also be further explained in your physical therapy. Because of the credits you received before your accident, they are going to allow you to double up on your classes this year as a senior. This will ensure you can graduate with your friends. Since school started again last week, we *do* have some catching up to do. I have two important things to give you," Dr. Mellark said.

He paused, pulling out a black envelope with a strange, gold wax seal with the letters *BW*. He looked me directly in the eyes with a serious gaze. "That's for you to open in private while you have time at home. It's a copy of your…medical record," he finished in a whisper, shooting me a sly wink.

I thought that was strange. I looked at it. Those letters, on that bright gold. Is Blackwell a real person? Surely, it was a coincidence. My brain had likely fabricated him while it heard something subconsciously.

He reached for something else within his pocket. It was a petite, black box. I furled my eyebrows as I questioned its contents.

"This is very important. You are eighteen, and because of the circumstances you are in, this should help you get on your feet."

I opened the box as he nodded toward it. My eyes then widened, but I didn't understand the full meaning of what I was looking at. Inside lay a matte black debit card and what looked to be a dark gray cell phone. I could tell quickly that it was a new model, too. I looked up at Dr. Mellark as if to ask him for details.

"Inside is a prepaid cell phone. Your first ninety days are already active. Mr. King has also provided a prepaid debit card for you to get what you need and get on your feet. It holds a balance of 15,000 dollars, which should hold you off long enough to find a job and a place to stay.

"15,000?!" I asked, my mouth dropping again. It seemed to be my default facial expression now. That was a lot of money. I knew it could go quickly if I wasn't careful, but I was more than thankful that I wouldn't be completely on my own without any money or place to live.

"Yes. Use it wisely. I suggest planning what to do while you're in physical therapy. That is all I have for you today. Have a great day, Tony. I wish you the best of luck with your test," Dr. Mellark informed me, beginning to head for the door.

The doctor looked back slightly, not making full eye contact with me. "I assure you, you will want to read that record—alone," he said, leaving the room.

Huh, that seems off, I thought. He was very adamant about this being private. I pondered for a moment, my mind wandering to the other dilemma at hand; I didn't want to believe it. I was alone. I still didn't know what my friends were going through. Two years could change everything. I would have to couch hop with them, but I refused to live with them. As much as I would love to, I refused to be a burden on anyone now that I was given this second chance.

Looking around the room and finding the date, I realized that Talida, Shawn, and I would all be eighteen now. Aiden was now nineteen. I hoped they would still remember me. Although, I certainly wouldn't be angry if Johnny and his friends had moved on.

I asked myself if I should reach out to my family. To see if they would want me to move back in with them. Then I would at least have a roof over my head. I frowned, remembering what still felt like the night before. My father had hit me. Would that happen again? I loved my family, especially my mom and brother, but I knew in my heart that it would be better if I could find my own path. They would reach out if they wanted to speak with me. Plus, Dr. Mellark had already said they hadn't kept in contact.

I looked down at the letter, my hands starting to tremble with anticipation. I wondered what it said. I had always been a curious person, and the way the doctor acted about this paper piqued my curiosity.

A knock at my door forced me to quickly shove it under my pillow. I didn't know who I could trust if it was as private as the doctor made it out to be. A tall man with a darker complexion walked into the room, his auburn hair pressed together in a tight bun. "Hello, Tony. My name is Paul Heron, and I will be taking care of your leaving process. Are you ready for your examination?" he asked me, cutting right to the chase. I nodded, wondering what he was going to have me do.

* * *

After several tests on basic functions, he told me I would be able to leave in the morning. The exam consisted of several exercises and simple movements. Most of everything had been easy, except for my balance; I was going to have to push to earn that back. The assortment of exercises wore me out, and I fell right to sleep afterward.

Chapter 4

Visitors

I had already been awake for a while now, pondering the choices I would need to make soon. The idea of reaching out to my family crossed my mind again, but we had never really had the best relationship.

My parents didn't understand me. For as long as I can remember, I've always loved the different styles of gothic fashion. The style made me happy and has always been one of the ways I liked to express myself. It was very artistic and unique, which had always drawn me to it.

As for music, I listened to almost everything, my favorite being Gothic Rock, rating it only slightly above a genre called Industrial Pop. I could truly connect with all kinds of music, while my parents only listened to country and thought any form of rock was the work of the devil. They believed that liking this kind of music and clothing style made me a delinquent, when in reality, I wasn't anything of the sort.

My parents never supported me fully. Every time I had mentioned a plan for my life—a career path—they would only tell me how unrealistic it was and that I should go to college and become a doctor, a lawyer, or *something* successful. A "real job." They wanted me to live the life they'd missed out on. My dad had always wanted to be a surgeon while my mom had her eye on aviation. When they'd learned that mom was pregnant, they'd dropped their dreams, telling each other they would come back to them once they were better off.

They had never said to my face that I was the reason for their failure, but after many passive-aggressive actions and insults, I began to believe it. What good would a gothic graphic-designing delinquent be for two high-end parents anyway? If they were to ever go back to their goals, I would only hinder their success. Going back to that creativity prison would be nothing more than a mistake. I would be throwing my second chance away. Whether Blackwell was real or not, I would be taking his words to heart.

There was a knock at the door. "Good morning, Tony. You have a visitor. May he come in?" Paul asked. I smiled, still groggy. I was nervous to know who it was, but I had high hopes that it was either Aiden or Shawn. Maybe even my brother.

"Sure, who is it?" I answered, sitting on the edge of the bed. I no longer had an IV attached, which made me feel less burdened. As he entered the room, followed by another man about my age, my face twisted in confusion. I didn't recognize him at first. The man had brown skin and short brown hair with a thin frame and glasses. He looked nervous, and I peered into his eyes, trying to remember if I should know him or not.

"Hey, dude," he said as if he didn't know what to say. Suddenly, I knew who I was speaking with, and it confused me further. It was Milo Sanchez! The former bully and peer that I saved in the school fire.

"Hey," I said calmly. There was a slight tension in the air as I thought about what to say. My emotions were again split. I first felt anger, knowing he had been a bully, and he had left me in the fire after I had saved him. But, once I began to think about the situation, he probably thought I was following behind him. He was just as scared as I was in that smoke-filled room. I smiled, becoming more friendly toward him. "I wasn't expecting to see you here."

Milo rubbed the back of his neck. "I needed to come and apologize." He paused, letting out a harsh breath as he avoided eye contact. He rubbed the back of his neck again and then looked up to me. "The way I treated you and your friends wasn't right. I wanted to come and say that I'm sorry, especially for the way I treated Aiden. I also wanted to say how thankful I am that you saved me in that fire."

Milo reached down toward his leg and lifted his jeans up to his right knee. Underneath was badly scarred skin. I hadn't noticed an injury when I helped him, but the flames must have gotten to him. "This would have been worse if you hadn't have pulled that cabinet off me. I would have been dead, so I wanted to come and thank you, Tony. If there's anything I can do for you, let me know."

I nodded, my chest swelling with a mixture of happiness and accomplishment. "That really means a lot to hear. I'm not holding any grudges toward you. I'm glad I was able to help. What kind of person would I be if I turned a blind eye to you when you needed help?"

Milo laughed, bright white teeth flashing from his mouth. "A normal one, probably. The way I treated you guys—well, I'm not sure I would have helped. Especially if I was scared and fighting for my own life." His tone turned serious again as the wide grin shrank and his eyes focused on mine. "Thank you, Tony."

He held out his hand, and I shook it. "Of course. How's life been?" I asked, not sure what else to say. The entire conversation was strange, but I was oddly giddy at the same time. I *had* saved someone. That's what Grudge-match would have done.

"Well, you know. School." He threw his hands up. "But I got myself a car, so it's not all bad! Chemistry's kicking my ass, though. I do have to get going. Thanks for hearing me out," he said, turning to leave the room.

Upon him saying that, it reminded me that my license would have expired. I had just gotten it before the school fire. I didn't own a car, but my mom had let me get the license using hers. If I had been lucky, my parents were likely going to get me something, but I got trapped in the school fire instead. Hopefully, it would be pretty easy to get my license again once I made it through physical therapy.

Maybe I'd use some of that money to get a vehicle. If I got the right one, I could even live in it until I found a place to stay on my own. I then began to wonder if my friends were still living at home or in their own places. Unless something had changed financially, it was likely they were still at home.

There was another knock at the door, and two familiar faces entered the room. "Oh, thank goth!" I exclaimed. My worries were interrupted and forgotten because of the presence of two of my best friends, Shawn and Talida.

My chest filled with excitement to see them again.

Talida looked only slightly different; she had gotten a lot taller, but her hair was still short and cut to the bottom of her neck. Her fashion, on the other hand, was the biggest change. She had a pair of black, ripped jeans with a belt and an orange crop-top shirt with sleeves that fell down to her elbows despite leaving her shoulders bare. I smiled. The outfit looked great on her.

Then I focused my attention on Shawn, who looked *much* different. He had grown his hair out, and it was now long and frizzy underneath a leather do-rag. He had started to grow facial hair, and he smiled as we made eye-contact. He was wearing a matching leather vest that put his toned arms on display. Shawn also had on black jeans with a studded belt along with a tank top beneath the vest.

Before there could be any awkward silence, they both attempted to hug me. Shawn backed off and let Talida hug me first. As I held her in a tight embrace, she stifled a sob. "We thought you would never wake up," she said through her sorrow, barely audible. I hugged her back. It felt strange to me that it didn't feel like I'd been away for so long. It seemed like yesterday that we had been talking about surviving sophomore year. I still held her, though, knowing she needed it.

She peeled herself away, making room for Shawn to barrel himself into me. Wrapping his arms around me and slapping my back, I held onto him too. "Fuck, man, I thought you were gone." His voice was stranger than Talida's had been, and it was deeper, but I could still feel the restraint in his voice. He was on the ledge of breaking, and I had seen him in that stage before. There were tears in his eyes, but he refused to let them fall.

"I'm as good as new," I said. All the tears began to get to me. As they began to form in my own eyes again, all I could do was smile because I was back. I was finally back, and it was apparent that my friends needed me. All of my worries about them moving on without me were for nothing. The only person we were missing was Aiden, who likely wasn't able to get a ride. "How'd you guys find out about me waking up?"

"Shawn's cousin works up here. We've been visiting almost every week, waiting for this," Talida answered. I smiled again, but guilt settled in.

"You all know you didn't have to do that," I said. The idea of the two of them visiting for the last two years, wishing for me to wake up, devastated me.

"Best friends stick together," Shawn said. "We're just glad you're back."

They both looked me up and down as if seeing a new person. As they realized what was different, they were both confused. "Holy shit, you're pale!" Talida exclaimed.

"Dude, I was about to say the same thing, but I didn't want to be rude!" Shawn said. It was obvious he hadn't been sure of the change. With me being gone for so long, I was surprised they noticed. He turned toward Talida. "His voice is deeper too, right?"

I gave an uncomfortable chuckle. I hadn't seen the rest of my body, but my arm looked several shades lighter than I had been before my coma, and I had already been pretty pasty. "I'm glad I finally woke up. I guess I'm a born-again goth! How's everything been going?" I asked, unsure of what else to say.

Talida laughed at the joke, and then she stepped back to look at me. Their quick look toward each other revealed it hadn't been going well. I frowned, unsure of exactly why. It was apparent that I sounded like a stranger to them. They had been giving me odd looks since I'd begun speaking. From my voice to my new skin, I felt like a different person. "I guess my voice changed," I added. "It's weird to hear myself speak." They chuckled slightly and then looked at the floor.

"Well, Johnny and his friends beat us up pretty badly while you were away. I'm so tired of it," she said, her words trailing off. She sounded exceedingly happy to be a good distance away from them.

"For real," Shawn said quietly. They've got us on the edge of losing it. Not to mention Johnny and Grey are getting sympathy for the school fire."

"What do you mean?" I asked. My eyebrows furled, and I began to question if I had missed something. *Sympathy? For what?*

Talida scoffed. "Oh, get this. Johnny and Grey are claiming that the school fire and you being put in the hospital gave them a form of PTSD. It's a crock of shit. If you ask me, I think Johnny started the fire to begin with!"

"The bullying stops when I come back," I said harshly, determined to be different than I used to be. Whether or not I still had to deal with them, I couldn't bear to see my friends this way. "As soon as I go back to school, he will never bully us again. I'm going to defend you guys, and if we stick together and are all willing to fight, it will be four against three. How's Aiden handling this?" I couldn't stand the thought of seeing my friends get hurt again. I *wouldn't*.

Talida looked down at the floor, seeming devastated by the question. Shawn looked away. "It'll be hard to stand up to them. We've spent so long being their victims," Talida said.

Why didn't she mention Aiden? My stomach began to dance into knots. Like when you know something terrible has happened, but you don't know exactly what. "What about Aiden?" I asked in a low voice, knowing she had avoided the question for a reason. Shawn had stayed silent. Unfortunately, I was too curious for my own good.

Talida began to tear up, and Shawn clenched his fists. They both looked at me as if I should already know the answer. "Tony…" Shawn's voice cracked, spilling the pain from within his throat. "Aiden was killed in the fire," he whimpered.

Talida started to cry. "There was a body, and I didn't want to believe it was true, but they found his ring," she added.

I choked on the words I wanted to say as my insides clenched. "His Grudgematch one we got him?" I asked, barely able to squeeze out the words. She nodded, falling into melancholy as Shawn averted his gaze again, looking like he wanted to hit something.

I knew the pain was going to linger for a long while. *Why wasn't I there?* I asked myself, knowing I had been able to save one person from the flames. Why did my friend have to be taken by that damned fire? Why hadn't I heard him? Talida threw herself around me, sobbing into my shoulder. I hugged her, tears finding their way out of my own eyes.

"I'm sorry I wasn't able to save him," I cried. "I should have been fast enough."

Shawn interrupted me, shaking his head. "There wasn't anything you could have done. There wasn't anything any of us could have done." As Talida let go, she looked up at me with her glassy blue eyes, which shattered upon meeting my gaze. Sighing before speaking again, her lip quivered.

"I miss him," she said, trying to pull herself together again. She sat down on a chair over on the side of my bed, nearly breaking down. Shawn couldn't bring himself to sit, apparently in his own world of sadness. The tension coming off him could have been cut with a blade.

"They're saying that you got knocked out by falling wood," he said.

I shook my head. "No, that's not what happened. I thought I was going to die in that fire. I started to hallucinate, and I couldn't breathe. I got splashed in the face by something, and I passed out."

My entire face felt tight as I tried to hold myself together. Whether it was the fact that our friend had been ripped away from us or that my other best friend was crying next to me, I didn't know. Anger rose inside me, and my veins started burning with hatred. It was an emotion I didn't experience often, and it was beginning to freak me out.

"I can't believe someone would do that..." I said, my mind wandering without being able to bring words to my mouth. In all honesty, I was speechless, and I had never dealt with this kind of thing well. If I found out that it had been Johnny, I would lose it. I knew that Rob and Grey had been in the gym across the school from where the fire was, but where had Johnny been? I started to change the subject; if these thoughts continued, I would be screaming and throwing a fit in front of my best friend, and I didn't want to scare her. "How have you both been?" I asked, scratching the top of my hand. "Despite everything that happened."

Talida slowly stopped crying as she tried to regain her composure, wiping the tears from beneath her wet eyes. "Well, we've struggled these last two years. A lot has been going on. Not a lot has changed on my end other than becoming a little more comfortable in my own skin. My father has started to make more money due to opening up a hibachi restaurant last year, so he was able to splurge to get me new clothes. It's been going okay. I help my dad out part time, so I have enough to buy school supplies now. I've been saving up to get a car when I graduate."

"Oh, wow, I didn't expect him to be able to do that," I said. I knew it had to have cost a lot to open a restaurant to begin with. How Talida's family pulled the money together to do that, I had no idea. "What's it called?"

Talida smiled. "It was difficult for him to open. He named it Blazing Sakura. It's not super fancy, but the food's good. He's using a bunch of family recipes." She then looked to Shawn so he could speak.

"I got my license," Shawn said with a grin. "It's not much, but my parents bought me an old Dodge truck shortly after your accident. I painted it myself and have been working on it. You've got to hear the speaker system I put in it!" I laughed. In all these years he hadn't shown a sliver of interest in cars outside of video games.

"You'll have to show me. I didn't peg you as a car guy," I said, punching him in the shoulder.

"Me either, but as I started working on it myself to save money, I found I really enjoy it. Plus, you know how much I like customization when it comes to building characters. Not as much fun as video games though." That time, we all laughed. "Oddly, I've been fixing people's vehicles for extra cash. My dad helped me clean out our garage so I could make some extra money over the summer without getting a job. After your accident, I had to find a way to cope with everything going on. Turns out, cranking on cars and then coming inside and playing video games was the right move. I really missed you man."

"I missed you both, too. I'm sorry for not being there for you," I said. I knew I didn't have a choice, but it still bothered me.

Shawn shook his head. "You had no control over going into that coma. We're just glad you're back."

"What do you say we go out to lunch?" Talida asked, interrupting what could have been more grieving. "We've got a lot to talk about."

That was an understatement. I still needed to bring up staying at one of their houses before going to physical therapy.

"What time is it?" I asked, looking around for a non-existent clock.

"It's 11:30. I'm down. Anything sound good?" Shawn asked with another grin. I could tell it had been a long time since he had given a true smile. "It's Friday, so everything's pretty open."

"Blazing Sakura is closed today, though," Talida said. "We didn't have enough people to cover today, and my father decided it was best if I came and saw you instead."

I don't know how they handled me being away for that long. *Two years is a long time.* "Well, I haven't had a burger in two years," I replied, chuckling, trying to bring some light on the situation. Hibachi sounded amazing, but it would have to come another day.

"That sounds good," Shawn replied.

"Burgers it is," Talida answered, starting to loosen up. "I have a little bit of extra money, so I'll get my own."

"I have enough to cover us," Shawn added. "I got a good chunk of money fixing someone's truck last week."

I shook my head. "Actually, it's on me. I'll explain on the way."

Chapter 5

A Solid Plan

I laughed as I practically fell out of Shawn's truck. Talida jumped out shortly after, not nearly as amused. "Holy hell dude, you drive like a nut!" she said.

Shawn's driving had been horrific, but amusing all the same. Shawn laughed. "Listen. I'm just trying to spend as much time with my two best friends as I can. I told you to hold on," he said.

I wanted to tell him to be more careful, but didn't want to kill the mood. We had fun on the way here, but I was sure he'd be getting a nasty ticket sometime in the near future. As we headed into our favorite steakhouse, Braxton Hicks, we were quickly seated and the others started to talk.

"Okay, so you explained what happened. You've got a new phone and a chunk of money. Have you thought about what to do after physical therapy?" Shawn asked me. Because they had been visiting me in the hospital for so long, both of them knew about what had happened with my parents.

Shawn apparently had strong words for them, which Talida had mirrored.

Needless to say I wouldn't be hearing from them again.

"I was actually wanting to know if I could stay with one of you over the weekend. Then I have to go back to the hospital. Afterward, I'm not sure what I'm going to do. I'm homeless, and that money will go away quickly if I have to find money for rent. That's *if* anyone will even rent to me without a job history."

I picked at my fingers, nervous about my near future. I had hoped I would be able to move out of my parents' house quickly, but it being thrown at me like this was a lot different. I had no idea how to be an adult, let alone starting without a home address. How was I supposed to find a job when I didn't have my own transportation or home? At least I had this new phone and money.

"You can sleep on my couch if you can't find anywhere else to go," Talida said, smiling. "It's not like it'll be the first time you've slept over. I know my father isn't a fan of it, but I don't think he'd make you live out on the street."

I nodded. We usually hung out at my house or Shawn's due to her family being weird about gaming and their daughter hanging out overnight with two boys. They didn't mind us swearing over at her house, so that part was okay. I had always felt slightly judged there due to having unconventional views and interests.

Shawn's house wasn't any better. While they tried to push Shawn to strive for a better future, in doing so, his mom had put him down for a long time. His family was very religious and hated the music we would listen to while hanging out. They disliked swearing, and they would prevent us from watching certain shows or playing certain games due to them "being part of the devil's intent." No witches, wizards, or ghosts in that house.

Shawn's mom also didn't like Talida, a foreign girl that cut her hair short and cursed. Luckily, his dad had usually kept her at bay before she could lash out. He was supportive and the reason Shawn had gotten into metal and video games to begin with. When visiting, we would usually just keep his bedroom door closed so that they wouldn't hear what we were doing. Shawn would keep his Metallica or my Gothic Rock quiet enough for them not to notice.

That's why we usually wound up at my house. While my parents didn't agree with what I wanted to do, they were pretty lenient on what we chose to entertain ourselves with. There were good memories there. Some I would never be able to relive now that Aiden and my family were out of my life. Getting the four of us together to hang and jam out to music. I remembered Aiden getting upset after the third time we replayed Shawn's favorite Metallica song, which he didn't happen to like very much. Aiden would then try to drown it out with a song on his phone. That was a losing battle. I grinned, being lost in old times.

Shawn rested his elbows on the table as he sat across from us in the burgundy booth. "Actually, he can stay with me. I talked to my parents this morning about it and they said he can stay as long as he needs. Albeit, on the couch, but that's better than nothing or wasting that money on hotel rooms," he said.

Just as I was about to speak, our waiter came and handed us our drinks.

We had all ordered our default sweet tea, and then ordered burgers. Once she left, I started to talk.

"I really appreciate you both. I'll room with Shawn this weekend, but I won't be a burden on you guys after my therapy."

Shawn looked like I had just hit him in the throat. "A burden? You're never a burden. You're our best friend. We're not going to let you live on the street."

"I get that," I started. "We're all going to stay close, but I need some time to get my life figured out. This is a second chance, and I'm going to go for my dreams."

"Don't put yourself in a bad position trying to be self-sufficient," Talida said, looking worried.

"I won't. I promise! It'll be fun."

"Well. If you're determined to not live with us afterward, I have an idea," Shawn said with a grin. He put his arms down and stared directly at me.

Talida looked toward him, wondering what he was thinking. As I made eye contact, he continued.

"Now hear me out first before shutting this down. You still want to be a graphic designer, right?"

"Right."

"And you want to have your own lifestyle where no one can tell you what you can and can't do?"

I nodded, resting my own arm on the table and I rearranged my feet beneath.

Talida's eyes widened as she seemed to connect with this idea.

Shawn lifted a finger. "With that money, buy some camping supplies and live—"

"In a van!" Talida interrupted.

"Under the bridge," Shawn finished.

Hearing that they had two completely different ideas, I began to cackle. Shawn and Talida both looked toward each other in confusion and they realized their error.

"Both of those are strong ideas," I said. "But both have issues. I don't have a license, and we're still in the middle of summer."

"He can't live under a bridge!" Talida exclaimed. "The only good option would be by the train tracks and that's way in the southwest. If you lived in a van, it would be way cheaper than a hotel, and you could be mobile. Shawn has a good start to an idea though. You're not starting off with very much money, so you could buy a cheap van *and* some camping supplies. That would keep you afloat for a while as you look for a way to make money."

As she spoke, there was a glimmer of hope in her eyes. It was a solid plan. Sure, I could get an apartment, but after buying everything I needed, I would run out of money quickly. Shawn started to nod in approval. She's right. I can help you learn how to drive too. We should be able to get your license pretty quickly."

"Don't I need logged hours or something? And proofs of residency."

"Not if you lie about it. As long as you *know* how to drive and can pass your test, surely that'll be fine in your situation. I'll call and get some information while you're away. As for the proofs, just use my home address. I'll have my parents switch a bill to your name or something."

I let out a sigh of relief and then smiled. Thinking of living in a van by myself and being able to drive around actually made me happy. I didn't think that would be the route I took, but here we were.

"That being said, we should plan that out. The van will cost the most, but what are you going to do for money?" Shawn asked.

"I haven't thought about that. Honestly, maybe freelancing my graphic design? I've got to come up with a portfolio if I'm going to be applying to companies anyway. I could sell designs. If that doesn't work, I could help you fix cars or work with Talida if they have an opening. I don't mind working."

The thought of working with one of my friends made the idea of having a job better. I knew I would have to interact with people I didn't know, but I couldn't let that stop me.

"Okay, but to do that you need a tablet. Are you going to use part of that money to buy one?" Talida asked, bringing up a good point. I slapped my forehead. I forgot I didn't have any of my stuff from before the coma.

"Shit. Yeah, I'd have to. I'll need internet too, but I can splurge on better phone cards to use their mobile Wi-Fi. Unfortunately, it can't be a cheap tablet either."

As they rambled off a list of the items I would need, Talida brought it upon herself to start writing everything down. "I'll do some research and see how low we can get all this stuff," she said, smiling.

"That being said, what do you need for physical therapy? Do you need school supplies beforehand?" Shawn asked.

"That's probably best. I'm honestly not sure what else I'd need. They'll provide me a room, and I can get cheap takeout if I have to as well." I looked down at myself. The hospital had provided me a set of clothes, but they were *not* to my taste. "I'd kill for some new clothes too."

Shawn laughed, followed by Talida. As they looked toward each other, and then nodded, they smiled. "We can't have our best friend looking like some rando. We need our gothic freak back," Talida said.

I chuckled. "So new clothes are in order after eating. With your driving, I'm not sure where we are. Are we close to After Dark?" I asked. After Dark had always been one of my favorite places to go. It was a strange place. The main building was a 24 hour coffee shop and clothing store that sometimes had live, goth entertainment. It was a place that those who liked the night life enjoyed here, and the store had many different clothing lines that all fell into the category of alternative clothing. The ambience there was always amazing, and clean. It was one of the few places I felt comfortable as my strange self in Old Belmont. Where others like myself tended to visit.

The buildings attached to After Dark had been planned by the owners to become a nail salon and tattoo shop. All of it was supporting the umbrella of alternative people. Goths, punks, emos, you name the scene, and they were welcome. Unfortunately, the nail salon and tattoo shop hadn't opened before my coma, although it wasn't legal for me to get a tattoo at that point anyway. I would have liked to avoid trying out all the nail parlors around the city if it had been open, though. I had a hell of a time finding a place that would give me what I wanted.

"Actually, it's right down the street. Blazing Sakura is too."

"Oh, hell yeah!" I exclaimed.

* * *

After a good lunch and some quick school shopping, Shawn surprised me with a new set of acrylic nails, matching the short black stilettos I had before my coma. We stopped by After Dark and I got a few sets of clothes. I also found a gothic, cotton trench coat with buckles down the front and a set of knee-high Demono combat boots that had metal plates going down the shins.

Shawn and Talida decided it would be best if we had a "Welcome Back Party" together, so they picked up a cake and a new movie to watch while Shawn's parents were at work on a late shift. We would have the house alone for several hours, which made Talida and me super excited.

The idea reminded me of the parties my parents used to throw. We would invite our whole family over for a bonfire or cookout two to three times a year. Halloween especially. My parents owned a couple of acres in the southeast, just barely inside the city limits.

I then thought about my grandma. My favorite person on my dad's side. Grandma Jude was completely different from my parents. She supported me, and she thought that a career path like graphic design would be perfect for me. I had always enjoyed working on the computer, making art and gaming. I couldn't do any programming, but when it came to designing and throwing pictures together, I excelled. She also—unlike a lot of my family—supported my fashion and music taste. She saw them for what they were: artistic music and a clothing style that I enjoyed. They were simply the ways in which I felt most comfortable expressing myself to others.

I told myself that I would contact her when I got the chance to see how she was doing. The ride to Shawn's house wasn't silent, but it was quiet enough to give me time to think. After reminiscing about family, I questioned when Johnny would jump me after I came back to school, knowing for certain he would. "Dude, I'm so excited your parents are out of town tonight," Talida raved on, leaning forward from the back seat and putting one of her hands on each of our shoulders.

I smiled. It wasn't often we had a chance to hang out by ourselves, despite us spending the day together. This would give us a good opportunity to unwind and hang out without the world's prying eyes. We had always been paranoid about mentioning certain subjects in public, and here, we would have full freedom.

We pulled into Shawn's long driveway, trees on either side.

His parents owned about ten or eleven acres of land a little bit further out than my parents'. This included two small fields and a wooded area with a creek that went around the property. We had explored the woods around his house many times. They were a place of solace away from his family when we needed time alone. There were many memories of the three of us hanging out by the flowing creek in the dead of night. Aiden had usually stayed inside, afraid of exploring the dark woods. In truth, it was probably a poor choice to do so, but we always had fun.

We went inside Shawn's trailer house after climbing the stairs of his wooden porch. It was a small home, with a small television in the corner of their living room. They had a corner couch and a small wooden table in the center of the kitchen. To the right of the entrance was a hallway that led to two rooms, Shawn's bedroom and a bathroom. To the left past the kitchen was the master bedroom and a back door.

I scrunched my nose as the familiar scent of cigarettes entered my nostrils. Cigarettes and cats. I had forgotten about this part of Shawn's home. I tried not to judge, but I hated the scent. I loved their three cats though. Aiden had been the only one to actually say anything about the odors of the house, which Shawn's parents had taken as an insult.

Shawn sighed. "Sorry about the smell, guys. I tried to ask them to smoke outside today, but they apparently didn't want to." He was just as aware as the rest of us. He had tried to get his parents to stop smoking, but that was like talking to a wall expecting it to move. "I'm going to grab something from my room, and then we'll hang out!"

Talida smiled. "I'll come with!"

"I'm going to use your bathroom real quick," I said, heading that way. I didn't actually need to use it, but I was itching to read the letter I had received. The weird dreams I had of Blackwell and then Veka went through my mind again. I didn't understand what the strange visions meant, if anything, but they weighed heavily on my mind.

Especially the one with Veka. Why would I have had a dream about a man chained to the wall, being tortured by the cloaked figure? And the prisoners, were they meant to portray something? An inner confrontation?

That might be it. Maybe it was meant to show that I would wake up to a change. One where I was no longer a prisoner.

Was the dream with Blackwell real? I looked down at the letter, staring at the golden seal. It gave me a slight sense of unease, but then excitement.

My hands shaking with anticipation, I opened the letter in the comfort of my solitude. My eyes darted back and forth, soaking in the words in front of me, and then I stared at them in disbelief.

Heroic Healing Hospital
1500 S. Flint Avenue
Old Belmont, MO, 65899

Dear Tony,

What you are about to read may feel absurd, and at the very least, fictional. My name is Blackwell, and I am writing to inform you that something spectacular happened in the two years of you being comatose. Your vitals had risen to a point where your body should have failed. Your doctor and I were baffled, so I had him take a blood sample for advanced experimental testing at my lab. When the test results came back from the lab, they showed strange changes in your DNA. This is highly unusual, and we decided after repeating the tests and getting the same results, that we should not reveal these findings to anyone until you had recovered consciousness.

The tests indicated that you possess great strength. However, there are traces within your blood samples that we are not able to identify. That leads us to believe you may have more abilities than strength. Because of the results, I asked Dr. Mellark, a doctor who could be trusted to keep this secret, to come up with a story to transfer you to my private hospital, Heroic Healing Hospital, or Triple H. After your transfer, he took over observing you during your coma. He will also oversee your physical therapy, which is very important; this is where you will learn to exert a proper amount of force with your enhanced strength to fit in with society.

I'm sure you will probably disregard this letter at first, but when you learn the truth, I want to invite you to a personal meeting regarding joining a growing group of extraordinary people like yourself. We are calling this group Project Barricade. It was formed to keep the world safe from criminals. Threats exist out there, and you would be a perfect asset to the team against them.

Once you have completed your physical therapy, Dr. Mellark will give you directions as to how to reach me. I look forward to seeing your progress, and I hope that you will consider joining our fight against evil.

I wish to meet you, Tony. You are destined for great things in the hard times to come. Don't underestimate yourself because you are more valuable than you think.

Sincerely,
Blackwell

Chapter 6

I Don't Know My Own Strength

Was this some kind of elaborate joke? I didn't know what to think after reading that letter. It seemed serious, and it made sense, without all the super-power crap. I questioned if Johnny had somehow pulled this off as a prank. What better way to make fun of a geek than to make him think he has superhuman abilities right after making fun of them?

Except it wasn't right after. This was two years after that bullying session. I then remembered the dream I had before coming out of my coma, which gave me chills. That's the same name as the guy in my dream. Blackwell. How would I have heard that name subconsciously if he wasn't real? Obviously, I didn't have superpowers. I think I would have noticed something like that already.

I folded the cream cardstock paper, put it back in its black envelope, and then stuck it back into my pocket. I scoffed, shaking my head as my eyes rolled to the back of my skull. How would Johnny get the doctor in on it if this was a joke? I shook my head, not wanting to think more about it. I needed to find out how I was going to defend myself against him when I returned.

As I left the bathroom, I realized I was forgetting something.

"I forgot something in the truck, but I'll be right back inside," I said, having remembered my cell phone was still outside. One of the things we planned to do tonight was get everyone's contacts updated. We had joked around by saying we would take funny pictures for each other's contacts too, which may or may not have ended up as part of the actual plan instead of a joke.

"Okay, we'll be in the kitchen when you get back," Shawn said from his bedroom.

Someone knocked on the door. As I walked toward the sound, my heart dropped. I wondered if Shawn's parents had come back earlier than planned, or maybe they were receiving a package. It was kind of late for that. A genuine smile grew on my face as I thought about enjoying time with my friends again. Even if one wasn't here to enjoy it with us.

"Coming!" I yelled. As I opened the door, my mood spiraled down to anger. Johnny stood in front of me, a smirk resting firmly on his face. Of course, he brought his thugs. "What are *you* doing here?" I asked. My fury was peaking, and he hadn't even spoken yet. I stepped out and slammed the door. I didn't want the others to get involved or hear what I was about to say.

"It's good to see you again too, Tony. We're glad you finally woke up. Your friends aren't nearly as much fun without you," he said as they all continued to chuckle.

"How did you find this house!" I exclaimed, my clenched fists shaking at my sides as I tossed his comment to the side. Before Johnny could respond, I heard loud bass pumping from the living room. As I realized it was my favorite Industrial Pop song, I almost disregarded the three of them entirely.

"Rob is very good at finding addresses. To be fair, we checked Talida's house first," Johnny answered. "Turns out, the school's computer system isn't as hard to hack as I thought. Did you know that the principal's password is SafePlace? It sure is his number-one priority." He chuckled, verbally spitting in the face of the school.

I pushed Johnny, and he slammed into his friends behind him, hard. I was immediately surprised that I had knocked him off balance, but it didn't take me long to return to the statement I needed to make. The words had been stirring ever since I'd woken up in the hospital. "Listen up, assholes. If you *ever*, bully me again, I swear I will make sure you never come back! I am tired of your shit, and I will not be dealing with it anymore! The coma changed me, and now I know who I am and what I have to do!" I yelled with rage.

Johnny's group went silent for several seconds, processing what I had just promised. Johnny started to laugh, his eyes bulging with disbelief. Soon after, his thugs followed with their own demeaning cackles.

As quickly as it began, it all stopped. Johnny's eyes flashed in anger as he took a step toward me. "Just because you were asleep for the last two years doesn't make you any different than when you went under. I'm sure your family would be a lot happier if you had just stayed asleep—or finally quit breathing. Welcome back to reality, Tony; the reality where you are just a worthless *freak* who can't stand up for himself, and I have control. You think just because you lifted a cabinet off some kid that you're a changed man? What a fucking joke," Johnny said, pushing himself into my space.

I tensed up my face, trying to look strong, but in truth, I wasn't sure what that should look like. "Reality," I stepped forward, "has changed," I said in a stern voice. It was apparent Johnny hadn't learned of the truth with my family abandoning me, or he would have used that information against me.

"Keep it up, and I'll end your reality," he whispered as he leaned in toward me. A low chuckle escaped Johnny. One that sent chills down my spine and sent my mind into a panic. As he grinned, turning his back on me, he left with the other two in tow.

As I saw them disappear in a shitty red Mustang, fear started to make an appearance. What was I going to do? I'd never been able to stand up to him before. What makes me think I can do it now? *Maybe he's right...*

I clenched my fists, causing my knuckles to go white. No, I couldn't think like that. I'm different than I used to be! If I don't make a change now, my life is never going to progress. It's going to continue to be a shit show where I don't make a difference in the end. I tried to raise my sinking confidence. *You can do this.* I needed to get through the physical therapy and find a way.

"Is everything okay, man?" Shawn asked, walking outside.

I had mostly calmed down. It was enough to quit shaking, but my breathing was still erratic. "Yeah, everything's alright," I reassured. He didn't need to know about this interaction. It'd ruin the mood. I pointed toward the cloud of dust. "Just neighbors making a wrong turn."

"Okay, just making sure. I thought I heard yelling," he said. He seemed worried, looking around.

"I'll be inside in just a sec," I said, forcing a smile and heading out to the driveway. He headed back inside with a nod.

When I got back to the truck, it was already almost dark. Everything sat in the shadow of dusk, in shades of purple and gray. A fog was rolling in, and it gave an eerie feel to the surrounding area. I peered through the trees, wanting to take pictures of the sight. It was beautiful, and creepy.

I smiled, and then my eyes focused on something in the distance. Far in the trees, downhill, stood something strange.

A figure.

I panicked. My entire body began to tingle, I wasn't sure what to do. I rubbed my eyes, and when the figure didn't go away, I could now see its glowing yellow eyes beneath a black cloak. As I thought about just running back inside, my body decided I needed answers. I was oddly drawn toward it.

"Hey!" I screamed, running toward him. As I rampaged forward, getting closer to him, I felt a cold chill. "Who are you?" I asked loudly, not sure I wanted an answer. I had reason to believe his name was Veka, but that didn't tell me what he was or his intentions. I ran faster. Faster than I had ever been able to run before. *No, I need answers.* This time, I wasn't in a dream.

Then I tripped over a rock.

I quickly got back to my feet and looked forward. The figure was suddenly right in front of me, peering down at me with his piercing gaze. I heard a scratchy cackle that terrified me. In reaction, I sent an uppercut in his direction.

But then he wasn't there. Instead, my curled fist struck a large tree in front of me.

BOOM!

The tree uprooted and launched itself upward, spinning vertically through the air.

I put both hands on my head in a mixture of astonishment and horror. "*What* the *fuck?!*" I exclaimed, my jaw dropping to the ground, followed by everything within my chest. I couldn't believe what I had just seen. For a split second, my mind relinquished the memory of the figure that had just been here.

It took a minute to register what had happened as the tree slammed down near the creek in the distance, creating a noise that the entire city had probably heard. I ran into the woods to hide myself, worried that I could be caught.

The first feeling I had was one of terror; I had already been freaked out, but the act of uprooting the tree had scared the hell out of me. It was the equivalent of a jump-scare. The second emotion I had was delight as I realized what this meant. "I do have superpowers!" I threw my fist in the air in triumph. "The letter is real!" I jumped in excitement. "I'm going to change the world!"

I walked up to another tree; I needed to see it again. I *had* to. This tree was much smaller because I didn't want to uproot the old ones. I wrapped both of my hands around the trunk and lifted. Sure enough, the tree pulled right out of the ground as if it were a simple weed. I threw it like a spear toward the other, and it landed with a loud CRACK!

I smiled. After all these years of being told I would never amount to anything, maybe this ability would change that. I couldn't let anyone find out about this power, but I could use it to a point where no one would notice a difference. Hopefully. I sat down on a fallen tree, thinking about how I would confront Johnny in the near future. My adrenaline-high quickly dissipated back into the reality of life. He'll never stand a chance. I still couldn't fight, but if I could land one punch—just *one*—it'd be over. After these next few months, I'd be able to control it. Now the only problem would be how to avoid getting expelled.

I caught myself straying away from the thoughts of a hero and running into a forest of evil. I could easily end him so he would never hurt anyone again. With this strength, I could watch him choke on his own blood. No one could stop me.

I snapped myself out of the evil thoughts. No, I couldn't do that. If I did, then I would be giving in to what everyone already thought about me. I'd be delinquent scum like Johnny and his friends. I will defend myself, but I refuse to be evil. The bullies would learn to fear me, though, because after today, I would never let anyone be bullied in front of me again.

I chuckled. "Bring it on, Johnny!" I yelled at the sky, smiling in determination. I put all the force I had into my voice. I wanted him to hear it. I wanted everyone to. "You will know pain when I see you again!"

As I remembered my friends inside the house, I quickly ran up to the truck and pulled the door handle. I needed to hurry inside. Talida was already standing on the porch, appearing frantic. "What the hell was that?" she asked. Her eyes darted back and forth, searching desperately for an answer.

"What?" I asked, hoping she hadn't heard me screaming.

"That loud bang? There were two of them!"

"That tree just fell down there!" I lied, pointing toward the creek. I wasn't going to tell them about the figure, and definitely not my newly discovered powers. "I'm coming in though. Let's start the fun!"

Chapter 7

Getting the Hang of Things

It was now early morning on Monday, and it was time to return to the hospital. I had a blast over the weekend with my friends, and Shawn had started to teach me how to drive again. Surprisingly, it was pretty easy to get used to again. My brain seemed to remember everything I had learned before the coma, despite being gone for two years. Shawn was convinced that, after my physical therapy, I could easily get my license again. He and Talida had also promised to help me find a nice van when I returned.

When they dropped me off, they were also informed that I wouldn't be able to have visitors. They understood that they couldn't visit, though I'm not sure what exactly they were told. It wasn't explained to me either. I was really confused, and I didn't want to leave the good company I was in. These two months were going to kill me.

I walked toward the glass doors as my new boots clinked against the pavement. It had been slightly chilly this morning, so I took the opportunity to wear my new trench coat as well. It felt good to be able to express myself out in public again, though it made some people uneasy…I looked over as a lady hid her child behind her, scowling in my direction. I shook my head. You'd think she'd never seen a goth before in this city of forty thousand people.

As I looked up at the large hospital sign, I realized it didn't have the full name. There was just a bright-blue LED sign of three *H*s overlapping above. As my mind wandered about how they kept the public out of this hospital, I then questioned if that was the case. *They might need the public to keep it open.*

"Tony! It's good to see you again. How was your weekend?" Dr. Mellark called from the door. He walked in my direction, snapping me out of the funk I was putting myself in. I forced a smile.

"It was good! I got to spend a lot of time with my friends and get some things figured out," I said.

"I'm happy to hear that. Let me show you around. The sooner we get started, the quicker I can get you back to your life," Dr. Mellark said. I nodded, giving a grin as I followed him to the right. "You'll be mostly staying on this side, with the exception of the cafeteria to the left. You will receive three free meals a day while you are here. Due to your transfer to this specialty hospital, Blackwell is taking care of your bill. Here at Triple H, we try to keep the public out. Everyone that works here is under an oath of secrecy to Blackwell. This facility is labeled as for specialists, and you have to have a referral, which only I can give." He continued. "There are a lot of directional signs, so you shouldn't have any issues finding where you need to go."

So, Blackwell's real. I looked down the hallway ahead of us. Silver-colored hexagon tiles ran down the length of the floor, and bright LEDs lit up the entirety of the building. The normally red-colored signs were oddly blue here, and the words were lit up as well.

"On the right is a weight-training room, where we will test what kind of strength you possess." I looked in that direction, seeing through the glass door to the room beyond. Assorted weights lay within, with several benches, but I couldn't see much else as we continued forward.

"Besides getting a baseline on your new abilities, we will also retrain your muscles to work the way they need to now. You may feel weakness in certain areas, and when you do, let us know." Dr. Mellark walked quickly with a fluid grace to his steps. He seemed to glide across the floor in a care-free stride as he talked freely with his arms.

"The next door on the right, which is further down, is to an area for overall body training. This is where we will work on regaining your balance and flexibility. On the left are several rooms where you will be able to stay, along with the restrooms." Dr. Mellark quit speaking, looking at me to see if I had any questions. I managed to glimpse the LED signs for the bathrooms, along with a couple of rooms with a sign that said "Lodging" above them.

As I noticed his glance, I thought for a moment, wondering if I was going to need to know anything right away. "So, since I have super strength, how am I going to be able to use the weights? Won't they all just be super easy for me to lift now?" I asked, unsure of how they were supposed to help.

"That leads me to the other part of what I need to inform you about. To answer your question first, we have special weights that will give you some resistance. This is the EPT Wing, standing for Enhanced Physical Therapy.

This hospital is under the eyes of Blackwell, the master of Project Barricade. As we find others with powers, Triple H will be able to help those who are in need of special surgical care and enhanced therapy. While he does have a battle medic, the medic won't be able to heal them all at once, therefore they'll likely send the wounded here. That will also help him keep Project Barricade under the radar," Dr. Mellark informed.

"That's very helpful for this group he's starting. Is he going to be able to find enough superhumans to fill a hospital though? Am I not the only one?" I asked, knowing the letter alluded to others, but it didn't confirm how many.

"He's found a small handful. Not many, but as of right now, he's found three others. As for the hospital, he plans to have ground forces. Agents, special forces—whatever you'd like to call them. He'll be requiring this hospital in the future," he said. I nodded. This was a lot of information, but it also intrigued me. Blackwell must be pretty serious about this if he's going to build a hospital for them. *How does he afford that?*

"That's neat. It will be cool to see it grow. I did want to tell you that I'm interested in joining. I thought about it a lot Sunday, and I want to be a part of making the world a better place," I said, smiling. How could I pass up an opportunity to be a superhero? I could never have dreamed that I would be put in this situation.

"That's exciting! Welcome to Project Barricade. All we ask is that you keep it to yourself and not let others know about your powers. I will be helping you along the way as you get up to speed." Dr. Mellark shook my hand. "Now, since the change in your strength was sudden, you may struggle with certain normal actions. Since you didn't have time to grow into your abilities, you also didn't have the time to learn how to restrain them. I'm assuming you didn't have any issues over the weekend?"

I shook my head. "Well, I thought I saw something and ended up hitting a tree. It uprooted and I launched it into the air. No one saw it though. A couple little things like snapping a plate in half and breaking the door handle. Other than those, I haven't been having many issues," I said. Honestly, I thought I would be having a harder time, but so far, things only seemed to happen under stress.

"That's phenomenal..." Dr. Mellark stated, staring at me for a moment. As I was a little weirded out, I opened my mouth to say something else, but was interrupted. "That's a great start, I mean. I would have thought you would be having struggles with those basic functions a lot more than you are. Seeing as you aren't having these battles, we can move on to a more specific area of your recovery."

As he led me into the weight room, I looked around, seeing several benches with black rubber weights on the top two rows of the shelving behind them. On the bottom two rows, sat weights of the same shapes but in a vibrant azure blue. Against the wall were several kettlebells and dumbbells, also of two different colors. Further down there were punching bags, which I definitely hadn't seen through the window.

"First thing's first. The black items are of normal weight. They're here to allow you to understand what normal weights feel like, giving you a basis for normalcy. This will help you reach your main goal here, which is to slip into society unnoticed and protect your secret identity. The black weights range from a pound to one hundred, while the blue are significantly different." He reached for a black dumbbell, easily lifting it from the rack. As he reached for a matching blue one, however, it moved about as much as the concrete building.

I chuckled. "Is that what Thor's hammer is made of?" I said. Dr. Mellark let out a chortle.

"No, but you give it a try. Lift this black one, which is twenty pounds, and then this blue one," he said, pointing to both. I walked over to them, lifting the first. I held it up to my face, as it seemed weightless. There was weight to it, but it didn't strain my body at all. Throughout the weekend, I hadn't lifted anything that struck me as odd, so it had been difficult to notice.

"Whoa, that's weird," I said. "I can feel the weight, yet it doesn't really matter. It's like I entered a real-life creative mode." I sat it down and wrapped my hand around the blue weight to lift it. As my eyebrows furled in confusion, I realized that this one felt normal, like what the black one *should* have felt like.

"You see what I mean?" Dr. Mellark said.

I nodded. "That's weirder," I said, laughing again. I curled it, being confused as to why this one felt normal to me. Obviously, I knew I had powers, but it was a shock factor for sure. I set it back down and picked up the next one, labeled Level 2. This one had quite a bit more resistance, as though it weighed sixty to eighty pounds. I had to use both of my hands to lift it but not without a struggle.

Dr. Mellark's eyes opened wide in awe. With a visible gasp, words sputtered out of his mouth. "Um—okay, put that down very carefully," he said.

"How much does this one weigh? It feels very heavy," I said as I sat it back down with a crack.

"That," he started, making sure I had picked up the second one. "Is the equivalent of a small car. About two tons."

I gasped. "Whoa, really?!" I asked, excitement taking hold. "I can lift a fucking *car*?" I looked back at the weight in astonishment, wondering what else I could do.

Dr. Mellark looked at me. "Looks like you can! That's splendid," he said, putting his hands on his hips. I looked over to the other weights, wondering how far I could go. As I reached for another, he stopped me.

"Hold on, Tony. You'll have access to the others later, but this is what I want you to do today. We will be focusing on this for the week. I want you to use black weights and compare them to normal objects on an average day. We will compare them so that you can understand what they feel like. Now pick up the one-pound weight."

I reached for the first dumbbell, and he began to speak again. "This one weighs a pound. It's roughly the same as a can of soup. Keep this in mind as we go further with the tests." I thought about it, comparing it to the item I would normally find at home. This was going to be difficult. "Also, some comparable items you probably have and hold would be paperback books, a loaf of bread, keyboards, and tablets."

I nodded, letting him know I was taking in the information to consider. "Will I hold real items in my therapy, or will it just be the weights? I'm worried that when I'm stressed, I will break real items, but I don't think these weights will break as easily," I said. How was this supposed to help me if I left afterward and still broke stuff because I wasn't used to them?

"This is for weight comparison in particular. This is a good place to start as you figure out weight again and what you need to keep in mind when lifting things that would normally be difficult. We will get to specific items later. When you leave, you will be able to handle your strength under stress along with being able to do things normally again." Dr. Mellark then handed me a slip of paper.

As I read it, I realized it was a workout regime, giving me everything that I needed to do for five days a week. It showed that Saturday and Sunday were rest days.

"We will meet in either this room or the body training room, where we will put you on a set schedule to get your muscles moving again. I will show you your room for the night, and tomorrow we will try out the punching bags to see how hard you can hit. Then we will try to reduce that so you will know how to hit more like a normal person," he said. I smiled, excited to receive my results tomorrow.

Dr. Mellark showed me to my room, and after spending the rest of the day exploring the wing, I laid down to rest. Now lying on a decent bed, I pulled out my phone for a moment and plugged it in to charge. As I pulled up Talida's number, I saw her contact picture was of her sticking her tongue out, eyes crossed in a funny face attempting not to smile. She was labeled as Tally. It caused me to chuckle since they hadn't let me look at the contacts.

Hers was funny, but I guffawed when I saw what Shawn had done. His head was tilted forward, his forehead appearing massive. The photo was slightly blurry, and he looked absolutely psychotic with his teeth bared. Almost unable to control my laughter, I texted our group chat.

Me: *First day down. It doesn't seem too bad. Going to be a lot of stretching haha*

Tally: *Woo! 60ish days to go! Miss you already! Shawn is already looking at vans.*

Shawn: *It's gonna be a long two months! Get out soon. What do you think of this one?*

Shawn sent an ad for an old minivan. It was an ugly, rusted brown color with 400,000 miles on it.

Me: *Hell no. No, no, no. Final verdict.*

Tally: *Oh my god! What is that!?!*

Shawn: *It's $400! We could paint it!*

Me: *Okay, go back to square one. Try to find a cargo van. One with space that I can build into. Nice try, but that is horrific! I've got to go to sleep. They have me waking up at the crack of dawn!*

Tally: *Okay, good night!*

Shawn: *I'll keep trying haha! Night man.*

I pulled the covers up over my shoulders and frowned. While the conversation was entertaining, my own pessimism reminded me of Aiden. Between him and Talida, logic was always at play in our plans. While Aiden was normally pessimistic, he always had good points.

As so many different thoughts plowed through my mind, I knew it was going to take me a while to fall asleep. Knowing that Blackwell was a real person had me stressed, along with seeing the cloaked figure in real life. Unless I was about to wake up from an extended dream, things were starting to not make sense. I tried to push the thoughts to the side. Once I met Blackwell, I would talk to him about everything.

* * *

The next morning, I wobbled into the weight training room. While I had gotten a good night's rest for once, it was still stupid early. It was a struggle for me to get up in the mornings, so waking up at the crack of dawn for training was going to kill me for sure.

I was also never a breakfast person, but as I noticed I had forgotten dinner, I told myself it would be a good idea to grab some before training. I also told myself that if I was going to be training to be a superhero, I should probably start eating healthier. I had no idea how my new body would react to food once I started using my abilities, but I decided on a bowl of scrambled eggs and sausage.

"Good morning," Dr. Mellark said.

I forced a smile. "Morning," I said groggily, trying not to seem cold. After some simple stretches, which were more of a struggle than they used to be, we headed over to the punching bags. The first one he led me to was a large, sky-blue bag with several massive chains holding it securely to the ceiling and floor. To say it was intimidating would be a huge understatement.

"Whoa," I said, looking it up and down. "What kind of monsters are you letting punch these things?" Dr. Mellark burst into laughter.

"You're the second person to go through this course. You'll likely meet the first over at Blackwell's hideout when you arrive. These bags can withstand extreme amounts of force, perfect for your enhanced strength," he said.

"Wait, someone else has super strength? Do the other three as well?" I asked, not sure why the information had caught me off guard.

"Only one of Blackwell's new recruits wields enhanced strength. Calls himself Steel Cowboy. He is physically insane, to say the least. Seems like a good man as well. When you are ready, hit the bag as hard as you can, and I will tell you how hard you hit it," he said as a yellow light began to flash near the top of the bag. I nodded, getting into what I thought would be a good stance to fight in. As I looked it up and down, I prepared myself. Clenching my fist and gritting my teeth, I sent my punch into the bag with a loud, low-toned *BANG!*

"Sheesh!" Dr. Mellark exclaimed, looking at a laptop he had set up. "Yeah, you've got some work to do to bring that down!" He spun the laptop around to show me the number, revealing 10,341 PSI. Knowing it was a lot, my heartrate spiked, but I wasn't sure how it compared to a normal person. Seeing my confusion, the doctor began to explain.

"That is roughly fifty times the strength of an average person and thirty times the power of a very strong punch. In other words, if you hit a normal person at that strength, you would kill them. I want you to try again, but hold back this time," he said.

I looked at my hands. It was crazy to believe I *literally* had lethal weapons in front of me. I grinned. Johnny wouldn't stand a chance. Knowing I needed to not kill him, I pushed that thought aside.

I lifted my fists, sending another one into the bag while trying to hold it back. "7500," Dr. Mellark said. I sent another one into the bag, holding back further. "7400." Another one. "7200." After several punches, each landing in the same range, I began to get aggravated.

"How am I supposed to hit softer than that?" I spouted, pacing now, and wondering how to lessen my punches.

"Don't stress over it. This is your first day. We have two months to put you into the normal range. I believe it'll take a month, and then we will spend the second half working on your form. I don't want you flicking people out of consciousness," Dr. Mellark said, chuckling at his remark.

"I don't know if I can do this," I said, putting my hands against my face and wanting to scream. I'd never get out of physical therapy if I couldn't even figure out how to lessen my punches.

"Listen, Tony. I know that if you've ever been taught how to punch, they've told you to follow through with them, but I'm telling you otherwise. Try to hit the bag, but as soon as you feel it, pull back," he said, remaining calm despite my frustration.

I sighed, settling into my stance, and I hit it once again, this time trying to yank my fist back when it connected with the leather-like bag.

"See, that's a start. That one bumped it down to 5600. We can work with that. With just one statement, we've knocked your strongest punch to nearly half its strength. This is your first day! We can do this!" he said. The words seeped into my head, boosting my desire to continue. I didn't know the reinforcement would affect me as much as it did, but I was starting to gain my confidence back. I wasn't used to being encouraged by anyone other than my friends.

"You're right," I said. "I can do this." After several more attempts and a lot of aggravation, we left the strength room for the day. The rest of my evening was filled with learning my workout routine, which had proven to be difficult and tiring.

To my surprise, the food from the cafeteria was excellent. There were many choices, ranging from American food to Indian with several options from each. After sitting down and enjoying a great bowl of chicken korma accompanied by some garlic naan bread, I headed to my room. I was able to rest a while before heading to bed. Confidently, I was ready to try my hand at balance in the morning.

* * *

On my third day, I walked into the body training room, less groggy than I had been the morning before. Rubbing my arm, I realized I was sore from the strength tests and workout. This was going to take a lot out of me. I knew I was going to have to deal with the aching for a long time. I couldn't remember the last time I had worked out. Gym class had been bad enough, but a daily routine? Somebody needed to put me out of my misery. The only saving grace was that it was a workout to get my muscles back in shape, and not one to push my limits. That—I'm sure—would come when I reached the hideout with Blackwell.

This room was quite a bit different than the one for strength training. The edges were mostly covered in brightly colored padding. There were several balance beams, one with a wall to the left of it. A strong metal bar, also padded, jutted out as a handrail.

The rest of the room was filled with an assortment of bars and mats, some areas seeming to be made specifically for stretching. Maybe this area would be easier on me. *Then again, my balance is still dicey.* The slightest bump could knock me to the ground, so I had been diligent with my surroundings.

After Dr. Mellark greeted me this morning, he led me over to the balance beam with the railing. "This is where I will test your balance. The bar is for you to support yourself if needed. I need to know which side you're having the most trouble with," he said. "Other than that, on the days you're here, we will focus on flexibility and stretching your body. While it may sound easy, I assure you it will be equal to the strength training, if not more uncomfortable. Don't underestimate what will be done here."

I cringed. I wasn't sure how stretching could be worse than strength training, but I took his word for it. *Prepare yourself,* I thought. I stepped onto the beam, already unbalanced. As I took a step forward, I was forced to grab the bar immediately. My stress was beginning to rise as I tried not to fall. I took another step, but my body was being yanked to the right. I grabbed the rail and fell backward, my strength ripping the bar from the wall and almost knocking myself out with it.

I groaned, now on the ground with tunnel vision. *You've got to be kidding me,* I thought, knowing I was going to have a giant knot in the middle of my forehead.

"Are you alright?" Dr. Mellark asked, frightened. He rushed over to me, lifting the rail off me with a struggle. "I greatly apologize. I underestimated how strong the bar mount should be to cope with your strength."

"It's okay—I'm alright. So, what do we do now?" I asked, standing up. I winced as the pressure sent a sharp pain through my forehead. The bruise was beginning to form under my skin already.

"We will move to the stretching. When you lost your balance, did you feel it more on a certain side?" he asked me.

"Yeah. I wasn't up very long, but when I fell, I felt like I was leaning to the right. Where are we going to stretch?" I asked. The doctor pointed over to the other mats, a clearer area than the rest. It was the area I was looking at earlier. I gave myself a pat on the back for guessing what it was for.

I followed him over. He first had me doing basic arm and leg stretches, but then we switched to yoga. Unfortunately, Dr. Mellark was right when he told me this wasn't going to be easy. I struggled with the positions, and I had even more problems with my breathing. I would have a long way to go to hit the flexibility and balance marks he wanted. After stretching to a point I thought was impossible and doing my evening workout, I enjoyed a bowl of seafood Tom Kha before heading to bed.

* * *

During the two months of hard work, I was slowly able to reach my goals. They had put me through multiple stress tests to see if I was able to keep my composure. After handing me several fragile items to hold without breaking them and forcing me to hit punching bags at normal power, all while having to restrain my strength, I officially passed the stress test. It was a slow process; I had fallen countless times trying to regain my balance, and I don't know how many normal punching bags I had ripped from their chains, slamming them into the wall.

During the final test, I was able to consistently punch around four hundred PSI, somewhere between an average person and a boxer. The hardest part of the process for me was handling technology. I broke test phones several times, applying too much pressure on the screen and cracking them. I had unfortunately shocked myself on numerous occasions, pressing my fingers through the electronics of the test phones.

"Well, you've passed everything that we wanted. It took you about two months, which is right on time," Dr. Mellark said, handing me what appeared to be a thin, black tablet without a brand marking.

"Put your thumb in the middle of the bottom of the screen, and it will log you in," he said.

Log me in? What did that mean? I followed his instruction. There was a flash of light, turning into a solid white line before the device became active.

"Welcome, Tony. I am MIRA, your Mobile Information Retention Assistant. Rerouting you to rendezvous point," a strong, female voice said.

"That's neat, what else can MIRA do?" I asked him, very interested in the system.

"MIRA, as she said, is your Mobile Information Retention Assistant. She can be used as a GPS and many other things, along with being able to record and analyze different objects and people in real-time. She will be a part of all new members' training, installed somewhere within their suits. Once you are in Project Barricade's system, she will also track your health in relation to your powers, and help you hone your abilities in the training room," Dr. Mellark said, proud of the system.

"Wow, sounds helpful."

"I'm sure it will come in handy. As for me, that's all the information I've got for you. Friday, after you're back to school, Blackwell has requested a meeting with you around 7 pm. When it's time to head to the hideout, turn the tablet back on and MIRA will show you the way. I'm sure Blackwell will have a lot more to say. Good luck with your introduction, and I wish you the best on your journey. It was good to be a part of your process, Tony. I'm sure he has big plans for you, and I look forward to seeing what kind of hero you become," Dr. Mellark said as he waved goodbye and turned.

I looked down at the tablet. If it was strong enough to power the MIRA system, perhaps it would be good enough for my graphic design as well. I put my finger on my chin in thought. "Wait, can I ask a question about this tablet?" I called out. He stopped and turned his way back to me.

"Any questions are welcome if I can answer them."

"Would I be able to use this covertly? Like, for graphic design?"

He smiled. "I assumed you would be wondering that. You see that switch on the top left? While the tablet's horizontal." I looked down at it, seeing that there was a small switch I could flip. It reminded me of the mute buttons they had on older model smartphones. "If you flip that stealth switch, it will mute MIRA audibly. She understands that by flipping the switch, it means you are possibly in public, and the tablet will be usable for things other than hero work. You can simply ask her to install whatever programs you want. Something I will add to that: when that switch is flipped, you will still receive notifications from MIRA like you would, only they'll show up like locked text messages."

"Wow, that's really going to help me out a lot. I was trying to figure out how I could swing buying both a vehicle and a tablet while leaving money for everything else. Thank you, Dr. Mellark," I said, grinning. I looked back down at the tablet, seeing the full potential of what I could do with it. He nodded and walked back around the corner, bidding me farewell.

Flipping the switch on my tablet before placing it into my bag, I was now sitting on a bench waiting to be picked up. *Tomorrow's the day,* I thought, looking at my phone and realizing it was Monday. I grinned, knowing I now had a proper hold on my power. Tomorrow was the day my life would change forever. I'd be able to see my friends again. *And...* My thoughts focused on the bullying, knowing I would never allow it again.

And tomorrow I get to beat the hell out of Johnny.

It's been a long time coming.

Chapter 8

Confrontation

Content Warning: Contains sexual harassment and bullying.

I sat up, groaning as I gathered the strength to turn off my alarm. The gurgled battle cry of a fantasy creature repeated over the speaker of my phone, rupturing the calm that I had been enjoying. I flailed my hand, managing to hit the right button, bringing sweet silence back into the room. I fumbled off the couch, then made my way to Shawn's restroom to get ready for the day, peering into the mirror.

I gazed into it for the first time since my coma; I was scared at first, not knowing what I was destined to see. As my eyes scanned my body, I looked skinnier, but despite my new power and body, my eyesight was still horrific. I wouldn't be able to find my way out of a lit room without my glasses. My body composition also changed; along with shedding some of the weight I had been dealing with before, I also felt much healthier. Even stronger. I didn't have huge muscles or anything of the sort, but I could see potential in my new, broad frame.

A clean slate. A vessel to chisel into a hero.

After taking a shower, I went to brush my teeth. For some reason, it felt as if I was punched in the jaw. Both sides ached. I probably needed to see the dentist again. I reached for my toothbrush. I prepared it, and then opened my mouth, only to drop it into the sink in shock.

"No fucking way," I said to myself, pulling up my top lip. Sure enough, I had two long canine teeth. "I have fangs!?" As my mind fell into amazement and then panic, I questioned what this meant for me. I didn't have powers because I was a vampire, right? I hadn't noticed the fangs before. That would explain the pain. After realizing I'd been in the sun all day at the party eating garlic fries and hadn't craved buckets of blood, I assumed I wasn't a vampire. I'd have to ask about that. Plus side, I no longer had to find a dentist to have fangs done. They had been something I had been interested in for a while before my coma. I would have had to wait until after graduation, and I would have had to hide it from my family. I'd planned to get several piercings and tattoos as well, which I could now act upon. Only after my graphic design work took off. The last thing I wanted was to bar myself from working by making it more difficult to get into in the first place.

After getting dressed, I reached for my white foundation. As I realized I no longer needed it, I chuckled. I put on some eccentric eyeliner and met Shawn in the living room, ready to go. We took his truck so we were able to park in the parking garage by the school.

On our way to the cafeteria, I noticed the entrance to the old freshman hallway. It was sealed off with a wall and still scorched. *That's so weird to see,* I thought, knowing what had happened.

I looked down the new hallway that had been built to replace it. Sadly, Talida wasn't there. It was unclear if the construction was still in progress or had been given up on. I was surprised to see that the Junior hallway wasn't closed, since it was on the second floor above the freshmen hallway.

As I worked my way through the line to grab my breakfast, I was informed by the lunch lady about some new rules the school was implementing this year. After eating breakfast, we were free to go outside and visit with our friends until the bell rang for classes. Unfortunately for me, that meant I would probably have to face Johnny earlier than I had hoped. *Shoot,* I thought, not wanting the confrontation this early.

I had been left to my own thoughts since Shawn was quiet this morning. It wasn't unlike him due to how early it was. He was just now starting to wake up as we headed for a table. I turned to him, and he put his phone away as he caught my glance.

"Okay, it's weird that Talida isn't here yet," I said. Normally, she would be the first one in the building due to having to find a ride to school. I had thought it was kind of odd that Shawn didn't insist we pick her up on the way here, since he had his license now.

"Oh, I was too tired to tell you. Tuesdays and Thursdays, Talida helps her dad prep for the lunch rush at Blazing Sakura. She'll be here on the bus," he said, his words still glazed with wishful slumber.

"Oh, that makes sense. I didn't think to ask due to being tired myself," I said. He laughed.

I sat down at the table and looked at my food. We were having nasty, frozen cinnamon rolls and stale cereal for breakfast. "You want my cinnamon roll?" I asked. "I hate these things."

Shawn laughed. "Gimme," he said playfully, reaching his hand out. "I have no such hate."

After scarfing the cereal for much-needed sustenance and chugging a decent carton of orange juice, we dumped our trays and headed for the door. Just as I wondered where Talida was, she came running behind me, throwing her arm around me with a side hug.

"There you are!" she said, smiling.

"I was beginning to wonder if you skipped today," I said back, laughing. For as long as I can remember, she had never missed school. With her parents being anal about her education, she was lucky that she was rarely sick.

She giggled. "Oh yeah, I *always* skip. Especially when my best friend comes back after two freakin' years," she said sarcastically, nudging me in the arm. She gave Shawn a quick hug and I noticed what she was wearing. She wore black leggings and a matching black crop top, covered by a jacket that seemed more like it was for exercise. She had come prepared for what we thought was going to happen today, avoiding the stiffer jeans she normally wore.

I looked at them with a serious gaze. "You guys have to see this. I found them this morning," I blurted out. I hadn't told Shawn yet either, despite being at his house for the revelation. I questioned if it were a good idea to tell them about the physical changes I was finding, but as far as I knew, they didn't correlate with my powers. They looked at me in confusion as I held open my mouth. Her eyes bulged as she saw them first.

"What?" she asked in surprise. "You have fangs? Are you a vampire? You have the pale skin to match." I laughed, shaking my head.

"Nope. Not a vampire, unfortunately."

"Dude! That's awesome," Shawn added, letting loose his low guffaw as he wondered what to call me. "Come on, Dracula, let's go outside."

The statement sent Talida into a fit of giggles, which turned into a cackle when I replied. "Well, so far so good with the daylight. Maybe I'm closer to Blade."

"With the trench coat maybe! I'm gonna hit the restroom before heading out though. I'll see you all outside."

We nodded. Surely, he would be outside before Johnny started anything. He probably wasn't even here yet. I crossed my fingers, hoping that our interaction would be later in the day rather than in the morning.

Talida and I headed outside through the gossiping crowd that was in front of the door. Outside were several benches and tables, along with a cheap basketball court above a small field to the left that most people didn't seem to use. The field went around the corner of the building to a place students didn't linger. There wasn't anything to do over there, but that's where we headed to hopefully find some peace. There were a couple of students hanging around outside, but most of them had stayed in the cafeteria. As we started talking, we saw Johnny and his group exit the school. We tried to avoid their gaze, but they immediately noticed and trudged toward us. With their lips pursed and eyes squinted, they were ready for a fight. "Welcome back, dickhead!" Johnny bellowed.

Shit.

"I was wondering when they were going to show up," Talida mumbled under her breath. Fear started to appear in her eyes. "Could really use Shawn right now."

"Yeah," I started, my voice cracking with adrenaline. "Looks like they're all hyped up too. Too late to send him a text I think." I looked at her rather than the bullies. There was something we needed to ensure in order to get through this. "Whatever they do or say, we can *not* throw the first punch." She nodded in agreement despite appearing to want to go in swinging. That scared girl afraid to defend herself from two years ago wouldn't exist after today. I could see it in her eyes.

"You still think you're tough, Tony? Bring it!" Johnny yelled, getting close enough for me to smell the cinnamon on his hot breath. Spit shot from his mouth as he spoke, as if he were a rabid animal. He put his hands on my shoulders, giving me a shove as he initiated the fight. My adrenaline immediately jolted from the confrontation; fear of what was to come flooded over me.

This is it, I thought. This is where I needed to prove myself. I pressed my lips, ready for what was about to happen.

"Eat shit, Johnny! You're no tougher than he is!" Talida yelled, attempting to be as close to him as Johnny was to me. I could see her fists shaking as they were balled against her sides.

"Since when do you want to fight, you fucking *nip*?!" I frowned in disgust at the terrible racist slur. He seemed surprised, as if hearing her interjection was the last thing he expected.

Johnny burst into laughter as Rob and Grey walked up beside him.

"We'll do whatever we want. It's three against two." Rob, the disgusting piece of shit that he was, brushed his knuckle up the front of her breast and grinned.

She slapped his hand away. "Hands off, asshole," she said. But her voice was waning. I could see that the move made her extremely uncomfortable as she didn't know whether to hit him or back up. He lifted his hand to likely repeat the motion.

I pointed my trembling finger at Rob, needing to step in. "You leave her alone! And leave her fucking race out of it," I yelled back at them, my voice failing me as it fragmented.

"The only thing she's good for is eye candy," Grey said. He looked her up and down. "And there's plenty of that."

"What are you going to do about it?" Johnny asked, taking another step closer to me as he looked me in the eyes. I clenched my jaw. They would never touch her again. Inches away from my face, the heat radiated off his skin, sizzling in his wrath.

My adrenaline turned to anger—fuming anger that I didn't have before my coma—and it was shooting through my body. It was difficult to hold back my clenched fist as I waited for him to throw the first punch, but the energy inside of me was telling me to kill the three of them. "Make another move and find out," I growled. To my surprise my voice didn't crack. There was no wavering as I glared back at him, more determined than ever to end this, once and for all.

He smiled as he turned around to punch Talida in the jaw. I could no longer control myself, and that's when my superhuman powers started to kick in, showing me that better reflexes had come with strength. My right arm swung up, and I pushed his out of the way. He missed her, and I used my left hand to swing a low jab into Johnny's side. Talida stumbled back, alarmed, and she followed with a strike to Rob's face. After that move he made, she now knew who she was targeting. Rob grabbed his nose, grunting as blood began to run over his lips. He grabbed Talida, tossing her to the ground.

As I glanced over at the edge of the building, I saw Shawn poke his head around the corner. We made eye contact, and his facial expression changed completely from calm to "what's happening?" Johnny was bent down in pain, groaning, and now Grey was heading toward me. I backed up, sending a piston-like punch to Johnny's face. He was forced back several feet, slamming into the muddy ground and leaving a rut as he slid between two students, knocked out cold.

With my focus purely on the bullies, I hadn't noticed that we had drawn a crowd. The few students outside were now circling us, and more were pouring out of the building, running our way. Some students cheered as a couple others let out boos. A small few pulled out their phones and started to record, attempting to get closer to the fight for a better view.

Talida wrestled with Rob as she tried to get back on her feet. Suddenly, Shawn sprinted across the school grounds, dividing the students around us and jumping into the fight with a loud, familiar grunt. "*Nyagh!* Revenge of the freaks!" he yelled, punching Rob in the face.

I spun backward, landing a clumsy kick to Grey's head, sending him to the ground on his hands and knees. Rob fled from Shawn and ran up to me with some sort of bear-hug thing. I grabbed his head from the back, pulling it down toward me as I kneed him as hard as I could without killing him. He fell to his back, holding himself in extreme pain. I may have used more strength than the average human, so he was probably looking at a concussion.

Shawn helped Talida off the ground, giving her a high-five as they backed away from the confrontation. While my attention had been pulled away, Johnny had woken up, and I was now heading directly for him with clenched fists.

"Listen, you punks!" I yelled, inching toward the three bullies. Anger manifested inside me. I thought of turning them into a pulp while I had the chance, but words would have to suffice.

"If I *ever* catch you worthless kids bullying anyone again, I will *ruin* you!" I yelled at them. The three of them sat against each other, trying to work their way to their knees. Then Johnny had the gall to laugh.

"You think because you got lucky this time that we will stop? You forget who's in control!"

"Shut up!" I hissed, storming toward him. Any will to hurt them with words withered away as I realized they thought they still had a chance. "I kicked your ass!"

"Yeah, but we'll be ready for you next time." Johnny coughed, and Grey shot him a look. "Next time, I'll make sure I target your skank first while you aren't around."

"I said shut up!" This time the words were a bellow and caused Shawn and Talida to look my way. I kicked him in the face, knocking him back to the ground. As he tried to stand, the other two were already on their feet. I kicked Johnny again. Every memory of them bullying me and my friends flooded into my mind. *They won't do it again*, I thought.

"Hey, wait—we give up! You won!" Rob said, trying to pull me away from Johnny, who I was now closing in on. I turned around sharply, grabbing his hand and peeling it off my shoulder. I twisted it backward with a snap. *Just like he did to Shawn's pencil when we first met,* I thought, chuckling. I made sure it was the one he had groped Talida with before asking myself if he needed the other one snapped too. He fell to the ground with a scream of pain, holding his new wound. Grey took a quickened step toward me and then stopped.

"Wise choice," I sneered. As Johnny was still grunting in pain, laying on his side now, I kicked him a third time. And then again. The few recording the video suddenly stopped as the students stopped their cheering.

"Ow—stop!" he yelled, frightened now. I didn't care. Not after the years of torment he's put us through. I needed to send a message, or they would continue to retaliate against me.

"You will never hurt my friends again!" I screamed. I sent another kick, this time hearing the snapping of a rib after a *THUNK*.

"Dude, he's had enough!" Grey said. I backhanded him. Hard. It was enough to send him in a twirl behind me with another loud crack. Shawn and Talida looked concerned. They started to approach, and Johnny started bawling.

"Please, stop!" Johnny cried, choking and coughing.

"Like you stopped for us all these years? No." I bent down and punched him in the mouth, hoping that would shut him up. He still yelled out, and as I remembered him slamming Aiden into a locker and throwing his stuff across the hallway, I hit him again, hearing another crack. "I want to hear you cry."

"Tony, please! I'm sorry," Johnny wheezed.

"No, you're fucking not." I bent down near his face, looking him in the eyes. The warmth of fury filled my fists, and they seemed to have a sort of numbness in them. "But you will be."

I never wanted to hear his voice again. *WACK!*

I could kill him right now. With these powers, who could stop me?

WACK! Through all the horrible memories, I wasn't going to stop. Suddenly, Shawn was in front of me with clenched fists. In my rage, I almost nudged him to the side.

"Get out of my way, Shawn," I growled slowly.

"Tony, he's down and out. That's enough," he said calmly, raising his hands.

"They killed Aiden!" I bellowed. Shawn shot a glance at Talida, who was now wide-eyed. She stayed quiet, letting Shawn try to talk me down.

"The fire did that. We don't know if they had any involvement."

"I'm blaming them!"

"Tony, we hate them as much as you do, but I can't watch you kill Johnny! He's a shitty human being but throwing your life away for his isn't worth it! Come on, man. I just got you back in my life! Now put out the damn fire!"

His words struck me hard. They were enough to knock me out of my blood-blinded haze, and suddenly I realized the fault in what I was doing. This isn't what I wanted. I stepped back, looking at the three bullies in horror of what I was close to doing.

Johnny was crying and in pain, Rob was holding his butchered hand, bone splitting through his skin, and Grey was backing away, mouthing the words "Holy shit."

Their eyes bulged in horror from what they had seen. Their gazes made me happy, along with a thrill that I knew I was guilty of enjoying despite the atrocities I had committed; the tables had turned, and now *they* were afraid of *me.*

It took me a moment to realize the new origin of their fear. *Wait, fire?* As I looked down, I realized my arms were blazing with bright yellow and white fire. As I was struck with fear, along with the quick realization that I had unlocked another ability, the flames dissipated as I shook my arms. I looked around. The students had seen that. *I have to act quickly.* They had all seen it.

I managed to let loose a chuckle as I reached for my backpack. "Enjoy the theatrics? It's super flammable," I yelled out, reaching into the side of it and tossing a can of body spray on the ground. Some of the students laughed, while others stared at me in fear. It seemed as though they believed the lie, staring at the can on the ground. As I calmed down, Talida ran up to me.

Shawn and Talida looked at me with hesitation. I was worried they would hate me for how badly I had beaten the bullies up, yet they still smiled.

"When did you—how did you…? What…? Whatever happened to you in the coma, I want some of that!" Talida said, laughing and trying to raise the mood.

I forced a smile. Was she talking about my powers…? My stomach tightened. Surely, I hadn't given myself away already. Hopefully, she had believed the lie as well.

"How did you get the nerve to fight back?" she asked.

My body relaxed, now knowing she was talking about the fight. "I don't know what happened," I lied. As much as I wanted to, I couldn't tell them the truth. If I had learned anything from superhero movies, it was that once they knew who I was, they would be in danger.

"I can't believe you just did that! When did you learn those moves? How did you flip Grey like that?" Talida asked, just as amazed as I was about how well that went. We won. I stared at them in disbelief. *We actually won!* I thought, screaming internally with excitement as my body fell into an impenetrable calm.

"I winged it," I said, chuckling uncomfortably. I looked down at my hands, and then at the bullies. "I can't believe we won. Just like that, all these years of suffering are over."

"It took all those years to finally get the courage to fight back. You changed, dude, and we wouldn't have been able to do this without you," Talida said, smiling. "Though I do think you may have gone a little far. They were done a long time ago." I gave a grin back. I realized that our decision to fight back together would have been enough, even without my powers.

"They wouldn't have stopped. I almost lost myself, though. I don't want to become the bully. But they needed to know they can't do this anymore."

"Did you light yourself on fire for aesthetics using *my* can of body spray?" Shawn asked. He let out a short laugh, knowing I wasn't going to turn on them again. "That's the boldest thing anyone has ever done in a school fight! You're a badass, dude!"

"Yeah, um," I said, starting to fidget with my fingers. "That probably won't go so well with the principal. Neither will breaking their bones."

As we walked around the corner, the crowd around us turned silent as their shocked faces filled my view; the faces of all the people that only knew me as a geek and a nerd. A low-life delinquent. Now I was something else to them, and they didn't know what to think. They probably thought I was a monster. I'd be expelled for sure.

"Teacher alert! I'm out!" Shawn yelled, blending into the wall of students as if he had a power of his own. The crowd in front of me dispersed, leaving just a teacher standing there. Mr. Graves. A normally easy-going art teacher if he hadn't gotten word that I butchered the three bullies.

Somebody had called for an ambulance, and the EMTs were rushing up to the boys on the ground. They got Johnny and Grey on the backboards and put them in the vehicle. I had no idea when they'd come back, if at all.

Mr. Graves had his arms crossed, ready to scold me. "Tony," he called out angrily.

I walked over to the teacher, questioning where the conversation would lead. "Yeah?" I asked, grinning from ear to ear. I tried to hide my visible ecstasy, but it was no use; standing up for myself had been invigorating. The teacher pointed toward the paramedics, who were talking to Rob.

"I know you were the cause of that! Both of you need to go to the office—now!" Mr. Graves said firmly. I was sure I'd be kicked out of school, but I wasn't sure if I cared; I had just gotten the revenge I had always wanted on Johnny, and I couldn't be happier. Knowing I had almost killed them, on the other hand, was jarring. I nodded, walking into the side door to head up the long hallway to the office. As we sat on one of the red benches, waiting for our names to be called, Talida looked at me.

"That was crazy," she said with a smirk, laughing a little bit. It was the first time I had seen her happy after a fight, and it was strange. It was almost as if we had slipped from reality for the moment.

"Yeah. That fire stunt horrified them, though," I said. "Maybe they'll finally leave us alone. It'd be crazy to have a normal senior year, wouldn't it?"

"Yeah, it would. Though Johnny and Rob looked pretty messed up," she said. She looked at me, questioning me. "How did you make the fire? I didn't see the whole thing, but Shawn was pretty thrilled with it."

"Well, don't tell Shawn this, but I soaked my hands with the body spray he lent me in the bathroom. I just waited for the right time to light it. I found a lighter on the way inside," I said, relieved of how smoothly the lie rolled off my tongue. We both laughed.

"Well, thank you. We really needed that fight to go our way," she said. She relaxed as if I had taken a huge weight off her. I smiled, and the only thing I could think of was how desperately I wanted to feel this again. With us fighting back, we had completely transformed our world. Hopefully for the better. "Thank you again for standing up for me. Rob was—awful."

"I couldn't have done it without you guys," I said. "I wouldn't have had the courage to fight back. As for Rob, let's just say I was excited to see that it was his right hand on my shoulder." She gave me a bothered smile. "He won't do it again. Don't worry." I gave her a short hug.

Principal Jackson came out of his office and called me in, cutting the conversation short. "Tony Jensen?" he asked for confirmation, looking up from some paperwork.

"Yeah," I reassured, taking a hard look at the floor, hoping that I wasn't going to be kicked out of school. The reality of the situation was starting to hit me, and I turned to Talida. "Make sure he knows about that part," I whispered. "Good luck."

"Johnny again already?" he asked as I entered his office to sit.

"Yeah…and I won this time." In my head there wasn't a reason to get into the details unless he asked. Principal Jackson knew me, and this was not usually how my fights concluded, although I had been warned the last time. His eyes widened.

"I have to say, even with your many visits with me in the past, this isn't what I was expecting today. What did Johnny do this time to deserve three broken ribs and a broken collar bone?" he asked. I cringed as he turned to his right, making sure his recorder was on.

"He came up to me saying 'bring it' and 'you think you're tough?'" I paused and thought about it for a moment.

"My friend, Talida, told him to stop getting in my face, and he started yelling, 'Since when do you fight?' He called her an awful, racist name, and I tried to stop him from yelling at her. Rob—" I put my hand on the back of my neck as I tried to think of how to explain it. "Rob groped her. Johnny tried to punch her, and when I blocked him, I got angry and hit him. They've been bullying us for years now, and I finally snapped," I said. "I had to make sure they wouldn't do it again."

Mr. Jackson sighed. "I'm going to need you to explain what you saw with Rob. Can you elaborate?"

"They started calling her eye candy and saying they could do whatever they wanted with three against two. Rob bounced her boob with his finger, and was going to do it again before everything started. That's why I broke his wrist."

"Was it worth it?" Mr. Jackson asked, not seeming bothered or even surprised.

"Every last second of it," I said without hesitation. I honestly didn't regret any of it. "If it gets me kicked out of school, well, that's the way it's gonna be!" I looked up at him with a confidence I hadn't been able to tap into before.

The brief thought passed through my mind that I wouldn't be coming back to school. I would be living in a van doing graphic design while my friends graduated. Part of me was excited about this idea. I could focus on my superhero training while they finished out school.

Mr. Jackson laughed. "I do recall our last visit, but luckily for you, the cameras caught this one. And to me, it looked like Johnny started that fight. I can sway that in your direction, but that doesn't mean this is over. We will have to contact their parents and hope they don't press charges."

My eyes widened, not having expected the statement. Just as I accepted my fate, it was flipped back around. "Wait, really? I'm not getting expelled?"

"Not this time, but you will need to continue to stay out of trouble. I think I can help you. I can get him out of school for numerous things—sexual harassment is one I can hopefully pin on the three of them. They could be out of school for a while as long as the board backs me," Principal Jackson said. I smiled. Maybe I would get out of this one. "You can leave, but I'm going to have to kick you out of school for two 'recovery' days. Go ahead and tell Talida to come to my office so that I can cross-examine your story with hers."

I nodded, shooting a smile. "Thank you, Mr. Jackson. I'm sorry for causing you so much trouble." A sense of relief came over me as I walked out of the office; he could have easily used this as the last straw to expel me like he had warned me about years ago. I wasn't worried about Johnny or Grey, but I'd be lucky if Rob's parents didn't press charges.

"It's no problem at all, Tony. Keep your head up," he replied as I closed the door.

"Talida," I said, looking around to see where she was. Sure enough, she hadn't moved and was slouched into the red bench.

"Yeah?" she answered as she sat up straight.

"He wants to get your side of the story," I said.

"Okay. Did he expel you?" she asked, worried.

I shook my head. "I'm kicked out for two days, but this fight was on the cameras," I said, smiling.

"Only two? Sweet!" Talida said back excitedly. She had been expecting the worst. At least a week. She stood tall, heading into the office to confirm everything I had just said.

Chapter 9

Persevere

After Talida's time with the principal and several calls to the school board and parents, they had finally reached a verdict. Johnny and his group had unfortunately been kicked out for two days as well, which was unexpected. The board decided to cut all of us some slack with a foreboding warning of expulsion.

As I thought, both Johnny and Grey's parents decided not to press charges. It took the principal a long time on the phone call with Rob's mother before he talked her into dropping the charges she wanted to put on me. On my way out, I glanced at the clock, noticing that I had been in the office for about an hour.

I trudged through the hallway, looking for my class. Finally, on my left was a sign on the wall by a classroom that read, "Mr. Karson." As my insides clenched at the horrible memories of this room, I reminded myself that this was the beginning of a new life.

One where I was confident. One where I could make a difference. I walked in.

I stood up front, looking at all the students in the classroom. Most of them I knew, some of them I didn't, but Shawn caught my eye, waving at me excitedly from the back.

"We have a returning student," Mr. Karson started to say, interrupting the lesson he had been teaching.

Mr. Karson's desk was on the far-left side of the room in the corner as you walked in. A whiteboard hung on the same wall, and the seats were on the opposite side. He got up, walking toward me. "This is Tony Jensen; he just woke up from a coma," he said, pointing toward me. I waved to the class.

Someone knocked on the door. Mr. Karson walked over to the door, opening it to see who it was. "Yes?" he asked.

"Johnny Coleman, Grey Proctor, and Rob Baskin won't be in your classes for a while. They've been suspended for tomorrow and Thursday and are currently in the hospital with significant injuries," a female voice answered. I quickly recognized it as one of the office ladies.

"What in the world happened?" Mr. Karson asked.

"They were severely injured in a school fight this morning."

I put my hand over my mouth to muffle my laughter; it was one of the first times I had laughed in school, let alone this hard.

"Okay, thank you," Mr. Karson said back politely.

The lady walked away, and she headed back up the hallway to the office as Mr. Karson closed the door. "Anyway, back to business. Find a desk," he said to me. I walked to the back and sat next to Shawn, who was now laughing as he looked up at me.

"I didn't expect to win that fight. I definitely didn't expect you to go ape on them afterward," he said. I chuckled back.

"Yeah, me either. They surely didn't see that coming. I didn't expect to only get two days suspension either," I said, hoping that we'd never have to deal with them again.

Shawn let loose a loud guffaw, his face becoming a dark maroon as he ran out of breath. He slowly stopped laughing and looked at me with a serious gaze, releasing a disappointed hum as he seemed to be mentally trapped in a different thought.

"What's wrong?" I asked, wondering what could possibly be bothering him right now.

He looked up at me, his eyes revealing a new pain. "You worried me out there, man. I didn't think you were going to stop. I've never seen anger like that come from you. I know there are rumors that Johnny started the school fire, but there's no proof, and he denies it. I'm sure if it was him, he would be bragging about it. I don't know... I just miss Aiden."

"I'm sure he would have. I wasn't thinking clearly out there. I'm sorry if I scared you. This isn't like me to feel that angry toward them, despite what comes out of their mouths. I guess I just snapped," I said back, wondering how a single person could be so evil. Why would anyone put lives in danger like that? "I miss him too. It's not fair."

Shawn smiled, but I could still see the sadness in his eyes. This was a pain that was going to last quite some time. "On a better note, do you see that girl over there in the corner?" he asked, pointing to a girl with long purple hair. She looked to be of East Asian descent with almond eyes and a curvy figure.

I nodded. "Yeah, what about her?" I asked, not recognizing her. I had never seen her before, so she must have been a transfer student.

"I'm going to ask her out after school. After being in that fight, I feel so rejuvenated and empowered. I feel more confident in myself, and people say confidence is key," he said.

I smiled. "I hope that works out well for you. Do you know anything about her? What she likes? Do you have any similar interests?" I asked. Personality was the most important aspect; without good personality traits or similar interests, there wasn't anything worth fighting for.

"I haven't talked to her yet. I know her name is Alexis, but look at that backpack; it's hers," Shawn said, pointing to a dark-purple backpack against the wall with a familiar symbol on it. The symbol was that of two intertwining phoenixes. "It looks like she's a huge fan of Grudgematch, and I think that's going to be my conversation starter. I've got a new watch with that symbol on it." Shawn tittered and muttered under his breath, "I have no idea what I'm doing."

"Everyone has to start somewhere. I'm sure it will go fine, especially if she is as much of a geek as you are," I said, grinning. He looked back at me with a smile.

"You know how I am with girls. I'm so awkward—and look at her! She's so pretty!" He stopped, as if wanting to change the subject before he got too flustered.

"Anyway. Dude! You knocked out Johnny with, like, two punches. Everyone knows that by now. Why don't you go get yourself a girlfriend? This is the perfect time to do it!" Shawn said, nudging my shoulder with his fist while smirking. "People won't blow you off right now; you have their attention."

"I don't know. I just haven't found the person that I click with like that," I said. I had to make a strong emotional connection with someone before I could think of them in that way.

"Well, isn't there anyone you think is kind of hot at this school? Worst case scenario, you don't connect well and have to break it off."

"Honestly, I'm not even attracted to anyone. Some people are pretty, sure, but I've never been able to think about anything more than that," I replied, questioning if it was strange. *I know I'm a little different,* I thought.

"Okay, Mr. Demi-sexual, do as you wish," Shawn said sarcastically, joking with me. I chuckled, but I was unable to argue his accuracy. I was definitely on the asexual spectrum, and demisexuality was close to what I was. Without having a significant other, who's to know? I hadn't thought far enough ahead to even know if I would end up with a man or a woman but neither had I had any experiences with either. When it came down to physical appearance, the human body in general was interesting.

"Who knows, man. Maybe, maybe not," I said, laughing. As the teacher began to speak, we decided to listen.

* * *

After several hours of going to different classes without anyone bothering me, the loud bell rang, dismissing us. Was I going to be able to pull off double classes? I headed outside to my bus with my mound of catch-up homework. Talida and Shawn ran in my direction, interrupting my worry.

"See ya Friday!" Talida yelled, rushing off to her bus. She was in a hurry today. She wasn't normally in that much of a rush to get home.

"Dude!" Shawn said. I turned to look at him, seeing him sprint from the opposite direction as Talida. He had an excited look on his face, and his eyes were beaming. "I have a date tonight! She told me she had thought about asking me out, but she was too shy! Today is freakin' amazing!" He screamed at me, more excited than he had ever been.

"Awesome! Good luck, man!" I yelled back, giving him a high-five. "I'll take the bus back to your house so you can go get ready. It was good to see everyone happy for once. In fact, Alexis might be really good for him. I never thought that all three of us would be as thrilled as we were today. Life was finally going to give us a break. Was this going to be the turning point for us?

"I'll see you there. My parents need some help before I go out, so I'm going to rush back!" Shawn said, heading to his truck.

"See you later! Get to know each other. We'll talk tonight!" I yelled back.

I boarded my bus and sat down. Now that I was alone, I began to think of the letter I'd received from Blackwell. I didn't know how I was going to pull off the hero training and school. I would get quite a bit less sleep, and it would be hard to hide it from my friends. I would have to find an excuse to get out of the house and meet him Friday night. I knew that Shawn's parents would be disappointed with me for getting kicked out of school, but they likely wouldn't start a fight or anything.

On the other end, I now had two free days. I questioned if I would be able to get my license tomorrow, and maybe buy a van Thursday. That would get me out of Shawn's house by Friday, which would make it easier to get away that night. Maybe I could borrow Shawn's truck for that. I would have to ask him about it.

Once I arrived at his house, I was lucky to see that his parents were working late again. Shawn was already in the shower, so I was now questioning if joining Project Barricade was a good idea. Was I ready for that? As Shawn exited the bathroom, I headed toward his now closed bedroom door.

"Hey can I ask you a question?"

There was a moment of silence from the other side. As I heard rustling, he answered. "Sure. You can come in. I'm just finding a shirt." I entered, walking into his room and looking around. Not a lot had changed. He still had the cobalt blue walls and desk in the corner attached to a whole bunch of game systems. As I looked closely at the ensemble of video games on top of a home-built wooden shelf, I saw the ring. Aiden's Grudgematch ring rested near the top, next to more Grudgematch paraphernalia and a photo of the four of us hanging out, years ago.

Shawn caught my gaze and let out a sigh. "It fits well up there, doesn't it? I didn't want to lose it at school or chance Johnny stealing it, so it's been up there." His words were somber, as if it still hurt him to look at it. It sure hurt me to see it, knowing that our friend was gone.

"Yeah," I said quietly. "It does fit well up there. Good picture of us too." I smiled.

"So, what's your question? Sorry to distract you." He smiled, and I mirrored him.

"Okay, so I know you need it tonight, but can I borrow your truck tomorrow to try and get my license in the morning? I figured since I'm suspended for the next two days, I could get my license and find a van Thursday."

He paused in thought, his eyes narrowing. "Hold on." He reached into his closet and pulled out a black and red collared shirt. "Do you think this looks good with these pants?"

I laughed. "Yeah, and it all looks better since you shaved off the neck stubble."

He smiled and buttoned the shirt, tucking it into his nice black jeans. "Okay to answer your question, I have another question. Do you think you're ready? You just started practicing before physical therapy." I sat on his bed and nodded. I was ready. Despite being in the coma for two years, it still felt very recent. It was like I picked up where I left off.

"I know I'm ready. I went over the information so I can pass the written exam again too."

"Okay, awesome. No, you can't borrow my truck," he said with a laugh. "That would be illegal."

I was taken aback by the answer. Not that I expected him to agree no matter what, but the way he was speaking led me to believe it might be a yes. I tried to hide the disappointment in my voice. "Oh okay. No problem."

"I'll drive you," Shawn said. "I'll be sick tomorrow, and I'll take you up there. Don't argue. Let's get your license."

I let out the breath I was apparently holding. "Oh, thank goth. I didn't know what I was going to do. But you really shouldn't skip classes. I don't want to put you behind."

"It won't matter. I don't have any tests tomorrow, and it should be easy make-up work. I've still got a while before my date, and I don't really want to be stressing out about it for another hour, so let's talk. I think I found a van for you. I haven't told Talida because I want it to be a surprise. It's got new wheels and everything." He pulled out his phone and I smiled, eager to see what he found.

"Badass, let's see it!" I exclaimed. "But it better not be like that last one."

He laughed, and I wasn't sure whether I should be more worried or re-lieved. He showed me the ad on his phone, and I started flipping through the pictures. I was immediately turned off by the van just by the price. $6000. "Now, it's still ugly, but they put new wheels and tires on it beforehand. I know what you're thinking. That's kind of expensive, but it's on the cheaper end for these big vans. You'd have to drop the entirety of what you have for a nice one. *But*, there's potential in this one, and it's a diamond in the rough."

"How so?" I asked, biting the inside of my lip. At least I didn't have to spend more on a tablet. I saw that it was a white van with peeling white paint. It was long—which was a good thing for my plan—and had a high roof on it.

"It has low miles and is being sold because they didn't want to do van-life. They started building it out and stopped due to changing their mind. Which means it has a lot of the expensive work already done inside. It has an electric hookup, and a solar panel."

I nodded in approval as I flipped through the photos. There were a couple of ideas I had for it if I got it, but I liked the wheels. They were large black and silver ones, making it look a little less run-down. There were no windows other than the ones on the back of the van, which would be good for my privacy.

"There's a fridge already in it, too," I said as I flipped through another picture. "I actually like this one." I looked at him, smiling.

"Wanna go check it out Thursday?"

"I would love to."

The idea of getting my license, the van, and joining a team of superheroes made me super excited. When Shawn left for his date, I told myself I would design a super suit. Before that though, Shawn decided it was best if we played a few rounds of Immortal Fighter. I lost four out of five, but we still had a lot of fun. I had heated up a frozen burrito out of his freezer and was good for the night.

"Well, I'd better go pick her up. Do I look okay?" he asked me.

I nodded. "You look fine. You've got this! Go have fun," I said, smiling. He put his hand on my shoulder, and then turned around to leave the room. Once I heard his truck turn on and leave, I rushed to pull my tablet out. I needed to start installing programs. I should have done it earlier.

After audibly asking MIRA to install four programs, one for photo editing, painting, print media, and vector projects, I was surprised to see that it was already connected to its own internet. It was fast. Way faster than any other internet I've ever connected to. All four of the programs were installed within seconds. I pulled out a stylus I had bought while school shopping, and sat down at Shawn's desk.

I looked up at the photo of the four of us, and then the Grudematch ring that had belonged to Aiden. I was doing this for them. For my new family.

I started to make sketches of how my super suit would look and what material it would be made of. After throwing four or five designs to a folder I was naming the digital trash bin, I decided to have a debate in my head as to what I wanted. On the current clean document, I wrote down a small list of my wants on the side where it would be out of the way of the design itself. It needed to make a statement. I rested my chin on my fist. It needed flexibility, and I needed to be able to maneuver in it without sacrificing armor. Maybe also a hint of technology? Not enough to hinder me if the electronics break. My first design wasn't quite right, so I trashed it as well.

I drew a second design, this one a little better, but still not quite what I was looking for. It needed a dark element. *Maybe a gothic touch,* I thought. Red and black was cliché, so I didn't want to go in that direction.

I wanted something that wasn't too dark; something with a vibrant accent color, but not too bright. I smiled as I looked around Shawn's room, catching a glimpse of the bandana in the corner. *Let's do charcoal and purple.* I didn't see that one quite as much. I made a few changes to the design I had just drawn, and it was much better.

* * *

The suit would have a dark gray, skintight material as a base. I decided that I would have a purple belt, purple thigh guards made of some sort of metal, and then I would have a pair of combat boots similar to the boots I wear now that go up to my knees with purple plates going up the center of my shins, centered on white straps. These boots would have a white, nonslip sole that would lead up the front of my foot to a spike. I would have a white design throughout the body of the suit.

As for the upper body, I started the design with a pair of rounded pauldrons that I decided would be purple. Directly underneath them, lying over my biceps would be a second layer that I would make white.

I decided to have a purple, four-pointed star shape, almost resembling a cross on the center of my chest. Two curved swerve designs would lead from the top into a gray and purple cape with a white line separating the colors. Heading downward with the curves, there would be three rib-like shapes in purple on both sides.

The mask was what I had been having a hard time with for most of the design period. I decided on a purple mask with black eyes, having an eyebrow furl with a serious gaze, even a little angry. I decided I wanted purple pupils and white glowing irises. Looking at them, they reminded me of the totality of a solar eclipse. This mask would have four spikes on the top, the outer two connected with a curve, and the center two with a point.

I also wanted to have a filtered mask for the lower half of my face. This piece would have a pointed oval shape in the middle of it. It would have four exaggerated white teeth shapes on top and two on the bottom, overall giving a fierce look to my suit design while being able to filter toxins from the air. If I was ever going to get stuck in a fire again, I would have to be able to breathe. I realized this would make it more like a helmet, so I drew it to where it would cover the back of my head as well. I even gave the helmet a small point at the back of the head so that I could pull my hair up into it. My head would be completely covered.

Looking at what I had, it didn't feel finished. I couldn't figure out what made the design incomplete, and then it all clicked. The back of my head was boring. *What would fix that?* My eyes widened as I drew a gray hood that would attach to the helmet and base of the suit. I smiled, moving on to the next piece.

I wanted to have something on both of my wrists, maybe the electronics that I had debated before, but I hadn't decided on them yet. I decided that I would have fingerless gray gloves to match the body of the suit and not interfere with my fire abilities, if that was even an issue that mattered in real life. Not to mention I didn't want to wear full gloves with my pointed fingernails.

I smiled. "It's perfect!" I exclaimed to myself, looking at my creation in awe. I couldn't wait to see this in person.

To wear my creation. To defeat evil in my own style and lurk in the dark of Old Belmont. It seemed as if a lucid dream had just been launched into reality. I was finally going to make a difference! But how was I going to get it made?

I started to think of a name for myself. Something that would not only make sense but also motivate me to be a better person. A name came to me. I would never give up; no matter what happened, with these abilities, I would never give in to my enemies. No more bullying, no crime against innocents, and if I could help it, there wouldn't be any evil either. I wouldn't stop until I rid the world of wickedness!

I will never give up. I will always push through, therefore I *am* Persevere.

Chapter 10

Living Space

After a much-needed night of rest, I awoke from a hard sleep. Turning off my alarm, I heard the groan of Shawn waking up as well.

"Oh shit, is it time to get up already?" he asked. We had stayed up for quite a while talking about his date. It had gone super well, and they already had a second one planned for Friday night. He told me that she went by Alex, and they had a lot in common. I had been super excited for them.

I stretched my arms over my head. I had fallen asleep next to Shawn. I could have gone to the couch, but at that point in time it was too late for me to care. "Looks that way," I grumbled. The thought of getting my license today acted like a cup of coffee to me. It woke me up slightly, but mostly just made me jittery.

As we both got up and got some clothes on for the day, Shawn frowned looking at his phone.

"What's up?" I asked, slightly concerned.

"The seller of the van is busy tomorrow, but we can look at it today if we get done quickly enough," Shawn said. "I know that wasn't the plan, but if you like it and get it today, we could get it set up a little better for you tomorrow."

I thought about it for a moment. I didn't like things going against plans, but this one could work in my favor. "Alright, let's do it."

* * *

That morning had gone well. We ate a quick breakfast, and then I passed my driving test. After receiving my freshly printed license, we headed out to meet with the seller. Shawn was driving us there, and I glared at my new prize. "Man, do all ID photos have to look completely horrific?" I asked.

"Oh, come on, man. It's not that bad."

I didn't smile at first, practically shoving the photo in his face. He broke out laughing, which made me crack as well. "Okay, it's kinda bad."

"I swear they do it on purpose."

As we pulled into the location, it made us both uneasy. It was far in the north of Old Belmont, near some of the warehouses. I found myself exceedingly happy that it was bright outside and not anywhere near dark. The address the man had given us led us to the back parking lot of an old warehouse with a view of the BAM! fulfillment center across the street.

BAM! was a huge brand for online shopping. They had about everything we would ever want or need. If my graphic design didn't pay off, I'd likely be trying to find a job there.

"This isn't sketchy at all," Shawn remarked, scratching his knee.

"Do you think this is where we're supposed to be? This place looks almost abandoned."

"It's the right address. Oh, there's the van!" Shawn pointed in the near distance, around a corner, where a man was leaning against a large white van. He parked the truck, and we looked at the seller for a moment. He didn't seem too out of place, despite the way he was looking around erratically. He looked at the cigarette he was smoking, and then he tossed it against the ground. As he turned and looked in our direction, I could barely make out the color of the bandana he had tied around a loop on the dark jeans he was wearing. He had another one tied around his neck, above his bare chest.

A green bandana. The color of pine.

"Okay, man. I think we should leave," I said. My eyes widened in fear as I heard Shawn's truck door close. He was already outside heading toward the man! I wanted to hit something in frustration. He could be so oblivious sometimes. How? How was he not scared to approach this man? I knew it was bad to judge by appearance, but that bandana told me everything I needed to know.

That green bandana signified that this man was an open member of the Mandiri; a dangerous gang that had been running rampant around Old Belmont. I was surprised to see him in this area. It was a well-known fact that this gang was heavily involved in Northeast Old Belmont. So much so that we always tried to avoid that area when we weren't going to Talida's house.

I stepped out of the truck, only to hear Shawn yelling toward the man. "Hey, sir, are you here to sell that van?" he called out. My adrenaline spiked as the realization hit that I had almost half of my financial gain in my back pocket. If this man planned to rob us, I would lose almost everything. Not to mention the worry I had that my friend was in danger. These gang members shot people for looking at them wrong. It took me a split second to remember that I had the power to stop someone like this, but I couldn't show my cards. Not here. Not yet.

"Yeah," the man yelled out sharply, pulling himself away from the van and starting to walk toward us.

"Dude!" I hissed. Shawn looked at me with confusion. I pulled my volume down to a whisper and worried that my words would be shaky. "We need to be careful. Did you not see the bandana?"

Shawn then looked down at the man's belt, his eyes growing wide. "Alright. I see what you mean. I may have fucked up."

I pushed myself to the front as the man approached, giving Shawn a glare of warning. "How are you? I'm Tony. We came to look at the van." I tried to look the man in the eyes, but my gaze fell on his waistband, and once I saw a pistol hanging out of it, I couldn't pull my stare away.

I ripped my gaze away from it, meeting his gaze. It didn't seem like he had noticed, or maybe he expected the reaction. "Not too bad, man. Here, let me show you around."

To my surprise, he turned his back on us and headed back over to the van. As I looked over to Shawn, he shrugged, mouthing "two against one." I tried not to let out an exasperated gasp as I mouthed back the words "he's got a gun!" He cringed, and then the man stopped.

"I was going to go out on my own and live in this thing, but it turned out I didn't have the patience. Good van, though. Lots of cargo space too if that's what you're looking for." As he showed us details on the van, I couldn't help but question how many bodies this man had probably shoved in the back of it. To my surprise, the interior was clean. Bare minimum parts, but it had wiring for a battery setup behind the driver's seat and a fridge. An outlet had been built near the fridge as well. I would have to figure out how much power it could handle.

"This seems nice," I said. It was a genuine comment, but I was still focusing on his movements. I would reveal myself to Shawn if the situation required it. I would not let another one of my friends get hurt.

"It drives well, too. Wanna take it a couple blocks?" he asked.

"Honestly, I'm good. I'm interested. I've driven one of these before. You wanted six thousand for it?" I asked. Shawn looked at me in confusion. I just wanted to get this situation over with. In the end, I didn't really have an option. I would have to either live in this van or attempt to walk away, which might anger the man. I had watched my parents buy enough vehicles to know what to do in terms of actually buying it. I could spot if he was trying to do something illegal with the deal.

"That's what I'm asking. I can pull out the paperwork if you're ready to buy. It's got a clean title." The man stopped talking and looked at the two of us practically shaking in our boots. "I wanna let you both know I'm just trying to sell a van. I don't attack children. I'm not here to swindle you either." He looked around to make sure we were alone. "I've been trying to get enough money to get out of here. I'm trying to pull away from this life in Old Belmont."

I nodded. "I understand. Forgive us for being a little paranoid." He laughed. It was a gruff, hearty laugh.

"I get it. Now, I'm gonna ask you again. Do you want to take this for a test drive?"

* * *

We ended up taking the van out for a drive. After pulling over and scolding Shawn about putting us in a position where we could have been hurt, he had told me to pull over. Shawn had mentioned the van was going to need some maintenance, but it was still a great deal. I bought the van, leaving with no conflict and a lighter wallet. The situation had given light on what I thought I knew, pushing me to hold onto my belief of not judging someone based on their appearance.

We arrived at Shawn's house after legalizing my new purchase, only to realize it was almost dinner time. We had made pretty good time today. I had expected to be forced to do all the paperwork tomorrow. This way, I could focus on getting camping supplies and making the vehicle more comfortable.

My thoughts were redirected by a loud gurgle from my stomach.

I walked over to the duffel bag I had been using for my belongings, grabbed a clean pair of clothes, and continued toward the bathroom to take a cool, refreshing shower. It took about half an hour because I enjoy the sensation of the water droplets hitting my skin and the feeling afterward of being totally clean.

Plus, unlike a lot of other people in my city, I had gauged ears, which took longer to clean as well. Unfortunately, my family or doctors had taken them out during my coma. Luckily for me, my earlobes had only shrunk two or three sizes, which I was thankful for; the idea of stretching them again from nothing was daunting. If everything went quickly, I would be able to have them stretched out again in no time. Maybe I'd go a little bigger this time.

After my shower, I blow-dried and combed my hair, only to decide that I wanted to try something new with my newly found reason to live. I picked up my new electric razor, took a deep breath, and shaved my left and right temples, leaving the rest long. I grinned, liking the new look, realizing that it fit well with my black, round, full-framed glasses. Then I walked into the living room to greet Shawn's parents.

"How are you all doing?" I asked with a smile. I wasn't sure what else to say. We didn't have a whole lot in common. "Thank you both again for letting me stay here for a couple days."

"It's no worry at all," his dad said. "How'd buying the van go? I see you brought it back." Shawn's mother caught a glimpse of my hair, shaking her head but not making a comment.

"Pretty good! It drives well, and I think I can do a lot with it," I replied, smiling. "Shawn's going to help me get some maintenance done on it. I'm getting camping supplies tomorrow."

He nodded, smiling at his son as he picked up a glass and filled it with milk. "Good. Glad you found a solution."

I caught a whiff of something delicious cooking in the kitchen—something with the pungent smells of asiago and cheddar cheese, accompanied by the potent aroma of green chili. "What's for dinner? It smells great,"

I asked, walking into the kitchen. It had been a while since I'd had such a delicacy as a homemade meal. It reminded me of the ones my family would make nearly every weekend. Ever since I could remember, my family had always cooked well.

Food was one of the best ways my family had understood each other. You could say it had been one of the only stable bridges in a land full of broken ones. Many topics I liked to talk about would have concluded with dead ends or arguments, but we had all been passionate and positive when it came to food, and we all seemed to enjoy most of the same kinds of dishes.

I missed them, despite the issues I had before my coma.

"Chicken enchiladas!" his mom said, reaching into the oven and pulling out the long pan nearly overflowing with the tasty goodness.

I looked at it, seeing the cheddar cheese nicely browned and gleaming with deliciousness atop the perfectly folded burritos. She took a spatula, splitting the enchiladas apart from each other with a tender crunch, letting the dark-red enchilada sauce seep further in between them, still bubbling and letting off steam.

"This might be my best batch yet," she said, smiling as she looked at the finished product.

I smiled back. "They do look extra delicious," I said, my mouth salivating with a mischievous desire to devour the entire pan.

"There are two enchiladas for everyone; I couldn't fit any more." She lifted two enchiladas and put them on a square black plate with green accents. She then put a dollop of sour cream off to the side, along with some

Spanish rice. She handed me the first plate, and I sat down at their table. Shawn's father had made it himself. It was a dark, rectangular wooden table with a shiny finish.

Man, only two enchiladas? I'd be in trouble if my first villain ever figured out my weakness for food. I chuckled to myself.

After the meal, Shawn and I decided that it would be best if we watched a movie together. We invited Talida, and she rented the brand-new *Heroes of the Ancients* movie, which was a strange but fulfilling —and rather enjoyable—mashup between superhuman culture and the demigods of ancient Greece.

It was ironic that I couldn't tell anyone I was about to become a superhero when my entire friend group enjoyed the culture around them. It made me wonder if I was doing the right thing by not telling them.

* * *

Thursday had gone quickly, mostly due to the amount of work Shawn and I had accomplished on the van. Shawn had school, so I had taken it upon myself to gather the materials I thought we would need. The basic ones anyway. Wood, batteries, some insulation, and a toaster oven air fryer combo. I was able to find a twin-size memory foam mattress at All-Mart as well.

With a lot of the time-consuming tasks already done, Shawn showed me how to change all the fluids when he got home, and I got the electricity working inside. It would be plenty to power everything I needed. At this point, my tablet wouldn't need to be charged for quite some time; it was still 99%. We rushed through the maintenance so that we could get the walls up and insulated, along with a roof AC that Shawn had found in the garage. We next got a bed set up, and Talida stopped by after school to bring me some bedding as a surprise. She had bought dark purple sheets with a black comforter that had a witchy design on it.

We had worked diligently to make this van feel like something more like a home, and I was feeling comfortable in it already. Looked like I wouldn't need camping supplies after all.

This was it; this was the start of a wonderful life. I had pulled the van off a back road and parked at the edge of a forest. It was public land, and I would be safe parking here for the night. I looked at the ceiling of my van, pulling the comforter over my shoulders. I was comfortable in the soft bed, feeling as if I was lying on a cloud. I was cozy. I was content. For the first time in a while, my future was feeling bright. *Now to meet Blackwell.*

Chapter 11

Introductions

School the next morning had been strange. There was no sign of Johnny, and my feelings from the night before about a brighter future were seeming to manifest in front of me. This had been the first day I had gotten through without a single person bullying me.

After my mundane yet very different day, it was time to meet with Blackwell. I parked in the same spot I had the night before, right outside a forest in the southwest quadrant of Old Belmont. It was still pretty close to Shawn's house, and my parents' house if they still lived in the same place.

I exited my vehicle and made my way down a small gravel road. I zipped up my trench coat and attached a leather mask to one of its straps. It was a mask similar to a human muzzle that I had found at After Dark. I liked the aesthetic of it hanging against my coat. Due to a cold front coming in, it was windy, causing tonight to be abnormally chilly for the summer, which had me extraordinarily excited.

I put on a pair of round, black prescription shades; the sun was at that awkward height where it shone directly into my eyes, giving no mercy as the beams assaulted my face. I wished the sun would go away on this otherwise perfect day. As I continued toward the city on an old gravel road, the bright-yellow light streamed through the trees, lighting up the road as if to brighten the path to my quest.

I looked at my tablet I had brought with me, and when I turned it on and flipped the stealth switch, I saw in large white words: "Shall we begin?"

MIRA's voice spoke the on-screen question. Seeing that the tablet had no buttons to press, I replied vocally: "Yes."

"Do you have a created alias?" MIRA asked.

I paused for a moment. *Does this make it official?* I thought to myself. Did it mean a hero's name? "I am Persevere," I replied clearly, grinning.

"Welcome to Project Barricade's Initiation Phase, Persevere. Let's get you to Blackwell so that we can get started."

A detailed map appeared on the screen, taking no time to load. A bright-purple pathway lit up, showing me directly where I needed to go. I tried to pinch the map to zoom out and see a broader view of the journey.

"Would you like a trip summary?" MIRA asked.

"Yes, please," I replied, caught off guard by the sudden question.

"Head north for two and a half miles, then head east for one mile, into the forest. Then you will arrive at your destination."

Wow, almost three miles. That was going to take at least an hour if I walked quickly. I was excited to see that I was in the same area as the hideout. My excitement turned to worry as I began to think about meeting Blackwell. I wasn't good with professional meetings—plus, the idea of meeting someone who was going to be leading an important group of people was terrifying. What if I made a bad first impression? What if he didn't want me either?

Not to mention that crazy dream I had about him during my coma. What did all that mean? I could see now that this second chance involved my new abilities, and I could conclude that the reason he said I was different was due to the same situation.

I started to head north, and after a while, MIRA told me to start heading east. Sure enough, I started to head into the forest.

As I stumbled around in the dark for a few minutes, I began to get freaked out. *What if I get lost?* I didn't know what was out here. I began to hear every little sound around me, and while I normally wasn't afraid of the dark, I was terrified of being in the middle of a forest without a light source. I could use my fire abilities, but I didn't know if I could control it just to have light. It could get out of control easily.

"Turning on the flashlight," MIRA said, startling me to the point of almost throwing the tablet. My heart raced, and I could hear it pound against the inside of my chest. A bright white light came on from the top of the device's camera, almost as potent as a small spotlight.

Oh, that's much better, I thought, now having an idea of where I was going. "Thank you, MIRA."

After a while of trudging through the forest, my phone rang. I pulled it from my pocket to see who was calling, and it was Shawn. I smiled, silenced it, and shoved it back into my pocket. I knew he was my best friend and all, but I had to be getting close. He likely wanted to talk about his date tonight. It was his second date with Alex, and he had been blowing my phone up about it all day beforehand. I looked around for anything that might catch my eye. I couldn't chance running into Blackwell while I was on the phone.

My phone vibrated, letting me know I received a text, and I checked it.

Shawn: *Call me ASAP, IMPORTANT news!!!!*

I guess it wouldn't hurt to make a quick call. I frowned, hoping that everything went well on his date. Just to make sure he's okay. I called him back. "Hey man, how'd everything go?" I asked in an eager tone.

"Alex is amazing! I think I'm in love with her," Shawn said in a super happy, rushed voice.

"Whoa, slow down," I said, chuckling. "What happened? And does she think the same way?"

"We got into a conversation about our favorite video games, which we found out are *practically* the same ones. Then we started talking about Grudgematch, and it's her favorite character of all time! I found out that we have a similar family situation too. You know how that is. At the end I told her I had a really good time and wanted to do it again, maybe take her to the arcade. She was excited and said she wanted to do the same. She kissed me, dude!" he yelled, fumbling over his words.

I smiled. "That's awesome! It sounds like the two of you really hit it off! Congratulations!" I replied, truly happy for him. I wasn't thrilled about her having the same family situation; I knew that he was talking about being looked down upon or judged. By what I saw of her appearance, her family probably thought she was going through a phase. Whether that's what it was for her or not, I didn't know.

"Dude, I'm going to protect her with my life. I think we have another person to add to our friend group. Do you think the freak pack would mind?" he asked me with a nervous chuckle.

"I'm sure Talida would be okay with that; if she clicks with you, I doubt *we'll* have any problem with her," I said.

I proceeded through the woods, and as I looked forward, I spotted a figure in the distance. Leaning against a tree stood the man that I knew as Blackwell. He was dressed in his black armor, just as I had seen him in the dream. A shiver went down my spine as I questioned if this man were going to be friendly, or if my dream would lead me astray. "I'm going to have to let you go, man. I'll see you tomorrow at school. I'm glad to hear that everything went well," I said, my voice seeming unstable and concerned.

"Is everything alright? You sound kinda weird," Shawn asked me, picking up on cues that I didn't mean to leave.

"Yeah, everything's good. I looked outside my window and saw something weird." I laughed, trying to ease the conversation. "Sleeping in this van for the first time is going to be strange."

"Okay, I'll see you at school then. If you ever need to talk, give me a call, though. You're acting a little off," he said, seeming legitimately worried. "You're always welcome back at my house."

I hated making him feel that way. "For sure! I'm doing fine—just a little tired. I know I'm welcome. Have a good night, man!" I waited for an acknowledgment, and then I hung up.

I gathered up my courage and headed closer to the man. Before I could greet him, he held out his hand.

"You must be Persevere. I'm Blackwell, the founder of Project Barricade, and it's good to finally meet you in person; I'm sorry it's under these strange circumstances. There's nothing to be nervous or worried about." His voice was calm, and it sounded deep and amplified as if there were a voice changer in his helmet.

His suit looked like some sort of black crystal. He had a helmet that was similar to a knight's rounded version with six slanted ventilation slits on the lower part. A black, shining visor, topped off the piece.

His neck was covered with the crystal, and it had a curved, vertical ventilation slit on each side with a horizontal vent on the top and bottom. His suit had a cuirass that ended down by his waist with leg pieces that went down to his knee. He had solid-black crystal knee pads. Below them was another leg piece made of the unknown substance that overlapped with his tall boots.

A long black and gold sword rested on his back, seeming to somehow attach itself to the suit outside of an enormous black cape flowing freely behind him. He had thin shoulder pads that ended in a point, and under the suit was a scale-mail style of the crystal to make his armor thicker but at the same time, maintain the mobility of the suit.

His golden medallion with the *BW* engraved on it in black letters hung around his neck.

"Yes, I'm Persevere," I stated. I shook his hand. "How did you know my name already? Did your agent tell you?"

"No, no, no," he started. "When you uploaded your name into the MIRA system, it sent the information directly to me. She is a magnificent program, and she will help you greatly throughout your training period. Though, for now, let me introduce you to the others," he said, turning around. As he did so, a very bright light shone from the top of his helmet. It was brighter than the one from the tablet, and its light shone for what must have been nearly a mile in front of us.

In the distance I could see a crumbling, abandoned building that likely used to be a humble corner store. As we got closer, more details of the ruins came into view. The windows were cracked, and the foundation mirrored them. The fractures caused the building to appear off-balanced. The wood was falling in on one side, and the only thing that seemed to be somewhat intact, or safe even, was the doorway.

"Don't worry—the building is stable. It's made to look as though it's abandoned," Blackwell informed me, leading me through the entryway. The statement gave me some relief, for I had been worried about it falling in on us.

I skimmed the room. It was mostly empty, but the flooring was flat and recently renovated. A large desk, almost like in a hotel, stood near the center of the back wall of the room. Upon further inspection, this was the only thing inside other than a few decorations.

Blackwell motioned for me to come behind the desk. There was a crevice the size of a picture frame in the center of the wall he led me to. He placed my tablet into the space, and the section of the wall opened like a sliding door.

"That was cool," I said, impressed; hidden doorways intrigued me. *What could I put in a secret room?* I thought as we entered the hallway.

"MIRA will give you personal access to this hideout. If you ever need in to train when I'm not out here waiting to meet a new recruit, you can let yourself in," Blackwell said, giving me more information about the tablet itself and pulling it off the wall. He waved his hand, leading me into a pale stone hallway. "I do need you to promise me that you won't tell anybody about this; it's not exactly legal," he said, laughing as he tapped a brick on his left. I glanced behind me, and I heard a low creaking sound just as the wall started to reconnect.

That made sense; I'm sure the government would try to shut down any vigilante work. As we turned a corner, it felt as if we were descending. We soon went around another, and it was starting to get cold.

We finally stopped, and Blackwell placed my tablet on the side of what appeared to be another blocked doorway. This time, instead of a hallway appearing, there stood a massive metal door. A bright-blue light scanned the two of us, and the door creaked, opening from the center to reveal an enormous lobby room with another desk. Behind it on the left was a shelf, and on the right sat a small computer system.

Blackwell retrieved the tablet, holding it at his side. "You'll no longer need this today, so I will hold onto it for you. I'll give this back to you once you leave. You will gain further access to MIRA Monday as we further your introduction," he said, looking in my direction before heading forward. I nodded in agreement, thankful I was going to be able to bring it back with me.

Blackwell pointed to a long hallway on the left. "That is where the physical and mental training is; that's where you will go every day to get your daily training completed. Consider this a second round of schooling where you will learn about your powers, along with getting information about how to properly use them depending on the situation you are in. A cafeteria is also in the works," he said, putting his hand down.

He pointed to a hallway on the right of the desk area. "That is where you and the others will get to know each other after your training. It includes the briefing room, social study, and a living quarters under construction," he said, pointing to each room. I looked to the end of the hallway, seeing large glass doors. "All the way down, we have a medical wing. Much more private than Triple H."

I felt overwhelmed with the thought of having to remember where everything was. As I stressed over the bombardment of information, Blackwell continued to talk. "Over on the other side of the room is a teleportation system that will be installed once we get more established," he said, pointing toward some teleportation chamber–looking platforms.

Before I could geek out over the teleporters, Blackwell started to walk over to the hallway on the right. "Your assignment for today is to complete a suit design and put the information about special things you want added. I will construct and improve it with connectivity to the MIRA system," Blackwell said. I nodded. "I would also like to introduce you to the heroes and give you a chance to get to know each other. I saw your design you built with the

MIRA tablet and took it upon myself to print it off this morning. Here you are." Blackwell quickly walked up to the computer system and handed me a printed photo of the suit design I had created.

Slightly relieved that I wouldn't have to draw it out or something, I followed him into a room in the hallway on the right. If I remembered correctly, this would be the social study. Tables and chairs were scattered in this room with three people already inside.

"This is Red Kelvin. He's a pyrokinetic. Unluckily, during a wildfire when he was young, his parents became victims of the flames. We are not yet sure if he was the reason for the fire, but either way, he had no control over it. You can get the rest of the story from him," he said, pointing to a guy slightly taller than me with smooth caramel skin and sponged, dark-brown hair.

Seeing Red Kelvin's appearance, I concluded that he was about the same age as me. He was very skinny, but he was also toned, showing me that he must have trained for a while already. He smiled at me and waved. I smiled, returning the gesture.

Blackwell pointed at someone else who was a few inches shorter than me. He was a stout guy with considerable muscles, showing the veins clearly in his arms. He also appeared to be about my age, maybe a year or two older, and he had short russet hair with brown eyes.

"This is Steel Cowboy. He specializes in super-strength, having received his abilities from an experimental drug. I'm sure he'll also tell you the rest of the story if you ask," Blackwell said.

Blackwell then pointed toward a tall woman quite a ways behind Steel

Cowboy with a white pixie cut and high cheekbones. She was dressed in name-brand clothing. She was definitely older than me, about twenty-five or so, and she had the outer appearance of an athlete. While not looking like she'd be a tomboy, I got the vibe that she had likely enjoyed volleyball.

"That's Nikki. She's a telekinetic and very friendly. Doesn't really have a crazy story, but she's a computer programmer." Blackwell waved his hand in front of him. "But enough of superhero backstories. I will leave and let you guys work on your suits while you socialize," he said, walking out of the room and shutting the heavy, metal door as Nikki waved and gave a warm smile.

Chapter 12

Meet the Gang

I walked over to the three of them, Red Kelvin being the first one I app-roached. His eyes were gray with red specks in the whites of them, catch-ing my attention. While his face was mostly clear, other than the shortly cut facial hair, I could also see red specks in patches on his skin as well, one of which went up his neck to almost touch his squared jaw. It looked like a rash I had seen before, but it lacked the usual characteristics of burn scarring. As for the specks in his eyes, I wasn't sure.

"Hey, my name's Tony. How'd you all end up here?" I asked.

The other two glanced toward each other before gesturing toward Red Kelvin.

"Tell him the story!" Nikki said in a warm voice, nudging Red Kelvin with a smile. Red Kelvin smiled back as if they had already been through this conversation.

"Okay, I'll introduce myself first. I've given myself the name Mason Kelvin. After my parents passed, I was found by the authorities and put into foster care. I had no luck in getting adopted." He gave an uncomfortable chuckle as he rubbed the bumps on his neck. "I guess nobody wants to adopt a kid with what looks to be a nasty health problem. It's merely cosmetic, but no one saw it as that.

Over the years I learned that I could control fire—and even conjure my own. I kept this a secret from everybody else and began to experiment, starting in the foster family's bathroom. I haven't been able to try anything big with it yet, but I have good control. Not that long ago, somebody adopted me and then brought me to meet Blackwell.

He asked me if I wanted to help him and be on his team, so I accepted. Project Barricade *officially* started yesterday," he said in a strong yet calming voice, looking back down at his drawing. He was a bit shy, and he sounded like he didn't talk to people a lot, but after hearing his origin, I could understand why.

"Well, hopefully, you'll be able to find your full potential here. I'm sorry to hear that they judged you for how you look. I know how that is. I didn't know that this group started just yesterday. Who was the first to be recruited?" I asked, looking at them. It was weird to be in a group that was likely illegal, just starting, and full of superhumans. I would have never thought people like us existed outside of comic books, let alone be one of five, if Blackwell had powers.

Mason glanced up from the picture he was drawing, and my eyes dropped to examine the design. It looked a lot like him. Two black straps were going from his shoulders to his waist on both sides that crossed in the middle. Straps crisscrossed his arms and legs, resting tightly over a red spandex suit, which started at his neck. Red flames danced upward along the bottom of a pair of black shoes.

"I was the first superhuman to be recruited. Steel Cowboy was second,"

Mason said.

"Oh okay. That's a cool suit," I said back.

Seeing his design, I made a mental note regarding my own suit. Maybe I should start my suit at the neck. I marked the design change on the design I had been given. *I like that.*

Steel Cowboy stood up, stretching out his hand for me to shake. "Hi. I'm goin' by Steel Cowboy. My true name's Corbin Sawyer," he started. He had a country twang in his voice, leading me to believe he was from somewhere down south.

"I took a weight-trainin' class in school, and the 'cool kids' always picked on me for bein' weak. I wanted to be stronger, and I resorted to findin' a dealer offerin' experimental steroids. Some bullies caused my self-esteem to drop so low I was okay with tryin' 'em. When I used 'em that night, I already started noticin' results in my muscle mass by the next day. I went to school the next week and decided to test my new muscles in class. I realized I could lift heavy weights real easy. After about a week of no side effects, I came home one day and realized I could pick up my dad's truck. I stopped takin' the steroids, and my muscles, along with the strength, stayed with me. As of today, I don't know the limit of my strength, but I wanna find out," he said.

"That's crazy. I also dealt with bullies. They're the reason I have powers, actually. Did Blackwell send you a letter after that?" I asked.

He nodded. "Yeah, he sent me a letter, but I refused. A few weeks after, I came home to a group of thugs. They attacked me, and I barely got away. I realized after that, I needed to join Project Barricade to better myself, and I look forward to helpin' people with my gift."

I looked at his picture, and it looked just like him, but he was wearing different cowboy boots and had a metal casing around his forearm.

"Cool picture," I said.

"Thanks! My skin is tough, so I don't see a point in wearin' armor or nothin' like that. I wanted a lasso, but if I can have somethin' on my wrist that I can shoot to latch onto my enemies, that could work well with my strength. I feel I should have some sorta ranged attack," he said, writing his name in the top left corner of the paper. "What's yours look like?" he asked.

I took the piece of paper from the desk that I had put it on and showed it to him. He smiled.

"That's pretty sweet," he said, taking a pause. "You one of them graphic designers? They do neat work," he asked, showing interest in the drawing.

I smiled. "Yeah, but I haven't had a chance to show it off yet," I said as Nikki walked over to take a look.

"Well, it's awesome. You need to keep up with that," Nikki said, raising her hand to give me a fist bump. I looked up at her, realizing she was the same height as me. Her piercing eyes held a resemblance to emeralds, shining brightly in the well-lit room.

She made eye contact with me and smiled. "I'm Nikki Blain. I don't want to go by a hero name, but you guys have picked interesting aliases. I was actually caught using my telekinesis in public by one of Blackwell's agents, and when they confronted me about joining, I figured I'd see where it took me. I love computer programming. I've created several apps and programs just to test them out, and I'm actually helping Blackwell with the MIRA system. I'm super excited to be able to use my abilities to help you guys and work as a team. I want to take down criminals instead of hiding my abilities," she said.

She's someone I can talk to—cool, I thought. She would be easy to carry on a conversation with. She had a very kind voice and seemed to know who she was and what she wanted. She also exuded confidence without sounding uptight, which was sometimes a thin line to walk.

"But enough about us; tell us about yourself. How did you get here?"

"Well, I'll start by saying that I've been bullied my entire life. On the first day of my sophomore year, I had a particularly bad session of bullying, and on the second day, I went to a bathroom to hide from those involved. There was a school fire, and I was able to save someone, but unfortunately, I wasn't able to get out. When they found me, I was taken to a hospital where I lay in a coma for two years. When I came to, I was told one of my friends had been taken by the fire, and I discovered that I have these powers. My family has left my life as well. My doctor sent me to Triple H where they taught me how to control my strength," I said, trying not to think about Aiden. I didn't want to cry in front of these strangers.

"Wow, that's nuts! I'm really sorry about your friend, but what powers do you have?" Mason asked, his eyes wide wanting answers.

"I went to Triple H, too!" Corbin exclaimed.

"I've triggered fire abilities and super-strength so far. I think there may be something else, but I'm not sure. I think it's very interesting that you're a computer programmer, Nikki. I tried to get into it, but it wasn't my style, so I decided to try graphic design. So far it better fits my niche," I said, setting my gaze on Nikki.

She grinned. "That's great! I was the same with graphic design. I connect with the numbers more than the art process," she said. "It usually tends to be one or the other." She looked down at her paper, which was still blank. She chuckled as she attempted to draw the base for her outfit. "I don't know that I care to have a suit. I know I'll need *something*, but I'd prefer to keep myself on the down-low rather than throw myself out in public, you know?"

She paused for a moment in thought, and with a shake of her head, she looked back up at me. "I guess that's the point of having an alias, though. And being on a team. But holy crap, wow! Fire *and* super-strength?! You're going to be a beast!" she exclaimed.

I smiled. "Thanks! I hope I can hone my skills so that I can help people. I know for certain I'm here to make people feel safe. I don't want people to feel alone like I did. I want to remind myself to never give up, and that's the emphasis I'd like to make with my name. I'm going to be known as Persevere. I look forward to working with you all. We're going to make an awesome team," I said excitedly.

"Damn right!" Corbin added, eyeing me up and down. "Did you add all that cosmetic work yourself?" I questioned what he meant for a moment and then remembered I looked strange.

Before I could answer, Mason jumped in with his own comment. "Are you a vampire? I like the getup." he said. I chuckled.

"No, actually. I stretched my own ears, but after the coma, I found that my skin lightened. I got fangs soon after too. It freaked me out a little bit, but no cravings for blood or intolerance to light. I cut my own hair, though."

Corbin smiled. "That's cool. It's different, so I was wonderin'. Good to meet you, Tony."

"I'm glad you asked!" Mason said. "I didn't want to sound offensive for asking why you look like that, but it's wicked! In a good way!"

"I hope it didn't sound rude. I meant no offense," Corbin added.

I smiled. "I didn't take any. It's expected. I'm already goth, and I had always dreamed of looking like this, actually. I took it as a question of curiosity," I replied. "So, I know Nikki likes computer programming, but what do you two like doing?" I pointed toward the men.

This time Corbin answered first. "I like to hunt, but I find someone who wants every piece that I don't use so that nothin' goes to waste. Other than that, I helped my pa with his ranch before I moved out of the coop. I don't really know what I want to do now. I moved away from the ranch when I turned eighteen."

"That's cool. I respect that you use every piece rather than hunt for sport. How old are you now?"

"I'm nineteen. I've been living on my own for about a year, but I quit my job to move into the hideout. The rest of the rooms are still under construction, but me and Mason got lucky. I'm doin' Project Barricade full time while I figure myself out."

"Fair enough. What about you, Mason?"

"I have two things I really enjoy in my free time. I like to shoot hoops and go paintballing. Or airsoft. Either are fun," Mason answered.

Nikki's eyes lit up. "I love basketball! We should see if we can get one in the training room," she said. "I'll play one-on-one with you."

"That's awesome. I'd be down to go paintballing sometime too," I added. "I've always been bad at basketball, though."

I continued to a desk, sitting down to add things to my suit. The conversation had died down as the others focused their attention to their own designs. I liked the group. They all seemed very friendly.

I wrote down the information that I had been debating on the back of my design. I wanted the whole suit to make me fireproof, and I would like the gloves to be pain resistant. I hoped to be able to transfer the fire from my hands to the outside of the gloves, along with having some electronics on my wrists.

As I finished brainstorming bits and pieces of information about the rest of the suit, I set the paper on a desk near Corbin and questioned what else I could add to the design. After deciding that I was finished, I headed toward the doorway.

"I'm going to turn in my design. How are all of yours going?" I asked, looking back toward them.

"I think I'm going to leave it up to Blackwell," Nikki said, standing up. "I may need some help on the creative side of this. If he pulls out something slutty, we'll have to have words though." We both laughed at the comment. "This is real life. Female superheroes don't all have to be dressed up in skin-tight outfits with their boobs out."

I smiled at the comment, completely amused. "I can't agree with that more. I'm a huge superhero fan, and I get so tired of seeing it. I can't tell you how many books about the subject I've tried to read that just end up as male-reliant harem stories with flat female characters only written for sexual comments." I paid attention to her face as I said the words, making sure I wasn't going to offend. When she started to laugh harder, I knew I was in the clear.

"What, you don't like it when their breasts boob boobily down the stairs?"

I groaned. "That is the *worst!*" There was a moment of silence as I scratched my neck. "Well, if you want any help, I could try to come up with something for you. I'm trying to do graphic design as my source of income and am hoping to focus mainly on character designs. This would be a perfect opportunity, plus I could help make sure it's what you want."

She grinned, rubbing her shoulder. "I'd like that. I could use all the help I can get. Can I text you about it once we leave?" Nikki asked.

I nodded. "Sure! I'll consider it my first project and get it to you tomorrow." I gave her my phone number.

The two guys stood. "Done!" they exclaimed.

We walked out into the hallway, heading back to the front desk as we explored our surroundings. It was an interesting place, and I was curious to know if we could roam the hideout before we got our suits or if the place was off-limits until then. Being with the other heroes wasn't too bad. They were going to be a fun group.

After a few minutes of straying off to look around, I headed to the desk. "I've got my suit drawn," I said, seeing the other heroes walking behind me, also looking into rooms on their way. *We're all nosy*, I thought with a chuckle.

"Put them here," Blackwell declared. I put mine on the desk, then Corbin, then Mason and Nikki. Blackwell looked them over with curiosity.

"Interesting," he said to himself quietly, placing them into a blue folder. "I'll have your suits by Monday. You can make adjustments at any time. As for you, Nikki, if you decide on a suit between now and tomorrow, get that design to me and I'll see what I can do. Anyone with a MIRA tablet can upload new designs to the system. From now on, class training is from 9:30 to midnight. That's short, but you will learn a lot in that time. Today was just to introduce you to each other and to let you get a feel for the hideout. It will be better if you begin training in your outfits, so that is all I have for you today," he said.

"I'll see you tomorrow, future heroes. Just remember, before you receive your suits, don't do anything rash. You need to stay on the down-low until you're ready for the repercussions," he said. Everyone headed for the doorway.

"It was good to meet you guys," Mason said, standing next to the doorway to give his farewells.

After goodbyes I headed into the forest to make my way home. Now alone, I started to think about what was in store when I returned to school. Was I going to have more issues with Johnny? I knew I shut him down last time, but was it too good to be true that he'd be out of my life now? I wasn't worried about Johnny physically, especially with his broken bones, but I didn't want to have to deal with him anymore. All he could do from this point on is become a nuisance.

I quickly turned toward the city. I was thirsty and wanted a drink for my walk home. I knew that there was a gas station a couple of miles from these woods. I walked this far, I might as well get something for the few miles back. I thought that maybe I should go to my van first, but I liked adventure and a walk sounded fun.

As I got closer, I became thirstier. Did I want a mango Toxin energy drink? A peach Power Armor would be better for me. Especially if I was going to start training soon. I didn't have school tomorrow, which made me debate making the extra trip up to After Dark for a coffee.

Soon I saw the gas station and decided that's where I would stop. It was the last one out of town in this direction, and it was near an apartment building. It had several buildings close to it and a few businesses behind it. As I neared the gas station, I could hear yelling. *What the hell?* I thought, looking around for the source. It sounded like it was coming from behind the building.

"Get him!" a man yelled.

"Don't let him get away!" another screamed. The voice was harsh and rasp, creating a malevolent vibe around me.

No, no, no, I thought as my reality clashed with what Blackwell had instructed. He told me not to do anything rash, but if someone was about to get hurt, I had to do *something*. Right? I inched closer to take a look from the corner of the building. As I peeked around, I could see a middle-aged man, short and scrawny with shaggy short hair and a goatee, getting jumped by four other guys.

I couldn't sit here and watch this. I clenched my fists. What should I do? I didn't know how to fight! I looked away for a moment, thinking it may be best if I left. I didn't know what would happen if I tried to help or what would ensue if I didn't. I had no idea why this guy was getting jumped in the first place. I took a deep breath, mentally preparing myself for what was to come as the man screamed desperately for help. *Fuck it.*

I looked around for something to cover my face. I then realized that I still had my leather mask I kept attached to my trench coat. I hadn't worked up the courage to wear it in public yet, but the night life in Old Belmont wouldn't care. It was a mask similar to a human muzzle, like something you'd see in a horror movie. I threw it on, hoping to hide my identity. I jumped out from the corner of the building, walking toward the men with clenched fists.

"Step away from him!" I yelled in the angriest voice I could muster. They stopped and looked at me, startled. Seeing them that way threw off my focus. *Now what?* I thought, unsure of what to do next.

"Who the hell do you think you are, freak?" the first guy asked, wearing a tan hoodie and dirty jeans. "The sex dungeon is the other way, kid." He looked at the others and laughed at his own joke. A green bandana hung from his belt loop, making me keenly aware of the situation at hand. This man they were attacking might not have done anything wrong. He was likely in the wrong place at the wrong time.

The other muggers kicked the man, who was now on the ground unable to stand. They started chuckling and walking toward me.

"My name is Persevere, and I demand that you—" I started, pausing for a moment as my words faltered. *You're slipping up. What are you doing?* I asked myself. "I demand that you...fuck off!"

My inner voice screamed in embarrassment. *NO—that doesn't make any sense, you damned idiot. Really?* I stood still, attempting to look strong even though I now wanted to crawl under a rock and die.

The men started to laugh hysterically. "You think you're a superhero or somethin'" the one from the back asked. "Get out of here, kid, while you still have the chance." The first guy seemed to tighten his muscles, looking tense. He turned and muttered something to the others, making me uneasy. That probably wasn't good. As they realized I wasn't going to leave, one began to speak.

"Well, well. Looks like we have ourselves some fresh meat," the one in the back said.

The man in the hoodie glanced back at them. "You guys know what to do," he said in an irritated voice as if they should have already done it. The other three men charged at me, instantly jumping into attack mode.

Oh, no. The first guy threw a punch, causing me to grin as I successfully dodged his blow. I wasn't so lucky with the next one that hit me in the side of the head. My ears rang, breaking my train of thought. The third guy landed a solid kick to my side, making my muscles tighten. I forced myself to breathe through the pain. This was so much different than the school bullies.

I grunted, but I didn't allow myself to fall. I swung at the first man I had dodged, hitting him in the chin and watching him fall to the ground unconscious. *Oh, crap,* I thought. *Hit lighter.* Their leader looked surprised for a moment, and then he jumped into the fight, attempting a low jab. I blocked it with both of my palms, stopping his punch mid-swing.

I received another kick to the side, and this time, I fell to one knee as I got punched in the face by the others. There were too many of them, and I wasn't trained to fight. I tried to focus again, and this time, my vision and focus started to clear up. *Come on—focus,* I thought.

I suddenly had the urge to swing my arm to the right, almost sensing the next attack before it happened. Sure enough, as soon as I swung my arm, it blocked the man's swing prematurely.

"I hate bullies!" I yelled. My focus was tuned, and my body seemed to have a mind of its own as I blocked the next five or six swings. My emotions rose inside me, but it wasn't only anger; there was also confidence. It was confidence that I now knew I could make a difference.

I raised my hands, looking at them in disbelief. *How did I do that?* I thought, unsure of how I was able to block them the way I did. I threw my arms down to my sides, bright white and yellow flames rising to my shoulders from my fingertips. To my surprise the flames didn't seem to bother my coat. "This world has too many people like you!" I yelled at them. The three men jumped back, terrified and confused. One of them pulled a pistol and aimed it at my chest.

My reflexes reacted to the pistol, swinging my right arm against the barrel of the gun as it went off twice, shooting the ground to the left of me. I managed to relieve him of his gun in one swift movement. As the other man took a swing, my flaming fist cracked against his nose, knocking him out cold with an explosion of embers as the blow scorched his face.

I swung my right foot, roundhouse kicking the other guy in the side of the head, sending him to sleep with his friend. As I looked at the leader of the group, I could see the terror in his eyes as he began to back up.

"No, please! Don't hurt me," he yelled. "I don't know what you are or what you're after, but I have money—and drugs!" the man said. "I'll turn myself in!"

You'll turn in alright, I thought through my anger. He couldn't harass people if he was dead. I shook my head, distancing myself from the evil thoughts. I wanted to be a hero, not a villain. The police would find him unconscious, not dead. *Still breathing, please.*

He got about six or seven feet away from me, and then he reached for something in his back pocket. Not sure what it was, I reacted the best way I thought I could.

"Yeet!" I screamed.

I chucked the pistol that was still in my hand, which hit him in the chest and made the gun go off in my direction.

I jumped into the air, letting loose a horrified yelp, mortified by the bullet flying toward me. A moment later, I realized that I hadn't been hit, and I watched as the gun pattered against the ground as quickly as their leader did. The man was now wheezing and trying to catch his breath, for the small, wrongly used projectile had knocked the wind out of him.

"I'll tell you what I want, you worthless thug," I started, attempting to bring my composure back. "I want justice. I want this city to be rid of all the criminals and scum just like you. I want you and every other maggot to know my name and fear me," I said, walking toward him with my fists clenched, exhilarated. I smiled, almost maliciously. "Tell your gang that Persevere is here, and the Mandiri had better watch their backs."

I looked around, seeing a large bin full of flammable trash. I threw my arms toward it, sending a fireball exploding toward the rubbish. It lit up in flames, and I looked back at the leader. "Have a good night," I said.

I punched him in the face as he attempted a scream, knocking him unconscious.

The man who was getting mugged was able to stand up, and he looked at me wide-eyed. "Thank you!" he yelled, limping away.

"It's what heroes do!" The fire and the victim would get the police here before the thugs woke up. It would be best if I left before I was noticed.

* * *

I smiled. It was good to be a hero. Now I had to find an excuse for the bruises.

2

The Team Behind His Back

Chapter 13

An Eventful School Day

I held my backpack close, running to the front doors of the school as the near-black sky dropped buckets of freezing rain on us. It was a stormy Monday morning. One that had quickly shown me I would need to replace my wind-shield wipers.

"Get to the base!" Shawn said, flying past us with a burst of random noises, his arms swinging behind him in the wind.

Talida chuckled, following Shawn in the same manner. "Run!" she said, pretending to fear for her life. Her fake fear added to Shawn's video game role-play.

The two of them shot toward the school, only to be slowed down by Shawn slipping on the grass and gliding across the mud with his face. Talida and I exploded into laughter, and she bent over, unable to contain herself. She tried to regain her breath, but with the way Shawn had fallen and slid with his legs behind his head, she was only thrown into an assortment of attempted breaths and snorts as the situation repeated in her mind.

My jaw hurt, but this time, it was from all the laughing and not from Johnny beating us up. Or was it the mugging last Friday night? That night's situation seemed as if it were a dream. The memory was a fever dream, and while my body was sore, I almost forgot that it had happened.

Shawn grunted as he slowly lifted himself from the mud. "That hurt," he said quietly, chuckling through his wheezing.

At this point, Talida and I had made it under the stone portico of the school, soaked to the bone. We stood close to each other as we tried to catch our breath and stay out of the way of other students. Shawn walked toward us, his shoes squelching and face still mostly covered in mud. I pulled a black washcloth from my backpack and handed it to him.

I had done the same thing Shawn did just a few years ago. I had slipped on the grass, covering myself in mud, and I had to wash my face in the school bathroom. It was humiliating, and at least this way Shawn could clean up.

"Thanks, man. This isn't really how I wanted to see Alex this morning," Shawn said, continuing to chuckle. His face turned serious, looking at my face again. "I still can't believe you tripped and fell out of your van."

I had lied to Shawn and Talida this morning, attempting to explain the heavy bruises across my body. I had panicked, and told them I fell out of my van. It wasn't believable in my mind, but they didn't bat an eye. The real explanation would have gotten me a lot of questions.

Talida grinned. "Is *Alex* going to be sitting with us for breakfast?" she asked, nudging him in the shoulder playfully as she emphasized her name.

Shawn finished cleaning his face, then looked at Talida with a serious glare. "Yes. She is. Don't you *dare* embarrass me further than I am right now," he scolded, holding his gaze until they both cracked out in laughter.

"I'll tell her all about how I kicked your ass at Immortal Fighter," Talida said, lifting her eyebrows up and down to solidify her threat.

"I swear to God that didn't happen!" Shawn laughed, nudging her back.

I stared up into the blackened sky, watching the clouds float across. Last time it was this dark, we had a tornado warning. It might be a short school day.

The three of us entered the building and headed toward the cafeteria for breakfast.

"Man, I hope they're serving those sausage biscuits today like last week. I can't handle any more soy pancakes," Shawn said, preparing himself for disappointment.

I caught myself occasionally looking around, as if I were afraid Johnny was going to come up behind us and assault us again. But it was over. He couldn't hurt us anymore. "It's going to take a while to get used to a normal school day," I said.

"Yeah, I keep checking behind me too," Talida said, mirroring the fear that still lingered in all of us.

It seemed too good to be true. After years of torture, I was having a hard time believing it was over.

As we walked down the black and red tiled floor, we could see the entrance to the cafeteria; it was an uphill ramp under a brick arch. Walking up to the long line, I could smell the sausage biscuits, and my stomach began to grumble.

A crack of thunder filled our ears, and half of the room screamed as the lights flickered. I smiled; storms had always been the bane of my productivity. I could sit and listen to thunder and watch lightning for hours without realizing it. I began to get giddy thinking about it.

Shawn looked around, trying to find Alex, but he couldn't spot her. "She must not be here yet," he said, his mood dwindling.

"I'm sure she'll be here soon." Talida grinned, trying to cheer him up. "With all these storms, I'm sure some of the buses are going to be late. You know the flooding causes several of the roads to be blocked off around here."

"You're right. She probably got…"

"Hey, Shawn!" The high-pitched tone of her voice filled the cafeteria, and Shawn's eyes lit up.

Alex rushed over to us, hugging him quickly.

She turned to look at us with a happy grin, her bright-green eyes gleaming at the sight of us all. "I'm Alex! It's good to meet you guys!" she said, throwing out her hand to me.

Such high energy, I thought. She was a good match already. "It's good to meet you too, Alex. I'm Tony." I shook her hand firmly, and she turned around to face the others.

"Hi! I'm Talida."

"How long have you known each other?" Alex asked, her gaze drifting smoothly to each of us and ending on Shawn.

"About eight years—if you don't count the two that Tony slept through," Shawn answered, nudging me in the arm, trying to make light of the situation.

"I wouldn't have if we weren't dealing with that shitbag…" I started.

Just then a harsh, angry, bellow of a voice projected out from across the cafeteria. "Tony!"

Alex's face turned white, recognizing the voice. We all did. As Shawn rushed in front of Alex, he got ready to fight. *Perfectly timed,* I thought.

"Speak of the devil, and he will appear," Shawn muttered through grinding teeth.

"Stay out of it. Let me handle this," I said, shooting them a glare to make sure they knew I would take care of the situation. I couldn't have my friends getting kicked out of school again. I'd take the hit. I had a whole new future to look forward to, whether I graduated or not.

As I looked toward the origin of the yell, all I could see was Johnny furiously storming my way. I put one foot back, preparing myself for the assault.

As I looked at Johnny, I couldn't help but notice his two black eyes and bloodied lip. *Those aren't all from me,* I thought, unsure of whether to be happy as my heart dropped. Someone else had been hitting him.

"You took everything from me!" he screamed at the top of his lungs, his voice ragged and cracking in fury. He grimaced, the pain from his broken ribs showing in his limp. "My friends left me, the school thinks I'm a joke, and my family no longer wants me!"

My stomach knotted. This was desperation I had never seen from Johnny before, and while I knew he deserved every bit of his pain, I couldn't help but relive what he had put me through all these years. I even related to him. I had been excluded from school activities, the school thought me a loser, and my family considered me a failure.

I swallowed the lump in my throat as he got closer to us. "You deserved what you got, Johnny. I was merely defending my friends."

"I'll show them. I'll show all of them that I can beat you!" Johnny said, lunging himself full force toward me despite his injuries.

I ducked out of the way of his swing, not wanting to fight back if I didn't have to this time. As all the anger and sadness bellowed from his throat, he took another wild swing, this one slamming into the wall behind me with a loud snap.

He didn't even flinch, I thought, knowing his hand had to have broken.

"I'm not weak! You're supposed to be afraid of me!" Johnny said, his words erupting between tears. His words rang out through the roar of the cafeteria cheering on the fight, and everything slowed. It was almost as if the world itself had been reduced to a crawl. Why was I not mad at him? I knew damn well I should be. Why did I feel bad for him? This isn't what I wanted.

"I will make your life hell, and then I'll *kill* you!" The determination in his voice made me flinch, and his words tightened my body. As I was thrown into a defensive state, I grabbed his arm mid swing, yanking him toward me. Slamming his body against the wall, the impact resulted in a loud *CRACK* that came from his bones. Competing with the ear-piercing sound was John-ny's gasp for air as the wind was ripped from him.

Alex shrieked, covering her mouth with her hands.

"Oh my god!" Talida exclaimed in awe, confused at my sudden show of strength. A short, nervous chuckle left her lips.

Johnny lifted himself from the floor, his anger still visibly flowing through him as his face glowed a deep red. He came at me again with a scream, favoring his left wrist and trying to elbow me.

I stepped to the side, pounding my knee into his stomach and dropping him to the floor.

"It's over, Johnny. Stop!" I yelled.

"I won't!" he said through his teeth, lifting himself again and throwing a punch.

I curled my fist, projecting it into his side. As he fell to the floor, groan-ing in pain, he once again tried to lift himself.

"This is pathetic. Stop! You've lost!" I yelled back. He was making him-self look like a fool. I frowned, upset that he wasn't going to give up.

Johnny slowly got back on his feet, spluttering through his tears. His eyes were bloodshot as he glared, his lips quivering as he threatened to break down. "I can't," he cried. "All because of you, my mom is beating me again because she thinks it will 'toughen me up.' I have to make sure you suffer. I have to make sure she won't hurt me anymore. I will take everyone you love away from you. I swear!"

Johnny sprinted to the entrance of the cafeteria and was confronted by the security guard. Wrestling with the guard, Johnny was thrown to the floor, which he used to his advantage by tripping the guard. He then stood back up and ran out the door into the torrential rain.

Shit, he got away? I thought, worried about the threats. Where was he going? I could take him myself, but what if he decided to start hurting other people?

All my friends heard him say that, so I didn't have to worry about them.

We got to the front of the line, and a teacher approached me, this one I didn't know. *Here we go again,* I thought with a scowl. Why couldn't I just be left alone?

"I saw the whole thing, so I understand that you didn't start that fight, but the principal will need to see you in his office after breakfast," the teacher said.

I nodded. "Alright."

We sat for a moment in awkward silence, not knowing what to say. Shawn looked at me, acting like he was about to crack up.

"Okay, since no one else is going to ask, how the hell did you do that? You threw him against the wall like he was some of the cafeteria's garbage! I didn't even see a strain in your face," he said, chuckling.

A lump formed in my throat. I didn't think about hiding that. I had been too wrapped up in the moment. "It must have been the adrenaline," I said, heat forming on my face with the thought of exposing myself.

"Was it the adrenaline, or did that coma give you superpowers? That'd be a pretty cliché origin story. I mean, you do look like a vampire now," Talida interjected. I lurched forward, nearly spitting out my food. Trying to calm myself, I latched onto the bar underneath my table, squishing it accidentally. *Oh no,* I thought.

I laughed nervously, trying not to react to the now-damaged table. "I wish!" I said, knowing that my words were heavily exaggerated—and too loud. I winced internally but begged my body not to show it.

"You seem kinda nervous, Tony. You alright?" Shawn asked, his demeanor changing as if he was worried he'd said something wrong.

Yes, totally fine with the two of you exposing me. Damn your intuition, Shawn, I thought in my head.

"It's a little unnerving that Johnny has threatened us and disappeared into the storm, isn't it? I don't think he could cause any harm, but he's out for revenge. I would warn your families, just in case," I said.

The others nodded. "Yeah, I will for sure," Talida added.

"Okay, hopefully we can break the tension here," Alex started, a little alarmed herself. "Shawn and I have talked about it, but do you guys want to go to the football game this Friday to watch the band? I feel like we all need to hang out!"

I looked at Talida to see what she'd say. "I sadly have to finish a research paper, but you guys should record it so I can see!" she said. "It's due next Monday, and I procrastinated."

I frowned, knowing I had hero training about the same time as the game. "I really want to go, but I have my first graphic design project to finish. I'll try to finish it by then so I can go. That'd be super fun if I can manage to finish it beforehand. Of course, I need to see what the principal has to say this time," I lied. I had finished a design for Nikki after the mugging, despite it being late. She loved it, and had even paid me for my help. I was excited to see the finished products tonight.

I grabbed my hair. I was so tired of dealing with Johnny. Why couldn't I just do my schoolwork and hang out with my friends? "Man, standing up for yourself can really make you *feel* like a delinquent here, can't it?" I said.

Shawn sighed. "Hopefully you can finish that paper early and hang out with us, Talida. Hopefully you can get away too, Tony. Yeah, man, it's ridiculous that when you defend yourself, you still get kicked out of school. I'm going to be pissed if the principal takes you out of school again because Johnny couldn't keep out of your business. *He's* the bully. Kick *him* out. Hell, expel him completely after this," Shawn ranted.

We were all in the same boat. How long could I keep this up if Johnny came back? He might not actually come back to school this time. I should probably notify the police just in case.

"So," Talida started with a huge grin, "did Shawn tell you that I beat him multiple times in Immortal Fighter when I was at his house the other day?" she asked, trying to light-heartedly stir things up with Shawn.

"No!" Alex exclaimed with an exaggerated gasp, turning to stare at him with her mouth agape. She attempted to repress a smile as she pretended to scold her boyfriend. "What the hell, Shawn? When did this happen?"

In an alarmingly swift force of motion, Shawn willingly thrust his face down into his lunch tray. *CRACK!* He screamed into the table, muffled by the mashed potatoes now covering his mouth. Talida and Alex cackled as I begged for a breath of air myself.

"You're fucking crazy!" I said between gasps. He began to chuckle as his face turned red. "She beat me like a week ago," he said, wiping the food from his face as he shot Talida a playful glare.

"I told you I'd do it," Talida silently mouthed, smiling as she wiggled her eyebrows.

"In my defense, she's a gamer too!" Shawn defended.

"You told me when we started dating that you were the master of Immortal Fighter. Not Talida, not Tony—*you*," Alex scolded, giggling. She lifted her finger to point at him playfully, leaning forward. "You have to redeem yourself, buddy. I say this weekend…" She looked at Talida. "if you're all available, we should meet up at Shawn's place and play a few rounds."

"That sounds fun! I'll for sure see you there," I said, excited to see Shawn try to "redeem himself." I looked over to Shawn, and he mouthed "I hate you" to Talida, causing me to laugh again.

As the high-pitched ringing of the bell notified us that breakfast was over, we all dumped our trays. "I'll see you all later! Hopefully Friday night, too!" Alex said as she and Shawn headed off to their classes. I heard her distant voice as she made her way down the hallway. "I love your friends!" she told Shawn. I saw Shawn give her a quick side hug, and I turned to head for the office.

"See you guys at lunch," I yelled back, heading to what I expected would be my ultimate demise. *I'm so dead,* I thought as I stood in front of the opening door.

"Come in, Tony," the principal said from behind the door.

I stepped into the office, embarrassed to be back in this room. I didn't belong here. I didn't do anything wrong.

"Go ahead and sit down," Principal Jackson said, looking at a document in front of him. "I understand that Johnny ran up to you at breakfast and assaulted you?"

I nodded, folding my hands together. "Yes, and he threatened my friends, saying he would kill me," I said, hoping that the information would increase Johnny's chances of getting expelled.

"Did they seem like empty words?" he asked me, concerned.

"No, they did not."

"I'll tell you what. I understand that you had no control over this, especially since Johnny has been an issue at this school for quite some time. You, defending yourself for the first time, solidified that this issue was going to happen…" He thought for a moment, making my nerves shoot through the roof.

"I'm going to notify the police about this situation and the threats, and Johnny won't be returning to this school. Not only did he threaten lives, but he ran off school property, and he assaulted multiple people including our security guard. Johnny is likely going to receive a felony for this, and he may even receive prison time. I'm not going to punish you for something you had no control over. You are free to head to class after I notify the police," he said.

A weight lifted from my shoulders. I didn't have to worry this time. I sighed with relief. While my spirits lifted, they were quickly shot down by the results of the phone call.

"What a bunch of idiots," Mr. Jackson said. "I despise this small-city police force. They said they'd look for him because of the assault, but they can't do anything about the threats without physical proof that he's going to hurt someone. Without proof they are just empty threats, which teenagers are known for," he said, slamming his fist on his desk in aggravation.

"I'll have security keep an eye on you and your friends at the school, but in the meantime, I suggest keeping an eye out. They'll likely find him soon. You're free to go. Have a good rest of your day, Tony, and stay safe."

I headed toward the door, that lump forming in my throat again. Empty threats? Really? They wouldn't be so empty if someone got hurt. "Thank you for everything, Mr. Jackson. I appreciate it," I said, glad that he was at least willing to try to help. I headed to class, hoping that my day would go by quickly.

Chapter 14

The World's Biggest Threat

After a slow school day full of worry, and a reminder from my friends that it was Halloween, it was time to head to the hideout. I was a little bummed I hadn't realized my favorite holiday was today, but I promised to make it up to myself next year. My friends were busy tonight, so none of us were able to celebrate.

Usually, I would do *something* for Halloween. Whether that be something more normal like a costume, or something celebrating Samhain like a late-night meal or simmer pot with my friends. Maybe, if I got back early enough, I could squeeze in something fun.

I grabbed my black trench coat from a hook I had installed and reached for the black leather mask I had used during the mugging, then stopped. Maybe I shouldn't, now that I stopped the mugging. That would give me away if anyone recognized me. That'd be a sure-fire way to expose my secret identity before I even got my suit. I walked out the door. I thought about ditching the coat too, but I wasn't the only one walking around Old Belmont with one of these at night. Plus, it was Halloween!

Shawn's parents had decided they would keep the guns close, taking the threats very seriously, but Talida's parents weren't worried. Maybe Blackwell could help me out with the situation. Or maybe I could take care of it myself. But what do I do? There was no promise that the police would do anything for a first offense. They'd probably give him a "wellness check" and say he's just a troubled teenager who needed time.

As I continued through the woods in the rain, my thoughts about Johnny weighed heavily on my mind. I could kill him. Then he wouldn't be able to hurt anyone. I shook that out of my mind and wiped the rain from my eyes. Killing him would make me a villain. I had to find another way…but what if there wasn't another path?

I attempted to reassure myself. The police would find him, he'd probably resist, and he'd be taken away forever, I hoped. Deep down I knew that it was going to be a problem I would have to take care of myself. I doubted they'd even find him. My heart dropped, taking my confidence with it. My memory focused on his blackened eyes and what he had said before the threats. I knew a lot of the damage was from me, but it was apparent more had been done at home. Could I help him? That's what a hero would do. But how?

After a few minutes, a fog began to roll in, making me uneasy. I hoped this fog wouldn't cause me to go in the wrong direction. I mostly knew the way to the hideout, but I didn't have MIRA to help me if I got lost today. I still had my tablet, but MIRA had been momentarily disabled, likely due to getting our suits today. I was also trying not to use it due to the rain. I had no idea if it was water-resistant.

I stopped for a moment, trying to relax as I looked up at the sky. It was peaceful out here. A little eerie, but I tended to like that. I watched the rain fall and felt each drop hitting my face, one after another. *Alright, let's get to the hideout,* I thought, dropping my head as I continued to move forward.

After several minutes, the light rain had become a downpour, falling from the sky as if it were trying to escape the clouds like a prison. I continued forward, knowing I had to be getting close. I briefly cursed under my breath for wearing my nice combat boots, hoping the barrage wouldn't ruin them. My body shivered as the temperature dropped dramatically, bumps beginning to form as my skin became numb, cold, and wet. I was beginning to regret coming here tonight. I asked myself if I could control fire if I managed to create it again. There was only one way to find out.

I focused my attention on my hands, still not sure of what caused my fire abilities. I knew anger and adrenaline triggered it, but did I really need to tap into that every time I wanted to use my fire powers? As I focused on my hands, harder, and harder until they were the only thing in my mind, my vision flickered. *Whoa, what the...*

I was ripped from my normal consciousness, plunging into another dream-like state. I looked at my hands, which had a light blood splatter on my charcoal, fingerless gloves. I immediately felt immense sadness. My existing dread formed a waterfall of horror like something traumatic had just happened to me. Something unbearably horrendous.

As I hit the peak of my sadness, bright-white fire lit up my palms. The only thing going through my mind was the thought of killing whoever or whatever was in front of me. I wanted to tear it to pieces with my bare hands. I clenched my teeth, looking up to see that terrifying, recurring face, smiling at me. The familiar mustard colored, beaming eyes met my gaze. There were the two glowing nose slits, only this time, I could make out other features of his face.

The area around the slits in his nose was shaped almost as if it were the holes on a skull with hard ridges, curving down flush with his skin the color of a bruise. His teeth were stained with blood, and there was a smile that would haunt my nightmares with two large vampire fangs resting over his bottom teeth. This time I could see that he also had two charcoal-colored horns.

I stood in what seemed to be the hideout, but I was unsure. This creature from Hell reared his head back and let loose an abrasive cackle. Upon hearing it, my vision blurred, everything became oversaturated, and I was yanked backward, crashing into my body and being thrown back into reality.

I gasped for air, my heart hurtling through my chest, and I couldn't decide whether I had been holding my breath, or if whatever I just saw horrified me to the point of an anxiety attack. After a few minutes on my knees, questioning what I had just witnessed, my heart began to slow.

What the fuck was that? There was that face again. My heartrate began to spike again, and I began hyperventilating. Everything going on recently, mixed with this, was just too much. Was I having visions? That face. That horrifying face.

The image of that face began flashing in my mind, from the many times

I'd seen it over the last several years to the most recent appearances. I remembered the figure in front of my television in that dream at school, and now this "vision." Why was it that each time I saw this face, it got worse? I was closer to it. Closer to seeing every detail of whatever this figure was. *Am I going to die??*

My body felt as though someone was crushing it with an unwanted, forceful hug. I couldn't breathe. I couldn't think. I couldn't even regain whatever composure I had before the vision. I was trapped within a tunnel of my own fears. Only one thought was bouncing around in my mind. Was this creature going to kill me?

"Tony!"

The voice rang out in the distance, bringing me back for a quick moment, but it wasn't enough for me to recognize it.

"Are you alright?" Corbin hollered. He sprinted toward me from the hideout entrance, helping me up.

"No," I replied without hesitation. While my hyperventilation had stopped, it was still on the brink of returning. I had never dealt with this before. Was this an anxiety attack?

"What's wrong?" Corbin asked, trying to help as much as he could.

"I need to…" I spouted, trying my hardest to form coherent sentences, almost failing in my attempts to claw back to reality, "speak to Blackwell."

Corbin looked concerned. After all, he knew that I had collapsed, and now I could barely speak, looking hysterical.

"Everything's fine. You got friends here. We're here to help you out,"

Corbin consoled. I stood up straight, pulling away from him. I had been leaning on him, but I was slowly regaining my strength. I pulled myself together. Well, at least more than I had been.

"I don't know what happened. I was focusing on my hands...trying to trigger my fire abilities to warm myself up, and suddenly, I was launched into a dream. I think I've been having visions, and I think Blackwell is in trouble," I said, trying my best to explain what was going on without sounding insane.

The first vision that I had experienced rushed back to me, and mixed with this new one, I no longer knew what was important and what wasn't. We all had powers, so I couldn't sound that crazy, right?

"Whoa, that's nuts. What'd you see? Why do you reckon he's in trouble?" Corbin asked me.

I leaned in toward him. "There have been many instances where I've seen the same horrible face. Often in my dreams. Once, in what I'm thinking was a vision that I had during my coma, and now, seeing the face in more detail. In all of them, this face has yellow eyes and glowing slits for a nose like a skull.

At the time of my coma, I went through a vision of Blackwell speaking to me, right before a vision involving this figure. I went into a room where a man was chained to the wall. It said that it was going to kill the man's 'special forces,' and that he was going to watch each of the members die," I said quickly as if the information was going to leave me.

I grabbed the sides of my head, trying to stabilize my breathing. "I also think I saw the figure at my friend's house. I tried to hit him but he disappeared. I don't know what's real and what's not."

Corbin looked bothered. "No shit? That's either a strange coincidence or it's somethin' Blackwell needs to hear. I say you go to Blackwell about this right now, just in case. If you've seen the creature's face in your dream, maybe that's somethin' you could check to rule out if it's serious or not," he said.

I nodded. "I'll check it out. I appreciate you helping me like this. You're a good friend," I said, truly appreciating him.

"'Course! I always help a friend in need. That's the way my pa raised me. If you ever need to talk, just reach out. I'm always here," Corbin said, holding out his hand.

I smiled and reached for his hand, replying with a firmly gripped handshake as he grinned back at me. My strength had returned, and my body was no longer shaking.

As we walked into the hideout, Blackwell was waiting. Seeing that I was soaking wet and covered in mud, his body language suggested that he was confused.

"Did you make the trip alright?" Blackwell asked, sounding honestly concerned.

"It's been a long day," I started. "May I talk to you in private before we start today?" I shot a glance at Corbin, who nodded in approval.

"Of course," Blackwell answered, opening the door for Corbin and then handing him back his tablet.

Blackwell waited until the wall closed in on itself again, and after making sure we were alone, he began to speak. "What's bothering you, Tony?" he asked, seeming very down to earth and approachable now.

I paused, my words clinging to the back of my throat. Now that I was talking to him, I wasn't sure how to start this conversation. How do I start this conversation?

"I'm worried…about your safety," I started.

Blackwell cocked his head and stepped back. "What do you mean?" he asked, utterly disconcerted by the statement.

"I don't know where to start—I guess from the beginning? Before my coma, I used to have nightmares of this cloaked figure with glowing yellow eyes. One of the last nightmares I had before my coma, the people in the dream called him Veka." I saw Blackwell's pose shift as he heard the name. It was an uncomfortable movement, but I kept talking.

Not wanting to stray off-track, I avoided the dream I had of speaking with Blackwell. I wasn't sure how I saw him before we met, but his words within the dream seemed private. Obviously, if he had somehow reached out within my coma, he would have known about what he said. I decided that I wouldn't bring it up. "During my coma, I had a dream that I was following Veka down a black brick hallway. I saw several people behind bars suffering, but we ended up in a room with a man chained to a wall."

Blackwell leaned forward, suddenly more interested than he was before. "That is—alarming. What else did you see?"

"In that dream, Veka told the man he would kill his 'special forces', and that he would watch all of his members die." I grabbed the back of my neck. My next words sounded crazy in my mind, but I forced myself to speak them. "This could be a huge coincidence, and most of it could have been pulled out of my imagination, but I'm worried that the chained-up man is a vision of your future," I told him, seeming to rush through the words like it was a disease I was trying to expel.

"Is that all that you saw?" he asked. His words were pleading for more information. They came out almost harsh. "I need to know everything."

"When I was at my friend Shawn's house, I thought I saw this 'Veka' standing in the woods. I ran up to him to try and get answers and tried to punch him. He disappeared, so I don't know if it was real or not. What worries me is that just outside, I was trying to summon my flames and had another one. I've never had a dream while being awake, and it freaked me out. I saw my hands, in fingerless, dark gray gloves, splattered with blood, and the figure was cackling. It looked like we were in the hideout. That's all I've seen."

Blackwell rubbed the bottom of his helmet in thought. "Hmm, that does seem very...disturbing. Veka is real, although I'm unsure how your mind manifested his image," he started, making my stomach jolt into my chest.

Oh no, I thought. But who is Veka? What is he?

"This being is powerful, and I will inform Project Barricade about him tonight after training. Don't dwell on him too much for now. It is highly possible that your imagination revised the face you've been seeing and created this face with the help of the nightmares. As for seeing him in the woods, it may have been a mixture of your nightmares and the manifestation of your powers. When your body starts to react to having them, sometimes it does strange things. You'll notice once you start training, your appetite will be dramatically increased as well."

Blackwell stopped talking, looking down at his feet for only a moment. He started to tap his finger on the desk next to him, as if debating whether or not to say something else. "As for this man chained up by Veka, you believe it could be my future? I need you to keep this a secret, but I am going to reveal my true face to you in order to solidify if I am in danger or not. You can tell me if I am the person you've seen in this dream."

My head cocked back in surprise. He hadn't shown anyone his face since I arrived. Why would he go through all this trouble now? "Are you sure? I can tell you what the man looked like in the vision."

"It will dwell in your mind until you are truly certain this face wasn't mine," Blackwell informed. "I am doing this to ease your mind—and my own." He reached for his helmet, lifting it from his face with a hiss while my body tingled with anxiety.

Thump…thump, thump.

My heart beat faster the closer his helmet was to coming off. As he lifted the helmet and held it near his waist, I was relieved. It wasn't the same face. It wasn't him. Not even close. I let out a large sigh of relief.

The man who stood before me looked strikingly different than the one in my vision. He had slicked-back, medium-length black hair on top of his pale, flushed skin. His face was cleanly shaved. He had a large nose and low, thick eyebrows that sat above piercing, jade-like eyes, which had a completely different glow to them.

As the man looked into my eyes, I saw his nerves slowly dissipate.

"It's not you," I said, a smile following my release of fear. "Thank you.

I'm still not sure what to think of these dreams, though. Should I trust them?"

"That is for you to decide. I personally wouldn't give them much thought. While that vision definitely sounded concerning, I think it was your mind playing tricks on you. My agent who was keeping an eye on you during your coma may have mentioned Project Barricade, which your mind could have latched onto. As for how you saw Veka in these dreams, I have no clue," he said, putting his helmet back on.

"Thank you for that, Blackwell. I needed that reassurance."

"Anything to help, Tony. I want you to be sure of what's going on. For now, I urge you to simply see these as dreams. You are a very creative person; therefore, I believe that your mind is building these scenarios in your head based on what you have subconsciously heard. As for you being launched into these dreams, I believe it is your body reacting to the changes it's going through right now. You have a lot of new emotions and a lot of new abilities, so surely your mind would also see it as different," Blackwell said, putting my mind at ease. It was clear that he believed I saw these images, but his words rang true.

My mind was reacting to change, and with that change, my creativity was boosted to create these visions? That made sense.

"So where do I go from here with all of this? How big of a threat is... Veka?" I asked.

"It is up to you to decide your fate, but I can tell you that I see a bright future, Tony. With multiple powers, you can do a lot with them. With your kind of passion, who knows where it will take you? I do want you to reach out to me if you have any more dreams, though."

Blackwell stopped for a moment, pondering my last question. With hesitation, he spoke. "Veka is our biggest threat. The *world's* biggest threat."

My stomach lurched. "So, this isn't going to be something we can clear up right away, is it?" I asked. This creature, this monster—Veka… What did he want with us?

"No. This won't be cleared up for quite some time," Blackwell said. "But first thing's first: We've got to get you heroes training. Let's head inside and get to work."

Chapter 15

Where's My Super Suit?

I stood firm, feeling as though I needed to push through the feelings stirring inside me. *Heroes are strong, and so are you,* I thought, swallowing the fist in my throat. Whoever this Veka was, we could defeat him together.

"I think I'm ready to begin our training, now that all of my drama is over," I said, still uneasy but much calmer than when I had arrived.

"I'm glad I could help clear up these dreams you're having. Let's meet up with the rest of the heroes in the lobby," he said, walking toward the wall and setting my tablet against it. As the door opened, we headed inside.

Upon finishing the descent, the other three heroes stood next to the desk, eager to see what was in store.

"How is everyone doing?" Blackwell asked, his voice piercing through the light chatter and silencing the room. He looked around the room slowly as his arms rested near his sides.

"Doing well, Blackwell. How about yourself?" Nikki asked.

"Not too bad," Mason said.

"Great."

Blackwell looked at each of us in approval, seeing potential in Project Barricade. "It's been a long day for me, but it's time I show you the training room."

Mason threw a fist up in excitement. He had been waiting to use this area for a while now.

"But before we get to that, I have even more exciting news. Your suits are finished and ready for you," Blackwell said, stepping behind the desk and reaching underneath. He retrieved four duffel bags, personalized for each hero.

"Alright, the first member of Project Barricade, we have Red Kelvin, our pyromancer!" he said, tossing a duffel bag covered in a red-to-orange gradient. Mason caught it, immediately unzipping it to see what was inside.

"We have our second member, the colossus up from Texas, the Steel Cowboy!" Blackwell tossed Corbin a brown leather bag. It looked to be lighter than most, but Corbin hadn't wanted a whole lot to begin with.

"Our third member—who took forever to adjust to having an alias—we have Whirl, the telekinetic!" He tossed Nikki a white, textured bag. She had been eagerly waiting to view the contents. She shot me a smile. I had been the only one who had known she'd picked an alias, as was shown by the excitement in the room.

"Last but not least, we have Persevere, our one-man army!" Blackwell projected, throwing me a royal purple bag with a gray handle. I smiled, also super excited to see what was in store for us.

"Now follow me, heroes," Blackwell said, a lot quieter than he had been moments ago. Nikki and Mason rushed to zip their bags back up, and then the four of us headed after Blackwell. We stopped at the first door on the left.

"This is the hideout bathroom and locker room. Go ahead and change. When you're ready, meet me in the training room, and I will explain further. I will give a quick reminder to call each other by your aliases when in your suits. It'll be good practice for the field," he said, heading back to the hallway.

We headed into the restroom, looking around. Mason had been here before, but for the rest of us, this was new. Six stalls, if you could call them that, stood against the left wall. They were more like rectangular pods, and from our view, the doors appeared to close from the ceiling down.

"Those are interesting," I said, looking at the pods. "Are they just stalls, or do they serve another purpose?"

Mason smiled and looked at us. "They aren't completely online yet, but when you enter them, they recognize who is using it. If you press the button above the toilet, it will go into what Blackwell calls 'Archive Mode' where it will tell you your stats and skill levels on a scale of one to seventeen. It's pretty interesting. It's supposed to connect with the system in the training room so that when you come back here and 'check out,' it will tell you how much you raised or lowered your stats."

Corbin looked at Mason, and they nodded at each other approvingly.

"That's neat. That'd be a good way to keep track of everything, including progression. I like seeing statistics, so I think I'll enjoy that," Nikki said, heading toward them.

"Yeah, I didn't think we'd be getting character stats in real life," I said with a chuckle.

We each stepped into a separate pod, and I looked around. It seemed like a normal stall. As soon as I took a step further in, the door lowered with a swoosh, sealing itself. White LED lights turned on above me.

Slightly creepy, I thought, looking at the skinny rectangular plate above the toilet. I pressed the button. An electronic whir broke the silence within the pod, and MIRA's voice spoke out.

"Welcome, Persevere. Shall I begin with your base statistics?"

I stood still for a moment, searching for where the voice was coming from. I turned to look at the door. It became reflective like a mirror, and I replied, "Yes."

"Stand straight, and look into the beam," MIRA said as a blue beam appeared abruptly from the door. The light of the beam shone brightly into my eyes.

I jerked, alarmed, but for some reason, the light didn't cause discomfort. *How strange.* I was usually sensitive to light. This must be something rather unique.

"Base statistics saved. Suit up and report to the training room."

I frowned, sad that I didn't get to see the base statistics. I opened the bag with my suit, eager to try it on. I pulled the body section out first, wondering how I was supposed to get into it. Did it just stretch over? There wasn't a zipper or anything.

The pod dinged, and MIRA appeared again. "This is your base. Made of an experimental material Blackwell has designed called 'Titan Fiber.' It is bulletproof, sixty percent power resistant, and has climate control built into it for harsh weather survival. The cape is eighty percent power-resistant and bulletproof. The suit can, however, be punctured by a blade."

A smile formed across my face as I pulled the cape out of the bag. I'd always wanted to wear one, but never thought I'd be seriously putting on a super suit. "What does power resistant mean?" I asked, confused about what exactly it did to powers.

"Power resistance is the tolerance that your suit has against elemental attacks and strength attacks along with ray guns and other unique weapons. For example, if Red Kelvin hit you with a fireball, your suit would absorb sixty percent of the damage, but I highly suggest not getting hit at all. Another example, which may save your life, is if Steel Cowboy were to punch you with his enhanced strength and then launch you against a concrete wall, your suit would absorb most of that impact, causing it to be survivable," MIRA answered.

Obviously, I wasn't planning on taking a fireball to the chest if I had a choice. Against super-strength, though, that power resistance could be very helpful. I slid the suit on feet first after undressing, seeing that the suit was quite stretchy. Once it was on, it fit to my form nearly perfectly. My cape seemed to snap onto the body once I threw it over my shoulders.

It looked good. I looked at myself in the reflection of the door. I watched as I awkwardly flexed. Erupting into laughter, I realized how cringe-worthy my actions were. A bundle of cloth on the ground caught my eye. It must have fallen when I took out the suit. As I reached for the mass, I realized that they were my dark-gray, fingerless gloves, studs built into the knuckles. I hesitated to put them on at first, but after a moment, I slid them over my hands. *It was just a dream.*

The gloves fit well, seeming fluid with my movements. They weren't tough like some I had worn before, yet still had padding under the knuckles.

"What are the studs on the gloves made of?" I asked MIRA. I thought it was the same material as Blackwell's suit, but it was a matte black in contrast to the crystalline appearance his had.

"The gloves are made of Titan Fiber, while the studs are made of dyridanine. Dyridanine is a material heavily used by Veka and his Followers. Blackwell found it to be a very strong material, but hard to forge. Blackwell's suit was forged from dyridanine to combat Veka's forces."

He has Followers and forces? This kept getting better and better. I clenched my fist. What was Veka doing? What kind of horrible things is this guy capable of? I began to question everything I thought before. Of course, if I saw gang violence or any small crime, I was going to stop it, but what if I were given these powers to stop something more? Every hero had a nemesis, right? At least in comic books and movies they did. It was strange to me that these thoughts were even relevant. It made me want to pull out my hair and fall into hysteria.

I reached into the bag, pulling out my mask, which looked more like a helmet. It was made with two parts—the lower face piece which I assumed went on first, and then the pointed purple mask that covered the top half of my head. It had black tinted glass lenses. I put the lower piece on, and I was surprised at how roomy it felt. All the masks or helmets I'd worn before had been very restricting. It had a filter in the front with the large teeth designs I had wanted.

As I sat the top piece onto my face after pulling up my hair into a tight bun, the sound of air releasing startled me. The two pieces connected, forming an airtight helmet. As I peered into the mirror, I also noticed purple pupils light up on the lenses of my helmet, emitting a white eclipse-like glow around it. From there, it felt as if it was pulling fresh air into the mask itself.

"Your helmet has the ability to filter poisons and other dangerous fumes from your surroundings, along with allowing you to breathe underwater. Your mask has several different views." The voice stopped for a moment, and my vision turned green.

"You have infrared vision, pinpoint vision, and regular vision."

My eyebrows narrowed in confusion.

"What is pinpoint vision?" I asked. Instantaneously, what I saw changed to a black-and-white, lined vision.

"Now uploading example."

A small white loading bar popped up in my sight, and a video loaded up, showing me a scene of what seemed to be multiple people running toward me. As each person began to move, a white triangle outline bounced over each person, notifying me of their movement. As the people sprinted toward me, my vision gave me details of how fast they were running and their projected route to me.

"That's interesting," I thought as the vision turned back to normal. I was thrilled that what I could see wasn't tinted like the material. I had thought it was glass, but it seemed to be an electronic screen—and probably a lot more resilient than glass. I wondered if this was shatterproof. The idea of it shattering into my eyes turned my stomach.

I threw the hood over my helmet, hearing it snap loudly into place as if it were highly magnetized. It rested right behind my mask and didn't seem to obstruct my view at all.

I then pulled out my boots and smiled; they were exactly what I was looking for. They looked very similar to the ones I had gotten with Shawn and Talida, except the plates on the front of my shins were purple. The soles of the boots, along with the straps, were an off-white and came to a point on the front of my feet. *These are amazing.*

"Your boots have stats that are similar to your suit, and the plates are durable enough to enhance your attacks."

As I reached into the bag, wondering what was next, I pulled out a set of pauldrons, which were next to a pair of plates to go on the side of my thighs.

"The pauldrons, the leg plates, your hood, and your cape are magnetic to the suit. There are no straps for them, and they can't be removed until you wish them to be."

I put them on, and they attached themselves with a loud snap like the hood and cape. They were rather comfortable and didn't hinder my movements. I then put on my belt, followed by two electronics that were in the bag. The first was a small square screen with a purple border that I put on my left wrist, followed by a rectangular screen that I put on my right. Both had off-white straps.

"The rectangular device contains my MIRA system. Through the screen, I can give you access to an in-world and out-world GPS system, advice, and many other things you'll learn along the way. The square wearable needs to be calibrated by Blackwell, and it contains your choice of energy shield, along with minor electronic features like time, a cell phone connected to your helmet, and several others with a link to my system."

That's awesome. "Can I see my stats through the MIRA system on either of these items?" I asked. It'd be a neat addition to keeping track of my progress.

"Yes. It keeps track of everything for you."

Finally, the last thing in the bag was a large pistol with a purple, rectangular body. It had a nice, solid grip to it and appeared to have two barrels. On the side of the body was what seemed to be a selector to change the mode of the gun.

"This is your Blaze Ray. Blackwell will explain the different modes in your training. Now that I've given you a briefing on your suit, head to the training room."

MIRA shut down with another whir, and the pod door opened. I looked around, seeing the other three heroes talking amongst themselves, waiting for me. Then the conversations stopped. Mason, or should I say, Red Kelvin, stared at my suit.

"Hot damn!" Red Kelvin exclaimed. "That's awesome!" His suit had also turned out well. It had a snug fit, clinging tightly to his form, and I doubted that it would restrain his movements at all. He also had a sideways K in the center of his chest, seeming more like a symbol than a letter. This symbol was accompanied by a thin mask across his eyes to help maintain his identity.

Nikki's outfit was similar to tactical gear—looking more like a white swat member than a superhero—and she had a strap going across her chest, filled with intricate throwing knives. She also had a simple black mask around her eyes for likely the same purpose. Nikki smiled, happy to learn how everyone's suits turned out.

Corbin—Steel Cowboy—walked up to me. He had received a simple outfit along with a cowboy hat and dark-brown bandana. "Lookin' great, Persevere. Look what I got!" he exclaimed, showing me two large metal casings around his forearms. They were pretty heavy-duty.

"That's awesome. What are they supposed to do?" I asked, smiling back at him.

"Yeah! They're supposed to eject rope that I can attach to things. MIRA says it's made of Titan Fiber. Seems fittin', don't it?" he asked. As I looked at them, I noticed Nikki and Red Kelvin both had a MIRA system around their wrists, but Steel Cowboy didn't seem to have one at all.

"Hell yeah! I got a Blaze Ray. It has different modes on it, and Blackwell is supposed to tell me what they do," I replied, super excited to see what we could all achieve. "Do you not have a MIRA?"

He smiled. "I do! They built the system into the casin' on my arm and installed the voice transmitter into my hat." He waved his forearm, and I could see the screen clearly built on one of the layers of the casing.

The four of us headed through a door on the far side of the pod room, leading into the training room, where Blackwell was awaiting our arrival.

Chapter 16

The Training Room

"Welcome, heroes. You are now officially members of Project Barricade, and it's time to start your training. Each of you has a MIRA system, always available so that your progress can be tracked. It can also receive your mission briefings when away from the hideout. You've all been given the same system but in your own styles. I want to start your training by telling you about this room. There are five different areas." He pointed to an area similar to the strength room at Triple H.

"The first area is strength training. Alongside normal weight benches is a Maximum Energy Power System, a system designed to push your body to its limit, find where you stand, and realize your projected potential. This can be used for people with enhanced strength, along with those without it," he said, nodding at Red Kelvin and Nikki.

"The second area is for your endurance testing. We have treadmills and other endurance machines, along with our endurance tester. It's designed to determine how long you can keep pushing forward." I looked into the distance and saw what looked to be a tunnel entrance. I was overwhelmed when I saw how massive this training room was.

"Our third area is for speed where we have a looped track with no obstacles, along with a mile sprint. The tracks will exit the training room into a tunnel and bring you back to the start. We also have our speed tester, which is similar to a treadmill and will allow us to properly test super speed."

I looked to where he pointed next, seeing what seemed to be an extra room in the corner. There were stairs that led to a balcony, but I wasn't sure what it was.

"The fourth area we have available is our combat trainer. You can set it so that you can go against up to twenty enemies at once in whatever mix of melee or ranged attackers you want. This you can use as our arena, where, after you have your stats plugged into the system, you can even fight replicas of each other for training. You can see how you pair against each other or with one another. An advanced system is in the works where you will actually be able to battle each other using the MIRA system at max power resistance."

We then entered a new area, which seemed to be a lot of empty space. Maybe for ranged weapons? Blackwell lifted his hands as he strode forward.

"The fifth and final area is our range where you can use your weapons against dummies designed specifically for each of you to hone your accuracy and technique. I highly suggest using the range to figure out what you're doing, and then taking what you learn to the combat trainer to test how it fairs in certain situations," Blackwell finished, pointing into the distance. "I'm going to lead you into the range first. Let's see what you can do."

Upon entering the range, my nerves were beginning to show. I hoped he wouldn't make me go first. I didn't even know how to control my powers yet. I hoped that someone who had at least experimented with their abilities would be chosen first.

"Alright, heroes," Blackwell said, looking directly at me. I held my breath and let it out with a sigh when he turned his gaze to Nikki. "I would like to see Whirl test her knives first. Step over here, please," he said, directing her in front of a gray target about fifteen feet away.

"So, from what I understand, you want to use your telekinesis to throw your daggers, and your end goal is to be able to use all of them at the same time?" Blackwell asked for confirmation.

"Yes, sir. I feel like it could be very efficient if we ever had to go into battle. I could even use the same technique for disarming multiple people in the case of stopping robberies or muggings," Whirl said.

Did everyone come up with end goals? Why hadn't I heard of this? I thought, bothered. I guess they live here though. It had probably been an afterthought. I debated about asking Blackwell if I could live here as well, but I was beginning to enjoy living in my van.

"Alright, show us what you've got."

Whirl stepped forward in confidence. She focused on the target, then on one of the knives strapped to her chest. She closed her eyes, and the first blade slid from its sheath, rising into the air next to her head. It quivered in the air for a moment, and then eventually stabilized. Holding the first one, she used her power to lift a second, which she wasn't able to keep from quivering.

Whirl's face tensed up as she launched her arm forward, propelling the first dagger into the upper left area of the target. She followed through, turning her body and launching the second dagger, hitting the very bottom right of the target. She attempted to launch a third blade, but this one fell to the ground once it was unsheathed.

"Not too bad," Blackwell said. "You've got enough control to throw two daggers and unsheathe the third one. That's a good start." Blackwell plugged the information into his MIRA system via a tablet and moved his gaze onto Red Kelvin.

"You're up. For this one I want you guys to step back," Blackwell said, motioning us back behind him.

Red Kelvin looked over at me, just about as nervous as I was, and he gave me a look of fear. I shot him a smile.

"You've got this," I whispered to him, excited to see what he could do. He gave me a quick smirk and then stepped forward.

"Do you have a goal that you would like to reach at the end of your training?" Blackwell asked.

Red Kelvin paused in thought. He hadn't known about the goals either. "Um. I think I'd like to be able to throw large fireballs rather than small ones from a good distance and be able to project fire like a flamethrower. Maybe a good fifteen feet in front of me. Right now, my flames kind of go everywhere," he said.

It was a small goal in theory, but still sounded difficult considering I didn't even know how to conjure my fire without being angry.

"Sounds like a reachable goal. Let's see what you can do," Blackwell said, stepping back to let Red Kelvin do his work.

Red Kelvin took a deep breath in, letting it out slowly to reduce his nerves. "I can do this," he whispered to himself, shaking his hands by his sides as he looked in front of him.

"You can let loose on the blue targets," Blackwell said. Three blue targets popped up from the ground, and the gray target was released from its post.

Red Kelvin threw both of his hands outward, easing them together in front of him as a large ball of fire was conjured in between.

He had pretty good control already. I worried about looking like a joke compared to these members that already knew how to use their powers.

Red Kelvin launched the large fireball forward, but right before it hit the target, it dissipated into nothing, leaving only a few marks on the target. "Was worth a shot," Red Kelvin said, conjuring another fireball, this one much smaller, maybe the size of a softball. This one, looking much more solid, was able to be launched toward the target with force. The fire hit the target, destroying the top half.

Red Kelvin took a step forward, projecting flames from his hands, trying for a good range, but ended with just three feet of fire in front of him and about the same reaching behind him. He pushed harder, the strain in his face becoming clear. His struggles added a short burst of range, but he was unable to hold it as the heat sputtered into embers. Red Kelvin's fire gave out, and he stepped back, the beads of sweat growing on his forehead.

"Not bad. Stick to the small fireballs for now, and we will look into creating the bigger ones later on down the road. We'll figure it out. Same with the ranged fire burst; I think we can finesse it," Blackwell said.

"You're up, Persevere. Any goals in mind?"

Blackwell calling my name was like a punch to the chest. My nerves hit, and I didn't want to move. *Here we go,* I thought, knowing I didn't have much control. This wasn't going to be good, but maybe I'd surprise myself with my Blaze Ray.

"I would like to be able to shoot quickly with my Blaze Ray, control my fire, and be able to understand what I can do with my strength," I said, not quite sure what I wanted as of right now. Since I didn't know a whole lot about my powers, my main goal was to figure out how to use them.

"Sounds like a lot to figure out—and a lot to work on. I believe we can all reach our goals, and we will work together to make sure of that," Blackwell said, nodding to everyone. "Let's see what you've got. I want you to try using your fire abilities first."

I stepped forward, knowing that holding off on my attempt wasn't going to further my progress. I breathed in and let it out slowly, looking behind me at the heroes. Red Kelvin threw me a thumbs-up, smiling at me as he lit a small flame at the tip of his thumb.

"Give 'em hell, Tony!" Steel Cowboy yelled as I turned back around, ready for the attempt with my newfound courage.

I tried to think of fire, and I threw my arms to my sides. "Fire!" I yelled, seeing the blue target in front of me. I looked down at my hands only to see nothing. Just me, screaming and throwing my hands around. Shit. What was I doing? Why wasn't it working?

"It's okay," Blackwell started, beginning to chuckle. "Performance anxiety is normal." I once again caught myself internally screaming. "Jokes aside, it happens with beginners. You'll latch onto your abilities, so don't be too worried about it."

Red Kelvin stepped toward me, and Blackwell motioned him forward, allowing him to interject.

"You've got to feel the energy inside you. It's not based on rage, and it's not about thinking of the heat itself. What you've got to do in order to conjure fire is focus on the energy flowing through you, from your heart, and focus on releasing that energy from your body through your hands. You'll figure it out, man. What things have triggered the ability before?" Red Kelvin said, being very informative.

It must have taken him forever to figure this all out. I'd assumed it was based on anger and the emotions around it. Because, you know, fiery rage.

I nodded to him with respect. "I really appreciate that. It's only triggered when I was angry after fighting," I said. "That's the only thing that's ever prompted it. I had a lot of energy because I had just won the fight. Let me try that. I hadn't thought about it that way. Thank you," I said, giving a smile.

"Of course. I can't leave my teammate hanging, can I?"

Red Kelvin stepped back again, and I looked at the target. I closed my eyes, focusing on trying to find this energy Red Kelvin was talking about. I didn't feel anything at first, but as I pushed deeper, searching, I got a rush. It dwelled within my chest, swirling around inside, and I focused on trying to propel that energy to my fingertips to release it. Suddenly, I was very aware of the blood in my veins.

The energy seeped into my arms, nearing my fingers, and just as I thought it wasn't going to work, my hands expelled flames, traveling up to my shoulders as my eye sockets began to feel warm. *Whoa,* I thought. This feeling was much stronger than before. Even when I was exploding in anger, my flames hadn't been so powerful. I lurched forward, flinging a small fireball at the target in front of me. It engulfed the target, wrapping itself tightly around it as the bright-yellow flames along my arms dissipated. I smiled, anger not fueling me this time.

It worked! I thought. I knew how to use my fire abilities now.

"Yeah! That's how it's done, P!" Red Kelvin cheered, throwing his hands in the air in excitement.

"Go, Persevere!" Whirl yelled.

Steel Cowboy stood, grinning. "Good start!"

I pulled out my Blaze Ray, looking at the gun to make sure I knew how to shoot it. I wasn't quite sure, but I was confident I could figure it out. It had multiple different levels with a knob to switch between them, but they were only indicated by numbers. I stared at it, biting my lip, and then looked at Blackwell.

"How do I use this?" I asked, chuckling. An explosion of laughter left the others as they realized I had no idea what I was doing.

"It's alright. I didn't expect you to just start shooting," Blackwell said, walking toward me and taking the gun from my hand. "So...you have a minus sign, the numbers 1 through 3, and a plus sign. The minus is a charging mode, meant to recharge your gun while it's not in use. It can be used as a stun gun at this level. The gun is charged with your fire energy, hence the name 'Blaze Ray.' The gun is fully charged right now, but in the future, you will need to use your fire to recharge it." He pointed toward the knob, switching it to the minus sign after taking a step forward. He handed it to me. "Why don't you try that before I continue."

I held the gun in my hand like I would a regular pistol with my left hand under the handle and my right firmly around the grip. Reminding myself that it was on stun, I took aim, seeing through the greyed out sights. I pulled the trigger, and a small bolt of white energy leapt out of the barrel, striking the blue target with a ZAP! I was immediately confused due to not feeling the gun react to pulling the trigger. There was nothing. It didn't seem to leave much of a mark on the target either. Just a minor scorch mark. "That feels super weak, but you said the minus is a taser?"

"Yes. Used to tase human targets. It is your only non-lethal level on this gun," Blackwell answered, reaching out his hand and looking at the gun. I handed it back to him, and he pointed at each of the numbers as he spoke.

"Level 1 is considered the 'kill level.' It allows you to shoot simple yet effective rays. If you hold it, you'll have about two rays per second. Level 2 is stronger, giving you three rays per second if held, but level three is an entirely different situation. Level 3 will emit large explosive rays. If the trigger is held down, you will have a precision laser."

He turned to face me completely, as if his next words were important. He pointed toward the plus sign, making sure I was paying close attention. It was interesting seeing Blackwell in teacher mode, and he held my interest well. "The plus sign should only be used in dire situations. Upon pressing the trigger once, it will purge the rest of the energy in the gun as a powerful blast. It's very destructive. I'll show it to you further along in your training. For now, I want you to use level 1 and level 3 to feel the difference," Blackwell told me, handing the gun back to me.

I switched the gun to the first level. Upon reaching it, the line on my sights started to glow white, showing me that it was on "kill." As I took aim and pulled the trigger, I was pleasantly surprised when I realized this mode didn't have a kick either, and the sights were super accurate. I hit a little to the top right of my target. I took three more shots with it, forming a nice grouping.

I held down the trigger, getting the feel for shooting multiple rays. As I switched to level three, a whirring sound emerged from the barrels. As I shot, it caught me by surprise. It kicked hard, flinging the gun behind me.

"Shit!" I yelled, turning around to see where it would land. I was alarmed by a loud explosion, and I practically jumped into the air. I had totally forgotten that it would be explosive. I looked around the room, embarrassed.

Whirl jumped into action, catching the gun with her telekinesis long enough for me to grab it from the air.

Steel Cowboy grabbed Red Kelvin and started to shake him excitedly, maybe a little harsher than he had wanted. "Holy moly!" he yelled as Red Kelvin violently flopped in his grip. "Did ya'll see that?!"

"Thanks, Whirl," I said, chuckling under my humiliation.

I turned around to a destructive sight. I had missed the target I'd aimed for, but it had grazed the second, blowing half of both of them out of existence. It left the rest of the target scorched, and black marks lined the floor as well. I stared for a moment as the grin I was unable to hold back crept onto my face. "Let's do that again!" I exclaimed, quickly aiming for the nearest target.

An alarm sounded from Blackwell's helmet, and we all quickly turned in his direction. "Hold on, guys. I'm getting a breaking news notification," he said, putting his finger against the side of his helmet and answering the call.

I frowned. I guess I'd have to shoot it later. I put the gun down to my side, and felt it magnetize to my belt, yanking it out of my hand. I looked around to make sure no one had seen that. *Lots of little quirks*, I thought. I'd have to get used to those.

Blackwell violently threw his hand down in front of him. "Damnit!" he shouted, leaning his head back.

I saw Red Kelvin jump, and the tingling sensation throughout my body was telling me something was wrong. It was obvious that Steel Cowboy was alarmed, as well as Whirl. I hadn't seen this side of Blackwell, so I had no idea what was in store.

"Everyone needs to report to the lobby—now!" Blackwell bellowed. His voice trembled with anger as he turned abruptly to leave the training room, his cape swinging to the side. The rest of us followed him, worried, but also curious as to what was happening.

Was this our first mission? He may get angry when bad things happen. I knew I did. We stood in the lobby, ready for orders, and Blackwell turned on the television in the lobby and sharply looked in my direction. I turned my attention to the screen.

"BREAKING NEWS," the screen read. "Mugging Put to an End by Fiery Vigilante"

"Shit," I said aloud. I knew it was going to be talked about, but I didn't know it was going to make the news—or that it was caught on video. I was hoping that the story would spread across the nightlife.

The news video jumped to a shot of me blocking the muggers' attacks, and it stayed on me until I threw the fireball, which I now realized was sloppy.

Very sloppy.

"Tell your gang that Persevere is here, and the Mandiri had better watch their backs," I heard my voice say. The video hadn't captured my voice well, but the words were clear.

Blackwell's booming, angry voice cut through my focus.

"Was I *unclear* when I told you to stay low?" he roared, practically fuming. "And the same night I told you that? Are you *kidding* me?"

Everything in my chest dropped, and my throat tightened up. I hated being yelled at, and seeing Blackwell like this terrified me.

"No, sir," I said. "But what should I have—" Blackwell interrupted me, putting a tight grip on my shoulder.

I saw him calm down, and he changed his tone abruptly. "I apologize for losing my temper," he said in a calmer voice as his grip loosened. "You did the right thing, but the timing of this crime was poor." Blackwell lifted his hand from my shoulder and turned to the rest of them, who were equally as distraught as myself. He started to pace in front of us, looking at the floor while he did so. He stopped, looking at each of us again as he began to speak.

"I think it's time I told you why I asked that you stayed low." He let out a deep breath. "I should have explained this before, but I wanted to avoid the fear that this information will conjure. I wanted to wait until you've at least understood how to wield your abilities."

Blackwell turned off the television. There was a moment of thought-out silence before his words slowed. "Project Barricade has a major enemy faction that we're dealing with called the Followers, led by a monster who calls himself Veka. I can promise all of you will eventually run into a member or a battalion from this force, whether you joined Project Barricade or not." His gaze fell on Steel Cowboy, who had mentioned being attacked by a group already. I made the connection, but I wasn't sure the others had.

"Who are in the Followers?" Whirl asked calmly.

"Veka's forces are vast. While having android ground forces due to a lack of human supporters, our main threat is the Experiments. They are Followers who have devoted their entire existence to Veka's whims." He shuddered. "Some are people, others are not, and the rest can no longer be considered human. Veka is a universal plague. His Followers follow him blindly in hopes of promised power, and he has outposts on many different planets."

We looked at each other, partially in fear of what was to come. Knowing I had seen things in my dreams that supported what he was saying shook me to the core. "What does he want with us?" I asked.

"Veka targets anyone who calls themselves a hero. He thinks killing people is a game, and because you became known, there is a chance that Project Barricade will be found out as well, putting all the heroes in danger. He will do his damnedest to do everything he can to make us suffer, and he will be laughing and getting pleasure out of the entire experience," Blackwell finished, ending his gaze with me.

That whole dream I had about him made sense now. How were we supposed to stand up against this monster? If he had so many Followers, how would we combat them? My adrenaline caused my hands to shake. I was more terrified than I had ever been. This was a much bigger dilemma than a school test, and if any of my friends got hurt, it would be my fault. In fact, if anyone got hurt, whether it was from Veka or Johnny, it would still be on me.

I saw the faces of the other heroes, and they all shared the same emotion. We were all horrified to learn about who we were up against, and none of us knew what to do at this point, but they weren't putting the blame on me. Every one of them, including Blackwell, knew that I made the best decision.

"I got angry, because the reason I told you to stay low is so you wouldn't be on his radar yet. I don't want him to attack before I have the chance to train you," he said. "I'm upset that you were made public because if Veka sees it, he won't be blind to your powers, but I know that it was the best option in the reality of the situation. You are all beginning your own heroes' journey, and I will make sure I properly prepare you for it."

The room grew silent during a long pause. "So what do we do?" I asked, trying to spark up a conversation. Certainly, some hope existed, or we wouldn't have formed this group.

"We need to train. Get you guys up to speed with your abilities, and for now, pray that Veka doesn't come after you personally," he replied. "I do have some good news. Veka is so busy with his own aspirations that *if* you are put on his radar, he will likely send one of the Experiments after you first."

Red Kelvin looked devastated. "How is that good news?" he asked. "He's going to kill us." Red Kelvin began to freak out, and I walked up to him, patting his shoulder to calm him down.

"There's still hope. As a team, we stand a chance. As for the Followers, the Experiments are much less of a threat than Veka is. Just stick together. Make sure if you go anywhere in your suits, you're not alone, and you should be fine. We will train hard, and we will make certain that we stand a chance when the time comes to fight. I didn't want to worry you with him in the beginning, so I apologize for this conversation needing to happen now," Blackwell said. "All of you heroes have great strengths, and I will help you develop your strongest assets. Don't lose hope, because together we can defeat Veka and the Followers."

The heroes, although still distraught, felt a little bit better with that sliver of hope.

"I'm going to let you decide what you do for the remainder of your night. You can work on your training or stop. If you decide to stop, I ask that you stick to the regular schedule. Tomorrow I will go over your equipment, and we will each go over our powers together. In the following weeks, once we can use our powers to their fullest, we will continue to build ourselves as a team and hone our abilities," Blackwell informed us.

The heroes looked at each other, and Red Kelvin and Whirl decided to call it a night, hoping for a better tomorrow. Steel Cowboy decided to train, and I followed him to work out for a bit.

I stepped onto a treadmill since cardio was my weakest point. I started to jog in hopes that a good workout would thin out the numbness in my chest, but I was only confronted by my fears. With my thoughts bouncing back and forth between Johnny, Veka, and now Blackwell, questions flowed through my mind. Was Johnny going to hurt someone? What should I do? How many of us did Veka know about? Was Blackwell going to be alright? I began to feel a shortness of breath, but I wasn't sure if it was the running or my body falling into panic. Was I going to die? Throughout the hundreds of questions pushing their way over my inner walls, one persisted and stood over the rest.

Was I already on Veka's radar?

Chapter 17

The Apprentice

Johnny trudged forward, gliding on the wet grass and holding his swollen hand. "They're going to pay..." he said to himself, wincing in pain. As he climbed the hill in front of him, his foot slipped, sending him falling onto his wrist.

Johnny screamed in agony, clutching his injury as if squeezing it would make the pain go away. As he leaned against a tree, wheezing from his still-broken ribs, he looked into the sky while rain bombarded his face. "I can't go back home," he said as his face clenched. There were no more tears to fall, yet he still felt like he hadn't cried enough. His mother's voice rang in his head. When he was suspended and his mother found out what had happened, all hell had broken loose at home.

"You let him *beat* you?" his mother had screamed as she slapped Johnny across the mouth. "I didn't raise you that way. You're failing half your classes, and now you're getting beat up. You're never going to be good enough. I thought you were at least better than *one* person at that school, but here you are showing me you'll always be at the bottom!"

Johnny's memory faltered, for he didn't want to think about the rest. That had been when she started beating on him. His father was gone. Still physically there but so high on heroin that he might as well have been out of the house. His mother was abusing pills. The only way he ever gained any respect or peace was when he was able to say someone was beneath him. "Why?" Johnny said, looking into the sky. "Why have you always hated me, God?!"

Johnny slammed his good hand against the ground next to him in frustration as he reminded himself to breathe. "Why did you do this to me?!" he said through his sadness. "Why did you take everything away? You haven't given me anything in life, so why did you take what I made for myself?" he wailed, breaking out into uncontrollable sobbing. "Show me!" Johnny's voice strained through the pounding of the storm around him as he made his demands. "Show me why, God!"

He looked down at the puddle forming around him, nearly giving up in his rage, and his own reflection was clear as day in front of him. His lips began quivering in anger, and as his nose wrinkled, he roared, punching the cursed image. "You're not even real, are you?" He raised his gaze to what was in front of him, and as a clap of thunder filled his ears, the sky lit up to highlight a human-like silhouette in the distance.

Johnny gasped, surprised anyone was out here in this weather. Johnny wondered if it was the police looking for him; he almost wanted them to take him away. Anything to escape his parents' home. Away from the abuse, away from Tony, away from the demeaning looks of everyone at school. As the figure closed in on him, he realized it wasn't the authorities.

"G-god?" Johnny sputtered, not knowing what else this could be right now. The man was very tall, standing around 6'4", and Johnny could have sworn he saw glowing yellow eyes. He shook his head in disbelief. "Hello?"

He heard a chuckle that made him uneasy. Like a knife slicing through flesh. "I am not your god; I am something much worse," the figure said in a rough, scratchy voice. As the being came into focus, Johnny realized he *was* seeing him correctly.

Johnny's heart leapt out of his chest as the ragged voice pierced through the storm like lightning. "Who are you?" Johnny asked. The figure was close to him now, towering over him from beneath his cloak.

"You will know my name in time. I am not your god, but I will be your salvation. What is your name, kid?" he asked, his voice carving through the wind.

Johnny's mouth opened, and his eyes widened. Turning to sprint away, Johnny let out a terrified scream. He fumbled, falling over himself as he tried desperately to escape. Surely, he was hallucinating. Was it because of the pain? Everything ached.

A low chime rang out, and the being appeared a few feet in front of Johnny, shadowy smoke falling away from him as he stood with a six-foot staff. Johnny screamed again, turning in the other direction.

Following another chime, the figure appeared in front of him again. "Stop running and hear me out!" the scratchy voice snapped, reaching out with a clawed hand the color of eggplant and grabbing Johnny's head. He pushed Johnny to the ground then took his hand off Johnny's head.

He looked up at the cloaked being, staring at the creature that would likely end his miserable life. He stood back up, realizing the figure was going to allow him to stand. He took a step back with his arms raised out in front of him. He tried to speak, but his words were stuck in his throat. He took a second step, feeling the ominous, cold aura of whoever, or whatever, this creature was.

"I'll skip the pleasantries then. My Followers have had their eyes on you for quite a while, Johnny."

Johnny gasped in panic. Despite this creature's voice being higher pitched than expected, it was still a strong voice with no lack of projection. It seemed to have an inhuman echo as if the words lingered in the air after being spoken—even through the storm. Johnny began to sweat, but despite his dread, he felt the need to hear this creature out. It was as if he had something especially important to say.

"Who are you? W-why have you been watching me?" Johnny asked, stumbling over his words and stuttering through fear. Goosebumps settled on his arms as he clenched his fists, trying to look strong.

"I've been keeping a close eye on you and Tony, so I know of your connection to him. I have heard of your most recent encounters as well. You see, I'm looking for someone special. Someone who is filled with hate and willing to take any opportunity to achieve what they desire. My question for you is how much do you want to hurt those who have pained you?" His eyes squinted, and the details in them were illuminated to Johnny. Around his catlike, slit pupils was a crimson ring. His eyes emitted a mustard-like glow, and beneath them were two glowing slits for a nose.

"Why does it matter to you? It looks like you can handle your problems by yourself. Why do you care about Tony so much?" Johnny asked, his mind filling with questions.

He chuckled. It was one that matched the rumble of the thunder behind them. "I need someone I can turn into my apprentice. What fun is there if I do it all myself? I've been watching Tony because he now has powers. I will not elaborate on how he got them at this time, but as you've noticed, he is much stronger and can conjure fire."

"Wait," Johnny started, grabbing the sides of his head. "How hard did I hit my head? You, a cloaked figure with glowing eyes and purple skin are trying to tell me that the kid I pushed around got superpowers during his coma? Do his friends have powers now too? I must be losing my fucking mind."

The creature cackled again. "It's a long story, but no—his friends don't. You haven't lost your mind, but your eyes are being opened to a darker, unknown aspect of life. I can give you the power to defeat Tony, but I have to believe you're willing to follow through."

Johnny thought about what he wanted and looked into this creature's eyes for a sign that he could trust him. When he realized he was on his own, he sighed. "Can you give me fire powers like him?" Johnny asked, clenching his fists again; his anger toward Tony returned. Despite his previous words, he didn't actually want to kill Tony. He wanted the pain to stop. He wanted to control the life around him. Sure, making Tony suffer would be a bonus, and after the control Tony had ripped away from him, someone had to pay for it.

"I can promise you you'll be able to destroy him yourself. In regard to the fire abilities, I have something else in mind. Something I think you'll enjoy much more."

Without any more hesitation, Johnny smiled and nodded his head. "I'll do it. I have what it takes." Images flashed through his mind of being able to take on anyone he wished. If he had that kind of power, the world couldn't hold him down anymore. His family couldn't bully him anymore.

The creature smiled beneath his hood. "Good. Tony has labeled himself a hero, therefore I am obligated to destroy him, but it isn't enough to just neutralize him," he started. "Heroes deserve a hero's death, after all. They're all destined to fail, and I'm going to provide them *all* their own personalized suffering."

The statement made Johnny shudder, and he questioned what he was getting himself into. He realized he had nothing left to lose, and that this would give him a chance for revenge. He didn't care where this led him. As long as he ended with that power, he didn't care what it took.

The creature stretched out his hand, and Johnny grabbed it and shook it. He was once again surprised when it was cold, seemingly without a pulse. Was he even alive?

"My name is Veka, and I need to give you some important information, Johnny. Let's talk." He put his hand on Johnny's shoulder and slammed his staff into the ground, which emitted an echoing, metal chime as they disappeared into a cloud of dark smoke.

Chapter 18

Base Stats

I pushed through the crowd of rushing students exiting the school. Today had been a long Friday, and everyone was excited for the football game. I was hearing rumors about what happened to Johnny and wondering what the answer to that question was myself. Where did he end up? I doubt he went home, considering what he had said about his mom.

"I guess Johnny just couldn't handle the same kind of stuff he's been dishing out," a guy said, laughing.

"What a loser," a girl replied. "He'll never amount to anything in life, especially now that he's got *that* on his record."

"Did you see what Tony Jensen did to those guys? They were a mess!"

"That honestly scared me so much," a girl said.

The situation came close to bothering me. If it weren't for the fact that Johnny had been a bully for years, I would have empathized, and maybe even defended him. That was the same crap they used to say about me. I frowned.

He deserved it for what he's done to us, but I ruined his life, so I needed to fix this if I could.

"Tony! Over here!" Alex's voice rang out in the distance, and I searched for its location. I found her and Shawn standing over at the edge of the sidewalk, beaming in anticipation, so I hurried over to them.

"Where's Talida?" I asked, getting a shrug in reply.

"She went home early, but she wouldn't tell us why. She didn't look like she was feeling very well," Shawn answered, his voice giving away his worry.

"That sucks. I hope she gets better soon. It's not like her to leave early," I said, confused. I hadn't ever seen her leave early. I began to worry, thinking about Johnny. Did he do something to affect her? I shook my head. I was getting paranoid. She was probably just sick. "Did you see her leave?" I asked.

"Yeah, she was by herself. Her dad still doesn't have a car, so I think she walked. Do you think she's okay?" Shawn asked, giving me the impression that his thoughts were in the same place as mine.

"The police are watching the school grounds. No one has heard anything from Johnny, so I think she'll be okay," I replied.

"I swear if Johnny does anything to hurt her, I'll kill him," Shawn said, shaking his head.

"Count me in," Alex added. "I like that girl."

"I feel that." I sighed. This conversation wasn't making the situation any better. "There will be hell to pay, for sure. No one is ever going to mess with my friends or family again."

Shawn and Alex looked at each other and then at me. "Well, are you able to go to the game? We could all go check on her before grabbing something to eat." Alex said, smiling at me.

I frowned. I really wanted to, but Blackwell was going to be running us through our tests for our official stats. This last week had been getting us started with working out and learning how to use our equipment. Blackwell had been right about my appetite increasing after using my powers regularly. I was always starving, and with my limited amount of money, it was going to be hard to feed myself if the hideout cafeteria didn't open soon. "I can't today, sadly. I really wanted to, but I have another graphic design project to do. Hopefully, we can catch the next one!" I said excitedly.

While I wanted to enjoy the band's show at halftime, I needed to go to the hideout and train first. This was an important night. I needed to make sure I was ready for Veka if he or his Followers were to attack. I also wasn't lying to them. I had put myself out there online for graphic design, and I had been getting a steady stream of jobs out of it once I had uploaded a portfolio on a website Nikki had helped me create.

The two of them looked disappointed. "Darn, but hopefully next time," Alex said with hope. "We all need to hang out more; I like you guys."

"I agree. It would be a lot of fun," I replied with a smile. "I'm down to hang out tomorrow like we talked about. We could game and get to know each other more. I'm sure the two of you will have a great time, though! I'm going to go ahead and head out."

Shawn smiled and made eye-contact with Alex. They kissed, looking passionately into each other's eyes. "Have a good night then, man! We'll see you tomorrow. Hopefully, Talida will be back and feeling good by then. We'll check on her on the way to the restaurant."

"Thank you both, for real," I said. I waved goodbye and began to walk away from the school grounds toward my van. Part of me was worried about the game, but after the Johnny incident, the school had decided to inform the police, and they were doubling the guards for today's game. I didn't think anything would happen, but I was glad the school decided to have more officers on duty.

* * *

I made my way to the hideout, and to my surprise, I got there quickly. With all the drama, I had forgotten to talk to Blackwell about Johnny. I checked my phone and saw a text from Shawn.

My heartrate spiked as I opened the message.

Shawn: Talida's mom answered the door and told us she was okay and resting. Have a good night man!

I let out a sigh of relief. That was the information I needed. When I walked into the building, Blackwell was startled.

"You're here early. Did you come to train, or is something else on your mind?" Blackwell asked, breaking away from what he was doing to walk up to me. It was abnormal for me to be here during the day with school.

"Well, I came to train, but I also wanted to ask your advice on an issue I'm dealing with at the moment," I said.

"What can I help you with, Tony? Is it personal, or is it more of a generalized concern?" he asked, giving me his full attention.

"It's a little bit of both. I have been having problems with Johnny, a school bully, and he assaulted me the other day. While running away, he said he was going to kill me. I was wondering if you had any advice on the situation," I said, surprised that I was so comfortable talking to him.

"I'm aware of Johnny. Due to your file, and my Eyes and Ears, I know a lot about him. In regard to the threat, do you think he meant it, or was it something he said in that moment of rage?"

"I'm not sure. He said he would make my life hell. Apparently, he's been having problems at home, and I don't think he has anywhere to go. I mean, if it were just me against him, I wouldn't have an issue. Not with these powers. I'm worried about my friends and their families. I don't know what to do," I said. I couldn't be everywhere at once. I couldn't protect everyone. He *was* injured, though.

"Well, most likely he'll just go after you. But on the off chance that he goes after someone else, I'd watch your friends closely, and I would alert their families of the threat," Blackwell said.

"They told their parents, and they will watch for him, but is there another way to help my friends? I'm not sure if he'll figure out where they live and try to hurt them or not," I said, not able to think of anything else.

"I can have some of my agents patrol and keep an eye on your friends to make sure they stay safe. I won't be able to watch them while they are home, but I can make sure their trips from the school to their destinations are safe," he said.

I smiled. "That would make me feel better. I can't be everywhere at once, so having somebody check on them would be great," I said. "Thank you so much. On another note, what's the plan tonight with training?" I needed to stray away from thoughts of Johnny before I drove myself insane.

"I already finished the basic training with Steel Cowboy. He's improving with his equipment. We'll be doing a strength and speed test. Tomorrow night I will have you on the combat trainer after teaching each of you to fight with your weapons. I'll have each of you do basic sword training as well," he said.

"Okay. Why do we need to do sword training?" I asked, a little confused. If I ever had to go into battle, what good would a sword be against enemies with powers or guns?

"Most of our enemies use a mix of melee weapons and ranged weapons. Veka himself prefers a scythe and can teleport. It will be important to be able to combat his Followers as well because some of them won't be affected by our ranged weapons. A good example of that is your Titan Fiber suit. It's bulletproof, for the most part, though it can be punctured by blade," he answered. He opened the door to the hideout. "If you would like, I can go ahead and put you on the strength and speed tests. Then tonight it will be free range training."

I nodded, now understanding the schedule for the next few days. Maybe if I got through these tests, I could meet up with Shawn and Alex. "Okay, that makes sense. Sure, I'd like to be further along than I am right now. How is Steel Cowboy handling his rope thing?" I asked, curious since I hadn't seen what had happened recently. He had been struggling with it the last week. I don't think either of them told me what it was called. At least, I didn't remember.

Blackwell chuckled. "We call it his electric lasso. He's still struggling with it, having problems with the release once he latches onto something. He's been figuring out how to launch it, and he's getting better at that. Slowly, but surely, he's getting it under control. Red Kelvin has improved tremendously on equipping his shields." Blackwell had equipped Red Kelvin's suit with a shield on both arms so that he could battle people with weapons while using his fire abilities. Blackwell turned to head into the hideout, and I followed him down into the lobby.

After I changed into my suit, he led me to the strength test. Looking around, I could see what looked to be a giant rock column with a bench underneath. The column was held up by two giant metal claws on its sides.

"I think Red Kelvin and Steel Cowboy are in the library studying, but we can go ahead and record your base stats on the strength test," he said as we walked across the training room.

"That sounds good, how is it rated? Like, how are the stats created?" I asked, curious as to how we would compare to each other. It was something MIRA hadn't explained within the pod.

"Primary stats are on a scale of 1 to 17. That involves strength, speed, and reflexes. Seventeen being the best and one being frail. Four is about where the average human lies. Secondary stats are on a scale of 0 to 10 and encompasses things like skin durability, fire potency, and how long you can hold your fire. Any number on secondary stats are beyond a human's ability."

"Oh, okay. That's neat," I replied as we stopped walking.

"The first test is set up like a bench press, so go ahead and hop on. The way we do this is the machine holding the stone will adjust the load for each level. What you lift will gradually become heavier until we find where you lie on the scale. It will also press something into your skin to test your durability. Don't worry, it won't pierce you."

I lay down, looking up at the flat stone directly above me. *That's intimidating,* I thought nervously. Handles were built into the column for me to hold onto. Before I grabbed the bar, an extending metal arm on my right lifted and jabbed me with a metal rod. It caught me off-guard, and I jerked with an exclamation. "Ow!" Before I even got the word out, it pulled back and was over. Blackwell gave a chuckle.

"Looks like you're at a 3 on skin durability. Looks like you can take a punch. Not bad, Persevere. Ready when you are on the strength test."

As I wrapped my fingers around the handles, I looked over at Blackwell, who was waiting for me. "I'm ready," I said, not quite sure what to expect. I narrowed my eyebrows with determination. I had to give this my all if I were to see an accurate depiction of what I could do.

Blackwell nodded, tapping on his helmet. The claws moved, and the column began to get heavier. I held it up straight, waiting for it to go to the next level, and so far, I wasn't struggling. As the contraption shifted once and then again, Blackwell began to laugh beneath his helmet. I began to wonder if he enjoyed causing us pain. I started to hold my breath, the column becoming heavier than I could handle.

I began to breathe again, trying to control what was bearing down on me. I started to cry out, exerting my remaining strength into the column to prove to myself that I could do it. The threat of Veka loomed over my mindset, and I knew that I needed to push further if I was going to defend the reality that he threatened.

The column continued to grow heavier, and after one last burst of strength, my arms gave out and the claws caught the column, holding it above me just like when I had started. Blackwell was quiet for a while as his MIRA system processed what I had done.

With a grunt of confusion that quickly turned into excitement, Blackwell spoke. "Congratulations, Persevere. You've earned an 8.5 ranking. Very nice for your first test." He raised his hand to give me a high-five. After I reciprocated, I began to think.

Wow, that was pretty strong. If a human was a four, I wondered how much stronger an 8.5 was. I assumed it was a lot more than double, but how much weight could I lift?

"I'm okay with that. How much potential do I have? How do I grow from here?" I asked, curious as to how much I could improve myself.

"After training, if you weight lift and try hard, you should easily be able to reach a 10, which would be intimidating. As you get older, and your body matures, that can increase as well." Blackwell began to focus, putting his hand on the bottom of his helmet in thought. "I'm baffled, to be honest. 8.5 is amazing for a hero with multiple powers. Usually, powers become mediocre if more than one is flowing through the body. I'm at an 11, and I've been honing my strength for years now. That's with more than one ability as well."

I cocked my head. "More than one ability? What other powers do you have, if I may ask?" I asked. He had never mentioned having multiple.

I saw that this question made him uncomfortable, and it was starting to make me question what was going on. What wasn't he telling me? What would be so important that he couldn't tell one of his members?

After a short pause, Blackwell spoke up. "I also have enhanced durability of my skin and enhanced reflexes. Keep that between us, because if Veka gets wind of that information, he will find a way to combat it."

That made sense. I wouldn't want Veka to find out and develop new ways to defeat us.

"Let's go ahead and do your speed test. Keep in mind that your speed will be faster than a normal human since your strength will be exerted from your legs as well. Have you tried to run since you got powers?" Blackwell asked me.

Me? Run? That wasn't usually in my cards. I giggled to myself. "Other than using the treadmill last night, I've avoided running for a very long time," I answered, chuckling. "I didn't realize it would work like that. I mean, once you think about it that way, it all makes sense. What good would it be if you only had the strength in your arms?"

We walked toward the track, and I began to get nervous. I had seen movies where people weren't able to control their speed, and they ended up sliding into a wall or hurting themselves. It could happen to me. Something always goes horrendously wrong.

"Alright, so I'm going to have you do the straight mile. Once we find your burst speed, you can test yourself to make sure you can take corners in your daily training," Blackwell said as I lined up on the track, preparing to be timed.

Blackwell quickly counted me down, and I pushed myself off the starting line. My speed was pretty normal at first. I started focusing on what I was doing, pushing my feet against the ground as hard as I could. I accelerated, scaring myself with how fast I was moving, but my fear was simultaneously replaced by the feeling that I had never been stronger or lighter in my entire life. It felt great.

As I neared Blackwell again, he nodded in approval. "Nice job, Persevere. You've earned a 6 ranking on speed. Well done!"

After a couple of hours of training, the other heroes joined us. I had been shown some basic exercises to improve myself, and as I was doing them, the other heroes earned their ranks. Steel Cowboy received an outstanding 13 rank in strength and a 7.5 rank in speed, accompanied by a skin durability of 7! Red Kelvin followed up with a 4 in strength and a 4.7 in speed. Nikki lagged behind with a rank of 3.5 in strength and 4.5 in speed.

"Since we are running ahead of schedule, I'm going to go ahead and start basic sword training. Tomorrow we will begin to use the combat trainer," Blackwell said. We began to head over to a smaller area of the room, which had several dummies.

"I will be introducing you to the proper techniques to use with simple-bladed weapons. We will go over the basics, from holding the blade to swinging it, and then I will show you some more interesting techniques that I think will fit your abilities and..." Blackwell paused for a moment, putting his finger up to his helmet as he received a notification.

He spun around, looking the opposite direction as us. His other hand reached his helmet as he became distressed. I wasn't sure what was going on, but I could feel the energy shift within the room.

Blackwell's words rushed from his lips, emphasizing his desperation. "There's an attack on the high school. Three attackers wearing black cloaks and wielding swords. Persevere and…"

I interrupted him, my breath practically being ripped from my throat. "The high school?!" I exclaimed. *The football game!* My breathing turned to short gasps as I broke out into a cold sweat. "I have to go! My friends are there!" I pulled my Blaze Ray from my side and began to run out of the training room.

Chapter 19

Attack on Belmont High

"Persevere! We need to..." Blackwell's voice trailed off as I fled the room, ignoring whatever he was going to say next.

My friends were in danger. I didn't have time to plan this—I had to act. I sprinted toward the school, running as fast as I knew how. As I propelled forward, I shoulder-checked a tree, not having seen it. As it fell, I grimaced and continued forward, ripping through the forest like a rampant wildfire. Tripping over rocks and bouncing against trees, I pushed desperately to move faster.

Come on. Focus, I thought as I neared the attack. I arrived on the school grounds quickly, looking around haphazardly for the attackers. "Where are they?" I whispered.

As I ran toward the front door of the school, my heart was split by several piercing gunshots followed by a scream. *Three, four, five,* I counted, darting in another direction as I realized the noise was coming from the football stadium. I pulled my Blaze Ray. *No, no, no!* I thought, thinking the worst. I couldn't even yell for them; I'd give away my identity. *Fuck!*

As I rounded the corner of the building, adrenaline tearing through my veins, I could see what the commotion was about. One of the officers who was supposed to be watching the game was on his back, and there was someone on top of him. The person was tall, in a black cloak, and was trying to stab a blade into the officer. I knew that this was the time for a superhero. But what was the attacker? It was no man.

As I looked closely, I realized it was an android! It looked in my direction, and I could see multiple holes in its chest where it had been shot. Looking at the face beneath the hood, I saw glowing yellow eyes and a rectangular open mouth on what looked to be a matte-black face. It gave the appearance of someone wearing a mask, similar to that of a Japanese Oni.

"Oh my goth!" I exclaimed in horror as it stood. It had completely stopped what it was doing, turning its attention to me instead of trying to stab the man. It was obvious the officer had injured it, for it moved slowly and sparks shot from its chest. As I stood wide-eyed, not knowing what to do, the android stepped over the officer and took a step toward me. I looked to the man still on the ground who was breathing heavily and lying in a pool of blood. If I was going to save him, I would need to be quick. I didn't think he had been stabbed, but it seemed I was wrong.

The sight took my breath, causing me to become nauseated. "Just who we wanted to see," a voice spoke through the mouth of the android. It was deep and emulated.

It suddenly bolted forward.

My stomach lurched into my chest as I pulled the trigger on my Blaze Ray. Before the attack could strike, a black energy shield sprung out from its arm, blocking the ray I had sent toward it.

I quickly jumped out of the way of the oncoming swing and threw a punch toward the android from the side. I was easily blocked, and as it took another swing, I managed to block it with my shoulder plate. I pulled the trigger again, this time at its open leg. There was a buzz as it fell to the ground, losing its stance as it lost most of its movement capability.

It pushed itself back to its feet with a staggered stance, taking another bloodthirsty swing in my direction. I dodged, and in retaliation, I swung my fist at it, cracking the face plate of the android. It fell to the ground, and now I could see wiring and smaller plates, more of what made this thing tick. "Not bad for an amateur," a voice said through it.

My hand trembled, likely from adrenaline. I sent multiple bolts toward the android, and I must have struck something important because the light in its eyes went out, and it fell to the ground in a heap. I ran to the officer. "Are you hurt?" I asked, now standing over him. Looking down to see the damage, I could see that he had a large V cut into his chest. While he was losing a lot of blood, it wasn't going to be fatal, as long as help was on the way.

He nodded weakly, looking up at me in confusion. "Go help the others," he wheezed, trying to catch his breath.

I looked around, making sure there weren't any other attackers nearby, and I bent down, picking him up and leaning him against a wall. "Help is on the way," I said. "You're going to be alright."

Knowing I needed to get moving again, I began to look around, searching for clues as to where Shawn and Alex were, along with the other attackers. *The bleachers,* I thought, heading down the hill toward them. Blackwell said there were three of them, so two left. With one guard down, there were about five more somewhere. With the shields and the surprise attack, I questioned how the other guards were fairing. A multitude of questions revolved in my head, all threatening to tell me the chances of Shawn and Alex being okay were slim.

I heard fighting ahead, so I sprinted toward the noise. I thought I had heard gunshots while I was dealing with the android, but as I had obviously been busy, I wasn't sure. As my eyes connected with the source, I saw three football players that were beating another attacker against the ground with anything they could grab. Multiple gunshot holes were in it, so it seemed like the other guard had dispatched this android.

"Are any of you hurt?" I yelled.

A few of the players looked up at me confused, but they could tell I didn't mean any harm. The officer, on the other hand, pointed his gun at me and stepped forward. "On the ground!" he yelled. "Drop the weapon!"

"Wait! I'm not your enemy. I'm here to help!" I said, surprised as to why they wanted to attack me now. I knew why, but it still caught me off guard. I flipped my Blaze Ray to stun, my hand trembling again.

"Get on the ground!" he said slower this time. I didn't have time for this.

"Please, there are others in trouble! There's another attacker somewhere. I'm on your side!"

Seeing that I wasn't going to back down, and I was being put in the same group as the attackers, the officer took a shot. As a bullet bounced against my chest, I was terrified. As I stood there, gathering my courage to pull the trigger, thoughts began racing through my head again. I had to go. I needed to shoot him and find my friends. I wasn't killing him. I clenched my teeth, knowing it was my only logical option at this point, and pulled the trigger, shocking him into unconsciousness.

"I'm sorry," I said as the officer struck the ground. While the others lifted their hands as if they feared me, I lowered my Blaze Ray. "I'm on your side, but others need help. He'll be okay. I tased him. Are any of you hurt?" I repeated.

"A few cuts, but we're fine. We'll be alright here. That officer got the attacker down before he could do much damage."

"Okay—I'll go find the others!" I managed to reply, leaving their presence. I was glad they were able to handle the android. I was surprised I was able to take out that first one. They seemed pretty well trained for androids. And why did it speak to me? I turned my attention to the bleachers, needing to find my friends. *Where the hell are you?*

Chapter 20

The Locker Room

Content Warning: Contains loss.

"Hurry! This way!" Shawn hissed toward Alex, pulling her behind the bleachers. "We can hide in the locker room until this situation is taken care of."

"Are you sure?" Alex asked, her voice cracking amidst her terror. "Why is this happening?"

"I don't know. It seems like they're after something. Come on!"

As the two of them ran past the bathrooms and into the locker room, they frantically searched for a place to hide. They found a dark corner near the wall behind a heavy plastic table. Shawn wrapped his arms around Alex, both of them trembling.

"Everything's going to be okay," he whispered in her ear, holding her tight. He could feel her breathing shorten as fear began to take hold. "I'll protect you."

"Please. I'm so scared." Her words distressed Shawn. They had only been on a few dates, but he felt like he had been with her forever. He enjoyed her presence in his life, and he would do anything he could to make sure she stayed safe.

"I've got you."

Just as he finished those words, a man entered the room. Shawn and Alex quickly ducked down, trying to hide in the shadows. They didn't get a good look at him, but he was definitely different than the other attackers. This one was still cloaked but human. He wore a matte-black mask with a rectangular mouth. Two short black horns rested on the forehead.

There was a grim laugh as a bright light filled the room, revealing their position. Shawn stood up, wide-eyed. He had to do something. Anything. In an attempt to catch the attacker off-guard, Shawn shoved the table toward him. The man swung his arm upward, launching the heavy table against the wall with a slam.

While Shawn knew the table was plastic, it didn't seem like it should have been lifted that easily. There was something wrong with this attacker. He ran to the side as the man lunged toward him, slamming his fist into a locker next to him. Sure enough, the dark green metal bent easily under the power of his strike. Shawn nearly screamed as he saw the man now wielding a thin black blade.

Shawn could see the attacker's eyes latch onto Alex. He turned away from Shawn and swung his sword down at her. Shawn moved quickly, leaping in front of the blade.

"Alex!" Shawn bellowed, attempting to knock the sword out of the attacker's hand. In the process of attempting the block, he was cut across the face and let out a moan of pain. Alex had been wailing, but then she roared and threw a punch at the man's groin, trying anything she could to save their lives. She pulled back as if she had struck a wall.

The man stood there, having no reaction at all. He took another swing, this one leaving a deep gash across Shawn's arm. As Shawn screamed, the man kicked his legs, breaking one of his knees. He hit the floor with a piercing CRACK. As he lay there on his back, every breath of wind was knocked from him by a powerful blow to the chest. CRUNCH! Stronger than any man had the right to hit. What kind of monster was this?

With what strength he had left, Shawn raised his head and looked across the room. Anger, sadness, and complete horror swirled within him; he knew there was nothing he could do. He tried to get up, and that's when he felt the pain. The immense torture his many broken ribs were haunting him with. He tried to do anything he could to put himself between the man and his girlfriend. As he lifted himself again, his arm gave out beneath him, sending him back down with a crash. He was sure every bone in his chest was shattered. He couldn't breathe. Every tiny breath was an impossible chore.

The man grabbed Alex, and she was able to land an elbow to his chin and then his throat. He backed up, loosening his grip to grab his neck as the bottom of his mask split and fell off, revealing his mouth. She booked it to the door, screaming for someone to help. Before she could make it, he grabbed her again, this time stabbing her through the shoulder with his sword.

Crying out because of her pain, she was violently slammed against the ground. Looking over to Shawn her eyes were soaked with tears.

"Help!" she screamed through her agony. "Shawn, help!" She was silenced with a knee to her jaw. She was now on her back, right across from Shawn. He could see that she knew he couldn't help her, which made his chest tighten even more.

Shawn's soaked cheeks pressed harder against the chilled concrete floor as his body weakened and his vision wavered. He tried to rise again, to do anything to save this girl he thought he loved, but he was in so much pain and had lost so much blood that he couldn't form the words he wanted to speak.

His body felt heavy, as if the floor were trying to consume him.

The attacker jumped on Alex, ripping off her shirt and repeatedly slicing her across the chest. Shawn lay there, physically unable to intervene as blood splashed against his face.

"Please, stop!" Shawn whimpered weakly through his sorrow, pleading with the attacker to quit feeding his eyes with horror.

The attacker then changed to stabbing her in the chest, repeating this over and over. As Alex let loose the most mind-numbing, heart-shattering wails, Shawn could hear them become distorted as the blood filled her throat. The room slowly fell into silence as the gurgling screams dissipated, and the only sound left was the squelching from the blade entering and exiting her corpse.

For a moment Shawn hoped that his blood loss would kill him—not the attacker. Anything to be able to go with Alex would be a better option than living. He lay on the ground, questioning if he would be able to live the rest of his life without having saved her.

That is if he could survive at all. There was a glimmer of hope, knowing that if he died today, he would be able to see her again. His thought was interrupted by another person rushing into the room.

Chapter 21

Inner Turmoil

I exploded into the locker room like a powder keg, having heard the screams from outside. As my fingertips became numb with fear, I looked around, assessing the situation. I looked over to the corner, and I could see blood. Two people lay motionless on the ground with an attacker crouched next to one of them. I quickly noticed this attacker was human, and the top half of a matte-black mask with horns covered the top of his face, under a cloak like the others. My heart lurched, and my eyes began to burn in anger when I realized who was there. A shirtless woman with purple hair, and a man who had been all too eager to play video games with us tomorrow.

"Shawn! Alex!" I said, getting no answer in return.

The attacker stood up, his bloodied sword in his hand. As I stormed closer to him, I could see that Alex was…gone. My fist clenched, and a pit of rage began boiling inside of me. The sadness was still there, but the anger quickly masked it, and the only thought going through my mind was killing the murderer in front of me.

The attacker raised his sword, heading toward me. I switched my Blaze Ray out of stun, and I shot the wrist holding the sword. After two rays, the third one struck, blowing a hole through it and causing him to drop the sword. There was a grunt of pain, and he grabbed his wrist, covering the wound.

I gritted my teeth, sprinting toward him, wanting to see him mirror Alex's fate. My arms were consumed in fire. I threw a flaming fist toward him, which landed in the middle of his chest, knocking him to the ground and scorching a hole into his clothing. The man reached for a button on his wrist to enable an energy shield as he croaked for air, but I snatched that wrist. I squeezed, his bones snapping and caving beneath my fingers along with the electronic he was carrying.

I looked toward Shawn as the attacker screamed in pain. He was still clinging to life but barely. My thoughts were interrupted by a loud gasp from Steel Cowboy, who had followed me in. He ran toward us, wide-eyed under his bandana, seeing the horrible situation in front of him.

"Steel Cowboy, get Shawn out of here!" I yelled, pointing to Shawn.

Steel Cowboy ran over to him and then looked at me. "What about her?" he asked, horrified by all the blood in the room as he frantically looked around.

I looked at him, unable to tell him she was gone. I shook my head, and it was the only answer I could give.

He nodded, and I could see the dismay in his eyes. He grabbed Shawn and ran out of the locker room.

I turned back toward the attacker, knowing I now had him all to myself. I shot him a glance, one that I'm sure would have horrified me if I was on the other end of it. "You'd better start *fucking* talking!" I yelled, grabbing him by the hair and dragging him across the locker room. At that moment in time, I wished my grip was tight around his throat rather than his hair.

Yet, there was a moment when my senses came back to me amidst the anger. I was supposed to be a hero. I had to get my answers, and then I had to lock this guy up. I couldn't kill him.

I debated on whether I cared.

I had almost killed Johnny until I backed off, but this guy was different. He wasn't a bully. He was a murderer that had just taken my friends away from me.

A second wind of anger flooded over me as I caught another glance of Alex, and I slammed the attacker into the concrete wall, feeling his ribs snap. I had expected more, but it seemed as though this man was more durable than he should have been.

Good.

That meant I could let loose more on this man than I previously thought. After catching his breath, the attacker began to laugh.

"Why are you here?!" I demanded, beating his head into the wall.

He began to grin, blood slipping between his yellowed teeth, but would not answer. This infuriated me. As my eyebrows furled in fury, I punched him again, questioning why his skull wasn't caving like his hand had previously.

"Who are you after?" I yelled.

The man began to speak, and I took a moment to listen, my muscles tightening as my body pulsed with anger.

"We are after you, through your friends. Our masters told us to attack the couple, and you would show up."

I was taken aback, my emotions confused. Me? Why were they after me? It was my fault Alex was dead, and Shawn might be too? Were these Veka's goons??

I punched him again, this time enjoying the sensation of my knuckles mashing against his skull. After several more strikes against him, shattering his mask, I asked him another question.

"Why are you after me?" I asked. "What have I done to you?" I looked into the man's green eyes, his rough skin, and yellowed teeth peering back at me. Long gray hair was now matted around his face with blood and sweat.

"Our masters commanded it. A warning, if you will." The man grinned. "And there's nothing better than the feeling of a blade slithering through someone's skin. Especially a young woman who means something to the one lying next to her," the man replied, cackling uncontrollably now.

That was it.

That was the one thing the man had to say for me to completely snap.

I burst into an uncontrollable fit of rage, beating him against the wall with both hands, throwing a knee slam in when I could, feeling the man's blood splatter against my suit. I pulled myself away from him, yanking out my Blaze Ray to aim it at the murderer.

"Veka was right about you; you're no different than the rest of us, and you've got potential," the man said weakly, still having that taunting grin slapped on his maw. My blood rushed to my face, and it felt as if my skin was going to burst into flames. He was a monster. He didn't have the right to be locked up.

He deserves to die!

As I knew the thoughts going through my mind were ones of a villain, I didn't care. Why would a hero let this man live? Just so he could do it again?

An odd sense of calm came over me. Maybe not calm but a sort of numbness that scared me. It was as if my body had reached its limit and decided to shut down my emotions.

Why should I listen to him at all? With these powers I now possessed, did I have to listen to anyone?

The attacker laughed between coughs. "You're no hero." He spat blood on the ground next to him.

"Maybe I'm not. Who's to say?" The heavy words fell from my lips, and it took me a moment to realize they had been spoken aloud. They fell as if they were weighted stones, falling from a torn sack. The man's grin disappeared, as if he didn't expect me to say that.

Before the man could speak another word, I pulled the trigger on my Blaze Ray, blowing a hole through the man's head. I stared at the damage long enough for my actions to sink in. My breathing began to accelerate as I realized what I had just done. Why didn't I feel bad about it? He's dead.

I *killed* him. What had almost happened to Johnny came to fruition in this locker room. *I just killed a person.*

I turned to look at Alex, for my stupid mind wouldn't allow me to leave without seeing what the attacker had inflicted with my own eyes. I was appalled by the scene. Tears began to roll down my face. That man took the life of one of my friends and was about to do the same to Shawn. He didn't deserve to live, did he? Or was the killer right when he said I wasn't any different than him? Why did he say I had potential? What if he had loved ones?

My heartrate spiked. I was beginning to freak out. I was a murderer. I wasn't a hero. I was just another killer. I couldn't save Alex. I might not have saved Shawn. I was going to go to jail and never see my friends again. How could I get away with it? Do I just leave? No one could recognize me in my suit. Would I have to get a new suit?

I turned toward the door, looking one more time at the hole in the attacker's head and cringing. It was a horrible sight that I couldn't believe I caused, but I didn't have time to dwell on it. I had to make sure Shawn was okay. I left the locker room, hoping to find the others, and I was alone with my thoughts again.

What made me not a villain? I had fits of rage, I was working under the radar of the police and not with them, and now I had just killed somebody out of anger. Was I a hero? I saved that guy from being mugged despite my orders to stay low. My group and I have good intentions and are trying to help people, but if I didn't exist, would any of this have happened?

Was I the villain?

Chapter 22

Fragmented

I bolted toward the edge of the school grounds, trying to find the others. Did Steel Cowboy take Shawn to the hospital? Where did they go? I searched frantically for a sign. Luckily, my search was quickly ended by hearing the call of my name.

"Persevere! The football field!" Red Kelvin shouted. I quickly turned around and darted in his direction. Red Kelvin was standing there, waving me down. An engine roared in the distance, but I couldn't spot its location.

As I made my way closer to him, my pace slowed to a quick walk, and I saw his mood change from worry to fear. I couldn't tell what exactly had caused it, but judging by his gaze, it was probably my blood-covered suit. With hesitation, he asked "What...happened in there?"

The statement brought my emotions back into play, and my face heated as I tried not to lose my composure again. I locked up, and I was now in that middle ground between sadness and anger, teeter-tottering, my body deciding how to react. I couldn't make eye contact with him right now. I knew that if I did, everything would begin to rush out again, and I would remember... I would remember their lifeless faces on that concrete.

As I stomped past him in anger, I gave him a cold response, for if I gave any more, I would fall apart. Through gritted teeth I mustered, "Three people were hurt. Two by him and one from me."

Red Kelvin tilted his head in confusion. He had never seen me in this agitated state, and it was obviously worrying him. "We should take that attacker in for questioning by Blackwell. Surely, we can find out more than the police can. Does the other victim need medical attention? Blackwell has a medic on the field," Red Kelvin said.

I shook my head, but unable to say more.

Red Kelvin's eyes widened, and his mouth dropped upon his realization of what had just happened, but his response wasn't the one I expected. His fearful look became soft, almost understanding, but I didn't know how he could understand.

"I'm sorry, Tony," he said in a low voice, using my real name to emphasize his apology. "I'm sorry you had to do that, and I'm sorry that I wasn't there to help. If there's anything I can do to lighten the blow of today, please tell me. I understand what you're going through right now," he said, looking me in the eyes as he spoke.

There was true honesty in those eyes; it was a response that a true friend would give, and I knew that it was sincere. He had meant every word, but my mind was latching onto the question of how he could possibly understand what I was going through right now. My brain was taking this animosity toward the man who had just killed my friend, and turning it onto Red Kelvin, and I didn't know why. How dare he look me in the eyes and tell me that he understands!? He didn't see his friends lying on the ground covered in blood! Who the fuck did he think he was!?

"Stop!" I yelled, looking at Red Kelvin sharply. "You can never under-stand what—" I pulled my words back in, looking down at the ground and clenching my fists, wondering if my fingers were going to snap from my grip. I knew I didn't mean the words that were about to come out of my mouth but enough of them slipped out for Red Kelvin to put together the picture of what I was attempting to spout out.

What was wrong with me? My friend was trying to help. Why was I attacking him?

Red Kelvin didn't budge. He didn't take offense to what I had said, and from his body language, I wondered if he had even heard me. My lips trembled, and tears began to roll down my face as my teeth pressed angrily against each other.

"I don't mean that," I squeaked. I gathered the strength to put my trem-bling hand on his shoulder. My guard broke. The wall that had been holding everything in crumbled as my friend stood firm in front of me. "That's my friend Alex lying in there, man. Steel Cowboy took my other friend Shawn to Blackwell…and he might be dead too! I wasn't fast enough," I said, com-pletely breaking down in front of him as my cries were muffled by my hel-met. I remembered the last time I broke down and cried in front of people, and I would give anything to be back in that classroom getting bullied. Any-thing was better than this.

Red Kelvin had nothing to say. Instead he leaned under my hand on his shoulder and wrapped his arms around me. My body tensed, not expecting contact, but his accepting embrace was what I unknowingly needed to pull myself back together. This friend in front of me truly cared about what was going on in my mind at this moment, and he had dropped what he was doing to let me know that.

Red Kelvin pulled away, and I was able to stop crying. "Thank you," I said, looking at him in sincerity. "I needed that." He nodded in response like it wasn't a big deal, but he knew how much it had meant.

"Blackwell brought a plane. It's on the football field, and we need to leave. They've already got your friend with the medic. We need to go if you're ready," Red Kelvin said, making sure I was stable. I could hear the sound of approaching sirens, and I turned for us to run down the hill to the field.

Why did it take the authorities so long to arrive? The police needed to have been here several minutes ago. I looked at my watch. It had been about fifteen minutes since I had arrived. Was this normal? Was something else going on in town? If this was the usual time for officers to respond, then the world definitely needed us.

As we headed down the hill, the plane Red Kelvin had mentioned came into my view. It was large. I wasn't even sure we could call this vehicle a plane. It was about three school buses in length with a large cockpit at the front, and a wide door opening on the left side just behind the cockpit. The door was open, and Blackwell was standing halfway out, motioning for us to come close to him. The ship had large, long wings that curved underneath.

It had a ramp that led to the opening.

As I neared the ship, I noticed a large, charcoal-gray fin mounted on top of it that matched the rest of its body. The ship was surprisingly quiet, and I realized the sound I had heard before must have been when it was landing.

If the circumstances had been different, I would have been amazed by what looked to be a spaceship in front of me. In this moment in time, my mind didn't have time to react to it. It was still trapped in that locker room as I stared forward blankly.

"Get in! We've got to go!" Blackwell yelled out to us.

I stepped onto the sturdy metal ramp that had dug into the dirt in front of me. A look of disgust rested on Steel Cowboy's face. He was appalled by what he was seeing. I was standing covered almost head to toe in the blood of another. He could figure out exactly what I had done in that locker room; he was the only one who saw what that man had done to Alex. My mind rushed to the question of if Steel Cowboy would be the one putting me away for murder, as he would know I had killed the attacker when it was all over the news. As I looked at him, I understood that he wasn't appalled by me, just by the amount of blood.

"Are you alright?" he asked me hesitantly.

I shook my head. "Only physically," was all I could reply, being trapped in a box of my own emotions.

Steel Cowboy pulled back, not asking further questions. He understood that I was in pain right now, and it was apparent he had decided to give me space.

"Is Shawn alive?" I pushed the words out, not sure if I wanted the answer or not. He had been almost gone when I found him. My throat began to tighten again. The chances of him surviving that kind of merciless treatment were very slim.

Blackwell nodded. "He's stable. He's with Medic right now. You caught him just in time, Persevere. If you had gotten there any later, there would have been nothing we could have done. He was—badly injured."

Those words sank into my chest, reviving what little hope I had for myself being a hero. *I saved him.* A small smile grew across my face, and then the rest of his words settled.

"Who's Medic?" I asked.

"He's one of the other members of our group. I was able to call him in after I got notice of the attack. He's been with us a long time, but he's been away. He doesn't have any combat abilities, but he can heal wounds, and he's great with bioengineering. He's great at what he does, but healing Shawn's body will have depleted his power for quite a while. Shawn is going to be okay, but his forearm will need to be amputated. We discovered too late that there was a toxin in the attacker's blade. His arm won't be able to recover."

My heart sank, and a sharp pain grew in my chest. Amputate? My friend was going to lose his arm?

"Now, we do have an experimental prosthetic. One of our higher-ranking members had been working on it alongside Medic before they left. Medic will attach a nerve harness to the end of Shawn's arm once the lower area is amputated, and then we can attach the prosthetic from there. The nerve harness will attach itself to his nerve endings, and ultimately it will give him the ability to feel with his prosthetic. There is one problem. The prosthetic has an experimental fluid inside of it that was supposed to allow our previous member to withstand high levels of radiation. Medic states that it will be safe, but we're uncertain how exactly this will affect your friend," Blackwell said, worry dancing along his words.

"It doesn't sound like he has a whole lot of options. He wouldn't want to live without a prosthetic, but what kinds of problems can this create?" I asked, trying to weigh out his options.

"Well, we have calculated that there are three possible outcomes. Medic's fairly certain that the majority of the results indicate that it would give him abilities. Strength and speed, to be precise. There is a small chance that it would kill him, which is why it was never used, but Medic thinks he's found a way around that. Another small chance states that he would gain the feeling through the prosthetic but gain none of the abilities inside." He placed his hand on his helmet.

"The problem lies with the fact that we're unsure how he will react to having said abilities, and he will need weekly injections and testing to make sure that his body doesn't reject the fluid for at least six months. If Shawn decides he won't work with us and runs off to use these abilities, there will be no saving him," Blackwell said.

My heart leapt at the thought of Shawn being a hero. It would be great to have one of my best friends alongside me during my missions, saving people. I couldn't imagine him deciding to run off with the powers once he knew I was one of the superheroes.

In my mind Shawn could survive without the special prosthetic, but it was my fault this had happened in the first place; we owed this to him. Even if he didn't acquire abilities, I wouldn't be able to live with myself if he wasn't able to feel with his hand for the rest of his life.

But what if he died? That chance was small, but I wouldn't be able to live with myself if that happened either.

"We have already run a survivability test for Shawn. There's an 84% chance of success with the prosthetic. It's your call, Persevere. He's your friend, after all," he said, making it clear that a choice would have to be made by me alone.

Heavy thoughts filled my mind as the large door slid down to close the opening of the ship. As we began to take off, I was questioning if I was fit to make that decision for him.

"Shawn is going to need immediate medical attention at the hideout. What's your call?" he asked me, this time more urgently.

My mind went numb, knowing my choice would change Shawn's life forever...or end it. "Can he not decide when he becomes conscious?" I asked, not wanting to make a decision we both might regret.

"I'm afraid he's going to need the preparation before he wakes up. He's lost a lot of blood, and your choice will determine what steps will be taken."

I bit the inside of my cheek, not liking the answer that was just given to me. *Shit,* I thought. They were really going to make me decide.

"I think he should have the prosthetic. It's my fault he's hurt to begin with. I couldn't live with myself if he would have to live the rest of his life without feeling in his hand," I said.

Blackwell seemed a little shocked at first, and then he nodded at me in approval, tapping the side of his helmet. "Proceed with operation two," he said, his words rushing from his mouth as he looked in my direction.

"We have a prep kit and a nerve harness on the ship, but we will have to go back to the hideout for the attachment and our anti-rejection serum. The serum should keep his body from rejecting the arm while preparing his cells for the fluid within the prosthetic."

I nodded, taking in the information as my nerves became unsettled. Did I make the right decision? As the questions revolved in my head, it seemed as though he wished to say something else. "Is there something else?" I managed to say. He nodded.

"This plane will take us anywhere we need to go in the future. Welcome aboard the *Aegis*, Persevere." Blackwell headed to the cockpit. The *Aegis*? That was fitting.

After what seemed like an eternity, we finally arrived back at the hideout, having entered a large hangar through a thick metal door. I was surprised to see that the plane could hover, which made it easy to maneuver in tighter positions. Through the entrance was a wide tunnel that led into the ground. As we followed through this massive tunnel, we arrived in another large room where the *Aegis* parked.

"Shawn will be rushed into our medical wing where Medic will complete the procedure." I nodded, looking around and seeing that he had already been taken through a door on the side of the room. Blackwell walked up to me with Steel Cowboy and Red Kelvin close behind. My nerves calmed, knowing that Shawn should be safe now that we're here. Now that my mind had finally had a moment to settle from the horrific details of the day, I realized that Whirl wasn't with us.

"Where's Whirl?" I asked, curious as to why she hadn't come to the school with us. She would have been useful there, I'm sure. Blackwell led us through what I imagined was the medical wing. It was somewhere we hadn't explored yet, but I definitely didn't have the mindset to be curious at the moment.

"Whirl was sent on another mission. The school wasn't the only place that was attacked, and I fear there will be another attack soon. I'm not exactly sure what these attackers are after, though. Did they say anything to you?" he asked me, interested if I had gotten any information.

I thought for a moment, knowing damn well what the monster had told me, but not sure if I should repeat it. Any thought that I could possibly be off Veka's radar was quickly shattered. With a loud sigh, I decided it would be best if Blackwell knew everything. We were nearing the lobby now, having walked through the hallway quickly.

"Yes. He said that they were sent after Shawn and his girlfriend because they knew I'd show up. When I..." I trailed off, reliving the moment once again. I cringed in pain but continued. "When I was about to kill him, he told me that Veka was right; he said I wasn't any different than them. He said I had potential. He also mentioned that his masters sent him to do this. He named Veka specifically, but he very clearly said he had more than one master. Any idea who they might be? Or am I overthinking it?" I asked, not quite sure what he had meant by it. I had been in too much pain, with too much anger, to even notice he had said that.

"Veka has many powerful Followers and several high commanders. It's possible that he was making mention of one of his higher-ups, but they normally would refer to them by name rather than being so vague. It's also possible that Veka has a new commander, one that isn't well-known yet. I want to assure you, that I will do what I can to find more information about this attack, but we need to stick together, now more than ever. We are in a dangerous playing field, and we now understand that Veka is after you."

I nodded, my mind becoming grim with the idea that my friends were at risk right now.

Blackwell rushed to a room in the back of the hideout and came back with a wooden chest covered with purple lettering.

"In here—we have the prosthetic and the serum. Do you have any more friends we need to keep tabs on? I can make sure they are watched from one of my eyes or even one of the heroes until everything is a little clearer."

I thought for a moment, knowing that it was a good idea. My mind then jumped to Talida. With everything going on, I had completely forgotten she was home, and now my mind began to race again.

"My friend Talida. Can we check on her now? She went home from school early, which is unlike her, and…" My train of thought was derailed by Blackwell receiving another notification through the earpiece in his helmet.

"We'll check on her. I want to assure you that Shawn is stable and is going to be alright, but I need you and Red Kelvin to respond to a house fire northeast of town. It's a little over five miles north of here."

My eyes widened.

"Tony? What's wrong?" Steel Cowboy asked, fear ringing through his voice as he echoed the thoughts going through Red Kelvin's mind.

I tried to speak, but my body froze, not letting out more than a whimper.

"Goth damn it!" I mumbled weakly, sprinting toward the door of the hideout.

Chapter 23

Through the Fire and Flames

Content Warning: Contains mention of trauma.

"That's got to be Talida's house!" I said, my adrenaline making my body shake in fear. *This can't be happening,* I thought. *Not again.* This news was hitting me much harder than the news of the school attack.

A fire. It had to be a fucking fire. I couldn't lose another friend. Not after what I had just done. My mind began to play back all the memories I had with Aiden. How we talked during school lunch about minuscule things that didn't mean a lot back then. But they meant something now. I would give almost anything to have those small conversations with him again. I couldn't lose Talida the same way. In fact, I couldn't lose her at all. *I won't.*

I ran as fast as my now-empowered legs would allow me to, needing to reach her house, not caring if Red Kelvin was behind me or not. This time, I *had* to succeed. I lost Alex, I barely saved Shawn, and I wasn't about to lose Talida as well. Whoever was behind this, whoever was trying to hurt me by using my friends, was going to pay. Even if it was Veka himself, I was going to make him suffer.

I didn't try to push back the evil thoughts building in my brain. The only important thing was saving my best friend and dispatching whoever was calling the shots against me. Why was this vendetta so personal? What had I done to Veka that caused him to hate me this much? Did he think I was a threat to him? I couldn't imagine a student with strength and fire being much of a threat to an experienced overlord. I bit the inside of my cheek. It didn't matter what he was… I'd make sure he never hurt anyone again.

It was a short moment of believing I had the ability to defeat him, for reality always found a way to seep back in. I would have to train a lot more in order to stand a chance. If Blackwell couldn't kill him, then surely, I couldn't either.

I could see the flames from quite a distance as I approached the house. I sprinted toward the door. My body wanted to hesitate as I remembered being trapped in the flames at the school. As my hands started shaking, I wasn't sure if I was going to be able to go through that again, but then Talida entered my mind. She was my best friend, and I wasn't that helpless kid anymore. I wasn't *going* to be. If I wanted to call myself a hero, I didn't have time to wait.

I grabbed the door handle and yanked, releasing the door from its hinges and launching it behind me. It spun in the air until it was stopped by the trunk of a tree. I ran into the flames, searching frantically for survivors.

For a split second, I was afraid, but my fear quickly turned to awe. I was standing in this blazing inferno, being untouched by the flames that had once changed my life. I almost felt as if I was leeching energy from my surroundings, which created a thought. Could I extinguish these flames? If I had a little more training, could I get rid of fire instead of creating it? Could I gather strength from it? I didn't have time to experiment, so I ran into the back room to the right, which I believed was Talida's room.

Finding no signs of my friend, I backed out into the hallway, then searched the two rooms on the right, one of which was a bathroom, and the second was an office. I ran to the kitchen, and I saw what looked to be a human shape underneath a blanket. My heart sank. Any thought of breathing was taken away from me as I hurried over to what was most likely Talida's lifeless body. *No, please no,* I thought as I pulled the blanket from the object.

While it wasn't Talida's body, it was still a sight that was going to haunt me, as if I wasn't going to be traumatized by what I had already seen and done today. I believed the body was that of Talida's mother, but it was hard to recognize through her charred skin.

My nostrils were assaulted by the putrid, burning flesh. Seeing her mom like this boggled my mind and made me even more fearful for Talida's life. Her mom's throat had been slit several times, and there were multiple stab wounds to her chest.

Were these the same attackers? I wondered as I looked away and headed toward the master bedroom across the kitchen.

I saw movement in my peripheral vision, and my head jerked in its direction. I pulled my Blaze Ray out and made sure it was on a kill switch. Someone was escaping through the back door, and I ran in their direction. I investigated the master bedroom, which seemed to be empty, and then I sprinted out the door to find the escapee.

Scanning the backyard, I saw someone running. I raised my Blaze Ray, the first thing coming into view being vibrant hot pink hair, cut to the neck. The second thing I realized was that the person was naked and covered in ash.

I lowered my gun with a gasp. Was this my friend? "Wait!" I said. She twirled around, looking in my direction and confirming that this was, indeed, my best friend. *What happened to her hair?* I thought. I ran toward her, ecstatic that she was alive. As I neared her, she froze in fear.

As I got close, I eyed her up and down. I blushed, not knowing how to react. I held myself back from hugging her, knowing it would be awkward and crossing a line. I wasn't sure what she had been through, but I was glad to see she was alive and seemingly unharmed.

This wasn't the first time I had seen her unclothed. Due to how long we've been friends and how close we were, it normally wasn't a big deal. Never in this situation, though. That's what made it uncomfortable. I knew that she never meant for anyone to see her this vulnerable. As I looked closer to make sure she didn't have any burns, I was confused. There *should* have been burns, but her skin didn't even appear inflamed.

My harsh movements startled her, and she began running again with a squeal of horror. "Get away from me!" she said, attempting to half-heartedly cover herself.

Upon realizing she didn't know who I was, I felt stupid and started yelling her name. "Talida! It's me, Tony. It's okay!" I said. She stopped and glared at me with apprehension. Her bright eyes popped from her soot-covered face, and she crouched as if she were ready to start running again.

She swayed, her stance visibly weakened. She seemed cautious, questioning how, or if, it *could* be me. Seeing she wasn't going to run away immediately, I detached my cape and held it away from me. "Here—to cover yourself." I tossed her the cape and took a step back.

"If you are Tony, then why are you in a mask? You're not my friend; don't you dare act like him!" she cried out in distress. Her eyes darted back and forth between me and the cape on the ground. Her legs trembled, threatening to topple her to the ground with the act of a swift breeze. Yet she still held her fists against me.

As I took a moment to ponder how to react in this situation, I reached to detach my helmet, showing my face to her. There was no one else around, so I was putting my full trust in Talida with my identity. "It's me."

Her eyes widened and then fell to slits. "How do I know you're not going to hurt me too?" she asked through tears. "Everyone else has turned against me. How do I know you won't too?"

I was taken aback by the question, frowning. *What the hell?* I thought, looking into her broken eyes. I had never turned my back on her; she was my best friend. I stood there, not sure what to say. Somehow, from whatever had just happened to her, I had lost her trust.

"I've never turned my back on you. You, Shawn, and Aiden have been my best friends for as long as I can remember. What's going on?" I asked, not knowing what else to say since I wasn't sure what happened.

Tears fell from her eyes. "That didn't stop my dad...or my mom."

What she said made everything inside me tighten up. *What does that mean?* My mind chased for an answer to what had happened, questioning everything I had seen within her home and building its own conclusion of what had happened. I needed to know for sure. Did Talida kill her mom? That didn't seem like her. I couldn't imagine any scenario that would end with her killing her mother like that.

"I'm sorry for whatever happened. I'm here to help, not cause any harm. I was notified of a house fire, and I was sure it was yours, so I rushed to help. I want to protect my friend."

I paused for a moment, not wanting my next words to scare her away. "I acquired powers during my coma, and I've been trying to hide them from everyone, but someone knows who I am… Shawn was hurt… I don't know why, but they've targeted us. I saved him, and he's back with my master at our hideout. I can explain more on the way, but I need to bring you somewhere safe," I said, hoping she would trust me. "I'm sorry I didn't tell you."

She looked at me, startled. "What? Is he okay? Is Alex okay?" she asked, asking the question I hoped she wouldn't. As she now believed me, she cautiously picked up the cape, wrapping it around her as she trembled.

I shook my head, my throat tightening again. "They got her. I barely saved Shawn," I said, not wanting to give her the awful news.

There was an explosive cry from Talida as she broke down, falling to her knees and covering her neck with her hands. As she sobbed, I took a step closer to her.

"Why are they doing this?" she squeaked through her wails. "What did I do?"

"I'm sorry. I wasn't fast enough; I failed all of us," I said. "This is all my fault." The words stung as they left my mouth. I doomed them. Maybe if I hadn't made myself known from the mugging, they would have been okay. If I hadn't have thrown that damned fireball, maybe Veka wouldn't be after me.

I took another step toward her to try and comfort her, knowing I needed to at least pretend I was strong. She needed me right now. As I neared her, a pink glow began to emit from her hands.

"What...?" I started, confused at the sudden change. "What is that?"

She put her head down, grabbing her hair as her melancholy turned to distress. "I don't want to hurt you. I don't have control. I didn't mean to do it," she said, throwing me into a confused state.

"Control of what? Can you tell me what happened?" I asked.

She began to cry louder, wailing through her tears now. "I don't understand what I did. I don't understand what's going on! Why am I being punished?"

"I know it hurts, and I'm here for you, but I need to understand what happened." I pushed through my sadness. My best friend was sitting here, on the ground, crying her eyes out. She was naked, didn't trust me, and there wasn't anything I could do about the situation she was in or even my own. We had just lost a great friend, and Talida...had lost so much more.

"Something happened. I'm not ready to say what, but I woke up in my room confused and scared...and tied to my bed..." She trailed off, clenching her jaw and struggling to get the rest of the words out. "When my emotions got out of control, my hands caught fire, and when I started to try and shake it out, it only got worse. My house caught fire, and by the time the rope burnt, I ran out into the kitchen only to find my mom had been killed. I don't know where my dad went, but I don't care about him anymore," she said. "Fuck him!"

Her statement shocked me; she had always been close to her dad. He had always been a major part of her life. Since their family didn't have a lot of money, family was all they had, and Talida had created a tight bond with her father. What happened to destroy that bond so quickly?

Her hands caught fire with strange pink flames as she emitted another explosion of cries. Her movements became jittery, and it was obvious that she was terrified of herself.

"Talida. It's going to be okay," I said, hardly able to take my eyes off her hands. I was alarmed and not quite sure what she was about to do with the flames. Why were they pink? I had to calm her down.

How does she have powers?

I walked closer to her, attempting to hug her, but she abruptly shut me down.

"*Don't* touch me!" she yelled, holding herself with her shaking, flaming hands. "I'm sorry."

"Talida, I'm not sure what happened, but I'm here for you. You're safe now," I said, trying to relieve her of the stress. I tried to keep my eyes off her flames, but my attention was focused on them. "I think we can help you if you come back with me. With all of it," I said, lifting my hand slowly. With concentration, I conjured bright-white and orange fire in my hand. Her eyes lit up for a split second, but I wasn't sure if it was more fear or a spark of hope. She then looked at me in confusion, having a hard time with the fact I had powers. She'd be freaking out right now under different circumstances.

The flames vanished from my hand, and after a long pause, Talida nodded. She was able to bring her breathing back to normal, the bright-pink fire still lingering on her skin. She looked up at me. "Please…help me," she whimpered.

"Of course, I will. I don't turn my back on my friends. May I help you up?" I asked, trying a different approach. She was hesitant at first, but after a few moments passed, she nodded.

I grabbed under her arm, her muscles violently tensing as her body reacted to my touch. As I helped her up, my mind began to ease; it was almost as if I could feel her emotions melting away as the flames shrank to a small flicker and disappeared. Her trembling body began to yield, and she buried her head into my chest, crying and wrapping her arms around me. She took several moments to cry against me, and I held my friend close, making sure she was okay with it. I tried not to cry, trying to be the strong friend she needed right now. A superhero.

After several moments, I let go. Now calmed down, I called Blackwell to let him know to call off the *Aegis*. He and Red Kelvin were heading our way, but I felt it was best if Talida and I had some time to talk on the way to the hideout. I questioned if it had been the right choice, since she was unclothed, and we'd have to walk through the woods. After talking to Talida about it, she insisted we walk as well, hoping to clear her head.

As we headed toward the hideout, I slowly caught her up on everything that was going on with Shawn and myself. I didn't tell her a whole lot about Veka in order to avoid sending her into another panic, but I gave her the gist that someone was after the heroes. I was going to let Blackwell take care of giving her the rest of the information because I believed he could handle it much better than I would be able to. I could provide a personal level of comfort, but Blackwell understood much more about what was going on.

When we arrived at the hideout, I opened the door using my MIRA system, which Talida appeared to be interested in. She had mostly calmed down at this point, but it was obvious that it was going to take a long time for her to heal. Still, her old self was starting to shine through the dark.

"I can't believe you're an actual superhero. That explains so much," she said with a smirk.

I smiled. "Like that first fight when I got back to school? Or when I slammed Johnny against the wall, and you made the superpower joke? Yeah, that's why I almost spit out my drink," I admitted, chuckling. "I'll have you know, that table is broken now. I squeezed the bar underneath on accident." It was great to finally talk about the truth with someone. Not being able to tell my friends had started to eat me alive. We didn't have any secrets between us. In fact, we probably knew a little *too* much about each other.

There was a slight smile along with a flinch at the mention of Johnny. "Don't tell me too much. I'll end up being your accomplice!"

"Are you okay?" I asked, seeing the flinch. I suddenly cringed. *No, stupid.* Of course, she wasn't okay. "I mean…" I started, attempting to correct myself. She interrupted me before I could finish.

"I'll be okay, eventually. I've got a lot to work through, but I trust you," she said, looking up at me. Her eyes danced along my face as if she were scanning my intentions, but it was clear that she wasn't frightened of me anymore. "Thank you for being someone I can count on. You always have been."

"I'm here for both you and Shawn. It's going to be rough for a while, but I'm going to do everything that I can to make sure nothing else happens. Master Blackwell will want to talk to you alone, if that's okay. He's the leader training us to fight. There are five of us with abilities, including myself and Blackwell. He will want to understand a little bit more about you, and I'm sure he will use that information to help keep you and everyone else here safe," I said, a little worried about her being alone with him. It wasn't that I didn't trust either of them; it's just that I didn't understand what had happened to her, and I wanted to give her a warning beforehand.

She looked at me again. "I trust you. If you believe he's safe, I trust that," she said, smiling. "There is something I need to tell—"

Blackwell entered the room, immediately interrupting the conversation. "Ahh, you must be Talida. You're Tony's best friend, right?" he asked, walking toward us.

Talida nodded. "Yes. We've been friends for a long time."

"It's a pleasure to meet you. May I have a word with you in private?" he asked before looking at me for approval. "I'll have someone find you some clothes as well."

I nodded, feeling a little weird about my boss wanting approval from me on this. It felt almost as if I were the master here.

"Of course. It's good to meet you too." Talida looked over at me. "I'll tell you after," she said. What was she going to tell me? Was she going to tell me what happened? Does she know why we've been targeted? My mind raced with thousands of questions I was unable to answer. *Where do we go from here?*

A tall man with ebony skin and brown eyes entered the room just as suddenly as Blackwell had.

"Medic! Is there something you need?" Blackwell asked in a hearty, friendly tone. Talida stood next to him, and I held back before heading to see Shawn to overhear this conversation.

"Yes, actually. Shawn is in stable condition, but I must be prepared to deal with the aftermath. As I told you, he will require testing and injections weekly for a long time. I have been wanting to ask you for the schematic of that prosthetic. I have to have it in order to be able to better understand how I can proceed in the future. You should know that right now everything is going better for Shawn than I had hoped."

"I understand. I will send you the schematic after I deal with this situation. I was just about to speak with Talida."

"Thank you." Medic said, heading back toward the medical wing.

"One other thing. Are you aware of the update Isaac made to this prosthetic?"

Medic turned abruptly toward him, almost in alarm. By his body language, he had, indeed, seen the update, but I had no way of connecting these actions with an explanation. "I was made aware when checking to see if it was structurally sound."

Blackwell leaned in toward him and lowered his voice to a whisper. "Make sure that doesn't become a problem."

Chills went down my back as I was unsure what he meant. Was Shawn going to be okay?

"It won't be. I've taken the countermeasures to make sure this will work for him."

As I left the room, I headed to use the restroom before seeing Shawn.

Chapter 24

Loose Cannon

Blackwell had led Talida into the social room, where I assumed he would be interviewing her so that he could understand completely what had happened. My mind started to jump around again, landing once more on Shawn. I needed to go see him. Was the amputation done already?

I headed to the glass doors at the end of the right hallway, which was the interior medical wing that we had available. As I headed in, Medic met me at the door.

"It's an honor to officially meet you, Persevere. I'm Medic. You're heading to see Shawn, I presume?" he asked me.

I nodded with a smile. "Yes. Is he alright?"

Medic smiled, showing his bright-white teeth. "Yes. He is recovering now. I have completed the amputation and installed the arm harness. The shot was administered, and I had just attached the prosthetic arm. Shawn's body reacted strongly but well. There's no sign of rejection, and the fluid within the prosthetic is connecting to his cells as we speak. You can go in and check on him if you'd like. He's a little unsettled, so be careful," he informed.

I nodded. "Thank you, and it's good to meet you too. I appreciate everything you've done for him. I'm going to go check on him."

Medic nodded and bowed. "I'll get out of your way. He's down the hall to the left, first door on the right. If you need me, I'll be speaking with Blackwell."

I smiled. "Thank you so much." I headed toward Shawn, debating on whether or not I should put my mask back on. Talida knew who I was, so I might as well go all out and tell Shawn as well, right? Plus, if he was freaked out, he would need to see a friendly face. I frowned as my thoughts turned sour. If it weren't for the grief he was going to go through, he'd be super excited about my abilities. Maybe he shouldn't know who I am quite yet. I'd make a decision later. I put my mask back on and headed toward the room.

* * *

As I neared the door, I hesitated. I really didn't want to give him the bad news about Alex, and I also didn't want to go through what had happened for my own sake. I couldn't be selfish now. The information hurt, but my friends needed me. *Be the hero,* I reminded myself.

I slowly pushed the door open, and I saw Shawn attached to an advanced medical bed. He seemed to have restraints on his wrists and ankles, and this angered me. Shawn didn't need restraints; he was my friend. I'd have to have a word with Blackwell about this later.

The situation infuriated me. No wonder he was fucking scared. My thoughts tangled and twisted within my mind, and I eventually concluded that they probably restrained him so that he wouldn't harm the healing of his arm or attack Medic when he woke up the first time Maybe I was over-reacting.

As I neared Shawn, I realized he was sleeping. I was surprised that the cut on his face was completely healed, leaving no scar. His face was red and swollen, and his puffy eyes made it apparent he had already been told what had happened. I had never seen my friend like this. Never once had I seen him this distraught. Just looking at his missing arm, replaced by a dark-gray prosthetic, crushed me. It was a straight blow to my soul. I looked in surprise at the quick healing of his arm, and my mind began to wander again.

How could I call myself a hero when this was all my fault? Veka and whoever's working under him are after me. I couldn't possibly be a threat to him. Shawn and Talida were just pawns being used to hurt me. Why am I Veka's target? What are his motives? If I hadn't acquired powers, Shawn wouldn't be lying on this table, and Talida wouldn't have gotten hurt.

As I stood, contemplating the importance of my existence to a monster like Veka, I began to dread the situation I was about to get myself into. I put my hand on his shoulder.

"Hey, man. I'm here," I said quietly. Shawn began to stir, and his eyes jerked open. A moment of fear passed over his face, viewing his surroundings and seeing that he was restrained. His eyes then went directly toward me, turning straight to fuming anger.

"You!" he said. "Did you do this?! Did you put these restraints on me?"

His voice loudened as his anger deepened. "Do you like seeing me like this?! Did you kill her!?" He demanded an answer, and it was almost too much to bear before I remembered he didn't know who I was. Shawn shook within his bed, his anger manifesting into a violent rage.

I changed my voice in hopes that I wouldn't be recognized. "No. I saved you from the school. I tried everything I could—"

Shawn interrupted me with an angry laugh. "Why do I feel stronger?" he asked, his demeanor changing dramatically as he realized something was different. His words were almost an angry whisper as if his motives were malicious. His body quit flailing within the bed, but his breathing began to pick up pace. "I'm going to kill you...with my hands...slowly!" he spewed.

It wasn't his words that caught me off-guard in this situation; it was the fact that I knew he meant every one of them. It was an anger I had never realized he held within him. Something deeper than what any of the bullying had produced. This was something...completely different. Shawn was out to kill, and it reminded me of that locker room.

Okay, maybe the restraints were a good idea. Now I could talk to him and— My thoughts were interrupted by the restraints ripping from the table, flying into the air, and bouncing off the ceiling.

My whole body jerked, and my adrenaline told my body to run rather than fight. *Never mind,* I thought. My eyes widened beneath my mask, feeling the negative energy from him fill the room.

Shawn sat up, and I got a good look at his forest-green eyes. I saw the intent in them, and I knew I was going to be in a lot of trouble.

"Wait!" I yelled in my normal voice. He didn't recognize it through his blind fury, and he leapt toward me. He threw a punch, hitting me in the chest and knocking the air out of me, flinging me into the wall. *He's so strong,* I thought, realizing he now had super strength. As I attempted to recover, I was hit with another strike, this one directly on the side of my mask, almost knocking me senseless.

I was hit with another blow, and then another, before I was finally able to fight back. I threw a punch at him, landing it on him, and then I took another swing, this time completely missing my target. I was dazed, and having a hard time paying attention. Shawn was gone. "Oh, come on!" I yelled in frustration as I turned around, looking for him.

As soon as I looked behind me, a fist hit me square in the nose, and then I felt a solid punch on my back. The only thing I could see was a blur moving around me. *What the hell did they do to him?* I tried to throw a fireball to make him stop, but it was no use. It crashed into the wall, blasting through the sink and spraying water into the room.

My adrenaline pumped, and I tried to focus as I had done in the last few fights I'd been in. For some reason, I seemed to almost see his next move without even knowing where he was. I closed my eyes, and I knew that he was going to stop in front of me.

"Shawn! Stop!" I yelled, throwing my arms forward, grabbing both of his shoulders and turning him around, slamming him into the wall. For the quick second I had, I used one of my hands to yank my mask off. My face was wet, and I realized blood and sweat were running down my left cheek.

"It's me! I was at the school. I saved you!" I yelled. As he looked at me in horror, I let go of him, realizing fire had lit up my arms again.

"Tony? Why are you throwing fire like that guy on TV?"

"Do you really have to ask? You flung me into a wall with super strength and have teleportation or some shit now. I got my abilities while in my coma, and I was trying to keep it to myself." My patience had been destroyed by the fight, and I didn't have time for stupid questions. Nor did I have time to remember Blackwell telling me he might have enhanced speed. "I *am* the guy on TV!"

"Dude, why didn't you tell me!? You know I wouldn't have told anyone. I'm your best friend. Does Talida know? Is she okay?" he asked me, more confused than angry now. His anger had finally subsided when he realized I didn't have any part in what had happened before. At least, not the part he thought I had.

"She does now. Her family was attacked. I'm not sure what happened, but our master Blackwell is speaking with her. She is as okay as she can be right now."

Shawn slammed his hands against the bed, bending the frame. "Damnit!" he yelled. "Who's behind all of this? Why are they after us?" he asked me, looking at me with a sense of curiosity.

"A monster named Veka is behind it all. The attacker at the school mentioned having more than one master, and we don't know who that is; but they're after me, so they attacked you to find me."

The words poured from my mouth as I attempted to explain everything going on. As I rambled, the loose strings within my mind began to create a web of understanding. Only one person hated me enough to hurt my friends. Only one person knew who my best friends were that would have that kind of motive. Was Johnny behind this?

I knew he was angry with us, and he had threatened us, but was Johnny capable of the horrid things that had just happened? Is Johnny working for Veka? Why would a monster like Veka need a bully like Johnny? Surely, this whole situation wasn't caused by *him*. It must be because I have powers and Veka's targeting me.

Shawn's next words derailed my train of thought. He was now much calmer, and his solemn stance revealed he was dealing with what had happened.

"I can't believe I lost her," he murmured, looking down at the ground. "Everything was going so well. We were just…hanging out, making jokes about the football team, excited to see the band…holding hands." His words began to fragment as he choked and slammed himself down on the center of the bent bed. "I think I loved her, man. How can someone be so evil? What did we do wrong?"

Shawn's words hit me hard. I was tired of hearing that question. The three of us had lost a lot, very quickly. Whether it was Shawn losing Alex, Talida losing her family, or me losing the little bit of faith I had about myself being a hero, today had taken a toll. It was the kind of day I truly hoped none of us ever had to endure again.

"I'm sorry, man. I wasn't fast enough. I looked so hard for you guys, but by the time I got there…" My words stopped. No matter how hard I tried to say the rest of the sentence, it wouldn't come out, but Shawn understood.

"I should have been stronger. If I had these powers before, no one would have gotten hurt. I should have been better. I should have trained instead of playing all those *stupid* video games. I should have been ready for this, but I wasn't, and now I've lost someone that meant the world to me." Shawn slammed his fists down on the bed again. "Why did I have to go into that damned locker room!"

He looked back at me, on the verge of losing his temper again. "You should have been there! With your powers, you could have…" He stopped himself as my heart sank. His words hurt, and now I knew how they felt on the receiving end. I couldn't believe I blew up on Red Kelvin. Even though he seemed okay afterward, that wasn't right, I thought, not wanting to hurt people like I had already. He was right though. I should have done better…

"I'm sorry," Shawn said with sincerity. "That's not fair. You did everything you could. You saved me, and I'm grateful. I just wish it would have gone differently." There was a long pause as I questioned if I should respond or just let him vent. Shawn looked down at his hands, one of flesh and one of metal. I now realized that the space between the metal plates of his prosthetic forearm was now glowing purple, and he had studded knuckles.

"It's so weird; I have abilities now, and I can feel with this arm. I'm like a cyborg," he said, giving a slight chuckle. "I need to push myself from here on out. I'm going to be stronger, and I'm going to be faster until there's no one as good as me. I will never let one of my friends get hurt again. I can't be weak; I have to push my limits until I don't have any."

As I let him ponder everything that had happened, Blackwell entered the room.

"This is Blackwell," I said, sure that they had already met. I looked behind us, afraid to see the damage we had caused, but more afraid of our master's reaction. A sigh left Blackwell's lips, and I cringed, knowing he had now seen it.

"First of all, I would like to update you, Shawn. I have notified your parents of what happened and that we have it under control. There is a cloaking device, if you will, inside your arm to make it look like a human arm when you're around your family. I will need you to stay in the hideout for the next twenty-four hours to make sure your body doesn't reject it. Once you are cleared, I will need you to check in every week for the next six months to keep an eye on your vitals and make sure everything stays stable with your newly found abilities. This same time every week, we will give you an injection to prevent the fluid in your prosthetic from being rejected," Blackwell informed him.

Shawn nodded. "Sure. Um," he started, rubbing the back of his head in thought. "Since I have abilities like you guys, can I join your group? I need to help people. I need to make sure this doesn't happen to anyone else."

Blackwell and I were pleasantly surprised; it wasn't at all the reaction to all of this we thought he was going to have. Now we shouldn't have to worry about him going AWOL. At least not yet. Right now he's interested in working with us rather than against the idea.

"Of course. Training starts at 9:30 every night, ending at midnight, but you're welcome to be here anytime."

Shawn smiled. "Great. Where's the training room? I'd like to begin immediately. When can I meet the other members?" he asked, looking around and not seeing anyone else here. "I know there was that other man. The strong one that grabbed me."

I looked at Blackwell with concern. "Is he clear to do that yet?" I asked quietly. "Doesn't his arm need time to heal?"

Blackwell nodded at the first question. "Medic was able to heal him quickly. He's good to go, but I would suggest he takes it easy for the next few days." He then turned to Shawn. "I will give you a tour of the hideout, but first, I need you in the social room. Talida has requested she speak with both of you, and she has permitted me to overhear the conversation to understand more of what's going on," Blackwell said.

The two of us made eye contact as we glanced at each other, both of us uneasy. *I'm getting tired of feeling this way*, I thought, sighing.

Chapter 25

Crossing a Line

Content Warning: Contains mention of possible sexual
trauma. Kidnapping Explained.

Blackwell led us into his social room. This time, we entered into another, smaller room with a thick metal door. A small table sat in this room, and it was apparent that it was used for interrogations; the table itself had restraints on it, and it was heavy-duty and metal.

"First of all, I want to tell you both a little bit about why we are here," Blackwell began, looking mainly at Talida and Shawn. Shawn sat down at the table next to Talida, who was appalled by the fact he had lost his arm.

"I'm so sorry," she whispered to Shawn, who looked equally as distraught about her being unclothed. Luckily, the cape mostly covered her.

"I am the founder and leader of a group of superhumans called Project Barricade. We exist to take down evil, whether that be smaller groups of people like thugs or much more powerful enemies such as the one behind these recent attacks. His name is Veka, and we now know he will stop at nothing to hurt us. He's latched onto you, Tony, and we don't exactly know why."

Blackwell took a moment to pause, being interrupted by someone entering the room. "Here you are, sir," Medic said, handing him a pair of leggings and a t-shirt. As he quickly left, Blackwell handed the clothes to Talida and turned around. Before Shawn and I got a chance to avert our gaze, she quickly dropped the cloak and threw them on. By the time we got the chance to react, it was over. Shawn's eyes widened and his cheeks became red. It didn't bother me nearly as much as him, but he seemed flustered to the point of being mute. He made eye contact with me, and I nearly laughed.

Blackwell then looked around at each of us and began to slowly pace the room. "We need to train and prepare ourselves to combat Veka's forces. We need to learn how to use our powers to their maximum capacity. That way, we can stand a fighting chance against his Followers when they attack. Shawn, I already have agents looking after your parents, so they will be safe. If something were to happen, you'll be the first one to know."

He nodded as I sat next to my friends while Blackwell talked to them.

"Since the two of you have abilities now, I want to offer you a chance to join our team. I will personally overlook your training and do the best I can to help you hone your powers." Blackwell paused for a long moment while sitting down next to the rest of us, resting his hands on his knees. "Can you tell us exactly what caused you to gain your abilities? I need all the details you can remember so that we can find those responsible."

Talida hesitated to tell us what had happened. Tears quickly filled her eyes. "My father called the school and asked that I come home early. He wouldn't tell me the reason why, but I did it anyway, telling the school I wasn't feeling well. I thought one of my family members back in Japan might have passed, and I was worried." Her jaw tightened as she looked between us in fear. "I never would have dreamed it would have been something like this. Once I got home, my father looked concerned and offered me some tea. *Ojiisan* hasn't been doing well, so I feared that it was his time. I sat down and drank the tea with my father, and he was silent the whole time. He—he spiked the tea and started apologizing profusely for what he had done..." She paused for a moment, gathering her courage to continue speaking.

I was confused by the word *ojiisan*, but then I remembered Talida had explained that it was the term for grandfather in Japanese. She rarely mentioned him, but they had been close before she moved to Old Belmont. She still called him *Ojiisan*.

Her voice began to crack under the intensity of the situation. "My father kept repeating that he had to do it to save my mom. He kept repeating that someone was going to kill them if he didn't do it as I slowly drifted to sleep. I woke up, strapped to a metal table. I remember the smell of medical alcohol and rotting flesh." She shuddered, closing her eyes to think as she held herself.

"And what did you see while there?" Blackwell asked.

"I was too afraid to look around much. I saw someone crushing up orange pills. As my vision cleared, I saw he was mixing them with a liquid labeled 'Draco Serum.' He filled a syringe labeled 'B46' with the liquid and stared at me. His eyes were glowing yellow, and it was completely terrifying. He was with someone," she said, taking another moment to swallow her fear.

"I see," Blackwell said, seeming a little distraught. He tapped his gloved finger on the table. "The one with yellow eyes is Veka. Did you get a look at who was with him? Chances are the other one is the apprentice Veka has taken under his wing."

Talida then looked straight at me, and then at Shawn, sending chills down my spine. She knew exactly who it was, and so did we.

Her face became wet with tears, and she nodded.

"It was Johnny," she muttered as if she didn't believe it. "He was there, wearing a black cloak. He called me that racist name again, and he told me to go back to sleep. He said he would take everything from me and my friends, starting with me." There was silence as the entire room was filled with the intense anger growing inside of Shawn. His need to explode in a fit of rage was nearly tangible.

My heart dropped as my stomach threatened to expel everything inside. I knew Johnny was after us; he told us he would kill us, but I never could have imagined he could be this evil.

"They…took off my clothes. Johnny made remarks about what he wanted to do to me as he hit me several times. Then they injected the serum into many different places on my body." She paused for a moment, not wishing to go on.

"Were you able to see any indication of your location?" Blackwell asked calmly.

"I looked around at that point. I didn't get a good look, but it felt like I was moving. Black metal walls had bright-yellow lights. There was a bright-white light above me. Johnny then knocked me unconscious. When I woke up, I was in my house."

Shawn grabbed my leg under the table, looking at me with fury flooding his eyes. As he squeezed my leg, it became obvious that he was attempting not to explode until she had finished talking. I knew it was coming; with everything that had just happened, neither of us were taking this information well.

I allowed him to continue squeezing my leg and quickly realized that my leg was a lot more durable than it should be. I guess it made sense given that I have a durability of 3. As the anger was rising within me, it was taking all I had to bite down on my lip and not interrupt her or storm out to find Johnny. I thought he was a problem before, but he'd become so much worse, and he didn't know who he was working with. What could Veka possibly have offered him that was worth joining him? Was my death that important to him?

"When I woke up, my whole body ached, and I was tied to my bed, naked. I freaked out, and as I got more scared, fire started to fly from my hands. That scared me more, causing flames to explode from me and catch the house on fire. My hair somehow turned pink during the process. I struggled to break free, and I thought I was going to die. The ropes finally snapped. I ran into the kitchen and found my mom lying on the floor not breathing. I didn't realize I wasn't getting burned until after I was out of the house." Talida looked at me in horror. "When I saw that someone followed me out, I thought I was in danger again. Then you told me who you were. I thought you were going to frame me for my mom's death or finish me off."

After another long moment of silence, Shawn's grip loosened. I had a sigh of relief as I thought that he had pulled himself together enough to not completely implode. Shawn stood up, destroying any hope I had accumulated.

"Are you fucking *kidding* me?!" Shawn said. I clenched my fist, holding my tongue. I put my other hand up to my mouth in a fist, my curled fingers pressing against my upper lip. I needed to keep my mouth shut. *As much as you want to say it, don't.*

"The punk gets a power trip and thinks he can do whatever the hell he wants?" Shawn continued with his fists down at his waist. "And who is this Veka piece of shit? Johnny doesn't have powers; let's go fucking kill him!"

Talida began to cry; she had never liked conflict, and in the situation she was in, she didn't need any more.

"Shawn, I hate him as much as you do, but we've got to slow down," I said. There wasn't anything I wanted more than to hurt the person who terrorized my best friends.

"Tell me one reason we shouldn't go after him right now. He hurt us. All of us!" Shawn demanded, throwing his hands into the air.

Blackwell stepped into the conversation. "He's serving as the apprentice of Veka, who is a powerful being with the ability to destroy this entire organization by himself at this point in time. If we are to make a move, and I do plan to, we need to think it through and build a plan of action. We need everyone trained and ready to fight an equally powerful enemy with abilities. We will need to take out Veka's Followers and forces before we can take him on alone. You will get your chance for justice, but it will take time."

"Well, your organization has never had me! I want to go after Johnny first! He can't be allowed to be free. I want him in my hands!" Shawn said. He turned around to leave the room. "God damn it!" he screamed, launching his fist at the metal door in front of him. Everyone jumped from their seats at the sound of screeching metal. The door ripped from its hinges and flew toward the wall on the other side of the social room. It was heading straight for Steel Cowboy, who had heard the yelling.

"What in the…" Steel Cowboy said as he steeled himself. He caught the door from the air and slid across the room, leaving skid marks on the concrete floor.

Oh my goth, I thought, so happy that Steel Cowboy wasn't hurt. "Shawn, wait!" I yelled, trying to calm him down to the point of reason. I headed toward him. I knew I had to calm him down, like he had done for me.

"Leave me be, Tony!" he said. "I need space!"

I stopped in my tracks. He had gotten angry with me earlier when he attacked me, but it wasn't like him to throw things or hit things when he was enraged. He had always been quick to anger, but never like this. At this point I knew that I needed to leave him alone. The best therapy for him right now would be solitude. If Johnny were here, I'd be having to stop us both from killing him, but he was likely far, far away from us.

"And call me Fury."

As Shawn stomped past Steel Cowboy and disappeared, Red Kelvin walked into the room. A look of complete horror rested on his face, and it was apparent he had seen what had just happened. The room fell into an uncomfortable silence, and the only thing audible was Talida's muffled sniffling. Blackwell broke the silence.

"Give him a few minutes, Tony, and then go check the training room. I'm sure he'll find his way there," Blackwell informed. "Talida, there's a hallway on the right when you enter the hideout. You can find a room of your choosing to bunk in. They were previously under construction, but a few of them are ready. We will clear up the situation with the authorities in the morning. Let me know if there's anything you need to make your stay more comfortable. Our cafeteria is now open every day, all day, and whenever you are ready, I can begin helping you gain control of your abilities. If you have a suit design in mind, I'll make it a reality. Try to rest easy. You're safe here."

Talida nodded. "Thank you all for being here for me. I'll join you. I'll tell you if I need anything. Tony?" she said, looking in my direction.

"Yeah?" I asked, wondering what she needed.

"Please make sure Shawn is okay. I'll be alright, I just need some time as well," she said. "Thank you for helping me."

I nodded. "Of course."

Red Kelvin and Steel Cowboy walked closer, Red Kelvin's eyes trained on Talida, and his lips curled into a small smile.

"Are these new recruits?" Red Kelvin asked.

"What was that all about?" Steel Cowboy asked. He seemed annoyed by what had just happened to him.

"The new guy is Fury, apparently. His name is Shawn Dewman, and he is a friend of Tony's. He is under a lot of stress due to some sensitive information we had just spoken about. I apologize on his behalf." Blackwell motioned toward Talida. "And this is Talida, also a good friend of Tony's.

Fury has enhanced strength and enhanced speed, and Talida has fire abilities as far as we know."

Red Kelvin put his hand out to shake Talida's hand, getting to her before Steel Cowboy did. "I'm Red Kelvin, but you can call me Mason Kelvin. It's a pleasure to meet you, Talida. Any friend of P is a friend of mine," he said, bowing his head as she hesitantly shook his hand. She looked confused, and Red Kelvin quickly explained that my hero name was Persevere.

"And I'm Steel Cowboy. My true name is Corbin Sawyer, and it's great to meet you," he said, shaking her hand as well. "I look forward to gettin' to know you and hopefully workin' with you."

"Alright, guys, let's call it a night. You can go train or do whatever you like, but let's give Talida some space," Blackwell said.

I nodded. "Good night, Talida," I said, giving her a remorseful look. "If you would prefer to spend the night in my van with me, you're more than welcome."

"Good night, guys, I'll see you tomorrow. I think I'll take Blackwell's offer tonight. I need some time to think, alone. Thank you for everything," she said as she held my cape out in front of her. "Um, here's your cape." Her cheeks turned red, showing her previous embarrassment.

I nodded. "No worries. You needed it more than I did. I'll see you tomorrow." She smiled and headed to find a room.

I looked around. Once everyone except our leader had left the room, Blackwell turned in my direction. "Keep an eye on your friend. Anger will either be his motivation or his downfall," he said quietly as he exited the room.

He stopped at the entry, looking at the now empty frame that used to have a door in it, shaking his head in frustration. "I just installed that door," he said to himself with another sigh. "And that sink." Blackwell left the room.

As I headed toward the training room to work out a portion of my own anger, I questioned what I was going to see inside. I knew Shawn had found his way, and I wanted to avoid a confrontation with him, but I knew that I needed to work out too. I threw my cape over my shoulder, and it snapped into place.

Blackwell's advice settled in my head, worrying me. I couldn't let my friend fall because of an anger issue. I couldn't let him become one of the villains, and I needed to put my emotions in check too.

As I neared the still-open door of the training room, Shawn was loudly beating against something, grunting and screaming like an animal. With courage I entered the room, hearing heavy breathing as Shawn fell to his knees, trying to catch his breath. *Dude, what did you do,* I thought as I caught a glimpse of his blood-covered knuckles. At least, on his human hand. I looked at his punching bag, which was dripping in blood now. I realized he had blazed in, hitting the first bag he could find, because there were two obliterated bags strewn across the ground. He must have found the one for enhanced strength last.

Shawn looked over to me, bowing his head in shame as he realized everything he had just done.

"Are you going to be alright?" I asked him quietly, trying not to trigger him again.

"As long as you don't remind me, I will be," he said, still angry. He was finally starting to calm down, just not quickly enough. "Well, I really fucked that up. Some first impression, huh?"

I pressed my lips, knowing well enough he had made a terrible first impression on Steel Cowboy and Red Kelvin. Even Blackwell. No, especially Blackwell.

"Everyone loses control. We all have. Don't beat yourself up too much about it, man," I said, wanting him to know that not all was lost. "The only thing we can do is try to grow from it."

Shawn looked at me, skeptical. He rolled his eyes, scoffing. "That's easy for you to say; when have you ever blown up to the point that I just did?" he asked me in aggravation. "I almost killed the strong one…what's his name?" He sighed. "I don't even know how to control my strength yet."

The question annoyed me, but I knew that so far, my blowup had caused a lot more damage than his had, even if it was to the right person. I answered the easy question first.

"That's Steel Cowboy. He's pretty nice once you get to know him." Now it was time to answer the hard one. "That person that attacked you in the school…" Shawn clenched his fist, his teeth following suit as his anger returned, telling me that I needed to choose my next few words very carefully.

I adjusted my stance before continuing. "That piece of shit in there…I snapped. I didn't feel any regret for what I did, but I beat him until he was almost dead. He had told me I wasn't any different than Veka, then I blew his brains out. It wasn't what a hero should have done, but in the moment, it was the only thing I could do," I said. He loosened his hands.

"Fuck, dude," he mumbled, his eyes closing as his head dropped. "That's brutal, but I understand. What I felt back in that room...when Talida told us she'd been hurt... I've never felt that before. That, along with when I woke up and thought you were the attacker, is the darkest I've ever been in my own mind. Sure, I was pissed when Johnny would bully us, and when you and Aiden were lost in the fire, I was lost, but this...this is a new level. It's one thing to lose things you love from an accident, it's another to hear that your friends were targeted intentionally."

I gave Shawn a moment to process, and then he began speaking again.

"I want to apologize to you directly. I'm sorry I blew up on you. I shouldn't have snapped at you. You are one of my best friends, and I don't know what I'd do without you guys. I want to join your team, and I want to make sure we help people with our abilities. The only way I can feel good about being alive right now is if I'm able to save others from my fate. This can't happen to anyone else," Shawn said.

I nodded. "This next week I want to focus on training and stopping crimes. I want to have some real experience in the field rather than just in the training room. Talida is going to be okay. She just needs time and our support," I said.

"I really made a fool of myself in front of her, didn't I? I just...it feels..." He took a deep breath as if to ready himself or organize his words. "When I'm angry, there's a rush, and it feels as though I physically need to attack something. I'm just thankful that most of the time I can direct my anger toward something rather than attacking everything around me. Except today, of course," he stated, upset with himself.

"It didn't look good, but we all understand. You'll have a chance to correct the bad impressions. Just put it down as something you need to work on. Anger is a loose end that you can work on controlling as well, since it doesn't look like you're going to have issues controlling your powers," I said.

Shawn let loose a quiet chortle. "I whooped your ass too," he razzed, cracking a smile.

"Hey now, I got you back. If Blackwell hadn't have walked in, I would have ended you," I said, laughing now. He chuckled back and looked down at his bloodied hand.

"Man, I feel like the human part of me is going to hold me back. I need to minimize my limitations, but I've got to work with what I have. I'm not going to make the same mistakes as some other cyborgs in the shows I've watched," he said, laughing.

"Yeah, that didn't end well," I said back, knowing who he was alluding to. "Don't go trying to add upgrades to rid yourself of the human. Just work with what you have and become a better you."

Shawn smiled. "You're right. That's good advice. Let's get some rest. I shouldn't push myself anymore tonight. I'll see you in the morning, dude," he said, wiping the blood off his knuckles and onto his shorts.

"Have a good night, man. I'm going to work out a little bit before I hit the crypt," I said as he left the room. I looked around, deciding what to do first.

"Alright," I said, planning to do some basic workouts tonight. Maybe some cardio. Or some lifting? Tomorrow was going to be a different story, but for now I needed something simple. I wanted to figure out how to focus mid-battle tomorrow. I fought a lot better once I really focused. As my mind wandered through my past experiences, it was strange how much improvement I had seen when I fell into focus. Obviously, that was important during battle, but when I go a step further, it's almost as if I can see my enemies' next moves. It was a little weird, but awesome.

It was almost as if I could see the future.

Chapter 26

Redemption Calls

After an early, hefty breakfast, I spent some time paying attention to the news. My tablet was able to keep me up to date, but I ultimately shut it off. They had been showing the same video for the last two hours; a video of one of the attackers running through the hallway. None of the other information had been released, and I was tired of seeing it.

As I arrived at the hideout with my duffle bag, which I had been able to take with me, I sighed. I wondered how Shawn was doing today with this all over the news. At least he wouldn't have to see what happened to Alex again. I wasn't quite sure what he had seen to begin with.

I stepped into the lobby, and the television was on in the corner with all the heroes staring at the screen. Upon my arrival, they all looked at me in shock.

"What's going on?" I asked, looking at the TV myself.

A bright-red headline on the screen read: "Breaking News," and underneath the headline read: "Masked Vigilante Exits School During Attack." As my eyes widened and my breathing shortened, a video of me popped onto the screen, the news anchor narrating over the video.

"This man is dangerous and armed. If you see him, call 911 immediately to notify your local police department. We are unsure of his motive, and it isn't certain where this man's intentions lie. We are unaware if this attack is related to the threats received Monday by the school, but a previous student has become a suspect," he told the audience.

The first video that played was of me shooting the officer. Of course, they didn't show the video of me saving the first officer from the android. A second video continued on the left side of the screen, showing me leaving the locker room covered in blood and running down toward the football stadium. Luckily, Red Kelvin and Steel Cowboy weren't visible in either video. I clenched my teeth as I thought they were going to name me as the suspect, but as the screen changed, so did my worry; they had no idea who the person in the costume was.

My secret identity was safe.

A school portrait of Johnny popped up on the right side of the screen, and it seemed as though the news anchor was handed something. Probably more notes. As he cleared his throat, he began to speak again.

"Police are still searching for Johnny Coleman, who has become the main suspect behind the attack after recent threats to students at the school. His disappearance since then is alarming. Johnny Coleman is also a suspect for a housefire in northeast Old Belmont where Lenalee Yakitashi was murdered and her husband Hajime Yakitashi is missing and also a suspect. It is recommended that you contact your local police department or call 911 if you see him," he said.

I wiped the sweat off my brow, relieved that the police didn't know who I was under that mask, but then worry began to set in. They were going to look for me. For all they know, this guy in the suit could be Johnny, which means they think I'm dangerous and out to hurt people.

As I looked around, the heroes were still distraught but not quite as much as they had been before. With their gazes still trained on me, I began to become nervous. *I messed up,* I thought, thinking about that day. They probably didn't trust me as much anymore. They know I killed him, and they know that's not what a hero's supposed to do. I began to pick at my thumbnail, pulling at the skin around it.

As I looked around, I saw Shawn leaving the room grimly, and I knew the news had just brought back the memories of what he'd been through. I scowled, knowing I had been the one who ultimately hurt him. *Man, I really fucked up.* I started to head after him, but Blackwell stopped me.

"Don't beat yourself up, Tony. We will all have a slipping point. Many of us already have. Go ahead and talk to Shawn, and afterward, I would like to speak with you privately about where we should go from here," he said solemnly.

Is this what getting fired felt like? Was he going to kick me off the team? I was the only one seen on camera, after all, although I didn't know why Steel Cowboy wasn't shown. My shoulders tightened as I resisted the urge to hide. I wanted to be anywhere other than here with all these eyes judging me. What were they all thinking? Did they still trust me? Maybe they were just worried about how I feel.

"I understand. I'll meet you in there," I said, my words falling short through my disappointment.

His sudden change in tone caught me off guard. "Don't worry. You've just taken a step that the rest of us haven't yet, and we need to talk about it," he said, reassuring me that I wasn't going to be kicked out.

I nodded, gave a slight smirk, and then noticed that the heroes had stopped looking at me. They were now carrying on conversations with each other as I headed to Shawn.

"Hanging in there?" I asked him as I followed him into the social room.

"Trying to," he said, not even attempting to give me a smile. "I'm having a hard time now that you're on the news and they're trying to paint you as the bad guy. I'm happy that a few people spoke in your favor though."

I cocked my head. "What do you mean? I didn't see anything about people talking about the situation other than the news anchor."

Shawn then gave me a slight grin. "They questioned me and Talida this morning since I was involved. They figured out that I was the only other one in the locker room. I told them you saved me, and the man tried to attack you. I also told them that it looked like you were coming in trying to help people. Luckily, some football players also backed you up and said you helped them. Turns out, even the officers guarding the school said you were there to help. Even the one you shot."

A small fire lit up in my chest. The football players? They actually defended me? It seemed strange to me, in that dire situation, that the football players were some of the people to speak on my behalf. I ran to help them, and in return, they saw me as a good person, coming to give assistance. There didn't seem to be a clique barrier.

I smirked. "The football players, huh?"

Shawn snickered. "Don't let it go to your head. If they knew who you actually were, they would still be laughing."

I nodded, still smiling. "Yeah, for sure. Still an interesting feeling. Being a hero to people who normally wouldn't care about you?"

Shawn nodded. "That *would* be weird. I want to experience being a hero, which brings up an idea I had earlier," he said, his thoughts turning to a more serious tone. "These cops are going to be looking for you, right? So, I think we need to find a way to clear your name. They don't know what you're after, and they don't know if you're a good guy or an enemy right now. We need to find something you can do to make it obvious you're the hero in this situation. Also to prove that you're not Johnny. Blackwell spoke to me this morning about physical therapy, so I'll be dealing with that as well. Me and Talida both have appointments at Triple H."

I stroked my chin, humming in question. "Well, what do you have in mind? I don't want them to think I'm a villain, and I don't want them to think I'm Johnny. It doesn't look like they've put two and two together to know that I stopped the mugging either."

Shawn cocked his head. "Wait, I forgot about that!" He shook his head, chuckling. "Of course, it was you, you psychopath... Anyway, that actually makes it an even better idea. I say we team up and take out that gang! They were affiliated with the Mandiri right? If we take out that gang, not only would we gain a good reputation, but we would also get them out of the way. A lot of the smaller crimes would disappear if they weren't here to do them, not to mention the bigger crimes they do. Those assholes kill people for *looking* at them wrong," he said.

A fire burned in his eyes as he spoke about taking them out, and I couldn't help but wonder what he would do afterward. He wasn't going to lose himself, was he? I knew he was dealing with a lot, and he had always talked about getting revenge on the ones who hurt his friends and family. That wouldn't consume him, would it?

"We'll need to be careful, for multiple reasons. That gang is danger-ous, and we aren't bulletproof. Well—I am actually. Once they're alerted that we're after them—which I guess I might have already put into play—they aren't going to hold back. Once we start taking out more of their people and they know it's not a fluke, that's when the real stuff is going to start. We also need to make sure we don't lose ourselves to these guys. We're heroes," I said, wanting desperately to voice my concerns about him.

"I think it would be a good place to start. Taking them out will give us some real-life experience with fighting and dealing with actual enemies. Sure, it won't prepare us for Veka's Followers, but having *some* experience is going to help. I'm not going to lose myself. I know who I am and who I want to be, but I'll be damned if I let another thug stay out on the streets. I will stop at nothing to avenge Alex; Veka and Johnny have to die for me to be able to start moving forward with my life. I want to do this with you," Shawn said, already fuming at the thought of confronting them.

There was so much emotion pent up in both of us. I sighed as I realized

Shawn and I had the same intentions. It was justified in my head to stop these people, so why did it worry me when Shawn talked about the same situation on his terms?

I bit the inside of my lip as I scratched the top of my hand. I mean, I had already killed someone. My mind justified that in the moment too. There was a moment of silence as he let me think about the option, and I felt the pressure that *something* needed to happen. I sighed again. "Let's do it. Let's stop the muggings and dealers, and let's take down this gang."

A massive grin grew on Shawn's face, and his eyes lit up. "Hell yeah! We're superheroes!" he yelled. "I need to talk to Blackwell about getting a suit. Then we can catch some thugs!" Shawn paused for a moment to think. "Do we know anything about this gang? I know they call themselves the Mandiri, but how do we find them? When you were fighting them, did you notice anything that we should be aware of?"

I thought back to when I was stopping the mugging. Was there anything that caught my attention?

"Other than knowing they carry that particular shade of green on them, I don't really have any new information. I ran into them mugging someone late at night behind the gas station, and we already know that they are mostly in the northeast sector of Old Belmont," I said, jotting this down in my memory. It would be good to organize what we knew, despite it not being much. "I've got another idea. If we can interrogate some of these gang members, maybe we can get some information that we can use to draw out their leader." I smiled as I realized my excitement about the situation. *Finally, some real work.* Stopping that first mugging was terrifying, but it had felt fantastic.

"Dude, we're going to scare the hell out of these guys." Shawn shot me a sinister smile. "You can control your fire, right?"

I conjured a bright fireball in my hand and nodded, starting to enjoy the idea of taking a group like this down. The world would be a much better place without this group of thugs running the streets. These people were out here killing, robbing, and goth knows what else. We could put an end to it.

"Good. These guys will be terrified if we disarm them and show them that we have powers. We should be able to get information very fast." Shawn stopped talking for a moment as a new idea flooded into his already busy mind. He looked at me, and his smile widened. "We should get Talida in on this too. It'll be the three of us, taking out the bullies of the real world, being superheroes! It's like we were born for this, dude!" He held up his hand and gave me a high-five, hyping me up.

"Let's do it!" I shouted, now fully invested. "Let me talk to Blackwell, and hopefully he can tell us where to start. He doesn't want us out in public yet, but the school attack has made it obvious we're already on Veka's radar. The best thing we can do right now is get the proper training and experience so that we're ready when he attacks us."

Shawn nodded quickly. "Sure, go ahead and talk to him. I'm going to stay in here for a little bit and design the suit I want. It'll be pretty simple since I've already got the tech," he said, raising his prosthetic arm with a smile.

"I'll be back," I said as I turned to leave the room. My nerves began to set in as I neared Blackwell's office. What did he want to talk to me about?

Did he already have a plan?

Before I could knock on the door, Blackwell stepped out. "Ah, Tony. I thought you would be here soon. Could you walk with me? The others are in the training room."

I nodded, following him down the hallway.

"There's no easy way to start this conversation, so I'm just going to jump right in," Blackwell started sternly, crossing his arms. "I'm aware that the situation with Veka and his members is growing exponentially, and it is no longer a question if you are on his radar. With the attack on the school proving they are after *you*, the question now is when and where he will attack your friends to bring you out again."

My heart shot through my chest. While I had known this was probably the case, hearing Blackwell speak the words aloud was a whole different ballgame. As my thoughts began to circulate around when I was going to die, Blackwell interrupted them.

"I'm going to highly suggest the heroes take up some real experience with criminals, and I suggest we all start using the training room to combat real threats. It will simulate whatever you like. You can test yourselves against different abilities to see how you fare or to see what you need to avoid, but it will be an important step in your training. I—"

I interrupted him. Because of my nerves and the overwhelming urge that I needed to start doing something now, I couldn't help but speak. He had just taken the words right out of my mind. "Shawn and I have been talking about that."

Blackwell cocked his head, taken aback by the interruption, but it didn't seem to anger him. "How's he doing?" he asked back.

"He's alright. He wants to get real experience, and after his loss, he wants to avenge Alex. I wanted to run it by you, but we want to stop the muggings and robberies being done by the gang called the Mandiri. It's a big gang around here, and we think if we neutralize them, it would give us a lot of real combat experience and help the people of Old Belmont."

Blackwell paused for a long moment, and just as I thought he wasn't going to acknowledge the concept, he took a deep breath.

"I think that would be a great start, but not everything around here is what it seems. You need to be careful. I'll let you do it, but I ask that once you get more information and find a lead on who's running the gang, let me know. You need to stay low so that the gang doesn't find you, and Veka doesn't catch on. Ending a gang the size of the Mandiri will put a target on our backs, but it will be a great start to ending violence." There was a short pause as Blackwell thought. "I will involve the other heroes, and together we'll have a head-start on taking them down."

"So where do we start?" I asked him, wanting to rush into it. There was no point in hiding anymore. Veka's Followers already knew who I was.

"I'll start a game plan tonight. I'll plan multiple missions for each of you. We will split into groups and hit them hard sometime next week. I'm not certain who the groups will consist of, or how many we'll need, but I'll tell you when I decide. Talida talked to me this morning, and while she is going to be shaken up for quite some time, she wants to familiarize herself with her powers and join the team as well. She's embracing her struggle and wants us to call her Kasai in the field. She has given me a suit design, and I will be asking Shawn for one as well."

Whoa, I thought. "That's a lot quicker than I thought it was going to be. Shawn is drawing a suit design now. Is there any reason for her choosing the name Kasai?" I asked, curious about its meaning.

Blackwell grabbed the back of his helmet, unsure of whether he should answer. "Yes..." He leaned his head back as if the answer hurt him, which sent my mind into confusion. After a moment of silence, he began to answer me. "It means conflagration, which is..."

"It means destructive fire," I grumbled, interrupting him again. "Shit." I looked down and understood why this name had such meaning to her, but it sent me into a state of wonder, a state of panic. Was she out for revenge like Shawn and I? If she learned how to use her powers and decided to go AWOL, we couldn't save her either. Now I had two friends with powers and someone who has hurt them both.

"Is she alright? Do you think she is at risk of deserting us like Shawn is?"

"She is stable. I don't think she's at risk. While I believe Shawn is looking at his newly acquired abilities as a weapon against the person who caused them, I think Talida is accepting her powers as fate; she believes these powers were given to her for a reason."

Blackwell uncrossed his arms, brushing his finger over his gold medallion. "She has embraced who she's becoming, and she wants to take control of herself to make this world a better place with less toxicity. In regards to Johnny, she wants to bring him in for justice and confront him personally.

She wants an apology and wants to see him locked away forever."

As his words settled my racing mind, I began to think about how different the three of us were now that these abilities had brought our personalities to light. We were all hurt by Johnny in different ways, Talida and Shawn more so than I had been. Shawn had lost what could have been the love of his life, and Talida recently lost her friend and family, along with all the trust she could have had in them. I, on the other hand, lost a friend and have committed an act I never thought possible by my own hands.

The memory of killing that man in the locker room lingered vividly in my mind. That *grin* he gave me. That *laughter*. That *anger* as I splattered what filth was inside his head against the concrete wall!

Shawn is undeniably out for blood, and Talida is set out for justice, but where do I lie in this predicament? Somewhere in the middle? Or, when it came down to it, would I kill Johnny too? Half of me knew that taking a life was wrong and that I should, under no circumstance, kill a human being.

The other half wondered what would happen if I didn't send Johnny to his grave. Would he become a real issue? If we put him in prison, would he find a way out to hurt us again? If Johnny was working for Veka, he might be too far gone already.

I sighed. I had always bashed Batman for not killing the Joker when he had the chance. I had always thought if he had just killed the villain, he would have saved a lot of people. But now that I was standing face to face with the dilemma of whether or not to take a life, I didn't know where I lay on the spectrum anymore.

Since Batman didn't kill the Joker, and that in itself resulted in the deaths or injuries of so many people, did that make him a villain? A criminal? I didn't know the answer to that question. I hadn't thought I would ever have to be in a situation like this, let alone make the call on someone's life. If I didn't take Johnny's life, and a lot of people died, would it be immoral to let him live? Would I become the villain?

"Blackwell?" I asked, knowing that I needed to speak with him about this. "Do you think Johnny is too far gone to turn him around? He was involved with some horrible things, and what he did to Talida is unforgivable, but do you think killing Alex was *his* plan? Or was that something Veka decided?"

Blackwell thought for another moment. "Well, I'm afraid that's a complex issue. He did threaten you and your friends, and he's bullied you for years, which may be a home issue; they usually are. From what I understand, Johnny may have crossed a very personal line with Talida, but what may have been done, wasn't confirmed.

As for the attacks, Johnny hasn't had any personal involvement. It very well could be Veka acting on his hatred to target and eliminate you. While I do believe he could be a serious threat, it is possible that if we act quickly, we can prevent Johnny from becoming a killer. With the implications of what he did to Talida, if they are accurate, he may not be redeemable. Ultimately, it is up to you to decide what sets you apart from the monsters," he told me.

"I'm afraid of what I'll do to him if I see him again," I mentioned. "I lacked control in that locker room. I don't know if I can control myself against someone who might have done that to us. Do you think he could have planned something like that?" I asked. With each word, my heart shattered further. I couldn't trust myself with my emotions, and I damn sure wouldn't be able to control Shawn if we saw him.

"I don't think he was physically involved in the attacks, although he had probably given Veka the information he needed to find you. As for Talida, only she could tell you what was done. If you plan to pull Johnny out of the hole he's being led into, I would focus on not letting him go further. You've got to learn who you are before you can learn to control your emotions against a person falling into evil. That will come in time, and only then will we find out how you will handle it."

I bit the inside of my cheek. "Do you think he did that to her? Do you really think if we find him in time, we can keep him from becoming like Veka? I want to bring him to justice. I want him to find the help he needs for whatever has caused his life to be like this. I want him to pay for what he's done, and come out as a better person," I said, clenching my fist. "I want to save him." That's the better route. That's what I needed to be focusing on. Helping troubled people to become better before they become worse.

"If what was implied is incorrect, I don't think he has fallen past the point of no return. He is being consumed by hate and fear, and I believe you are the only one that can change his path. Shawn is reckless and lacks the mindset to turn him around. I can't say he's wrong about his mindset, but it is not what needs to be present if you are to do this. Talida's set on justice, and while she doesn't want to kill him, she in no way cares about where he goes from here."

My heart pounded in my chest. It wasn't too late.

"Johnny's a horrible person, but I can't just let him go down this path to becoming a true monster. He's already disgusting, and he needs to pay for what he's done, but I can't let him regress further. Where do I need to start?" I asked.

"You need to find Johnny, before Shawn and Talida, before he gets a taste for blood."

Chapter 27

Saying Goodbye

Content Warnign: Contains loss and grief.

The next week was nothing more than heart-crushing. I had spent my time trying to hunt Johnny, hoping that if I kept myself busy, I could prevent myself from grieving. It was no use. Now that Alex was gone, and Johnny was nowhere to be found, I had no other choice but to dwell on my sadness.

I spent a lot of the time trying to console Talida and Shawn. Especially Shawn. While he had been able to hold himself together at first, he was now going through the important steps of moving forward. The process was definitely not cut and dry like they told you at school.

The first three stages seemed to all happen at once, and now he was stuck in a depressive state. The only way Shawn felt he could cope with Alex's death was by becoming a better hero. That was something he had decided early on. Shawn had decided to take out his anger and sadness by running around Old Belmont, trying to find criminals he could stop in a make-shift suit while he waited for Blackwell to create his professional one. Despite how quickly Blackwell had said he could get them done, he had run into some problems with both the Fury and Kasai suits. Shawn had succeeded in finding criminals, but we hadn't gotten any leads on the Mandiri yet.

I was doing about the same, although I had always handled grief better than others. Alex was one of my friends, and losing her really hurt, but I wasn't the one that had been dating her. I seemed to be trapped in a stage of anger, blaming Veka and Johnny for her death and wanting revenge. I knew I needed to make sure I stayed heroic, but I couldn't help myself from hoping I would find Johnny in one of those alleyways. To put him in jail where he belonged. To break him away from Veka's strings. Not before I took out my anger and frustration on him though.

More than trying to stray away from our grief, we were trying to avoid the fact that Alex's funeral would be Saturday of this week.

Today.

Today was the day we all wanted to avoid but knew we couldn't. A time to say goodbye to our short-lived friend. She had fit into our group so well. I missed her already. I briefly blamed myself for gaining abilities. If I hadn't put Johnny in his place at school, would he have been pushed to running away and finding Veka? Would Veka have even known who I was?

"You look great, man," Shawn said solemnly. I had just arrived at the End of Beginning Church and Cemetery, where Alex would be laid to rest soon. It was in the southwest quadrant of Old Belmont where Alex's family supposedly lived. They had never told us directly. Shawn and I were the first ones here, and the hearse would be coming shortly. Due to the nature of her death, Alex's family had decided they wouldn't be having an open casket viewing. They stated that they merely wanted to put her at peace. Shawn and Talida were both sad about it since they had both been hoping to see her face one more time.

I, on the other hand, always thought open caskets were strange. Creepy even. I knew it was odd to think that, with my other slew of interests within the macabre. I was relieved when I heard there wouldn't be one. It just seemed weird to gather around the visible body of the person we cared about. She was a great friend, and I felt that I needed to be here to show my respect to her and her family, but she was gone. It was time to put her body to rest.

I stood tall as I realized my parents would have refused to come due to what I decided to wear to this funeral. They would have been embarrassed of me, but if I had learned anything in the time after my coma, it was that it was better if I was completely myself. That's what our friend Alex would have wanted. She wouldn't want me to come to her funeral and pretend I'm someone I'm not. My parents were no longer in my life, and I was surprisingly thankful for that. I missed my brother, though. He was someone I could have talked to at a time like this.

To be fair, I felt just as uncomfortable being this close to a church as my parents would feel to be alongside me. Especially with my new physical traits. Being an ex-Christian as of a few years ago due to clashing personal beliefs, alongside my new pale skin, fangs, and a gothic fashion, I didn't feel like I belonged here.

Under different circumstances, I would have loved to stroll through the cemetery, and despite my spirituality, churches had beautiful architecture that I admired.

Today, I had pulled my hair up in a high, tight bun. I wore black eyeliner and a gothic suit. It was a black tailcoat with pentacle buttons over a purple vest and a black shirt with a purple tie. I had a pentacle ring to match the suit on my right hand, and I had redone my black stiletto nails for the occasion. I wanted to look my best with my friends. Plus, putting effort into my appearance made me feel a little bit better about myself. It raised my confidence, and goth knows I needed that right now.

"Thanks. You do too!" I wasn't quite sure how to respond as I looked Shawn up and down. It was a rare occasion that I saw him dressed up, and he cleaned up well. He had slicked his dark-brown hair back in a low ponytail with gel and trimmed his facial hair. He wore a black suit with a purple vest and red tie. He wore sunglasses, partly because it was sunny, but mostly to hide his swollen eyes. He also held a black briefcase. The fact he had also chosen black and purple made me smile.

I also noticed he was wearing Aiden's Grudgematch ring as well. As I looked at his other arm, I could see the vague shimmer of the illusion around his prosthetic. If you weren't looking, you would never be able to see that something was different. It looked like a normal arm, and I could barely tell.

Shawn looked around. "Where's Talida?" he asked. As if in answer to his question, she walked up to us.

"Sorry. I was running a little late," she said. "My Uber never showed, and I had to find another one. If I had known it was going to be that difficult I would have gotten a ride from one of you two. Speaking of, are your parents here, Shawn?"

Talida wore a black funeral kimono with white floral flowers and a pair of flats. She had a hair pin holding the hair out of her eyes, and she had makeup on. It took me by surprise because I didn't think she even owned makeup. She had never worn it before, but it looked nice. "Wow, you both look great!"

Shawn answered first. "Thanks, you do too! No, I came alone. My parents were busy, and I walked here."

"Walked here? This is like fifteen miles from your house!" Talida exclaimed, forgetting about his powers.

"Yeah. I needed the walk, though. With my super-speed, the distance was nothing. I changed when I got here." He lifted the briefcase slightly as if to say that's what held his clothing. "Overall, I'm glad my parents were busy today. They're not great at support, and I will honestly need the walk back to clear my head. Thank you both for coming."

"Of course," I said. "I'll always be here for you both. She was our friend, and I wanted to be here to support you. If you decide you want a ride back, I can give you one." I had driven my van here, and I worried about his current mental health.

As I looked at Shawn, I could see how close he was to breaking. His face was tense, and there wasn't any hint of a smile. Normally, we could bring each other up, but today was not going to be one of those days. We stood in support of each other, but it'd likely remain a grim day. Then Shawn stepped forward.

He hugged me. As I hugged him back, I could feel his body shudder as he started crying against my shoulder. "I can't believe she's gone," he mumbled. The words set me off, causing my own lips to tremble. I couldn't stand to see my friend cry. Normally, out of our group, Shawn was the strongest. He was the rock. I usually didn't break down either, but lately I found that I was prone to it. It was like my wall had been destroyed.

"We're here for you," I said, trying to keep my voice strong. I was not going to break down at this funeral. I wouldn't let it happen. In my peripheral vision, I could see Talida wipe tears from under her eyes with the side of her hand. She stepped forward and hugged both of us.

"I know, man. I just wish she was too." Talida pulled away. I could see the words of Shawn tear apart her resolve. She was trying just as hard as us to hold it together. Shawn sniffed as I pulled away. "I'm sorry. I don't mean to cry." He threw his hand down in a fist. "I'm supposed to be stronger than this."

"There's nothing wrong with letting your emotions out. We're all upset, but you're hurt more than we are. Sometimes you've got to cry. We all do," I said.

"That doesn't make you weak," Talida interjected, making sure he knew that.

Shawn nodded. "I know." As we looked up, it was time. We could see the funeral procession heading down the road. He sighed as he stared into the distance, knowing this place would be swarmed by her family as soon as they parked. There weren't many family members, and her parents wouldn't invite anyone from school. With her death being public, where it took place, they were avoiding having classmates and whatnot show up out of nowhere.

They actually didn't invite me and Talida either, but Shawn had given us the address. It wasn't that they blamed us for her death, just that they wanted to keep this small, from what I understood. Shawn was the only one of us officially invited. He said he had met her parents once when they had first hung out.

Her family parked and began getting out of their vehicles. There were a couple of kids a little older than us, followed by their parents. Then two sets of grandparents stepped out, followed by what could only be her mother and father. I could tell by the misery in their faces. The bags under their reddened eyes. The mother had attempted to cover her face with makeup, but it was like trying to cover a black wall with a single layer of white paint. She hadn't added enough, and her tears likely washed most of it away.

Alex's mother was a short, Asian woman with thin light-brown hair. She was likely in her late forties. Her father looked about the same age, but he was a stout man with graying facial hair and a beer gut prominently showing under his umber overcoat. He met my eyes with a scowl that he then turned toward Shawn. As they approached us, I could see other family members frowning in our direction. I got the sudden feeling that we weren't welcome here.

"I don't believe we've met," her father said to me in a gruff voice. His piercing almond eyes stared down at me. I could feel the overtone of annoyance. He nodded toward Shawn, understanding that he'd likely be here. "My name is Dallas. I'm Alexis's father." The first thing I noticed was the whiskey on his breath. I tried to give him the benefit of the doubt, believing alcohol was how he coped with his daughter's untimely passing.

Talida stepped forward first, holding out her hand. "I'm Talida. I was friends with your daughter, and I'm best friends with Shawn. I'm sorry for your loss. Please tell me if there's anything I can do for you." He reached out and shook her hand, eyeing her up and down with a disapproving glance. He shook his head, eyeing her pink hair, and then turned to look toward Shawn.

I put out my hand, catching his attention. "My name's Tony. I was also friends with your daughter, and I'm one of Shawn's best friends too. My condolences, sir." Dallas's scowl turned to one of hate, and I was immediately confused. He shooed my hand away.

"I am aware that my daughter was going through a phase, but I will never accept her trashy friends. I see that she was involved in the wrong crowd. Surrounded by delinquents who wished to taint her future. I allowed Alexis to continue talking to Shawn because it made her happy in this brief phase of her life, and I knew that it would ultimately be temporary. I did not invite the two of you, yet you trespass on this dark moment in our family's lives." Dallas then turned his back on us, after briefly glancing at Shawn again as if he had more to say to him but decided against it.

So many thoughts went flying through my mind after his words. There were so many things I wanted to say. My first thought was to defend Shawn. He had done nothing wrong. When the time came, he tried to help Alex! And calling us all bad influences and telling us we were delinquents? How dare he!? We were friends with her because we had similar interests and cared about her!

Talida threw her hands down to her sides, her hands balled in tight fists as her face reddened. "How *dare* you?" she cried out. "Alex would have been lucky to have someone like Shawn in her life! He cared about her more than any other person could have!"

This was the one thing that was able to force a smile from me. As she let loose against this ugly man, her words mirrored my feelings. I wanted nothing more than to knock that mustache off his filthy face. Talida said everything I wanted to say to him, so I kept my mouth shut and let her do the talking. We weren't here today to fight with her family. We were here because we lost a close friend.

Shawn walked over to us as Talida finished. Dallas was gone anyway. As if we didn't exist. "It's okay, guys. We aren't here for him anyway. Nothing he thinks matters anymore." His words were heavy. While he was able to take the criticism, it reminded him that the future they had was gone. "Whether or not he approved of us no longer matters. He doesn't have a say in it…because Alex is dead." The vein in his head became visible as he tried not to let himself become a blubbering mess. "And he's right. He shouldn't be proud of me. He shouldn't care about me. I was there that day, and all I could do was watch her die."

The words made my throat clench. It was all I could do to not break down as I saw the pain in my friend's eyes.

Shawn stepped away before we could say anything to help him. He needed space, so we gave it to him. As the ceremony progressed, there were sniffles from a few of her family members, but most of them were able to hold themselves together. The area was quiet as the pastor spoke nice words about Alex and her family. It then moved onto family members speaking about how much they loved her, all while Alex's mother sobbed quietly.

I looked over to Shawn next to me, tears running down my own face. Maybe it was a bad idea to wear eyeliner today. I saw his clenched fist and his clenched jaw. The only thing I wanted to do was help him.

"I'm so tired of watching people I love die," he whispered, unable to speak any louder. His words shook me to my core, and he started to cry again. He looked at the ground, unable to watch the casket now being lowered into its grave. He held in his wails, trying to stay quiet in the crowd of Alex's family and friends. I stood there, the tears rolling now. I stood strong, though. Someone had to be there for Shawn and Talida. I could see that Talida was hurt too, but no one compared to Shawn.

I felt for Shawn. He had told me he and Talida went to Aiden's Celebration of Life. His family had taken care of the body privately, due to the severity of his death, but they wanted a ceremony to get some sort of closure with their family. That's why Talida and Shawn had gone, so that they could say goodbye to our best friend. Now he's at a second funeral for someone close to him.

That's why we were here today. To say goodbye. A poetic parallel to the hell we were being put through.

Suddenly, Shawn couldn't keep himself quiet anymore. He kneeled down, and in a burst of melancholy that caused me and Talida to jump, he screamed for her.

"Alex!" He grabbed the sides of his head.

"Alex, please come back! I fucking love you, and the only thing I want is to see your face again." He pushed his energy out in short bursts of sobbing, his face now on the ground as he seemed defeated. His crying grew to an up-setting crescendo as his sadness poured over the edge of his emotional cup.

As Talida and I saw Shawn, we couldn't control ourselves anymore ei-ther. "I'm sorry," I whispered, choking up. Talida wiped tears away again as she began to fall to the sorrow.

Today, I heard both of my friends crying. Today, I was lost in the failure of a superhero.

"I'm sorry I couldn't save you, Alex."

3

The Nemesis in His Shadow

Chapter 28

Under the Radar

"Okay, MIRA," I said as I wiped the sweat from my neck. "Let's try this same scenario again with five people. This time, randomize their location and give them enhanced strength."

The shielded computer system for the arena buzzed as it began to initiate an ambush scenario where I would be surrounded by five enemies. I had previously succeeded in defeating up to three, and I was now ready to step it up a notch.

I had been working on focusing mid-battle, which seemed to be the thing that saved my life during my last fight. I called this skill my Battle Focus; fighting was the only time I knew I could use it so far, and it was only when I narrowed in on myself or the enemy.

"Now initiating training sequence. Engage in 3... 2..."

As I focused on myself, MIRA's voice faded out, and I was now ready for the battle. During this stance I had created, I could almost sense my attackers coming. I saw one heading toward me from the front, and at the same time, I knew one was coming from behind, who was moving a lot faster than the first.

I turned around quickly, clearly seeing that the attacker was going to go in for a high jab toward my head. I crouched, dodging the jab, and struck the man in the stomach as hard as I could. The man went flying, disintegrating as I took him out.

I turned back around to the second attacker, and in my peripheral vision, I could see two more that threatened me. He went for a kick to my side, which I blocked as the other two came into melee range.

As they swung, I blocked one of them and was hit in the face by the other, causing my ears to ring and making me realize how much harder super-strength punches were.

As I honed my Battle Focus, it seemed as if everything slowed. I blocked a kick to my left and then a punch to my right. As an attacker behind me swung his arm down, I flung mine upward, my fist creating a large arc of fire behind my swing. The strike landed, killing him, just as I kicked the one behind me in the head, snapping his neck.

As I saw a weakness, I leapt into action against the fourth enemy, kicking his leg out from under him as I pulled my Blaze Ray. I pulled it up just in time to shoot the fifth attacker running toward me, and then I turned to shoot the one on the ground.

Not too bad, I thought. I just needed to focus sooner so I could avoid the first hit. My training had been going smoothly since I started using this newfound technique. In just a matter of hours I had been able to reach the point of being able to defend myself against three of them, and now I was able to defeat five while only being hit once.

I was in no way ready to fight Veka head-on, but this was a start.

Everyone's MIRA system began to emit the sound of a siren. *What's that mean?* I thought, having never heard it before.

I looked down at my MIRA system, which had the words "Mission Alert" in a bright-white box. "Blackwell would like all Project Barricade members to meet in the briefing room for their next mission," MIRA said aloud.

Weird, I thought. This must have been new for the system. As I turned off the arena simulator, the other heroes headed to the exit. I followed, catching up with them.

"Do you think this is about taking down the gang?" I asked. I had told them earlier about what Blackwell and I had discussed last week.

"That, or something entirely different. Could be anything at this point, really," Whirl said.

"Yeah, I wouldn't be surprised if it was another attack. Veka seems to be getting all riled up," Steel Cowboy added, cracking his knuckles. I had seen him moments ago beating against the punching bags like a walking tank, working harder than I had seen previously. It seemed like we were all training heavily, knowing that our lives were at stake now.

"I bet he got some more information about the gang. We're probably about ready to make that first attack," Red Kelvin added.

As we neared the briefing room, I wondered where Shawn and Talida were. I hadn't seen them all morning, and they hadn't told me that anything was going on. Surely, they were okay, right? With the recent events, my friends not telling me they were going to be gone had me a little freaked out.

As we entered the briefing room, we were immediately met by Blackwell, who ushered us in.

"Good afternoon, Project Barricade. Welcome to your first official mission briefing," Blackwell said as we sat down.

He wasn't mentioning Shawn or Talida, so he must know where they are.

"I'll start by telling you that this briefing will be about our first step against the Mandiri. We do have a few things to go over that aren't necessarily related, though. As you four know, we have two new members. First, I want you to officially meet Fury. Wielding super-strength at a 9 and super-speed at an astounding 14, along with the technological ability to spot weaknesses in his enemies, Fury will be a great asset. Like the rest of us, he has things to work on, but I believe he will mesh well with our team," Blackwell said.

As I sighed in relief, Shawn came out in his hero outfit, which caught me off guard. *Wow, his specs are better than mine!*

His whole outfit was a dark purple and red. He wore a purple do-rag mask that covered his eyes and nose with three red stripes, coming to a point on the front of the mask. As he turned his head to look at Blackwell, I noticed that the three stripes led into two strips, used to tie the mask. There was also a red line beneath both of his blacked-out eyes.

He wore a vest of the same purple with a black strap running diag-onally across his chest. This led down to his baggy red and purple shorts. The most eye-catching piece of his suit was his massive cape the color of dried blood, which rested around his neck and then split down the middle to a point on either side. That drew my eyes toward a set of large boots.

As he looked around at everyone with a solemn expression, I knew exactly why he had chosen the color scheme; I was positive it was a play on our favorite superhero. Grudgematch had always been in a purple outfit of the same shade. It was likely one of the reasons purple was my favorite color.

Using the color purple would definitely remind him of the strong connection he had made with Alex. It was a step toward accepting what had happened without letting it go. An homage of sorts to pay his respects to their fallen relationship.

Shawn waved. "It's good to finally be on the team, for real," he said, confirming my theory. He stood nervously, resting his hand over the black straps that covered his bicep. "Um, I'm not sure of what exactly to say, but I apologize for my poor first impression. I want to apologize to all of you. Steel Cowboy"—he paused for a moment, making eye contact with him—"I'm sorry for throwing a door at you. Red Kelvin, I'm sorry for almost running you over in the hallway. I was not in a good place mentally, and I'm just…sorry." Shawn walked over to where I was sitting, his large wallet chains clanking along the way. They accepted the apology, and he sat down next to me and raised his fist.

As I fist-bumped him, he gave me a small grin. "You like the outfit? It was our favorite color combo," he said.

I nodded, giving him a smile back. "Yeah. It's a nice touch. Ready to kick some ass in it?" I asked him.

He chuckled. "You have no idea."

Blackwell looked back at the room behind him. "Second, I want you all to meet Kasai. She has enhanced strength at a 7.5 and reflexes at a 9. She wields fire and a unique, related ability that we were able to unlock this morning during training. She can create dragon-like scales with her flames, and as we focus on melee training, she will be a great asset to our team there as well."

Talida walked out of the room behind Blackwell, revealing her suit and giving me an opportunity to see her hair again. It was strange to me since her hair had been the same since we were kids. However, the hot pink hair matched her suit perfectly.

My eyes were now drawn down her pink and orange suit. I first noticed the orange cloth going across her face with pink eye holes. Below that was what looked to be an orange, thick Titan Fiber suit with an intricate pink design going from her upper chest down to her abdomen. The design led to the top of a pink belt with the orange word "Kasai" in the middle.

Underneath the belt, she had a pink flame design along her thighs, leading to the top of her knees. She had a simple pair of orange shoes with pink flames along the front. My eyes were then drawn to her large cape. The cape was pink on top, but near the bottom, it turned to dark orange flames, which led about halfway up the side. Talida waved, wearing orange gloves with pink dancing along her knuckles.

"Hey, everyone. Thanks for inviting me to Project Barricade. Thanks for welcoming me," she said, her body language showing that she was definitely out of her comfort zone.

Talida ran over to us, a huge smile on her face that caught me off guard; I hadn't seen her smile like that in a long while, let alone after everything that had happened. She was definitely taking this differently than Shawn. I mean, they were both hurt, but she was trying to maintain her old self through her pain.

"How do you like my suit? I designed it last week when I was in a better headspace." Red Kelvin became noticeably flustered. *What's with him?* I thought.

I smiled back, along with the rest of the heroes. "It looks great!" I said, mimicked by Steel Cowboy and Whirl.

"It looks awesome!" Shawn said. "I love the color choices."

The words "You're smokin'" slipped out of Red Kelvin's mouth, and we all looked at him, becoming silent. Talida made eye contact with him as he realized he had spoken the words aloud. As I watched Red Kelvin's eyes double in size, he tried to recover himself.

"Because…you know…it's a flame-related design. You use fire, therefore there's smoke and you're…" Red Kelvin blushed as the rest of his face went pale. He conjured a small fireball in his hand and began twirling it around. "Hot."

Kasai giggled, putting her hand up to cover her mouth in disbelief. Shawn held his breath as he attempted to let the situation play out without him losing it. As he realized it wasn't going to work, there was an explosive burst of laughter, and the others chuckled right after him.

As I watched Red Kelvin dying of embarrassment, I could tell in his eyes he liked her. "Um…" Red Kelvin chirped. "I'm sorry…"

Talida continued to smile as she too began to blush. "It's okay," she said.

"I would like to say it is very flattering, and I hope that you like it," Red Kelvin said, trying to redeem himself.

"Thanks," she said back shyly, the visible skin on her face redder than I had ever seen it. She opened her mouth to say something else but was interrupted by Blackwell.

"Alright, now that introductions have been made, we need to jump right into business," Blackwell started, seeming to interrupt the embarrassing moment on purpose.

Kasai sat next to Shawn and me, and we all began to pay attention. We were ecstatic to be going on our first mission together. This would be the first time we've all worked as a team on something important, so we knew doing it well would make an impression.

"My eyes and ears have pulled together some information about the Mandiri, and we are led to believe that some sort of deal will be going on. We aren't quite sure what kind of package this is, but it is safe to assume we don't want them getting it. As of right now, we have two potential locations where this deal may go down. I'm going to split you into two groups, one of which will hit the northeast location near the Shadow Lake docks, and the second group will hit a northern area in the woods close to High-Rise Campground. The first group is going to consist of Persevere, Steel Cowboy, and Kasai. The second group will consist of Shawn, Whirl, and Red Kelvin. The goal is to intercept the package and eliminate the present members. We dispatch them, and we send that gang a message that they're in trouble. I don't believe interrogating these members is going to give us any information. According to my eyes and ears, they keep things pretty locked away. The only way we are going to be able to pull their leader out of the dark and end this gang is to force their hand. That's just what we are going to do tonight."

I interrupted him, confused. "Wait, we're going to kill them? Isn't there another way?" I asked.

All the heroes looked at me, wondering the same thing. The distressed faces around me made it obvious that none of us were ready for that to happen.

"The only way to clear these members off the streets is to take their lives. If there was another way, I would try it, but there's not in this case. We don't have enough solid evidence to put these people away. The authorities are scared of them, which is made worse because they don't have the evidence needed to arrest them."

"Then why don't we gather information about them so that they can be locked up? If we snap a few pictures and then beat them into submission so that we can take pictures of their faces, wouldn't that be enough? I don't think killing them is the right option. We need to do this right and put these criminals in prison!" I said with a raised voice. I felt that we were straying off the right path and heading into a darker one that would lead us to be on the same side as Veka. Was this the decision Blackwell had mentioned in the vision? Was this a test?

I can't let that happen. "These men are thieves or killers, and they hurt people to get what they want, but killing them isn't going to make us better than them. That would put us on the same level, and then what's the difference? What makes it okay to justify killing a person just because they're a killer? You're going to start a gang war, and we would be considered a gang," I said.

My mind bounced back and forth like a seesaw. On one side, I believed killing was immoral. I had always been taught that taking someone's life was an ultimate sin, and we should focus on repairing the broken. The ones that can't be repaired need to be punished in prison. Let them live with what they've done without stooping to their level.

The other side knows damn well that the opposing beliefs won't work. If a person has caused pain, taken lives, or destroyed lives around them, aren't we hurting other people second-handedly if we don't take their lives? Can we really tell other human beings that you can *buy* taking a life with only seven years in prison? If we know a monster exists, shouldn't we kill it before it kills again?

My mind fell into a rut; it was a rut I had been in only a couple of times, and it was the line of thought that created my evil temptations. I believed they deserved pain, and I was very willing to hand it out. Anyone bullying or physically hurting people for their wants deserved the same pain they put out.

"I understand your struggle; this is a hard situation, and unfortunately, as heroes, you're going to run into a lot of them. These people, these monsters that call themselves the Mandiri, *are* murderers—yes; but there's a lot of gray area within that as well. These men and women kill people of all ages for their gain, and sometimes that includes children and the elderly. They rape, take whatever they want, and they've decided that it is the life they're willing to live. Unfortunately, in this world that we live in, everything is not always black and white, but we do know that this gang is very dangerous, and the world would benefit from its destruction. These members won't be taken alive." Blackwell brought his fist up to his face before clearing his throat.

"I wanted to avoid a harsh subject due to its irrelevance in this situation, but it now seems like it may provide important information. As some of you may or may not know, the Mandiri also play a huge part in the human trafficking that is being done in Old Belmont. We don't know where the victims are going, but they're likely being used as labor to create whatever's going to be in the shipment tonight. Taking out these members tonight will not only bring their leader to light, but it will also bring us one step closer to shutting down the human trafficking going on. The Mandiri will stop at nothing to achieve their goals, and we must take action," he emphasized.

While his speech brought a lot to light, I still believed that we shouldn't have to kill them. We needed to keep them alive to gather information about where the captured people were being taken. Killing these monsters wasn't right, however horrible they might be. However irredeemable.

"He's right," I heard Fury say. "What if that's what the school attackers were after? What if they had taken some of our friends or family, and we never got to see them again because they were forced into slavery? This world would be better without people like this. We should take pride in being able to rid the world of these…these parasites!" he urged.

My heart dropped when Talida agreed with him. "I'm with Shawn. Maybe we should take one for the team and be the ones to help this world heal. Maybe if we kill these people, we won't have to kill the rest. I don't feel good about the idea of killing them either, but I also wouldn't want any innocent people to be ripped away from their families because of the bad intentions of some sick gang. The Mandiri are also a large reason the people of Old Belmont look down upon the northeast quadrant. The majority of their crimes are done there."

Blackwell cleared his throat. "I am going to let you lead the group on this mission, Persevere. I will let you ultimately decide what you are going to do, but in the end, we need all our members safe, we need to get the package, and more than anything, we need to send this gang a message. We need to instill fear into these people. They need to know that Project Barricade is here and in control," Blackwell said.

As I swallowed the lump in my throat, I nodded. I still didn't know what final decision I would make. I couldn't know until it came down to that situation. Red Kelvin looked at me with an apologetic nod, and it was apparent that he wasn't sure what to do either.

As I looked at Steel Cowboy, his focused glare at Blackwell confused me. When I saw his clenched fists, I wasn't sure if he was angry at him or at these gang members. Was there more to his past than I knew? I searched my memories, realizing I didn't know anything about his mother or past other than he had a problem with bullies in high school like me, and he had moved away from his dad's ranch.

As Blackwell continued to talk about the locations, I whispered to Steel Cowboy. "Hey, Corbin, you alright?" I asked. That startled him slightly out of whatever funk he was in, and he looked over at me. As he realized what had been asked, he pressed his lips together, shaking his head.

"Just a sec', guys," I said to the others next to me as I stood up to head to Steel Cowboy.

When I sat down next to him, he let out a large sigh. "I don't wanna talk about it," he said. I was confused. I began to realize that something had happened to him, but I still wasn't sure what.

"I understand. If you need to talk, I'm here for you. You were there for me when I had that panic attack, I'd like to be here for you during whatever struggle you're dealing with," I said, putting my hand on his shoulder. He jerked slightly, and as I began to question if I should have put my hand on him, he gave me a slight smile.

Steel Cowboy sighed again. "You're a good friend, and to be honest, I do kinda wanna tell you, but it's my own struggle to deal with," he said, taking a long pause as he drew a slow breath. "Um."

I looked him in the eyes, feeling the pain almost as if it had fallen directly from his eyes onto my chest. A vulnerable man sat in front of me; someone who had been deeply broken and didn't know what to do.

Steel Cowboy looked back at me. "The only thing I'll say is my family has some experience with human trafficking. I'd like to leave the rest for later, though. I don't wanna end their lives, but I can't let those involved leave without justice either."

"Don't worry, man. If you need to talk, I'll be here. We'll figure it out," I said again.

"Thanks. Let's power through this mission first."

Blackwell continued talking, and I began to listen. "Now as I've said before, group one will head to the docks and intercept the package if it arrives. There are several places that you can use to keep yourself hidden until it's time to strike. Keep in touch with the other group, and you both will need to attack at the same time to ensure that the other location is not tipped off before they are attacked. Notify the other group when you catch sight of the package and then strike cleanly. I will instruct your MIRA systems to give you the location where your groups need to go. You've got six hours and thirteen minutes until you need to be at your locations. I will let you decide what you want to do in that time frame. If you'd like to mentally or physically prepare, now is the time to do so. I wish you luck, heroes."

Chapter 29

Antithesis

Content Warning: Contains sex trafficking.

As my boots slid across the now-wet grass, I could see the area my group was supposed to be watching. A number of old, wooden buildings stood by the water, many of which had been abandoned long ago. With the crime in Old Belmont, it was dangerous to come to this lake anymore. With plenty of places to hide out, the docks were likely a hot-spot for human trafficking.

I wouldn't even chance going to the High-Rise Campground, which was north of here alongside the lake. It was a beautiful place, but the Mandiri had plagued northeast Old Belmont for a long time now. I felt bad for those that lived in the Bedrock Trailer Park, which was eerily close to the abandoned docks.

Before we got any closer, I looked at my MIRA system. I could see all the connected members' devices individually on my screen. When I spoke, my voice would carry to all of them. Blackwell had made sure everyone was equipped with a voice transmitter that we were able to adjust with the MIRA system. I tapped Blackwell's name, causing a red diagonal line to appear over his hero icon. He was now muted from my words, and I then began to speak.

"Mute Blackwell real quick." There were a couple of confused comments, but they all did as I asked.

"What's going on, P?" Red Kelvin asked from his end.

"This is my choice, but I need you all to follow my lead. I'll deal with Blackwell later, but I'm not killing these criminals. We'll get the package, send a message, and capture the gang members," I replied.

"What?" Fury asked. "Why the sudden change?"

"It's not right for us to kill them unless we have to. There will be more than enough evidence here to put them away. Once we capture them, we'll snap pictures and bring them with us as well. We're superheroes, not killers."

As many of the members agreed with me, Talida's voice came through. "I'm trusting you on this. Since this is just a gang and not Veka's forces, I think you're right to make that call." With everyone now on board, we unmuted Blackwell and continued forward.

As I looked around, my group following closely behind me, I could see a spot around the side of one of the buildings that looked to be an open alleyway. Focusing on this area, I stopped. "I think this is where it's going down," I whispered. "Look over there. It's right next to a dock, and there's quite a bit of room in that alley." I pointed toward it, and Steel Cowboy and Kasai nodded.

"Let's keep an eye out here," I said, motioning for the heroes to hide behind something close to us. As Kasai hid behind a large wooden sign that read Shadow Lake, keeping an eye out from behind her as well, Steel Cowboy darted toward the side of the closest building.

I inched closer, trying to find a good view while remaining out of sight. Suddenly, somebody poked their head out from around the corner. My heartrate shot through the roof as I practically leapt toward Steel Cowboy. *He didn't see me, right?* I wondered.

"There's people here. One might have just seen me," I whispered through the voice transmitter in my mask.

Kasai's quiet voice replied. "He didn't. I saw him look too. I can't get a good view on whoever else is over there," she said. "God, this is scary."

"No kidding," Steel Cowboy said.

"We are in position, Fury. There is at least one target here in the alley next to the docks. Anything on your end?"

"Nothing here," Fury replied. "Barren, actually. We found a spot where they'd likely meet. A clearing in between several trees, so there's cover, but no signs of anyone being here. We've checked the campgrounds too, and no one's even camping tonight."

"Alright, be careful, and keep your eyes open."

"You too, man. If you see the package, we'll do the best we can to reach your area as fast as possible." Fury's voice got super quiet for a moment. "What was that, Whirl?" Fury asked.

Just as I thought they had found somebody, Whirl replied. "It was nothing. Just a deer. The only thing on our end is a bunch of trees and animals."

"MIRA, activate infrared vision. Is there a way I would be able to see through walls?" I asked in little more than a whisper.

"Activating enhanced infrared vision."

I looked over to where I had seen the man peek out. Sure enough, there were thirteen people including the one I had seen. Before saying anything, I tried to see how they were standing. There was a chance that this could be a group of friends smoking or drinking in the alley, but as I noticed they were in formation, I became sure that they were from the gang.

"They're here. Thirteen people looking to be in a formation. One seems to be sitting on something near the middle. Four of them look to be holding their weapons."

As I thought about telling my group to attack them, I stopped when I realized the other half of the trade wasn't here yet. Three heroes against thirteen armed people wasn't optimal either.

"We'll be right there. Whirl, Red Kelvin—they're at the other location. Persevere has eyes on them. Let's go!" he yelled. They started to run, and then the audio cut.

I pulled my Blaze Ray from my belt, getting ready to attack but keeping my eyes peeled for the package. "Anything, Kasai?" I asked, locking my eyes on the group of people.

"A boat's coming in. Looks like a pretty big one."

As I looked over the water, I could see what looked to be a boat with a small cargo container on the back. It looked like a pretty big shipment. What the hell were they trading?

As the boat pulled into the dock, one of the men, the leader, motioned for three of the others to follow him. They headed to the boat. My heart jolted as I realized the man who was stepping out of the boat was very different than the rest of them. He was in a black cloak with a matte-black mask. Two horns and a rectangular mouth made this mask familiar.

Who the hell was that? That was the same get-up as the school attacker. I clenched my open fist, wanting so badly to fill it with fire and attack the man, but I knew I had to keep watching. Two more men stepped out of the passenger side, dressed similarly to the first man, and I realized these were *exactly* like the school attackers. *Great. One leader and two androids.*

As they began to talk, I quickly realized that I wasn't going to be able to hear what they were saying from where I stood. I looked around, but to my dismay, I couldn't get closer without being seen.

I saw the leader from the first group motion toward the back of the boat, and then point toward the alley they were in. The horned man walked to the back of the boat, opening the end of the shipping container attached to it.

My heart sank as I realized what was in it. My stomach turned, and my anger grew as I saw several distraught faces within the container, mostly women. "This is a damned slave trade," I whispered as he began bringing the people out onto the dock in chained cuffs. I clenched my teeth. *You've got to be kidding me.* "Don't make a move."

"You talkin' to us or yourself? We're under your orders," Steel Cowboy said with a similar look on his face. I could tell it was just as difficult for him to see this. He then put a comforting hand on my shoulder.

"Mostly myself."

"What's going on over there?" Fury asked through the sound of rushing wind.

"It's a slave trade, I don't know what the other end of the deal is quite yet."

"Ugh!" he grunted in disgust. "Do we have the go-ahead to kill these fuckers yet?"

I paused for a moment, knowing that the horned one and androids were under Veka's control. The Mandiri must be trading with Veka. "I'll give you the word. Wait for my call. We won't kill the Mandiri members, but as for the ones in cloaks, you have my go-ahead once I give you the order. Be careful, though; the other two are androids. They're the same as the attackers at the school, which means they're dangerous." There was a grunt in return, but he accepted the terms.

"Persevere, we have to move," Kasai said. "What's your call?"

"We need to know what they're being traded for."

As a fourth woman stepped out of the container, I heard a gasp next to me. As I looked toward Steel Cowboy, his eyes grew big, filling with tears and then anger as his face went from flushed to red. *Oh no,* I thought, looking at the woman, and then back at Steel Cowboy. *It isn't...*

"That's my ma!" Steel Cowboy exclaimed, barely able to hold himself back. "We gotta go! We gotta do somethin'!"

I nodded, and just as I was about to give the word to attack, a burst of black smoke caught my eye in the distance. "Whoa," I said. "Hold on. We'll save her, Steel Cowboy, you have my word, but we need to know what that was," I said, pointing toward the smoke.

As the smoke dissipated, it revealed three people. The first two were the same as the ones that stepped off the boat; androids in black cloaks and black masks with glowing yellow eyes. As the third one stepped forward, it felt as if my breath was crushed.

"What the hell?!" I exclaimed. The third man was in an outfit almost exactly like mine. The color choice was the only visible difference, for his was black and scarlet, almost the color of blood. With two glowing red rings for eyes, he sent a menacing glare to his surroundings. He started to walk toward the boat.

"Hold," I whispered. The men's voices grew louder, and we were now able to hear most of the words.

"It was supposed to be fifteen women, and you brought us nine!" the Mandiri leader yelled.

"Bring forth the pills," the horned man said, as if he was ignoring the first statement. The rest of the men came from the alley, carrying a large chest. As they sat it down, the leader started to yell again.

"Okay, here's the damned pills! Where are the rest of the women? This is a risky trade, and you know that! I'm risking my life to give these to you."

The chest opened, revealing several small pill bottles filled with bright-orange and white pills. The man dressed like me stepped forward, interrupting the argument and pointing toward the pills. "That's all we needed to know," he said in a familiar voice. As my boggled mind tried to wrap around the idea of what was happening here, my confusion and anger turned to a question.

Who is that? I thought. *I know that voice.* The leader of the gang members looked startled, for the strange man had come unnoticed, but the horned one seemed unphased. "Who the hell are you?" he asked, lifting his gun.

"These pills aren't yours to ship out and sell. You've breached your contract, and by the rules of Veka, there is only one penalty, and that is suffering," the man said.

The gang member's eyes widened. "What...what do you mean? Veka gave us these pills and wanted them shipped immediately. He said it was part of the plan..."

The familiar man interrupted him with a sharp tone. "No! He didn't, and I've been specifically told you would say that." The horned man nodded his head toward the person next to him, who ushered the women back into the cargo hold.

"Good," I said. "They're safer in that container. Prepare to attack. Fury, how close are you? We need to move, now."

"We're still about seven minutes out. If it's urgent, you may need to take care of it without us. If you can wait, we are close," he said.

With a cringe, I knew we were probably going to have to act before he'd arrive. What should I do? That was a lot of men. We needed to see how this was going to go down without losing the package.

The leader bit his tongue for a moment, nodding his head as he was visibly offended by the statement.

"Look around you, kid," he started, chuckling as he threw his hands in the air to his sides, suddenly changing his tone. "We've got our weapons drawn. Twelve people over here..." He pointed to his left at the original men who were with him, and then he motioned to his right to the two androids and horned man. "And you've got three people over there that *have* been trained in Veka's forces. You need to leave before you're riddled with holes..."

"Are you unable to see that the two guards I have with me are the same as the two he has on the boat? They're with us. It's thirteen against six, and I can take care of you myself. It's apparent you don't understand who you are dealing with." The man stepped toward the gang member. "I am Antithesis, and I'll be the last thing you ever see!" he said, swinging a fist down toward the man's face before he could respond. As his arm swung through the air, a shadowy mist enveloped his arm and solidified into a massive icy fist—the color of blood-tainted ice. The knuckles shot out in spiky shards, impaling the man's head and upper body, attaching him to the ground beneath him like spears of the chaotic substance.

I jolted, taking in the unexpected view. "Oh, my, goth!" I squeaked, still attempting to be quiet as a black shadow leaked off what was now a gang member's corpse.

Kasai looked at me from her location, and it was apparent that we were all debating if we could handle this enemy.

The cloaked men immediately pulled up assault rifles, opening fire on the Mandiri with energy bolts, making it known that they were enemies to the gang.

The gang fired back. Bullets struck Antithesis, bouncing off as he sprinted toward them. Three of them fell to the ground, dead from the volley of bolts the androids were sending out. Antithesis grunted as the Mandiri's bullets struck him, and then he lifted his arms, sending crimson veins of light into the ground. Immediately, these veins lurking across the surface erupted into chaotically placed spikes of red ice, impaling four more of the men.

Two of the Mandiri cowered in the corner, hidden from Antithesis, but where I could see them. As the gang was mowed down by energy bolts, Antithesis stepped over to the chest, grabbed the end of it with one hand, and walked toward the boat.

I made it known to the heroes that there were two more members in the alley. My team knew what I wanted done with them.

"Put this on the boat, and let's take this back to Veka," Antithesis said, handing the chest to two of his men.

This was it. We had to act now. "I'll hit the two with the assault rifles first with my Blaze Ray. Steel Cowboy, I want you to take out the one on the left holding the chest while Kasai takes out the one on the right. Then we'll go after Antithesis. Fury, come as quickly as you can—we have a problem. Kill anything with a cloak!" I held up my fist, and then threw it down, giving them the signal they'd been looking for.

I pulled out my Blaze Ray and aimed it at the first android with the assault rifle. As I pulled the trigger three times, set to kill, the trilogy of bolts pierced through the man. Two through the chest and one in the neck. Upon the second bolt in the chest, sparks flew, and its eyes flickered as it fell to the ground in a heap of metal. The others noticed, and the one holding the chest dropped it. The second one with the drawn weapon started to shoot at me.

I barely dodged the energy bolts coming my way as I shot toward the android. Steel Cowboy got his electric lasso gripped to the one on the left. Kasai came sprinting, and Antithesis latched his eyes onto her. As Kasai let loose her rage in the form of an explosion of pink fire, the one that had been previously holding the chest turned to look at her.

As it seemed the fire wasn't going to affect the android, she intensified the heat, focusing it on its chest. It seemed as if whatever wiring inside overheated, and it fell with a crash too, right before it could lift its weapon.

Antithesis laughed as it hit the ground. He let out a grunt as he threw his hands forward, creating a giant, spinning ring of ice with black veins.

"What the hell?!" Kasai exclaimed, sending a large burst of fire in his direction and leaping out of the way of the ring, which was now shooting spikes of ice from its center.

Antithesis turned to face my direction. "It's good to see you again, Tony," he said.

I gasped, unaware of how he knew me.

Then it clicked.

Time stopped as I put a name to the voice, and I felt as if my entire being turned to ash.

It's him.

Johnny is Antithesis.

I began to shoot at him, starting at the legs and arms first, for I wanted to take him alive, but suddenly he was somewhere else. My heart rate shot through the roof. I shot at him again, this time to the left. I missed again!

How did he do that?

"What are you doing, Johnny?!" I asked as he moved his icy fist, which seemed to absorb the rays I had shot toward him. His fist glowed brightly before turning back to that sickly red. Black shadow fell from his body in whisps.

"It's Antithesis now." Suddenly, he was right next to my face, and I imagined he was grinning beneath the copycat mask he was wearing.

Before I could say another word or attack him, his voice fell into a whisper. "*Your* antithesis."

I swung at him to strike him while he was close.

But he was gone. Far away from me again in a fraction of a second.

As Kasai heard the words, her reaction was much less subtle. "What?!" she said. "I'm going to make sure you pay for what you've done!" As controlled fury flowed through her, large, pink scales of nearly solidified fire covered her body. She threw herself at him, swinging at him with flaming fists, each one being blocked by a burst of his unique ice abilities.

Fury began yelling in my ear. "He's there?! I'm coming to you! I'm going to kill that mother-fucker!"

Steel Cowboy leapt into the battle, the anger flowing in his eyes as well. It was a different trigger for him. "You took my mother!" he said, thrashing violently at him with precision. His vigorous training was coming into play, but Antithesis blocked each of his strikes.

"So, this is…" Antithesis started, blocking one of Steel Cowboy's punches and kicking in his knee. As a loud *pop* sounded through the air, Steel

Cowboy screamed in pain and fell to the ground. "The Project Barricade..." He swung his fist up in an uppercut motion just as I landed a shot on his shoulder.

Antithesis was pushed back, the giant wave of ice shards he was going to send toward Kasai being pushed toward her right. It wasn't far enough, and Kasai's right side was struck by dozens of icy red shards. She leapt out of the way, falling to the ground as well with a whimper.

"Veka has been talking *so* much about," he finished. I lowered the Blaze Ray, running directly toward him, crushing the ground beneath me.

I threw a punch, enhancing it with all the fire ability that I could muster. An explosion of ice beneath Antithesis launched him into the air, shifting him out of the way.

Just as the large pillar of ice lifted him from the ground, my hand struck the wall, sending a crack all the way up in an explosion of yellow flames.

There was a battle cry from behind me, which then echoed in my headset. "I'll kill you!" Fury said, flying through the air above me and landing a punch to Antithesis's mask. Antithesis was knocked off the pillar, landing on his feet on the ground below with a powerful slam.

"What better way to end Phase One and Two than right here when they're both together," Antithesis said, shooting a glance toward the heroes that he had injured. What did he mean? What were Phase One and Two?

Kasai stood back up, only mildly injured due to the strength of her scale armor. She mustered another wave of fire, which Antithesis stood through, his arms raised in front of him. Fury ran into the flames, and as I followed him, I could see Fury throwing punches faster than I had ever seen him, landing several in between the blocked attacks.

Antithesis caught up with him, his reflexes kicking in as he blocked every future punch Fury threw at him. As I jumped into the battle, focusing as hard as I could on him, I kicked his legs out from beneath him and went in for a punch while he was on the ground.

There was another explosion of ice as a spiked pillar shot out. Fury was able to block it with a large energy shield from his prosthetic arm. He was thrown several feet away and struck himself on the head with his own shield.

I took another swing. Antithesis shot backward, my fist landing on the ground as his body was launched away from my attack. As he leapt back onto his feet, I tried an uppercut but was blocked by him. My Battle Focus kicked in, and I was able to avoid his next three shots. I focused further, trying my hardest to see how far this ability could go, and it seemed as if the focus guided my fist into his side, landing a powerful blow.

He grunted in pain. I blocked his next move and swung my body around with a strong roundhouse kick. He blocked that, and as I recovered, he attempted to hit me. His hit landed in my midsection, sending me several feet backward and giving me tunnel vision. *Oh, shit,—that's what super strength feels like,* I thought. He was so much stronger than me. Likely by several power levels.

"Hey!" Red Kelvin yelled from behind us. I smiled; now that backup was here, we would hopefully be able to defeat Antithesis or escape with our lives at the very least. None of us had expected Veka's forces to be here, let alone Johnny as a supervillain; a powerful one at that.

Red Kelvin came in running with his shields activated, seeming almost fearless. Antithesis turned once again toward Kasai and sent another wave of ice spikes from the giant fist he had created. "No!" Red Kelvin said, leaping in front of her and lifting his shields. He was able to block most of the ice, but the rest went around his shields, grazing the sides of his arms. "You will not hurt her!" he yelled with ferocity.

"What, is she your girlfriend? Did you find yourself a little play-thing to keep you entertained, Talida?!" Antithesis yelled, sending yet another wave of ice.

Red Kelvin let loose the biggest fireball I had seen from him yet, followed by another, and now Kasai was in on it. She followed his fireball with a volley of her own. They were lucky enough to miss the spikes this time, but now it was time for Fury and me to step in again.

I leapt at him, swinging my own fiery punches. I was trying my best to keep him away from Steel Cowboy, who had moved back and was now limping toward the shipping container. He used his electric lasso to yank himself toward the container. I smiled beneath my mask. He deserved this. We needed to help these poor people out of the container and get them out of here. *Let's defeat Johnny.*

I caught a glimpse of Kasai through the flames, seeing her normally pasty cheeks filled with red as she continued to unleash hell on Antithesis. Whether it was from the anger, the stress, or Red Kelvin saving her, I would probably never know.

Whirl ran to my left as though unsure of how she could help without hitting one of the heroes. She attempted to grab Antithesis with her telekinesis but he didn't seem to budge. She instead started moving the boards of the dock beneath him in what was likely an attempt to make him lose his footing. As Antithesis ran out of the way of the fire, he sent a large wall of spiked ice toward the two pyromancers, forcing them to leap out of the way, one to the right and one to the left.

When Whirl saw an opening, she launched all her knives toward Antithesis at once. Antithesis turned to block them with his energy shield and broke six of them with the shield, sending a large ice spike that hit Whirl's forearm. "Oh, no! Are you alright?" I asked her.

As Whirl screamed and fell to the ground, favoring her arm, Fury landed a punch to Antithesis' side, knocking him sideways and causing three of the knives to go into his leg. There was a yell of pain, just as I landed a punch on him myself.

He was vulnerable. We were doing it. We could still win this! Here's one for all the years you hurt me, Johnny! I jumped toward him and sent my fist as hard as I could into his body. Antithesis was thrown backward, sliding against the ground, bouncing along the way with a loud grunt of pain.

He quickly got up, and just as he got to his feet, he was hit with two fireballs, one from Red Kelvin and one from Kasai. Out of the flames, Fury came through punching and knocked him to the ground again.

Antithesis began cackling. It was a laugh that would haunt my future. I had never heard anyone laugh this hard, especially while they were getting their rear end handed to them. It was as if he had gone insane and his anger was the source.

Another explosion of ice, this one much larger than the rest, sent out a horizontal ring from him. "What the..." I leapt to a place that was safe as soon as the other heroes were out of range.

"This fight isn't over. You'll suffer Tony, but you won't be the first! I'll hurt your friends, and then their families, and then everything else you have ever loved," he screamed. "Every hero needs a nemesis, and you've created yours!" He made it to his feet, and in a blur of crimson and shadow, he was suddenly a hundred feet away from us. Large pillars of ice shot toward him and covered him with a makeshift dome that had dark veins that leaked shadow.

Antithesis tapped on his arm where my MIRA system would have been, and he disappeared within a puff of the same black smoke as when he had arrived. When I realized we were safe, I ran to Steel Cowboy, who was ripping the door off the shipping container.

"Ma!" he said through his pain, falling to his healthy knee. "I'm here." Tears were streaming down his face when I reached him. I ripped the chains off the prisoners and set them free.

"Fury, could you get those Mandiri members still hiding in the alley?" I asked as I checked to make sure they were still there. He nodded, then quickly ran over there with the chains and brought back the two members. I almost laughed, for he had dragged them along the ground with his super-speed after disarming them.

I looked behind me and saw Red Kelvin run toward Kasai while he yelled to find out if Whirl was okay. After he knew for certain that Kasai was alright, he sprinted to Whirl. Fury had luckily been able to take care of the bleeding by tying his bicep wrap around Whirl's arm.

"He really kicked our asses," I said to myself. As Steel Cowboy lay on the dock, unable to stand, I walked over to him. "Are you okay, man?" I asked.

"Physically, no; I need Medic. But knowin' my ma is okay…" A smile grew on his face, and he winced. "I couldn't have asked for anything else in my life to go this well. How are y'all?"

"Whirl is hurt, but Fury got the bleeding taken care of. Kasai is injured, but not nearly as badly as you and Whirl. Red Kelvin was grazed, but he doesn't seem phased right now. Fury and I are fine," I said, feeling the stinging pain in my side. "Well, we're pretty beat up, but there's nothing that won't heal quickly."

Fury came closer to us with the two Mandiri members, his skin practically steaming with the anger he had just experienced. "So, what now? Now that we know Johnny has a slew of powers, what the hell do we do with that? He damn near took us out by himself!"

I looked back at him, realizing that everyone was now near me. They were waiting for a response. They looked to me as a leader despite us already having a master. I was distraught by the notion. I choked. How could I be a leader? *What do I say?* I then mustered everything I could to attempt to convince my friends that I was worthy of them following me. As the words "I don't know" sat on the tip of my tongue, I pushed them to the side.

"There's only one thing we *can* do. We train, and then we do what we did here tonight again," I said.

"Get our asses reamed?" Whirl asked, her spirits low. Her pessimism struck a nerve with me, reminding me of Aiden. *Man, I wish he was still here with us,* I thought. Was he still alive out there somewhere? Is that another reason I was gifted with my abilities? Did I need to find him? Something in my mind hadn't settled ever since Talida had told me about his death. I shook my head, knowing things like that only happened in movies. My friend was gone. They had found his body.

"If Veka's other Followers are anywhere near as skilled as Antithesis, we are in a lot of trouble," Kasai said, raising her eyebrows in concern.

"We fight. Together."

Chapter 30

The Man in Chains

Several Hours Before the Fight at the Docks:

Johnny followed Veka down the dimly lit, brick hallway. His mind raced as he traced the oddly yellow flames of the torches that illuminated their path. Veka had told him the yellow flames were a failed experiment to create an inextinguishable flame, one of which he could use in a multitude of ways, but it hadn't worked.

"What are we doing down here?" Johnny demanded.

Veka chuckled lightly. "You will see. There are things here that you will learn to accept and things that you will learn to understand. For now, keep quiet and follow me. Soak it all in, and we will see if you have what it takes to achieve your goals," Veka said with a sadistic grin.

The comment unnerved Johnny, but he continued forward. This being couldn't show him anything that would stray him from regaining the control he once had.

As they continued down the hallway, the air became filled with the odor of mildew accompanied by the scent of death. Johnny's ears were filled with the sounds of people in pain and noises that could only be torture. He realized he was dealing with something much worse than he expected.

"Please, I haven't had food in weeks," a woman cried from a cell on the right. The screaming from what could only be victims of experimental torture turned Johnny's stomach, and he began to wonder if following this demon into its own lair was worth reaching his goal. He began to question if he would be able to bring himself to do it. Johnny avoided looking at the woman, not wanting to see what horrors lay within the cells.

"If you survive a few more months, I will set you free," Veka said in his scratchy, piercing voice.

A man in one of the cells grabbed the bars, which made a loud echoing sound. "Please, god of the damned, end my life." This man caused Johnny to look at who was moaning; an older man, appearing to be almost dead already, with a rotting, festering hand.

The atrocity made Johnny's eyes wander further; what other horrible things were in here? There was a man with rotting eye sockets, the skeletal lady asking for food, and several prisoners with open, festering wounds for who-knows-what reason.

Johnny had always been tough; he was the bully. He had control over certain aspects of his life, and he would stop at nothing to achieve even a small amount of inner serenity. It's what he craved. But this...this was something Johnny had never experienced. It was appalling.

Johnny looked at Veka, wanting to say something, anything, but he knew he couldn't back down now. He wasn't sure how Veka would react, so instead, he attempted to justify what was going on. He needed revenge on Tony, and as Veka said, this would all start to make sense.

As they reached the end of the corridor, Johnny could finally breathe. He had been on the verge of panic, but the horror was over, and now he needed some answers. He wanted to know why this demonic being was helping him, and if that were really the case at all. Did Veka bring him here to experiment on him as well? He continued to question whether this trip would be worth it as Veka laid his hand on what seemed to be a hand-scanner for a heavy metal, charcoal colored door.

As the scanner lit up yellow, the locks released and the door swung open, revealing another man who was chained to the wall by a large metal collar.

Veka cackled as the man turned to look at them. "Ah, good morning," Veka said. He reached out toward the prisoner and grabbed his black beard, lifting his head to look him in the eyes. "Is there anything I can do to make your stay more comfortable?" Veka asked, pausing for a moment to see if he'd respond. "Perhaps a television to watch your hopeless, 'special forces' fall apart? I can get you the best quality TV so that you can see every detail of each and every one of your members' deaths."

Veka let go of him and began to pace the room. He chuckled again, this time almost to himself. "You know, it's funny; you're just going to be locked in this room while my Followers do the work, and then I will kill you myself, ending this whole charade you created with just one, quick slash." As Veka grinned in anticipation of a response, the man yanked himself forward, stretching the chains as far as they could go toward Veka.

"You will not get away with this! I will escape, and when I do, you will pay for your atrocities. You're a monster, Veka!" he screamed with ferocity. Johnny was taken aback by the strength in this prisoner's eyes. He reminded Johnny of himself in a way; he wanted revenge. Veka had done something to this man, and now he wanted to make him pay.

"*I'm* the monster?" Veka said back toward the man. "You know damn well what you did to wrong me!"

The man didn't argue with Veka on that point, but he continued to talk. "Look at what you're doing, Veka! Look at those people in that hallway. Those are human beings, and you're watching them rot! You're experimenting on them, ruining their lives, and for what? Revenge on the few that have wronged you? Yes, you are the monster."

Veka stepped forward, triggered by something in the sentence. As he pointed a clawed finger toward the man, he was now screaming. "You started this! It was your race that decided to attack me and make me an outcast when all I ever wanted was help. I have plans back on my world that need to be fulfilled, and when I came to this planet seeking refuge, what did your race do? They attacked me. I searched for a man who called himself a hero, and he not only refused to let me speak but also slaughtered my mother in cold blood! Tell me, Asim, is that what a hero would do? Because of my interactions with you people, I will rid this world of ones who give themselves the title of hero, and I will use your bodies to further my research. You'll die in here, and it will be by my hand alone. As soon as you call yourself a hero, you've submitted to the rules of my game!" Veka seemed to calm down, but Johnny was terrified. As he attempted to keep his hands from shaking, Veka ushered him out of the room.

"So, who was that? What did he do?" Johnny asked, attempting to make some sort of conversation in hope that Veka wouldn't ultimately kill him because of his race too.

Veka shook his head. "He was a meddler. He was gathering a force to try and undermine me, so I'm going to find all the people that he was working with and slaughter them. I want him to watch," Veka said, having no sympathy for the man or the ones working for him.

Johnny cleared his throat. "So why are you here?" Johnny asked. "If we're going to work together, I'd like to…"

Veka interrupted him. "You work *for* me, not with me. I will give you the ability to achieve your goals, and in return, I ask that you help me with mine. I do see potential in you, but you're going to have to let go of everything you think is right and wrong," he snapped. Johnny stayed quiet for a moment, not sure if he should speak, and then it became apparent that Veka wasn't finished.

"I will tell you a little bit about myself, only because I *do* see that potential in you. I am from a dimension called Rek. I am a Kallyn, which is the major race on my world, and I was born into an immensely powerful, unique bloodline." Veka raised his arms as if to boast about his lineage, grinning widely. "Because of this, I was made an outcast, and they attempted to kill me in order to erase my lineage. They feared me taking the throne."

As Veka lowered his arms, his grin grew serious. "There are different categories of Kallyn. Four to be exact. My bloodline can be born with aspects of each of them along with qualities of what you humans call vampires, causing my world to believe that my bloodline would introduce the ultimate beings." Veka scraped a black claw against the brick wall, leaving a deep gash as his neutral face turned to a scowl.

"They hunted down my family to find me, and despite remaining hidden for some time, we were eventually found. I escaped and after some time, wound up here. I vowed to become an immortal to return to my world and avenge my father's death. He sacrificed himself so that the rest of my family could escape."

Johnny didn't know what to say for a moment. Then he felt that he had to break his silence. This demon loved to hear his own voice.

"I think I understand. What do you have against humans? I understand why you're against heroes, but what exactly did our race do?" Johnny asked.

"When I arrived here, I attempted to make connections with your race. My first interaction was long ago, and they tried to kill me. Tried to hunt me down like I was some sort of plague. We came to this world needing help. My mother had connections with the vampires' matriarch here, but when we arrived, her bloodthirst once again took hold."

Johnny continued to follow Veka down the hallway as he continued rambling. He paid little attention, but felt he should probably at least try. "We tried to search for help, and we heard rumors of a grand hero. Highly revered by everyone in his country. Instead of providing help, he called us demons, and my mother was slaughtered. I've been in the shadows ever since. Over these many years, I've seen the human race try to kill everything different than itself. I've lived through the witch trials, the crusades, and many others like them. Humans have proven that they fear progress. If you introduce a different idea too soon, they will revolt against it."

Veka turned to look at Johnny, continuing to walk fluidly, although backward. "I will be the first to admit my race isn't any better; in fact, most of my race is inherently violent. They kill everything and everyone who is different due to the fear that those people will become more powerful than them. Few families differ from that attitude, but because of my vampire mixed bloodline, I have a broader spectrum of emotional understanding than other Kallyn."

Johnny thought for a long while before responding. As the things Veka had told him swirled inside his head, some possibilities came to mind. He began to ask questions. "Are you…Dracula?" he asked him. Veka cackled, shaking his head in response.

"No," he said. "Dracula is a tale to scare children while introducing the world to the idea of a vampire. There is little truth in that tale. Vampires and witches, however, do exist."

As Johnny realized Veka wasn't going to answer further, he changed the subject.

"So, what now? Why'd you bring me down here? Are you going to show me how to fight Tony or what?" he asked him with a hint of annoyance. He crossed his arms, more uncomfortable than he let on.

"In due time. Right now, we need to educate you. Follow me, and let's talk."

Johnny followed him through a cell door. "Alright," he spat, rolling his eyes. He didn't want to waste his time on more education. Veka had already talked a lot.

"As I've already told you, you're going to need to forget everything that you think is right and wrong. So, what is your end goal?" Veka started as they headed down into a new tunnel. As Johnny was about to answer, he was quickly interrupted by Veka. "You want to kill Tony. But why do you want to kill him?"

Johnny held his tongue. As he realized Veka wasn't going to answer that question, he spoke up. "I don't want to kill him right away. I want to make him suffer, like I have my entire life. He took everything from me. He took the last bit of control I had over my life, and now I have to take everything from him to regain my respect."

Veka smiled. "You mention control. What exactly is it that you believe you had control over?"

Johnny became annoyed, hearing each of Veka's footsteps crunch against the ground. "What does this have anything to do with hating Tony?"

Veka slammed his fist into the wall, crushing the stone beneath his skin with a loud CRACK. He then turned to Johnny again. "I'm going to be asking you a lot of questions, and if you don't answer all of them, I can't help you. It is crucial that you reach down inside and find the ability to *answer* me!" Veka snapped.

Johnny's eyes widened, alarmed at how quickly Veka had lost his temper. After what he had seen in those cells, Johnny was beginning to think he shouldn't push him further. Johnny stopped for a moment to think. What did he have control over?

"I...I guess I had control over the school. Kids were afraid of me because I was stronger than them. I could manipulate them to do my homework and get supplies when I lost mine. I was able to beat up Tony and his friends every day, and it was that way for a long time. School was the only time I've ever felt that much control. I enjoyed knowing what was going to happen every day when I left for school."

Veka grinned a little wider. "There we go. Now we're getting somewhere," he said as he let loose another gravely chuckle. "So, you like control, and Tony took that away from you when he made you look like a fool. And because he took this away from you, your life fell apart. The two boys you thought were your friends left, and you disappointed your family, am I correct?"

Johnny scowled, angry that Veka was bringing all this up again, but he continued to push through the conversation. "Yes," he answered through his teeth.

"And how do you feel about yourself knowing that Tony took this all away from you?"

"I feel worthless...helpless." Johnny's fingers dug into the skin of his arms. These were uncomfortable questions, and he wasn't used to being forced to answer them. Hell, he wasn't used to being asked them at all. Veka was the first person to ask how everything made him feel.

"In order for you to be able to make Tony suffer and regain your life, you have to delve into your past and find the source of your loss of control. There are a few steps to regaining it, and once you have that back, you will be stronger than Tony. Human morals are in your way; you have become so caught up wondering if what you're doing is right or wrong, you don't take the time to think about how it will affect you in the end. That, in itself, shows a lack of power." Veka held up a clenched fist.

"What you crave lies in what's best for you, and only you. As soon as you bring someone else into the situation, you lose control by adding a variable. The step you are going to have to take is this: eliminate the need to ask how your actions will affect others around you. This will put you a step above Tony. He dwells on how the people he cares about are affected. You hurt the people he loves…" Veka stopped for a moment, reaching toward one of the yellow torches. The flames slowly seeped into his hand, until the previously lit torch was snuffed out. "And you've found his weakness." A large smirk grew on Veka's face.

Johnny thought deeply about this for a moment before he spoke. He hadn't been given people in his life that he cared about. Rob and Grey had been the only ones that he ever thought he was friends with, and he only cared about what they thought of him. "So, for me to hurt Tony, I have to hurt the people he cares about? But his family hasn't done anything to me, and they're out of his life now," he said, receiving yet another grin in return.

"It's a mindset that you will have to create. No, his parents haven't personally caused you pain, and he isn't close to his parents, so you will have to hit someone a little closer to his heart. Take it one step further and you reach the point where you can hurt his friends. That will devastate him." Johnny grinned.

"We've already hurt Talida with the experiment. Her trust will be gone for a while. Why don't we hurt Shawn next? That will hurt Tony," Johnny said.

"I've already deeply hurt Shawn. While we were dealing with Talida, I sent some of my men, and they attacked the school. Tony's retaliation will come later for you, but I want you to make sure you're ready to encounter him."

"Wait. What did you do to Shawn?" Johnny asked, not having known about the attack. The statement alarmed him.

"The attackers were taken out by Tony as 'Persevere,' but we made him slip. The leader killed Shawn's girlfriend, and in return, Tony slipped, and murdered the leader," Veka answered.

"So, Shawn is devastated, but what about Tony? How did it affect him?"

"Tony is probably on a downward spiral of doubting himself. He's weakened, and if we're lucky, on the path to becoming a villain. This is the time for you to rise and become who you were meant to be. Think only of yourself and how your actions will affect you because in the end, you are the only one you can trust. I am going to give you the ability to kill Tony and take what you want, but you are going to have to prove to me that you can use those abilities without the crutch of human morals weighing you down. You must regain control over your life before I can give you that power."

Johnny looked up at him. While he debated on his morals and what Veka would have him do, he was becoming angry that Veka hadn't told him of the attack. That wasn't something he would have chosen to do, and he didn't have any say in what happened.

"Let's look back on the conversation we were having about control in your own life. You know what you must do to Tony in order to weaken him enough to kill him, but what do you need to do to gain that power? Am I wrong to say your parents abuse you in one way or another?" he asked Johnny, getting right into the harsh questions.

"How do you know that?" Johnny demanded, distraught.

"Most bullies have similar stories. Bad home life, and then a reach for control. Tell me your story. Tell me everything wrong in your life. Let me guess—father's a drunk, and he gets a little too angry so he takes it out on you and your mom?"

Johnny clenched his fists. "Shut up!" he yelled.

Veka grinned as his yellow eyes narrowed down on him in a malicious glare. "No. I don't think I will. Tell me about them. What does your dad do to you?"

Johnny clenched his jaw this time, wanting to lash out against this monster for bringing up this subject. That's what he had always done. Every time his pain would be brought to light, he would attack the source. Yell at them, hit them, whatever it took for them to quit asking questions. But what about this time? What good would hitting this being do if there was no way to win?

Johnny loosened his fist. "You're wrong…"

"Tell me why I'm wrong."

"My dad is a drunk with a heroin addiction. My mom is always popping pills and hitting me when my dad's…not here. I told my dad once, and he hit me too for accusing her. She waits until he's high or drunk enough that he won't remember or understand what's happening. They degrade me. They put me down for anything and everything that I do, telling me I'm never going to be good enough..."

"Good enough for what?"

There was a long pause as Johnny was lost in a sea of negativity. His face tightened. "Good enough for them to love me," he said.

"Your parents are a large source of your shortcomings. The only way you're going to be able to regain the control you once had in your life is to confront them."

Johnny was quick to reply. "They won't listen. They'll only put me down again. My parents will never respect me."

"If they won't listen, then you must force them to do so. Show them that you are stronger than them. These people are weaker than you Johnny. They hurt you, worse than Tony ever would. Your only option is to eliminate the threat to your power," Veka said heartlessly; there was no sympathy for his parents' lives in his words.

"Wait, like, *kill* them?" Johnny asked, startled. "They have hurt me for a lot longer than Tony..." Johnny began rubbing his chin, not sure if he could justify killing his parents. They were terrible people, but was death really the only option?

"That is the only way. You still care about them, yes?" Veka asked.

"They are terrible; monsters. But they're still my parents. I can't kill them, but they won't ever see me again," Johnny replied.

"Your parents are dead weight. They could be doing these horrible things to people other than you, and since there is still a sliver that exists within you that cares about them, you are showing weakness. Killing your parents might hurt for a moment, but ultimately, it's the only way you can set yourself free. Kill them and all the people who doubted you or turned their back on you, and you will become stronger than Tony could ever wish to be. With that strength, you will be able to kill Tony. And that control you seek? You will hold it in the palm of your hands, and even I won't be able to stop you," Veka said, clenching the fist he held out in front of himself.

They neared the end of the tunnel, and their silence caused Johnny to debate on the subject at hand. He now understood what needed to be done. "Alright. I'll kill them. I need a weapon, though. I'm not strong enough to take them on," Johnny said, releasing the air that he had unknowingly been holding.

"How do I know you'll follow through? Show me you have what it takes. Prove to me that you deserve the power I can give to you," Veka said.

Johnny raised an eyebrow in confusion. "How can I…"

The wall next to them slid down from the ceiling, disappearing into the floor below it and revealing another man in chains. This one had fair skin with what seemed to be burn marks dancing along his right arm. As Johnny stared into this man's green eyes, the only thing he could see was defeat; this man was broken, mentally destroyed, or however else you'd like to describe a man who had lost all will to survive.

Johnny looked at Veka in shock as he realized what he was insinuating. Veka simply nodded in the man's direction and handed Johnny a knife from within his cloak.

"Wait—why do I kill him? What'd he do?" Johnny asked, not wanting to kill a man at all, let alone without a reason.

"Since this will be your first kill, I'll cut you some slack, but *never* question an order from me. Once you question an order, it may be too late to act, and I always have a reason for what I have instructed.

This man succeeded in assassinating one of my officers, and we've been working on breaking him for quite some time now. Seems he was gathering information for the meddler. I finally got the information I was looking for from him, so I decided that I no longer needed to keep him alive. Before joining my forces and assassinating one of my men, he was in a similar situation as your parents. He beat his daughter on several different occasions just because it made him feel in charge. He was no good for the real world, and he's no good for my Followers. Kill him, so that you can be one step closer to your real goal."

Johnny gripped the knife firmly, hesitating to go any further. His hand began to shake as he lifted the knife above his head. Johnny closed his eyes, not sure if he could do it.

Veka sighed. "How do you expect to kill Tony if you can't even kill this low-life scum? You haven't even made it to your parents yet, let alone him." There was a pause as Johnny bowed his head, partially in shame and also because he was pondering how to do it. "Are your parents right? Are you not good enough? Do you want to go home and continue to be a failure?!" Veka bellowed behind Johnny. "You're just a school bully, and you failed at that. Maybe your dad should beat you again to toughen you up. Maybe then you'll be able to at least control your trembling hands!"

"I'm good enough! They're wrong! Every single one of them!" Johnny clenched the handle of the knife in his hands and plunged it into the man's shoulder blade. "Fuck you!" Johnny said, blood spurting toward him and landing on his arms. Veka began to laugh hysterically, almost falling to the floor as Johnny continued to lose his temper and scream at this man he didn't even know. "You won't stand in my way!"

Johnny yanked the knife from his shoulder blade and stabbed it into the side of his neck, giving a smile. Blood filled the man's mouth as he cried out in pain, and Johnny stabbed again, watching the man's eyes become dim. The man fell over as Johnny hovered over the corpse. Johnny's muscles flexed, and he took several deep breaths, letting his anger fully take over. It was time to succeed. It was time to regain his life.

Johnny began to calm down. When Veka stopped laughing, he chuckled himself, grinning.

"How did it feel?" Veka asked, breaking the silence in a calm, lowered voice.

"It was amazing." Johnny looked Veka in the eyes and gave him the biggest smile he had seen so far. "I've never felt so much control. I feel invincible! I'll kill my parents. I'm going to take back what's mine, and no one is going to stop me. Send me after Rob and Grey next. Then I'll kill Shawn. I'll kill them all until I finally reach Persevere!" He stopped for a moment as he pondered. "I want to be everything that Tony isn't! I want to be everything he has ever feared. I want to be his antithesis!"

Veka smiled. "Congratulations, Antithesis. You're one of us." Veka's tone indicated his satisfaction. "And what a mess you're about to make. You are ready. No one can turn you around now." There was a moment of silence as Veka debated on what to do from here.

"What now?" Johnny asked, his eyes still wide in his newly created psychosis. He was still on an adrenaline high.

"I think it's time to finish Project Antithesis," Veka said. Johnny looked up to him, cocking his head.

"What's Project Antithesis?"

"Let me explain what I have been doing. What I have been looking for. I am working toward creating the ultimate superhuman to work for me. One that will be able to take out Persevere and the rest of Project Barricade, after making them suffer. Through my experimentation, I am creating a serum for this superhuman, and I have had a few successful attempts in the process." Veka showed a sadistic grin.

"Phase One was an attempt to give somebody superhuman strength in the form of a pill. I passed it off as an experimental steroid. One of Project Barricade's members, Steel Cowboy, got a hold of this steroid and was the first successful experiment. The pill more than works and gave him the strength that he desired. But then it was time for the next step. Phase Two was Talida. I mixed the pill's contents with a serum of a powerful pyromancer known as Dracomatch. This serum was called Draco Serum, and it was known to give the user aspects of a dragon. Talida now has super strength along with some dragon-like fire abilities, which I am unsure about. After several experiments with my powerful blood, we have gotten to you, Johnny. You will be taking the final step toward becoming the perfect superhuman. I will give you your abilities today, and it is time that I tell you your first goal. We must take out Phase One and Phase Two."

Johnny smiled as Veka led him back to the surface and they entered a room much larger than the ones he had been in before. This one had a very high ceiling and was filled with different vials and tables. The strong scent of medical-grade alcohol lingered in the air.

As they walked toward a table with straps attached for the feet, hands, and head, Johnny's high dissipated to anxiousness. "Will it hurt?" he asked. He wasn't sure what to expect.

"I'm not certain. Phase One didn't hurt, Phase Two left her body sore, and the multiple experiments I used for Phase Three were all over the place. What I'm about to do to you, no one knows what to expect from it."

Johnny's eyes widened as he took a large gulp. He wanted to ask about Phase Three, but couldn't bring himself to. "I understand...so, I was wanting to talk to you about something else as well," he started.

"Alright, you may speak."

"I miss having my friends by my side. I know I said I wanted to kill Rob and Grey, but I would prefer if they could work for me again. Is there any way to force them to do that? I could use help with my plans, just like old times," he said. There was a low chuckle.

"With your new abilities, I suggest giving them an option. Confront them. If they don't accept, bring them in anyway and we will find a solution. My way will take a huge toll on their bodies, but we can talk about that later. It is possible."

Veka took a dagger from beneath his cloak again, startling Johnny. It was the one he had recovered from the corpse Johnny left moments ago. He looked around, seeing if there was someone else Veka would have him kill.

"On the table. It's time," Veka said. He pulled his arm from his cloak and cut a short slice across his wrist, letting loose a short stream of mustard-yellow blood.

Johnny looked at him, confused. "What are you doing?" he asked as he climbed onto the table.

Without saying a word, Veka let the blood drip into a small vial. He began to strap Johnny onto the table, and Johnny worriedly repeated his question, this time with concern in his voice. "Why did you do that?"

"This is the final phase. I have the most powerful enhancement in this world, right here in my veins. If you survive this treatment, you will be on your way to becoming more powerful than the rest of my Followers, and you will crush Project Barricade beneath your feet!" Veka poured the small vial into a flask filled with bright orange liquid. He then used that mix to fill a syringe.

"You will go by Antithesis in the field from here on out, and I look forward to seeing the damage you cause along your quest for revenge," Veka said, starting to chuckle. As his laughter grew louder, he stuck the needle into Johnny's neck.

They sat for a moment, waiting for it to take effect. Just as Johnny began to calm down, thinking that nothing was going to happen, all the muscles in his body tensed. He screamed in pain; his entire being felt like the worst Charley Horse he had ever had in his life.

His muscles clenched further, burning, as if they were tearing from his bones. "Help!" Johnny screamed, unsure of what else to yell through the pain.

"There's nothing I can do for you except wait," Veka replied, numb to the pain he was causing him.

Johnny's body immediately slammed itself back onto the table from the small amount of slack he had in the restraints. The large metal legs of the table collapsed, causing it to fall to the floor.

As Veka stood with a large smile, intrigued, he began to talk to himself. "That is amazing. Look at what I've created."

Johnny let out another wail as he thought his eyes were melting out of his skull. Veka could see Johnny's eyes beginning to darken. The color within them turned to shadow, which then began to leak from his sockets. The pain subsided, and Johnny attempted to free himself of the restraints. Without any resistance, the restraints ripped from the table, as if they were made of paper.

"Whoa…" Johnny said as he stood, wobbling in place in a state of vertigo. "I feel so…" Johnny lifted his hand, pressure building within his palm. As a dark red frost covered his hand, he smiled. "Different."

Veka began to cackle as he wrote something down in a notebook. "Project Antithesis. Concluded. Successful. Final Phase: Shadow Frost." Veka turned his gaze to his new Follower. "Antithesis, I have a job for you. We are going to accelerate your training, and I want you at the Shadow Lake docks two hours after sunset. The Mandiri have stolen from us, and we are going to send a message during the next trade. You are going to fix our little problem. After that, we will go after Phase One and Phase Two."

Chapter 31

Debrief and Assess

Due to the injuries we suffered during our fight with Antithesis, we gathered our forces and waited for Blackwell to arrive with the *Aegis*. While we were waiting, those of us who were uninjured moved quickly to take incriminating pictures and obtain the evidence we needed to put the few that we had captured away for the rest of their lives. We had also gathered those who had been in the shipping containers. After breaking them free, we asked that they remain here with us so we could get them to safety.

It seemed that evil might be winning right now, but this small success made our efforts look to be worth it. Putting away bad guys and saving those in need. That was the reason I chose to be a superhero, despite not knowing about the true evil we would face.

Soon the *Aegis* arrived, and we loaded the prisoners and everyone else into it. Those that we had captured were held in containment. The people we had saved were taken to a room where they could relax. That done, all of

Project Barricade went to the main cabin to meet with Blackwell.

Blackwell stepped forward. "I apologize for not being there with you, heroes. I didn't suspect that Veka was involved with the Mandiri. I'm sorry that Johnny has become one of his Followers." Those words were aimed toward me.

"I worry that there isn't a way to save him anymore," I said. "He acts as if he's lost his mind. What can we do now?"

A black cloud hung over me as I not only worried about Johnny, but also the backlash I would likely get for undermining Blackwell's orders to kill the Mandiri.

Medic was already moving toward the most injured of our party to heal them the best he could before we reached the hideout. He could stop the bleeding and stabilize those badly injured. After a short time had passed, Medic whispered several things into Blackwell's ear.

Blackwell then turned again to our group and answered my question.

"You'll find the right path, but at this moment, it's time to debrief and assess the completed mission. I'll start by saying well done. Kasai's injuries are small, and they'll likely be healed before we reach the hideout. Unfortunately, Steel Cowboy has a broken knee, and Whirl has bone damage in her forearm along with having lost a lot of blood. Medic estimates that Steel Cowboy will be back to full health in about a week, and Whirl will do the same in two to three days. He thinks Steel Cowboy should take the time to heal more slowly. After some research, his own healing should strengthen Steel Cowboy's bones more than if he would get help from Medic. Medic will accelerate it the best he can, though."

Blackwell looked at each of us. "Despite your injuries, this mission was a success. You worked well as a team and came out on top, recovering both the shipment and the trafficked victims without any civilian fatalities. You did all of this while one of Veka's Followers was present. Rather than following the plan, you took your own path and kept some Mandiri members alive. They'll be questioned. Once you send me the photos you took, and we have all the information we need, I'll have a special team check them out and transfer them to a location where they will rot in prison. I'm impressed with how well you fought together today. If you ask me, ever since Kasai joined us, Red Kelvin has been fighting much harder as well," Blackwell said, shooting Red Kelvin a glance.

Both his and Kasai's faces turned pink. I chuckled, also having come to that conclusion. There were definitely some sparks coming from his end. Whether she reciprocated those feelings, I didn't know; we had been too busy for me to pay attention. Being my best friend, I would have to ask her later.

I sat down next to the others, who were sitting close together rather than being spread out like last time. They were all wearing their suits. Our team felt much more cohesive than it had been before this mission. Blackwell opened the chest we had received from the docks. "As you can see, this shipment is a chest of pills. To be more exact, it's a chest of titan pills—the steroids that Corbin used to gain his abilities. I'll have my men test these, but my guess is that they're half the strength Corbin was given. We believe that these pills were being mass-produced to give Veka's human forces superhuman strength. We don't know how many of these are left, or if he is still making them, but we do know, from what you witnessed at the docks, that a small group of gang members had stolen them from Veka. We will continue working in the interrogation room to find out if Veka is still working with the Mandiri."

"So, what's next?" I asked.

"After we get the Mandiri members sent off, I will reach out to the authorities and get the trafficked victims to safety. I'll put out a special directive regarding Corbin's mother, Mary, and she will be given government assistance to be relocated to somewhere safe," Blackwell said, nodding toward Steel Cowboy. He nodded back and smiled. "I'm sure you are ecstatic, Corbin. As for Project Barricade, now we rest. Take your win tonight. For those who were trapped in those shipping containers, you lived up to being heroes today. That should be a reward worthy of keeping that title. You made a difference, and it's obvious that you will continue to do so. Rest easy, heroes."

With that being said, we made our way back to the hideout. Shawn and Talida walked with me, hoping to set up a campsite with me and my van. I had been a hero today, and there would be a lot more work to do in the near future. I would have to figure out how to defeat Antithesis and Veka's Followers, but tonight, especially tonight, it was time for me to be Tony Jensen.

Epilogue

eka and Antithesis stood in the experimentation room. This time, no one was strapped to the table, and no one was being cut open. Veka had asked him to meet there, saying he had an important update to share. They then talked about what to do next.

"Will it work?" Antithesis asked, staring at the schematic Veka had extended over the small metal table.

"We will send Jen to take on Project Barricade soon. I've already given her the mission. Consider this a test run before our final blow."

"The cyborg?" Antithesis asked. Veka nodded, a wide smile resting on his face. As Antithesis looked closer at the schematic, something caught his attention. "Does Shawn know?"

"I believe you're going to have to be more specific with that question."

"This schematic states that an experimental fluid is introduced through the bloodstream using nanites. You also said that there's a mole in Project

Barricade. I'm assuming you passed on a fluid of your own to introduce into Shawn's bloodstream?"

"You're much smarter than I previously believed you to be. Yes. I passed to Medic an experimental fluid of my own, and he introduced that to the prosthetic, which carried it through Shawn's bloodstream with the nanites already within the piece. Fury is Phase 3 of the Antithesis project. Fury now has my blood flowing through his veins."

Johnny laughed. "That's brilliant. Medic's the mole?" he asked in surprise.

"He always has been. I'll admit, we jumped a few steps in the Antithesis project so we could continue with you, but Medic will continue to watch Shawn and record everything he can about the experiment."

"That's awesome. I'm not worried about myself; I'm stronger than any of those 'heroes.' What's this update on the schematic? You said we could target Shawn next to hurt Tony, and that's what I want to do." He pointed to a small piece that was circled, deep within the prosthetic itself.

"This update will allow us to destroy his confidence. We will emasculate him, and he'll be nothing but a husk who doesn't believe in himself anymore. That's where Jen comes in. We send her in to weaken Project Barricade, and then we make our move. With this upgrade. Now we simply tell Medic what needs done."

Veka and Antithesis joined in a unanimous cackle as they dreamed of the pain they would cause. This was yet another piece of Veka's game, falling into place, and right now, every piece was exactly where he wanted them.

About the Author

The Story Brought to Life

I never felt as though I had a place in this world as myself until I found the art of wordsmithing. I spent most of my childhood playing video games, reading, and pretending I was somebody else. Whether I was exploring the playground as Spider-Man, Thrall, or Sarah Kerrigan, my imagination has always run rampant.

I started writing my dreams down in journals, and the cartoons weren't enough for me anymore. While I loved the stories I was filling my mind with, they weren't the stories I craved. I started to write about my favorite characters meeting and the craziness that would ensue. I soon decided that writing was what I wanted to do for the rest of my life. When I got to that point, my family and friends told me that I should create my own characters, and that's what I set out to do.

Just before entering middle school, I created my first few original characters. I wrote stories involving them and their superhero, or supervillain, lives. Eventually, as the bullying got worse, I modeled a superhero after myself and created a world that I could escape into. Throughout middle school, I focused on becoming an author. There, I met two friends that would change my life, and my writing, forever. As the three of us powered through the worst years of bullying, I leaned on my writing as an escape more than ever. Throughout that hard time in my life, my family and those two close friends were all I had. They were my inspiration for the close-knit friend group in my series *Fray!*

My Interests

I've always been a huge fan of superheroes, fantasy, and sci-fi. My favorite superheroes have been Spider-Man, Batman, Deku, and the Teen Titans. Some of my favorite fantasy worlds have been Middle Earth, Xanth, and Azeroth. My favorite kinds of stories are those that involve a bullied kid who suddenly gets the power he needs to change his situation, or where normal people are gifted powers and decide to change the world in a positive way. That really interests me.

I grew up with a lot of negativity around me in school and in public. I was bullied for multiple reasons along the way; therefore, my books portray characters who are unique and against prejudice. Somewhere along my journey through school, I started playing World of Warcraft. There, I met the love of my life, a wonderful person who introduced me to a life I didn't know I was missing.

I consider myself to be a part of the Gothic community because I like the style and music of many people who fall into that spectrum. I've always loved the darker aspects of life. Halloween has constantly been my favorite holiday due to its macabre themes. I've grown fond of gothic fashion and express myself through my personality and clothing.

My Goal

My writing goal is to hit one million words in my series *Fray!* I have many books planned, and I hope to keep most of them around the same length, give or take. My personal goal is to set an example for others to see that they can reach their goals if they put their minds to it. I want to give others a means of escape. I want to share the world I've created throughout these years with all of you.

Don't give up just because people want you to change. Everyone has a path they are meant to traverse. Don't judge someone because they appear different; they may be your next best friend along your journey through life.

Keep being you.

Want to find more? Check out my website **www.Quillan-Ink.com**